ID0960270

The Ape Who Guards The Balance

Books by Elizabeth Peters

THE APE WHO GUARDS THE BALANCE*
SEEING A LARGE CAT*
THE HIPPOPOTAMUS POOL*
NIGHT TRAIN TO MEMPHIS
THE SNAKE, THE CROCODILE AND THE DOG*
THE LAST CAMEL DIED AT NOON*
NAKED ONCE MORE
THE DEEDS OF THE DISTURBER*
TROJAN GOLD
LION IN THE VALLEY*
THE MUMMY CASE*
DIE FOR LOVE
SILHOUETTE IN SCARLET
THE COPENHAGEN CONNECTION
THE CURSE OF THE PHARAOHS*
THE LOVE TALKER
SUMMER OF THE DRAGON
STREET OF THE FIVE MOONS
DEVIL-MAY-CARE
LEGEND IN GREEN VELVET
CROCODILE ON THE SANDBANK*
THE MURDERS OF RICHARD III
BORROWER OF THE NIGHT
THE SEVENTH SINNER
THE NIGHT OF FOUR HUNDRED RABBITS
THE DEAD SEA CIPHER
THE CAMELOT CAPER
THE JACKAL'S HEAD

*Amelia Peabody mysteries

Elizabeth Peters

·

THE APE WHO GUARDS THE BALANCE

AN AMELIA PEABODY MYSTERY

AVON
TWILIGHT

AVON BOOKS, INC.
1350 Avenue of the Americas
New York, New York 10019

Copyright © 1998 by MPM Manor, Inc.
Interior design by Kellan Peck
Visit our website at **http://www.AvonBooks.com/Twilight**
ISBN: 0-380-97657-9

To Joshua Gabriel Roland Brown Mertz

December 20, 1997

With love from Ammie

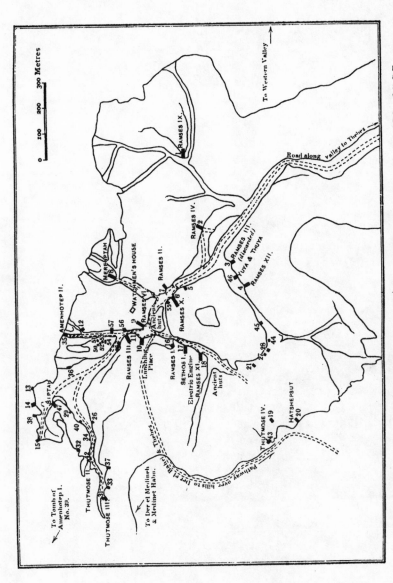

SKETCH MAP OF THE VALLEY OF THE TOMBS OF THE KINGS, 1907

Foreword

Students of the life and works of Mrs. Amelia P. Emerson will be pleased to learn that the present Editor's tireless research on the recently discovered collection of Emerson papers has yielded additional fruit. Certain excerpts from Manuscript H were included in the most recent volume of Mrs. Emerson's memoirs, and other excerpts appear here. The authorship of this manuscript has been determined; it was written by "Ramses" Emerson, but additions in various hands suggest that it was read and commented upon by other members of the family. The collection of letters herein designated "B" are signed by Nefret Forth, as she then was. Since the recipient of them is addressed only as "Dear" or "Darling," the Editor was originally in some doubt as to this individual's identity. She has decided to leave the Reader in doubt as well. Speculation is the spice of life, as Mrs. Emerson might say.

Newspaper clippings and miscellaneous letters are contained in a separate file (F).

The present Editor feels obliged to add, in her own defense, that the journals themselves present a number of inconsistencies. Mrs. Emerson began them as private diaries. At a later time she determined to edit them for future publication, but (as was typical of her) she went about it in a somewhat slapdash fashion and over a long period of time. Her methodology, if it can be called that, explains the anomalies, errors, and anachronisms in the urtext itself. Eventually the Editor hopes to produce a definitive, thoroughly annotated edition, in which these inconsistencies will be explained (insofar as it is possible to explain the way in which Mrs. Emerson's agile mind operated).

Of particular interest to Egyptologists will be Mrs. Emerson's description of the discovery of KV55, as the tomb found by Ayrton in January 1907 is now called. No proper excavation report was ever published, and the descriptions of the participants disagree in so many particulars that one cannot help suspecting the accuracy of all of them. It is not surprising that none of them mentions the presence of Professor Emerson and his associates. Mrs. Emerson's version, though certainly not free of bias, makes it clear that the Professor's suggestions and advice were deeply resented by the excavators.

Being only too aware of Mrs. Emerson's biases, the Editor has gone to the trouble of comparing her version with those of others. She is indebted to Jim and Susan Allen, of the Metropolitan Museum of Art, for making the unpublished manuscript of Mrs. Andrew's diary available to her; to Dennis Forbes, editor of KMT, for allowing her to peruse the galleys of his chapter on KV55 from his forthcoming book, *Tombs. Treasures. Mummies*; to Mr. John Larson of the Oriental Institute for answering innumerable questions about Theodore Davis and the storage jars; and to Lila Pinch Brock, the most recent excavator of KV55, for getting her into the place and telling her all about it.

She (the Editor) has also read practically every book and article written about the tomb. The (extremely impressive) bibliography will be sent to Readers upon receipt of a SASE. She (the Editor) has come to the conclusion that Mrs. Emerson's description is the most accurate, and that she was, as she always was, right.

BOOK ONE

OPENING THE MOUTH
OF THE DEAD

●

Let my mouth be given to me.
Let my mouth be opened by Ptah with the
instrument of iron with which he opens the
mouths of the gods.

1

I was inserting an additional pin into my hat when the library door opened and Emerson put his head out.

"There is a matter on which I would like to consult you, Peabody," he began.

He had obviously been working on his book, for his thick black hair was disheveled, his shirt gaped open, and his sleeves had been rolled above the elbows. Emerson claims that his mental processes are inhibited by the constriction of collars, cuffs and cravats. It may be so. I certainly did not object, for my husband's muscular frame and sun-bronzed skin are displayed to best advantage in such a state of dishabille. On this occasion, however, I was forced to repress the emotion the sight of Emerson always arouses in me, since Gargery, our butler, was present.

"Pray do not detain me, my dear Emerson," I replied. "I am on my way to chain myself to the railings at Number Ten Downing Street, and I am already late."

"Chain yourself," Emerson repeated. "May I ask why?"

"It was my idea," I explained modestly. "During some earlier demonstrations, the lady suffragists have been picked up and carried away by large policemen, thus effectively ending the demonstration. This will not be easily accomplished if the ladies are firmly fastened to an immovable object such as an iron railing."

"I see." Opening the door wider, he emerged. "Would you like me to accompany you, Peabody? I could drive you in the motorcar."

It would have been difficult to say which suggestion horrified me more—that he should go with me, or that he should drive the motorcar.

Emerson had been wanting for several years to acquire one of the horrid machines, but I had put him off by one pretext or another until that summer. I had taken all the precautions I could, promoting one of the stablemen to the post of chauffeur and making certain he was properly trained; I had insisted that if the children were determined to drive the nasty thing (which they were), they should also take lessons. David and Ramses had become as competent as male individuals of their age could be expected to be, and in my opinion Nefret was even better, though the men in the family denied it.

None of these sensible measures succeeded in fending off the dreaded results. Emerson, of course, refused to be driven by the chauffeur or the younger members of the family. It had not taken long for the word to get round the village and its environs. One glimpse of Emerson crouched over the wheel, his teeth bared in a delighted grin, his blue eyes sparkling behind his goggles, was enough to strike terror into the heart of pedestrian or driver. The hooting of the horn (which Emerson liked very much and employed incessantly) had the same effect as a fire siren; everyone within earshot immediately cleared off the road, into a ditch or a hedgerow, if necessary. He had insisted on bringing the confounded thing with us to London, but thus far we had managed to keep him from operating it in the city.

Many years of happy marriage had taught me that there are certain subjects about which husbands are strangely sensitive. Any challenge to their masculinity should be avoided at all costs. For some reason that eludes me, the ability to drive a motorcar appears to be a symbol of masculinity. I therefore sought another excuse for refusing his offer.

"No, my dear Emerson, it would not be advisable for you to go with me. In the first place, you have a great deal of work to do on the final volume of your *History of Ancient Egypt*. In the second place, the last time you accompanied me on such an expedition you knocked down two policemen."

"And so I will do again if they have the audacity to lay hands on you," Emerson exclaimed. As I had hoped, this comment distracted him from the subject of the motorcar. His blue eyes blazed with sapphirine fire, and the cleft, or dimple, in his chin quivered. "Good Gad, Peabody, you don't expect me to stand idly by while vulgar police officers manhandle my wife!"

"No, my dear, I don't, which is why you cannot come along. The whole point of the enterprise is for ME to be arrested—yes, and manhandled as well. Having YOU taken in charge for assaulting a police officer distracts the public from the fight for women's suffrage we ladies are endeavoring—"

"Damnation, Peabody!" Emerson stamped his foot. He is given to such childish demonstrations at times.

"Will you please stop interrupting me, Emerson? I was about to—"

"You never let me finish a sentence!" Emerson shouted.

I turned to our butler, who was waiting to open the door for me. "My parasol, Gargery, if you please."

"Certainly, madam," said Gargery. His plain but affable features were wreathed in a smile. Gargery greatly enjoys the affectionate little exchanges between me and Emerson. "If I may say so, madam," he went on, "that hat is very becoming."

I turned back to the mirror. The hat was a new one, and I rather thought it did suit me. I had caused it to be trimmed with crimson roses and green silk leaves; the subdued colors considered appropriate for mature married ladies have an unfortunate effect on my sallow complexion and jetty-black hair, and I see no reason for a slavish adherence to fashion when the result does not become the wearer. Besides, crimson is Emerson's favorite color. As I inserted the final pin, his face appeared in the mirror next to mine. He had to bend over, since he is six feet in height and I am a good many inches shorter. Taking advantage of our relative positions (and the position of Gargery, behind him) he gave me a surreptitious pat and said amiably, "So it is. Well, well, my dear, enjoy yourself. If you aren't back by teatime I will just run down to the police station and bail you out."

"Don't come round before seven," I said. "I am hoping to be thrown into the Black Maria and perhaps handcuffed."

Not quite sotto voce, Gargery remarked, "I'd like to see the chap who could do it."

"So would I," said my husband.

It was a typical November day in dear old London—gloomy, gray, and damp. We had come up from Kent only the previous week so that Emerson could consult certain references in the British Museum. Our temporary abode was Chalfont House, the city mansion belonging to Emerson's brother Walter and his wife Evelyn, who had inherited the property from her grandfather. The younger Emersons preferred their country estates in Yorkshire, but they always opened Chalfont House for us when we were obliged to stay in London.

Although I enjoy the bustle and busyness of the metropolis, Egypt is my spiritual home, and as I breathed in the insalubrious mixture of coal smoke and moisture I thought nostalgically of clear blue skies, hot dry air, the thrill of another season of excavation. We were a trifle later than usual in getting off this year, but the delay, occasioned principally by Emerson's tardiness in completing his long-awaited *History*, had given me the opportunity to participate in a cause dear to my heart, and my spirits soared as I strode briskly along, my indispensable parasol in one hand, my chains in the other.

Though I had always been a strong supporter of votes for women, professional commitments had prevented me from taking an active part in the suffragist movement. Not that the movement itself had been particularly active or effective. Almost every year a Women's Suffrage Bill had been presented to Parliament, only to be talked down or ignored. Politicians and statesmen had made promises of support and broken them.

Recently, however, a breath of fresh northern air had blown into London. The Women's Social and Political Union had been founded in Manchester by a Mrs. Emmeline Pankhurst and her two daughters. Early in the present year they had decided—quite sensibly, in my opinion—to transfer their headquarters to the center of political action. I had met Mrs. Pankhurst on several occasions, but I had not made up my mind about her or the organization until the shocking events of October 23 had aroused my wholehearted indignation. Meeting peacefully to press their views and hopes upon Parliament, women had been forcibly ejected from that bastion of male superiority—bullied, pushed, flung to the ground, and arrested! Even now

Miss Sylvia Pankhurst languished in prison, along with others of her sisters in the cause. When I got wind of the present demonstration I determined to show my support for the prisoners and the movement.

In fact, I had been guilty of some slight misdirection when I told Emerson my destination was Downing Street. I feared he might become bored or apprehensive for my safety, and follow after me. The WSPU had decided instead to demonstrate in front of the home of Mr. Geoffrey Romer, in Charles Street near Berkeley Square.

Next to Mr. Asquith, the Chancellor of the Exchequer, this individual was our most vehement and effective opponent in the House of Commons; he was an elegant and eloquent speaker, with an excellent classical education and considerable private wealth. Emerson and I had once been privileged to examine his superb collection of Egyptian antiquities. I had, as I felt obliged to do, made one or two pointed remarks on the subject of female suffrage, but it may have been Emerson's even more pointed comments about the iniquities of private collectors that irritated Mr. Romer. We had not been asked to come again. I quite looked forward to chaining myself to his railings.

I had feared I might be late, but when I arrived on the scene I found matters in a shocking state of disorganization. No one was chained to the railings. People were standing about looking confused; at the other end of the street a number of ladies were huddled together, deep in conversation. Evidently it was a conference of the leaders, for I heard the familiar voice of Mrs. Pankhurst.

I was about to join them when I beheld a familiar form. It was that of a tall young man impeccably attired in striped trousers, frock coat and top hat. His deeply tanned complexion and heavy dark brows resembled those of an Arab or Indian, but he was neither. He was my son, Walter Peabody Emerson, better known to the world at large by his soubriquet of Ramses.

Seeing me, he broke off his conversation with the young woman next to him and greeted me in the annoying drawl he had acquired when he had spent a term at Oxford reading classics with Professor Wilson, at the latter's invitation. "Good afternoon, Mother. May I have the honor of presenting Miss Christabel Pankhurst, with whom I believe you are not acquainted?"

She was younger than I had expected—in her early twenties, as

I later learned—and not unattractive. Firm lips and a direct gaze gave distinction to her rounded face and dark hair. As we shook hands, with the conventional murmurs of greeting, I wondered how Ramses had got acquainted with her—and when. She had been smiling and rolling her eyes at him in a manner that suggested this was not their first meeting. Ramses has an unfortunate habit of being attractive to women, especially strong-minded women.

"What are you doing here?" I inquired. "And where is Nefret?"

"I don't know where she is," said Ramses. "My 'sister,' to give her the courtesy title you insist upon, though it is not justified by legal proceedings or blood relationship—"

"Ramses," I said sternly. "Get to the point."

"Yes, Mother. Finding myself unexpectedly at liberty this afternoon, I determined to attend the present demonstration. You know my sympathy for the cause of—"

"Yes, my dear." Interrupting others is very rude, but it is sometimes necessary to interrupt Ramses. He was not as perniciously long-winded as he once had been, but he had occasional lapses, especially when he was trying to conceal something from me. I abandoned that line of inquiry for the moment and asked another question.

"What is going on?"

"You can put your chains away, Mother," Ramses replied. "The ladies have decided we will picket, and deliver a petition to Mr. Romer. Miss Pankhurst tells me they will be distributing the placards shortly."

"Nonsense," I exclaimed. "What makes them suppose he will receive a delegation? He has never done so before."

"We have had recently a new recruit to the cause who is an old acquaintance of his," Miss Christabel explained. "Mrs. Markham assures us that he will respond to her request."

"If she is an old friend, why did she not request an interview through normal channels instead of instigating this . . . Ramses, don't slouch against that railing. You will get rust on your coat."

"Yes, Mother." Ramses straightened to his full height of six feet. The top hat added another twelve inches, and I was forced to admit that he lent a certain air of distinction to the gathering, which consisted almost entirely of ladies. The only other male person present was an eccentrically garbed individual who stood watching the discussion of the leaders. His long, rather shabby velvet cloak and broad-brimmed hat reminded me of a character from one of the Gilbert and Sullivan operas—the one that satirized the aesthetic movement and its languid poets. As my curious gaze came to rest on him, he turned and addressed the ladies in an affected, high-pitched voice.

"Who is that fellow?" I asked. "I have never seen him before."

Ramses, who sometimes demonstrates an uncanny ability to read my mind, began to sing softly. I recognized one of the songs from the opera in question. " 'A most intense young man, A soulful eyed young man, An ultra-poetical, super-aesthetical, out-of-the-way young man.' "

I could not help laughing. Miss Christabel gave me a look of freezing disapproval. "He is Mrs. Markham's brother, and a sturdy defender of the cause. If you had deigned to attend our earlier meetings, Mrs. Emerson, you would be aware of these facts."

She did not give me time to reply that I had not been invited to attend their earlier meetings, but marched off with her nose in the air. I had heard the young lady praised for her wit and sense of humor. The latter appeared to be in abeyance at the moment.

"I believe they are about to begin," Ramses said.

A rather ragged line formed, and placards were handed out. Mine read "Free the victims of male oppression!"

A little crowd of spectators had gathered. A hard-faced man in the front ranks glared at me and called out, "You ought to be 'ome washin' of your 'usband's trousers!"

Ramses, following behind me with a placard reading "Votes for Women NOW!" replied loudly and good-humoredly, "I assure you, sir, the lady's husband's trousers are not in such sore need of laundering as your own."

We proceeded in a straggling line past the gates of Romer's house. They were closed, and guarded by two blue-helmeted constables, who watched us curiously. There was no sign of life at the curtained windows of the mansion. It did not appear likely that Mr. Romer was in the mood to accept a petition.

As we turned to retrace our steps, Miss Christabel hurried up and drew Ramses out of the line. Naturally I followed after them. "Mr. Emerson," she exclaimed. "We are counting on you!"

"Certainly," said Ramses. "To do what, precisely?"

"Mrs. Markham is ready to carry our petition to the house. We ladies will converge upon the constable to the left of the gate and prevent him from stopping her. Could you, do you think, detain the other police officer?"

Ramses's eyebrows went up. "Detain?" he repeated.

"You must not employ violence, of course. Only clear the way for Mrs. Markham."

"I will do my best" was the reply.

"Splendid! Be ready—they are coming."

Indeed they were. A phalanx of females, marching shoulder to shoulder, was bearing down on us. There were only a dozen or so of them—obviously the leaders. The two ladies heading the procession were tall and stoutly built, and both brandished heavy wooden placards with suffragist slogans. Behind them, almost hidden by their persons, I caught a glimpse of a large but tasteful flowered and feathered hat. Could the individual under it be the famous Mrs. Markham, on whom so much depended? The man in the velvet cape, his face shadowed by the brim of his hat, marched at her side. The only individual I recognized was Mrs. Pankhurst, who brought up the rear.

They slowed their inexorable advance for neither constable nor sympathizer; I was forced to skip nimbly out of their way as they trotted past. Christabel, her face flushed with excitement, cried, "Now," as the marchers surrounded the astonished constable to the left of the gates. I heard a thump and a yelp, as one of the wooden placards landed on his helmeted head.

His companion shouted, " 'Ere now," and started to the defense of his friend. Ramses stepped in front of him and put a hand on his shoulder. "I beg you will remain where you are, Mr. Jenkins," he said in a kindly voice.

"Oh, now, Mr. Emerson, don't you do this!" the officer exclaimed piteously.

"You two are acquainted?" I inquired. I was not surprised. Ramses has quite a number of unusual acquaintances. Police officers are more respectable than certain of the others.

"Yes," said Ramses. "How is your little boy, Jenkins?"

His voice was affable, his pose casual, but the unfortunate constable was gradually being pushed back against the railing. Knowing

Ramses could manage quite nicely by himself, I turned to see if the ladies required my assistance in "restraining" the other constable.

The man was flat on the ground, tugging at the helmet which had been pushed over his eyes, and the gate had yielded to the impetuous advance of the delegation. Led by the two large ladies and the poetically garbed gentleman, it reached the door of the house.

I could not but admire the strategy, and the military precision with which it had been carried out, but I doubted the delegation would get any farther. Already the sound of police whistles rent the air; running feet and cries of "Now, then, what's all this?" betokened the arrival of reinforcements. Mrs. Markham had prevaricated or had been deceived; if Romer had agreed to receive a petition, this forceful stratagem would not have been necessary. The door of the mansion would surely be locked, and Romer was not likely to allow his butler to open it.

Even as this thought entered my mind, the portal opened. I caught a glimpse of a pale, astonished face which I took to be that of the butler before it was hidden by the invading forces. They pushed their way in, and the door slammed behind them.

Outside on the street, matters were not going so well. Half a dozen uniformed men had gone to the rescue of their beleaguered colleague. Laying rough hands upon the ladies, they pulled them away and actually threw several to the ground. With a cry of indignation I raised my parasol and would have rushed forward had I not been seized in a respectful but firm grasp.

"Ramses, let go of me this instant," I gasped.

"Wait, Mother—I promised Father—" He extended one foot and the constable who had been coming up behind me toppled forward with a startled exclamation.

"Oh, you promised your father, did you? Curse it," I cried. But frustration and the compression of my ribs by the arm of my son prevented further utterance.

The constable Ramses had tripped got slowly to his feet. "Bleedin' 'ell," he remarked. "So it's you, Mr. Emerson? I didn't recognize you in that fancy getup."

"Look after my mother, will you, Mr. Skuggins?" Releasing me, Ramses began picking up prostrate ladies. "Really, gentlemen," he said, in tones of freezing disapproval, "this is no way for Englishmen to behave. Shame!"

A temporary lull ensued. The men in blue shuffled their feet and looked sheepish, while the ladies straightened their garments and looked daggers at the constables. I was surprised to see Mrs. Pankhurst and her daughter, for I had assumed they had entered the house with the other leaders of the delegation.

Then one of the police officers cleared his throat. "That's all very well, Mr. Emerson, sir, but wot about Mr. Romer? Those there ladies forced their way in—"

"An unwarranted assumption, Mr. Murdle," said Ramses. "Force was not employed. The door was opened by Mr. Romer's servant."

At that strategic moment the door opened again. There was no mistaking the identity of the man who stood on the threshold. The blaze of light behind him set his silvery hair and beard aglow. Just as unmistakable as his appearance was the resonant voice that had earned him his reputation as one of England's greatest orators.

"My lords, ladies and . . . er, that is . . . your attention, please. I have agreed to hear the petition of my old friend Mrs. Markham on condition that the rest of you disperse peacefully and without delay. Return your men to their duties, Sergeant."

Behind him I caught a glimpse of an exuberantly flowered hat before the door closed with a decisive bang.

Mrs. Pankhurst's was the first voice to break the silence. "There, now," she said triumphantly. "Did I not assure you Mrs. Markham would prevail? Come, ladies, we may retreat with honor."

They proceeded to do so. The mob, disappointed at this tame ending, followed their example, and before long the only persons remaining were my son and myself and a single constable, who drew the violated gates together again before stationing himself in front of them.

"Shall we go, Mother?" Ramses took my arm.

"Hmmm," I said.

"I beg your pardon?"

"Did you observe anything unusual about . . ."

"About what?"

I decided not to mention my strange fancy. If Ramses had observed nothing out of the way I had probably been mistaken.

I ought to have known better. I am seldom mistaken. My only consolation for failing to speak is that even if Ramses had believed me, the constable certainly would not have done, and that by the time I forced someone in authority to heed my advice, the crime would already have been committed.

Darkness was complete before we reached the house, and a thin black rain was falling. Gargery had been looking out for me; he flung the door open before I could ring, and announced in an accusing tone that the other members of the family were waiting for us in the library.

"Oh, are we late for tea?" I inquired, handing him my parasol, my cloak, and my hat.

"Yes, madam. The Professor is getting quite restive. If we had been certain Mr. Ramses was with you, we would not have worried."

"I beg your pardon for neglecting to inform you," said Ramses, adding his hat to the pile of garments Gargery held.

If he meant to be sarcastic, the effect was lost on Gargery. He had participated in several of our little adventures, and had enjoyed them a great deal. Now he considered himself responsible for us and sulked if he was not kept informed about our activities. A sulky butler is a cursed inconvenience, but in my opinion it was a small price to pay for loyalty and affection.

Taking Gargery's hint, we went straight in without changing, and found the others gathered round the tea table. My devoted husband greeted me with a scowl. "You are cursed late, Peabody. What kept you?"

None of us likes to be waited upon when we are en famille, so Nefret had taken charge of the teapot. She was wearing one of the embroidered Egyptian robes she preferred for informal wear, and her red-gold hair had been tied back with a ribbon.

Strictly speaking, she was not our adopted daughter, or even our ward, since she had come of age the previous year and—thanks to my dear Emerson's insistence on *this* young woman's rights—was now in control of the fortune she had inherited from her grandfather.

She had no other kin, however, and she had become as dear to Emerson and me as our own daughter. She had been thirteen when we rescued her from the remote Nubian oasis where she had lived since her birth, and it hadn't been easy for her to adjust to the conventions of modern England.

It hadn't been easy for me either. At times I wondered why Heaven had blessed me with two of the most difficult children a mother has ever encountered. I am not the sort of woman who coos over babies and dotes on small children, but I venture to assert that Ramses would have tried any mother's nerves; he was hideously precocious in some areas and appallingly normal in others. (The normal behavior of a young boy involves a considerable quantity of dirt and a complete disregard for his own safety.) Just when I thought I had got Ramses past the worst stage, along came Nefret—strikingly pretty, extremely intelligent, and consistently critical of civilized conventions. A girl who had been High Priestess of Isis in a culture whose citizens go about half-clothed could not be expected to take kindly to corsets.

Compared to them, the third young person present had been a refreshing change. A casual observer might have taken him and Ramses for close kin; he had the same brown skin and waving black hair, the same long-lashed dark eyes. The resemblance was only coincidental; David was the grandson of our foreman, Abdullah, but he was Ramses's closest friend and an important part of our family ever since he had gone to live with Emerson's brother. He was not much of a talker, possibly because he found it difficult to get a word in when the rest of us were present. With an affectionate smile at me he drew up a hassock for my feet and placed a cup of tea and a plate of sandwiches on a table at my elbow.

"Your eyes look tired," I said, inspecting him. "Have you been working on the drawings for the Luxor Temple volume by artificial light? I told you over and over you should not—"

"Leave off fussing, Peabody," Emerson snapped. "You only want him to be ill so you can dose him with those noxious medicines of yours. Drink your tea."

"I will do so at once, Emerson. But David should not—"

"He wanted to finish before we left for Egypt," Nefret said. "Don't worry about his eyesight, Aunt Amelia, the latest research indicates that reading by electric light is not harmful to one's vision."

She spoke with an authority which was, I had to admit, justified by her medical studies. Acquiring that training had been a struggle in itself. Over the violent objections of its (male) medical faculty, the University of London had, finally, opened its degrees to women, but the major universities continued to deny them, and the difficulty of obtaining clinical practice was almost as great as it had been a century earlier. Nefret had managed it, though, with the help of the dedicated ladies who had founded a woman's medical college in London and forced some of the hospitals to admit women students to the wards and the dissecting rooms. She had spoken once or twice of continuing her studies in France or Switzerland, where (strange as it may seem to a Briton) the prejudice against female physicians was not so strong. I believe that she was loath to leave us, however; she adored Emerson, who was putty in her little hands, and she and Ramses really were like brother and sister. That is to say, they were on the best of terms except when they were being rude to one another.

"Why are you wearing those silly clothes?" she now inquired, studying Ramses's elegantly garbed form with contemptuous amusement. "Don't tell me, let me guess. Miss Christabel Pankhurst was there."

"Not much of a guess," said Ramses. "You knew she would be."

"What does Miss Christabel have to do with Ramses's attire?" I inquired suspiciously.

My son turned to me. "That was Nefret's feeble attempt at a joke."

"Ha!" said Nefret. "I assure you, dear boy, you won't think it is a joke if you continue to encourage the girl. Men seem to find conquests of that sort amusing, but she is a very determined young woman, and you won't get rid of her as easily as you do the others."

"Good Gad!" I exclaimed. "What others?"

"Another joke," said Ramses, rising in haste. "Come and keep me company while I change, David. We will talk."

"About Christabel," Nefret murmured in saccharine tones.

Ramses was already halfway to the door. This last "joke" was too much for him; he stopped and turned. "If you had been at the demonstration," he said, biting off the words, "you would have been able to observe my behavior for yourself. I was under the impression that you meant to attend."

Nefret's smile faded. "Uh—I had the chance to watch an interesting dissection."

"You were not at the hospital this afternoon."

"How the devil . . ." She glanced at me and bit her lip. "No. I went for a walk instead. With a friend."

"How nice," I said. "That explains the pretty color in your cheeks. Fresh air and exercise! There is nothing like it."

Ramses turned on his heel and stalked out of the room, followed by David.

By the time we assembled for dinner, the two of them had made it up. Nefret was especially sweet to Ramses, as she always was after one of their arguments. Ramses was especially silent, as he seldom was. He left it to me to describe the demonstration, which I did with my customary vivacity and little touches of humor. However, I was not allowed to finish, for Emerson does not always appreciate my little touches of humor.

"Most undignified and vulgar," he grumbled. "Striking constables on the head with placards, pushing rudely into a man's house! Romer is an unmitigated ass, but I cannot believe that such behavior serves your cause, Amelia. Tactful persuasion is more effective."

"You are a fine one to talk of tact, Emerson," I replied indignantly. "Who was it who tactlessly knocked down two constables last spring? Who was it whose tactless remarks to the Director of Antiquities led to our being refused permission to search for new tombs in the Valley of the Kings? Who was it—"

Emerson's blue eyes had narrowed into slits, and his cheeks were becomingly flushed. He drew a deep breath. Before he could employ it in speech, Gargery, Nefret and David all spoke at once.

"More mint jelly, sir?"

"How is the *History* coming along, Professor?"

Nefret addressed her question to me instead of to Emerson. "When are Aunt Evelyn and Uncle Walter and little Amelia expected? Tomorrow or the next day?"

Emerson subsided with a grunt, and I replied sedately, "The following day, Nefret. But you all must remember not to call her 'little Amelia.'"

Ramses scarcely ever smiled, but his expression softened a trifle. He was very fond of his young cousin. "It will be difficult. She is a dear little thing, and a diminutive suits her."

"She claims that two Amelias in the family make for confusion," I explained. "I suspect, however, that what puts her off is the fact that your father is inclined to call me Amelia only when he is vexed with me. He generally uses my maiden name as a term of commendation and—er—affection. Now, Emerson, don't glare at me, you know it is true; I have seen the poor child start convulsively when you bellow 'Curse it, Amelia!' in that tone of voice."

Again Nefret intervened to prevent a profane utterance from Emerson. "Is it settled then that she is coming out to Egypt with us this year?"

"She has won her parents over, with David's help. Evelyn said his gentle persuasion was irresistible."

David flushed slightly and bent his head.

"She is the only one of their children who is interested in Egyptology," I went on. "It would be a pity if she were prevented from developing that interest only because she is female."

"Ah, so that is how you got round them," Ramses said, glancing from me to his silent friend. "Aunt Evelyn would find that argument hard to resist. But Melia—Lia—is very young."

"She is only two years younger than you, Ramses, and you have been going out to Egypt since you were seven."

In my enjoyment of the pleasures of familial intercourse I had forgotten my odd foreboding. Yet, had I but known, Nemesis was even then almost upon us. In fact, he was at that very moment in the act of ringing the bell.

We were about to rise from table when Gargery entered the dining room. His look of frozen disapproval warned me, even before he spoke, that he was displeased about something.

"There is someone from the police to see you, Mrs. Emerson. I informed him you were not receiving callers, but he insisted."

"Mrs. Emerson?" my husband repeated. "Not me?"

"No, sir. Mrs. Emerson and Mr. Ramses were the ones he asked for."

"Curse it!" Emerson jumped up. "It must have something to do with your demonstration this afternoon. Ramses, I told you to restrain her!"

"I assure you, Father, nothing untoward occurred," Ramses replied. "Where is the gentleman, Gargery?"

"In the library, sir. That is where you generally receive policemen, I believe."

Emerson led the way and the rest of us followed.

The man who awaited us was no uniformed constable but a tall, stout individual wearing evening dress. Emerson came to a sudden stop. "Good Gad!" he exclaimed. "It is worse than I thought. What have you done, Amelia, to warrant a visit from the assistant commissioner of Scotland Yard?"

It was indeed Sir Reginald Arbuthnot, with whom we were well acquainted socially as well as professionally. He hastened to reassure my agitated spouse. "It is Mrs. Emerson's evidence that is wanted, and that of your son, Professor. The matter is of some urgency, or I would not have disturbed you at this hour."

"Hmph," said Emerson. "It had damned well better be urgent, Arbuthnot. Nothing less than cold-blooded murder would excuse—"

"Now, Emerson, you are being rude," I said. "It was good of Sir Reginald to come round himself instead of summoning us to his office. You ought to have deduced from his attire that he was called away from a dinner party or evening social event, which would not have eventuated had not the situation been serious. We were about to have coffee, Sir Reginald; take a chair, if you please, and join us?"

"Thank you, Mrs. Emerson, but I am rather pressed for time. If you could tell me—"

"Nothing is to be gained by haste, Sir Reginald. I expect the thieves have already got clean away with their loot. I trust Mr. Romer was not injured?"

Taking advantage of the thunderstruck silence that followed, I pressed the bell. "But I believe," I continued, as Gargery entered with the coffee tray, "that you would do better to take a glass of brandy, Sir Reginald. Exhale, I beg. Your face has turned quite an alarming color."

His breath came out in a miniature explosion. "How?" he gasped. "How did you—"

"I recognized the leader of the gang this afternoon—or thought

I did. I concluded I must have been mistaken, since I had no reason to believe the individual in question was in England. However, your presence here suggests that a crime has taken place, and that that crime is connected with the demonstration this afternoon, since it was Ramses and I whom you wanted to interview. It requires no great stretch of the imagination to reach the only possible conclusion."

"Ah," said Sir Reginald. "The only possible . . . I think, Mrs. Emerson, that I will take advantage of your kind suggestion. Brandy. Please!"

Emerson, whose eyes had been the widest of all, turned and walked with slow, deliberate strides to the sideboard. Removing the stopper from the decanter, he splashed brandy generously into a glass. Then he drank it.

"Our guest, Emerson," I reminded him.

"What? Oh. Yes."

Sir Reginald having been supplied, Emerson poured another brandy for himself and retreated to the sofa, where he sat down next to Nefret and stared at me. Ramses, his countenance as blank as ever I had seen it, politely carried coffee to the others. Then he sat down and stared at me.

They were all staring at me. It was very gratifying. Sir Reginald, having imbibed a sufficient quantity of brandy, cleared his throat.

"Mrs. Emerson, I came to inform you of a startling piece of news which reached me scarcely an hour ago, and you appear to know all about it. May I ask how you knew?"

"I hope you don't suspect *me* of being a member of the gang," I said, laughing.

"Oh—well—no, certainly not. Then how—"

It is better not to commit oneself before one knows all the facts. I said, "I will be happy to explain, Sir Reginald. But first you had better tell the others precisely what happened this afternoon."

Mr. Romer's butler was the key witness, from whom the police had heard the story. He had not opened the door; in fact, his master had ordered him to lock it. He did not know how the lock had been forced. Caught off guard, he was overpowered by two heavy-set muscular women who had borne him to the ground and bound him hand and foot with ropes they took from their reticules. The other invaders had instantly fanned out into the back regions of the house.

Not a word had been spoken; the procedure had been planned with the precision of a military operation.

Lying helpless on the floor of the hall, he had seen a man wearing a long cloak and slouch hat bound up the stairs. Shortly thereafter another individual, whom he took to be his master, had descended the stairs and gone to the front door. Opening it, he had addressed those without in the words I have reported. It had been his master's look, his master's voice, his master's very garments, but instead of coming to the aid of his unfortunate servant, the soi-disant Mr. Romer had gone back up the stairs.

For the next half hour, only voices and sounds of brisk activity told him of the whereabouts of the invaders. When they reappeared they were carrying luggage of all varieties, including a huge traveling trunk. The bearers were persons dressed in the livery of Mr. Romer's footmen, but their faces were not the ones of the footmen he knew. They began carrying the baggage out. They were followed by the man who looked like his master, now wearing Mr. Romer's favorite fur-trimmed overcoat. The woman with him was one of the intruders; she was dressed like a lady, in a long mantle and large flowered hat. Arm in arm they left the house, and the door closed behind them.

It took the poor man over an hour to free himself. Creeping timidly and stiffly from room to room, he found the other servants locked in the cellar. The footmen were attired only in their undergarments. Mr. Romer, bound to a chair in his library, was in the same embarrassing state of undress. The cabinets which had contained his lordship's superb collection of Egyptian antiquities were empty.

"In short," Sir Reginald concluded, "the individuals who had entered the house assumed the livery of the footmen and carried the trunks, which contained Mr. Romer's collection, to a waiting carriage. The constable at the gate suspected nothing. He actually helped the driver load the luggage into the carriage. As for the individual whom the butler took to be his master—"

"He was the man in the slouch hat and the cape," I said. "I blame myself, Sir Reginald, for not informing Scotland Yard at once. However, I hope you will do me the justice to admit that none of your subordinates would have believed me."

"Very possibly not. Am I to take it, Mrs. Emerson, that you recognized this person, at a distance, and despite a disguise that deceived his lordship's own butler?"

"Not to say recognized," I replied. "The modern fashion of beards and mustaches affected by so many gentlemen makes an impostor's task laughably easy. It was rather an indefinable sense of familiarity in his posture, his gestures—the same sense of familiarity that had struck me when I saw the individual in the velvet cloak and slouch hat. He is a master of disguise, a mimic of exceptional ability—"

"Amelia," said Emerson, breathing heavily through his nose, "are you telling us that this man was—"

"The Master Criminal," I said. "Who else?"

Our first encounters with this remarkable individual had occurred when we were working in the ancient cemeteries near Cairo. Tomb robbing and the sale of illegal antiquities are of long standing in Egypt; the former profession has been practiced since pharaonic times. However, during the early 1890s there had been a dramatic increase in these activities, and it was obvious that some genius of crime had taken over the iniquitous underworld of antiquities dealing. I should say that this conclusion was obvious to Emerson and me. Police officials are notoriously dim-witted and resistant to new ideas. It was not until we found Sethos's secret headquarters that they were forced to admit the truth of our deductions, and even now, I am told, certain individuals deny that such a man exists.

Though we had foiled several of Sethos's most dastardly schemes, the man himself had always eluded us. It had been some years since we had last seen or heard of him; in fact, we had believed for a time that he was dead. Other miscreants, suffering from the same misapprehension, had attempted to take control of the criminal organization he had created. It now seemed evident that Sethos had rebuilt his organization, not in Egypt but in Europe—specifically, in England.

I was in the process of explaining this to poor confused Sir Reginald when I was again interrupted. I had been expecting an outburst from Emerson, whose violent temper and command of bad language have won him the affectionate Arabic soubriquet of "Father of Curses." However, on this occasion the interruption came from Ramses.

"Something told me by Miss Christabel Pankhurst, though without significance to me at the time, tends to substantiate your theory, Mother. Mrs. Markham and her brother did not join the group until after we left London in June. A number of other 'ladies,' friends of theirs, became active in the movement at the same time. They must have been the ones who entered the house with her. I was struck, at the time, by the fact that Mrs. Pankhurst did not form part of the delegation."

"Yes, but ... but ..." Sir Reginald stuttered. "All this is unsubstantiated, unproven."

"The proof," said my annoying offspring, anticipating me as he usually did, "is in the outcome. The thieves were not ordinary burglars; they were after Mr. Romer's antiquities, which form one of the finest private collections in the world. The Master Criminal specializes in Egyptian antiquities, and the notion of using a suffragist organization in order to gain entry to the house of a virulent opponent of votes for women is characteristic of Sethos's sardonic sense of humor."

"But," said Sir Reginald, like a broken gramophone record, "but—"

"If it was Sethos you will never catch the bastard," said Emerson. It was symptomatic of his state of mind that he did not even apologize for bad language—to which, I must confess, we had all become accustomed. He went on, "But I wish you luck. Nothing would please me more than to see him in the dock. We have told you all we know, Sir Reginald. Hadn't you better get at it instead of lolling around drinking brandy?"

From Manuscript H

Ramses opened the door of his room.

"You knocked?" he inquired in simulated astonishment. "Why this deviation from habit?"

Nefret swept into the room, the full skirts of her negligee trailing like a royal robe, and flung herself down on the bed. "Don't try to put me on the defensive, Ramses, I will not let you do it. How dare you spy on me?"

Involuntarily Ramses glanced at David, who rolled his eyes and shrugged, indicating that he had no intention of getting involved in the argument.

"An unprovoked and unwarranted accusation," Ramses said.

His cool response only made Nefret angrier. Color stained her cheeks. "The devil it is! You came sneaking round to the hospital to find out whether I was really there. Well, I wasn't, was I?"

"Evidently not."

They glared at one another. David decided it was time to intervene, before one of them said something really rude.

"I am sure Ramses only went by to see whether you wanted to accompany him to the suffragist meeting. Isn't that right, Ramses?"

Ramses nodded. It was the best he could do; a spoken "yes" would have stuck in his throat.

"You needn't have brought it up in front of Aunt Amelia and the Professor."

"You started it."

"By teasing you about Christabel?" Nefret was never able to stay angry for long. The corners of her mouth quivered.

"You know I don't give a damn about the damned girl!"

"Oh, dear, what an ungentlemanly thing to say. But she—"

"Don't begin again," David exclaimed. He never knew whether to laugh or swear or sympathize when the two of them got into one of these exchanges; Nefret was one of the few people in the world who could make Ramses lose his temper, and David was probably the only person in the world who knew why. Hoping to distract them, he went on, "You came at an opportune moment, Nefret; we were discussing the reappearance of the Master Criminal, and Ramses was about to tell me what he knows of that mysterious individual."

Nefret sat up and crossed her legs. "I'm sorry, Ramses," she said cheerfully. "I shouldn't have accused you of spying on me."

"No."

"It's your turn to apologize."

"What for?" He caught David's eye and got a grip on himself. "Oh, very well. I apologize."

"All forgiven, then. I am glad I came, for I am dying of curiosity about Sethos. To be honest, I had come to think of him as . . . well, not exactly a figment of Aunt Amelia's imagination, but an example of her tendency to exaggerate."

"Her fondness for melodrama, you mean." Ramses seated himself on the floor, Arab-style.

Nefret grinned and took the cigarette he offered her. "Neither of us is being entirely fair, Ramses. Aunt Amelia doesn't have to exaggerate. Things *happen* to her. She was holding something back, though. You can always tell because she looks you straight in the eye and speaks briskly and firmly. The Professor was concealing something too. What is the secret about Sethos that neither of them wants known?"

"I have told you some of it."

"Bits and pieces. It was from him you learned the art of disguise—"

"That is not entirely accurate," said Ramses. "I fell heir to Sethos's collection of disguises, after Father forced him to flee from his headquarters, but I had to reason out his methods for myself and improve on them."

"I beg your pardon," said Nefret.

"Granted."

"Ramses," David began.

"Yes. I have told both of you what I know of the man from my personal encounters with him. On all those occasions he was disguised, and very well, too; his impersonation of a crotchety old American lady was absolutely brilliant. At the end of that particular adventure he succeeded in abducting Mother, and held her prisoner for several hours. I don't know what transpired during that interval. I doubt that even my father knows for certain. That is why the mere mention of Sethos maddens him so."

Nefret's mouth hung open. "Good Gad," she gasped. "Are you saying he—she—they—"

"I doubt it," Ramses said coolly. "I have never known two people so attached to one another as my parents. It is very embarrassing at times," he added, scowling.

"I think it's beautiful," Nefret said with a fond smile. "No, Aunt Amelia would never be untrue to the Professor, but if she was in that evil man's power—"

Ramses shook his head. "She would not have spoken of Sethos

with such forbearance if he had forced himself on her. However, there is no doubt in my mind that he was in love with her, and it is possible that she felt a certain unwilling attraction for him. I saw the letter he sent her after we had got her back; he promised her he would never again interfere with her or anyone she loved. I suspect, though, that she and Father have encountered him again since. There were some very odd aspects about that business a few seasons ago— you remember, Nefret, when they went out to Egypt alone and we were staying with Aunt Evelyn and Uncle Walter."*

Nefret gurgled with laughter. "Do you remember the night we let the lion out of its cage? Uncle Walter was absolutely furious!"

"With me," Ramses said. "Not you."

"It was your idea," Nefret pointed out. "Well, never mind. But the villain in that case wasn't Sethos, it was somebody else. I forget his name."

"It is difficult to keep track of all the people who have tried to murder Mother and Father," Ramses agreed. "This villain was a chap named Vincey, and since Father shot him during their final encounter, we may reasonably conclude he was guilty of something. Father doesn't kill people if he can avoid doing so. But I still think Sethos was involved in that business, in a manner I can't explain."

Nefret scowled. "It's ridiculous, the way we have to piece things together from bits of miscellaneous information. Why do Aunt Amelia and the Professor try to keep information from us? It's dangerous, for them and for us. Uninformed is unarmed!"

She gestured vehemently, sprinkling the floor with ashes. Ramses removed the cigarette from her hand and extinguished it in the bowl they used for a receptacle. Its original function had been to contain potpourri. His mother knew he smoked, though he seldom indulged in her presence, since she disapproved. He knew he did it *because* she disapproved. David did it because he did, and Nefret did it because he and David did.

"I wonder if Sethos knew she would be there this afternoon," David said.

"I am convinced he did not know," Ramses said. "Mother had had very little to do with the WSPU, and her decision to attend this particular demonstration was made on the spur of the moment."

*The Snake, the Crocodile and the Dog.

"He must have seen her there, though."

"It is difficult to overlook Mother." They exchanged knowing smiles, and Ramses went on, "However, by the time she arrived it was too late to cancel the operation. No, David, I'm certain the encounter was accidental. He'll be careful to stay out of her way hereafter."

He fell silent. After a moment, Nefret said, "What does he look like? She's a good observer; if she spent so much time alone with him, she ought to have noticed *something.*"

"Not a great deal. His eyes are of an indeterminate shade; they can appear black, gray or hazel. The color of his hair is unknown, thanks to his skillful use of wigs and dyes. The only facts of which we can be relatively certain are his height—a trifle under six feet—and his build, which is that of a man in the prime of life and excellent physical condition. Though he speaks a number of languages, Mother is of the opinion that he is an Englishman. Not very useful, you must admit."

"Yet she recognized him tonight," Nefret said.

"That was odd," Ramses admitted. "I would think she had invented it, but for the fact that something unquestionably struck her at the time. She started to ask me if I had noticed anything unusual, and then thought better of it."

"You didn't?"

"I had not seen the fellow for years, and—"

"That's quite all right, my boy, you needn't make excuses. Six feet tall, in excellent physical condition . . . Hmmmm."

"Just what are you suggesting?" Ramses demanded, stiffening.

She put a slim hand on his shoulder. "Calm yourself, my boy. I assure you I meant no insult to Aunt Amelia. But if she was attracted to him, however unwillingly, the counterreaction will be even stronger."

"What counterreaction?" David asked.

Nefret gave him a kindly smile. "You don't know much about women, either of you. A woman may forgive a man for abducting her, and she certainly will not blame him for falling in love with her. What she will *never* forgive is being made to look like a fool. That is what Sethos has done to Aunt Amelia."

"I wish you wouldn't spout aphorisms," Ramses grumbled. "You sound like Mother."

"That is not an aphorism, it is a simple fact! Don't you see—the way Sethos used the suffragist movement struck a blow at a cause dear to Aunt Amelia's heart. It will give fresh ammunition to those male supremacists who claim women are too naive and childlike to deal with the real world. The WSPU will be mercilessly ridiculed for admitting a pack of criminals into their ranks—"

"That isn't fair," Ramses protested. "Sethos has deceived the keenest criminal investigators."

"Fair, unfair, what difference does that make to the press? And just wait until some enterprising journalist discovers Aunt Amelia was there. 'Mrs. Amelia P. Emerson, the noted archaeologist and amateur detective, attacked a constable who was attempting to prevent a gang of thieves from entering the house!' "

"Oh dear," David exclaimed, paling visibly. "They wouldn't!"

"She didn't actually attack the fellow," Ramses mused. "But it wasn't for want of trying. Oh dear indeed. Could we find an excuse to leave town for a few days, do you think?"

2

I am a rational individual. My emotions are under firm control at all times. Being only too familiar with the lies and exaggerations of journalists, I knew what to expect from those villains once the story of the robbery got out. I was prepared for the worst and determined not to lose my temper.

Nor would I have done if the *Daily Yell*, London's most prominent proponent of sensational journalism, had not printed a letter from Sethos himself. It had been sent to the newspaper in care of Kevin O'Connell, who was an old acquaintance of ours. At times I considered Kevin a friend. This was not one of those times.

"For once," Emerson remarked somewhat breathlessly, as I struggled to free myself from the steely arms that had wrapped round me, "I must come to O'Connell's defense. You could hardly expect him to refrain from printing . . . Curse it, Peabody, will you please put down that parasol and stop squirming? I will not allow you to leave the house while you are in this agitated state of mind."

I daresay I could have got away from him, but I would not have got far. Gargery stood before the closed door, arms outstretched and frame stiff with resolve; Ramses and David had been drawn to the scene by Emerson's shouts and my indignant expostulations, and I entertained no illusions as to whose side they were on. Men always stick together.

"I do not know why you are behaving in such an undignified manner, Emerson," I said. "Let me go at once."

Emerson's grip did not relax. "Give me your word you will come along quietly."

"How can I not, when there are four of you great bullies against one poor little woman?"

Gargery, who is not especially large or muscular, swelled with pride. "Aow, madam—" he began.

"Mind your vowels, Gargery."

"Yes, madam. Madam, if you want that reporter thrashed you should leave it to the Professor, or to me, madam, or Bob, or Jerry, or—"

Emerson cut him short with a gesture and a nod. "Come along to the library, Peabody, and we will discuss this calmly. Gargery, pour the whiskey."

A sip of this curative beverage, so soothing to the nerves, restored me to my customary self-possession. "I suppose you have all read the letter," I remarked.

Obviously they had, including Nefret, who had kept prudently out of the way until then. David said timidly, "I thought it a very gentlemanly and graceful gesture. An apology, even."

"A cursed impertinence, rather," Emerson exclaimed. "A jeer, a sneer, a challenge; rubbing salt in the wound, aggravating the offense—"

"He has a pretty turn of rhetoric," said Ramses, who had taken up the newspaper. " 'The honorable and upright ladies of the suffragist moment—a movement with which I am in complete sympathy—cannot be blamed for their failure to anticipate my intentions. The police of a dozen countries have sought me in vain. Scotland Yard—' " He broke off and looked critically at Nefret. "You find it amusing?"

"Very." Nefret's laughter is quite delightful—soft and low-pitched, like sunlit water bubbling over pebbles. On this occasion I could have done without the pleasure of hearing it. Catching my eye, she attempted to contain her mirth, with only partial success. "Particularly that sentence about being in sympathy with the suffragist movement. Considering that one of his lieutenants is female, one must give him credit for living up to his principles."

"What principles?" Emerson demanded, conspicuously unamused. "His reference to your Aunt Amelia proves he is no gentleman."

"He referred to her in the most flattering terms," Nefret insisted. She snatched the paper from Ramses and read aloud. " 'Had I known that Mrs. Emerson would be present, I would not have proceeded with my plan. I have greater respect for her perspicuity than for that of all Scotland Yard.' "

Emerson said, "Ha!" I said nothing. I was afraid that if I unclenched my jaws I would use improper language. Ramses looked from me to Nefret.

"What do you think, Nefret?"

"I think," said Nefret, "that Sethos does not know much about women either."

It gave me a certain mean satisfaction to find that Sethos had foiled Scotland Yard as effectively as he had fooled me. The inquiry had come to a dead end after Mr. Romer's carriage and horses were discovered in a livery stable in Cheapside. The individual who had left it was described, unhelpfully, as a bearded gentleman. The carriage had been empty.

I was in receipt of a courteous note from Mrs. Pankhurst wishing me bon voyage and hoping she would have the pleasure of seeing me again *after I had returned from Egypt in the spring*. Apparently she blamed me for the unpleasant publicity. A most unreasonable attitude, since it was not I who had been taken in by Mrs. Markham and her "brother," but of course it would have been beneath my dignity to point this out. I forgave Mrs. Pankhurst, as was my Christian duty, and did not respond to her message.

The press surrounded the house, demanding interviews. I was determined to have a little chat with Kevin O'Connell, but it would have been impossible to admit him without arousing the competitive spirit of his fellow villains, so Ramses and Emerson smuggled him into the house after dark, through the coalhole. He was still rather smudgy when Emerson brought him to the library and offered him a whiskey and soda.

I was at a loss to understand Emerson's remarkable forbearance with regard to Kevin, whom he had always regarded as an infernal nuisance, but I had come round to his point of view; if Kevin had withheld the letter, Sethos would have sent copies to other newspapers. I therefore accepted Kevin's effusive apologies with only a touch of hauteur.

"Indeed, Mrs. Emerson, me dear, I'd never have allowed the letter to be published if I had known you would take it badly," he protested. "It seemed to me a gentlemanly and graceful—"

"Oh, bah," I exclaimed. "Never mind the excuses, Kevin, I admit that you had little choice in the matter. However, the least you can do to make amends is to tell us everything you know about that impertinent missive."

"I can do better than that." Kevin took an envelope from his breast pocket. "I brought the original."

"How did you manage to get it back from Scotland Yard?" I asked.

"By bribery and corruption," said Kevin with a cheeky grin. "It is only on loan, Mrs. E., so make the most of your time. I assured my—er—friend that I would return it to him before morning."

After perusing the letter I passed it on to Emerson. "We might have known Sethos would leave no useful clue," I said in disgust. "The paper is of the sort that can be purchased at any stationer's. The message is not even written by hand, but on a typewriting machine."

"A Royal," said Ramses, looking over his father's shoulder. "It is one of the latest models, with a ball-bearing one-track rail—"

"That is a safe pronouncement, since none of us can prove you wrong," I remarked with a certain degree of sarcasm.

"I believe I am not wrong, though," said my son calmly. "I have made a study of typewriting machines, since they are already in common use and will eventually, I daresay, entirely replace—"

"The signature is handwritten," David said, in an attempt, no doubt, to change the subject. Ramses does have a habit of running on and on.

"In hieroglyphs," Emerson growled. "What an incredible ego the man has! He has even enclosed his name in a cartouche, a privilege reserved for royalty."

Kevin was beginning to show signs of impatience. "Forgive me, Mrs. E., but I promised my confederate I would get this back to him by midnight tonight. He would be the first to be suspected if it were missing and then I might lose a valuable source of information."

There were still a few confounded reporters hanging about the following day, when we expected Evelyn and Walter. Having dispatched the carriage to the railroad station in order to meet the train, we waited for an appropriate interval; Emerson then emerged, picked up a reporter at random, carried him across the street into the park, and threw him into the pond. This served to distract the rest of the wretches, so that Evelyn, Walter, and Lia, as I must call her, were able to enter the house unassaulted.

Walter declined tea in favor of whiskey and soda, but his reaction to the affair was less outraged than I had feared it would be. As he remarked to his wife, "We ought to be accustomed to it, Evelyn; our dear Amelia makes a habit of such things."

"You cannot blame this on Amelia," Evelyn said firmly.

"I can," said Emerson, brushing at the muddy splashes on his boots and trousers. "If she had not taken it into her head to participate in that demonstration—"

"I would have joined her had I been in London," said Evelyn. "Come now, Emerson, she could not possibly have anticipated that that—person—would be involved."

"We must give her that," Walter agreed, with an affectionate smile at me.

"It must have been frightfully exciting," said little Amelia (whom I must remember to call Lia).

She was so like her mother! Her smooth skin and soft blue eyes and fair hair recalled happy memories of the young girl I had found fainting in the Forum that day in Rome so long ago. But this young face, thank Heaven, was blooming with health, and the graceful little form was sturdy and straight.

Nefret gave her a warning look. "Don't get your hopes up, dear. Sethos made it clear that the encounter was accidental and that he would have avoided it had he been able. It will be a dull season, I assure you, with no exciting adventures."

"Quite right," said David.

"Absolutely," said Ramses.

"A very dull season," I agreed. "If Emerson means to go on with his boring work in the Valley. I wonder that you have put up with it so long, Emerson. It is insulting to us—us, the finest excavators in the profession—allowed only to clear tombs other archaeologists have abandoned as unworthy of interest. We might as well be housemaids, cleaning up after our betters."

Emerson interrupted me with a vehement remark, and Walter, always the peacemaker, interrupted Emerson, asking him how much longer it would be before we departed. I leaned back in my chair and listened with a satisfied smile. I had turned the conversation away from the dangerous subject. Evelyn and Walter would never allow their beloved child to accompany us if they believed there was danger ahead. Nor, of course, would I.

It was on the following morning that I received another communication from Mrs. Pankhurst, inviting me to an emergency meeting of the committee that afternoon.

Nefret had taken Lia to the hospital with her, and the boys had gone to the British Museum with Walter. Emerson had announced at breakfast that he meant to work on his book and must not be interrupted. I had looked forward to a long quiet day with Evelyn, who is my dearest friend as well as my sister-in-law, but after brief consideration I decided I must attend the meeting. Although Mrs. Pankhurst made no reference to her earlier note, I took the present invitation to be in the nature of an olive branch. It was quite a businesslike epistle, brief and to the point.

Evelyn, as ardent a suffragist as I, agreed I ought to turn the other cheek for the good of the cause, but I felt I must decline her suggestion that she accompany me.

"This is a business meeting, you see, and it would not be proper to bring a stranger, especially in view of the fact that I am not a member of the committee. Perhaps they mean to propose me this afternoon. Yes, that seems quite likely."

Evelyn nodded agreement. "Will you tell Emerson of your plans, or shall I, when he emerges from his lair?"

"He is rather like a bear when he is disturbed," I agreed with a laugh. "But I suppose I had better do so. He doesn't like me to go off without informing him."

Emerson bent over his desk, attacking the page with vehement strokes of his pen. I cleared my throat. He started, dropped the pen, swore, and stared at me.

"What do you want?"

"I am going out for a while, Emerson. I felt obliged to mention it to you."

"Oh," said Emerson. He flexed his cramped hands. "Where are you going?"

I explained. Emerson's eyes brightened.

"I will drive you in the motorcar."

"No, you will not!"

"But, Peabody—"

"You have work to do, my dear. Besides, you were not invited. This is a business meeting. I must do a few errands first, and you know how you hate going to the shops with me."

"One excuse is sufficient," said Emerson mildly. He leaned back in his chair and studied me. "You wouldn't lie to me, would you, Peabody?"

"I will show you the letter from Mrs. Pankhurst if you don't believe me."

Emerson held out his hand.

"Really, Emerson," I exclaimed. "I am deeply hurt and offended that you should doubt my word. The letter is on the desk in my sitting room, but if you want to see it you can just fetch it yourself."

"You are taking the carriage, then?"

"Yes. Bob will drive me. Why the interrogation, Emerson? Are you having premonitions?"

"I never have premonitions," Emerson growled. "All right, Peabody. Behave yourself and try not to get in trouble."

Having mentioned errands, I felt I must perform a few, since I never lie to Emerson unless it is absolutely necessary. They took some little time, and the early dusk was falling when I directed Bob to take me to Clement's Inn, where the Pankhursts had taken lodgings.

Fleet Street was filled with omnibuses, carriages, vans and cycles, each vehicle looking for a break in the traffic. Motorcars darted ahead of all rivals whenever opportunity served, the roaring of their engines adding to the din. Our progress was slow. When one particular delay prolonged itself, I looked out of the window and saw a positive tangle of vehicles ahead. The core of the obstruction appeared to be a coster's barrow and a hansom cab, whose wheels had become entangled. The owners of both were screaming insults at one another, other drivers added their comments, and from somewhere behind us the impatient operator of a motorcar sounded a series of frantic blasts on his horn.

I called to Bob. "I will walk from here. It is only a few hundred yards."

Opening the door—with some difficulty, since a railway delivery van had pulled up close on that side—I started to get out.

My foot never touched the pavement. I had only a flashing glimpse of a hard, unshaven face close to mine before I was passed like an unwieldy parcel from the grasp of the first man into the even more painful grip of a second individual. Initially I was too astonished to defend myself effectively. Then I saw, behind the second man, something that informed me there was no time to lose. The back doors of the van were open, and it was that dark orifice toward which I was being carried.

The situation did not look promising. I had dropped my parasol, and my cries were drowned by the incessant hooting of the motorcar. As the fellow attempted to thrust me into the interior of the van, I managed to catch hold of the door with one hand. A hard blow on my forearm loosened my grip and wrung a cry of pain from my lips. With a violent oath the villain gave me a shove and I fell, striking the back of my head rather heavily. Half in and half out of the van, giddy and breathless, blinded by the hat that had been tipped over my eyes, I gathered my strength for what I knew must be my final act of resistance. When hands seized my shoulders I kicked out as hard as I could.

"Damnation!" said a familiar voice.

I sat up and pushed the hat away from my eyes. The darkness was almost complete, but the streetlights had come on, and the powerful lamps of a motorcar silhouetted a form I knew as well as I had known that beloved voice.

"Oh, Emerson, is it you? Did I injure you?"

"Disaster was avoided by a matter of inches," said my husband gravely.

He pulled me out of the van and crushed me painfully to him, completing the destruction of my second-best hat.

"Is she all right?" The agitated voice was that of David, perched atop a cart that had drawn up behind us. Ignoring the curses of the driver he jumped down, accompanied by a rain of cabbages, and hastened to Emerson's side. "Professor, hadn't we better get her away at once? There may be more of them."

"No such luck," Emerson grunted. Scooping me up into his arms he bent over and peered under the van. "They've got clean away, curse them. I should have hit that bastard harder. It is your fault, Peabody; if you had not winded me with that kick in the—"

"Radcliffe!" Though the voice was distorted by emotion and want of breath, I knew the speaker had to be Walter; no one else employs Emerson's detested first name.

"Yes, yes." Tightening his grasp, as if he feared I would slip away from him, Emerson carried me toward the motorcar. It was our motorcar. Behind the wheel, watching with mild interest, was my son, Ramses.

"**P**remonition be damned," said Emerson. "It was cold hard reason that informed me you had been guilty of a serious eroror in judgment."

"In fact," said Evelyn, "it was I who convinced you, was it not?"

At one time she would not have ventured to contradict him, but (with my encouragement) she had learned to stand up for herself— not only with Emerson but with her husband, who had been rather inclined to patronize her. Emerson quite enjoyed her independent manner. His scowling face relaxed into a smile.

"Let us say, my dear Evelyn, that your doubts confirmed my own. After dismissing Peabody so cavalierly, Mrs. Pankhurst was not likely to—"

"Oh, curse it," I exclaimed. "You had no such suspicions or you would have attempted to prevent me from going."

Emerson said, "Have another whiskey and soda, Peabody."

He had bundled me into the motorcar, leaving Bob to extricate the carriage—not so difficult after all, since the entwined vehicles had untangled themselves with a quickness that might have struck some as hightly suspicious. The railway van formed a new obstruction, however. Its driver had disappeared, and so had the individual Emerson had struck senseless. This annoyed him a great deal, for, as he remarked, when he knocked people down he expected them to stay down.

When we stopped in front of Chalfont House we were set upon by our agitated friends, including Nefret and Lia, who had returned from the hospital too late to join the rescue expedition. They pulled me out of the vehicle and passed me from one pair of loving arms to the next—including those of Gargery, who was inclined to forget his station when overcome by emotion. The other servants contented themselves with shouting "Hurrah!" and embracing one another. We then retired in triumph to the library.

It was our favorite apartment in that large, pretentious mansion. Rows of books in mellow leather bindings lined the walls, and Evelyn had replaced the ornate Empire furniture with comfortable chairs and sofas. A cozy fire burned on the hearth and the lamps had been lit. Gargery drew the heavy velvet curtains and then sidled off to a corner of the room where, with our tactful cooperation, he pretended to be invisible. I would have invited him to sit down and listen in comfort had I not known he would be shocked at the idea.

I had a few questions of my own. Conversation had been impossible during the return drive; Emerson kept shouting directions and suggestions at Ramses, who ignored them as coolly as he ignored my complaints that he was driving too fast.

Now Ramses said, "I also found it difficult to believe that Mrs. Pankhurst would proffer such an invitation, and at such short notice. However, we might not have acted on such doubtful grounds had not Aunt Evelyn showed me the letter. A single glance informed me that it had been typewritten on the same machine as the one Sethos had used."

The only thing I dislike more than being lectured on Egyptology by Ramses is being lectured on detection by Ramses. However, a rational individual does not allow childish pique to interfere with the acquisition of knowledge.

"How?" I asked.

"Individual letters may become worn or scratched or cracked," Ramses explained. "These flaws, however minute, are reproduced on the paper when the key strikes it."

"Yes, I see." I promised myself I would have a close look at one of the confounded machines. One must keep up with modern advances. "So you could identify the machine that wrote that letter?"

"If I could find it. That is of course the difficulty."

"A difficulty indeed, since you have not the slightest idea where to begin looking for it."

"What difference does it make?" Evelyn demanded. "You have brought her back safe. Thank heaven you were in time!"

"There was ample time," said Emerson, who is disinclined to give heaven any credit whatever. "We went straight to Mrs. Pankhurst's rooms in Clement's Inn and learned, as we had expected, that she had sent no message. David wanted to go haring off to look for you, my dear, but I persuaded him of the folly of that."

"Yes, I know how impetuous David can be," I said, smiling at the young man. It had been Emerson, of course, who had wanted to drive furiously around London in a futile search for me.

"We had no choice but to wait for you near the designated rendezvous," Ramses said. "We had been waiting for a quarter of an hour at least before you came, Mother, and were, I assure you, on the qui vive, but we failed to recognize the significance of the entangled vehicles. It is a common-enough occurrence. I do not doubt that on this occasion it was deliberately engineered, and that the drivers of the coster's cart and the cab were Sethos's confederates, as were the individuals in the railway van. The operation was very neatly planned and executed. They might have got you away if Father had not leaped instantly from the motorcar and forced a path through the crowd."

Nefret, who was curled up in a corner of the divan, laughed. "I would like to have seen that. How many bicyclists did you trample underfoot, Professor darling?"

"One or two," Emerson said calmly. "And I seem to recall climbing over a cart filled with some vegetable substance. Potatoes, perhaps?"

"Something squashier," I said, unable to repress a smile. "I hope Bob can get those boots clean. You had better go up and change."

"You too," said Emerson, his brilliant blue eyes intent on my face.

"Yes, my dear."

Drawing my arm through his, Emerson led me out.

I assumed, naturally, that he was impatient to express his relief at my deliverance in his usual affectionate manner. On this occasion I was in error. He assisted me with buttons and boots, as he usually did; but once my outer garment had been removed, he turned me round and inspected me more in the manner of a physician than an impatient spouse.

"You look as if you had been over Victoria Falls in a barrel," he remarked.

"It looks worse than it feels," I assured him, not entirely truthfully, for the assorted bruises were stiffening and my shoulder ached like fury. I must have landed on it when the rascal tossed me into the van.

Emerson ran his long fingers through my hair and then took me gently by the chin and tilted my face up to the light. "There is a bruise on your jaw and a lump on the back of your head. Did he strike you on the face, Peabody?"

Not one whit deceived by the unnatural calm of his voice, I strove to reassure him. "I can't remember, Emerson. It was quite exciting while it lasted, you see. I fought back, of course—"

"Of course. Well, I have seen you in worse condition, but I am going to put you to bed, Peabody, and send for a doctor."

I had no intention of submitting to this, but after some spirited discussion I agreed to let Nefret have a look at me. The look of shock on her face told me I must present rather a horrid spectacle, so I let her tend to me, which she did as gently and skillfully as a trained physician.

"There are no broken bones," she announced at last. "But the brute handled you very roughly."

"I was fighting back," I explained.

"Of course." She smiled affectionately. "She'll be stiff and sore for a few days, Professor; I know you will make sure she doesn't overdo."

Emerson was more than pleased to assist me with buttons and ribbons. He insisted on putting on my slippers for me, and as he knelt at my feet he presented such a touching picture of manly devotion that I could not resist brushing the thick black locks from his brow and pressing my lips to it. One thing led to another, and we were a trifle late going down for dinner.

The children were in excellent spirits, particularly Lia, who could talk of nothing but our forthcoming voyage. I was amused to note that she was wearing one of Nefret's embroidered robes and that she had arranged her hair in the same style as Nefret's. It did not become her quite as well, but she looked very pretty, her cheeks pink with excitement and her eyes sparkling. The boys teased her a bit, warning her of snakes and mice and scorpions, and promising to defend her from those terrors.

They were so merry together that I did not notice at first that the child's parents were silent and ill at ease. My brother-in-law is a man I truly esteem: a loving husband and father, a loyal brother, and a scholar of exceptional ability. He is not very good at hiding his feelings, however, and I could tell something was bothering him. My dear Evelyn's troubled gaze kept moving from her daughter to me and back again.

They waited until after we had retired to the library for coffee before they broke the news. Walter began by informing Emerson that he had taken the liberty of reporting the incident to the police.

"What incident?" Emerson demanded. "Oh. What did you do that for?"

"Upon my word, Radcliffe, you take this very coolly!" Walter exclaimed. "A brutal attack on your wife—"

Emerson slammed his cup into the saucer. Not much coffee was spilled, since he had drunk most of it, but I heard a distinct crack. "Curse you, Walter, how dare you suggest I am indifferent to my wife's safety? I will deal with Sethos myself. The police are of no damn—er—confounded use anyhow."

I will summarize the discussion, which became somewhat heated. Emerson does not like to have his judgment questioned, and Walter was in an unusual state of excitability. It culminated as I had begun to fear it would, with Walter's announcement that he could not allow Lia to accompany us that year.

Everyone began talking at once, and Gargery, who had been shaking with indignation ever since Walter accused Emerson of negligence, dropped one of my best demitasse cups. Finding her father adamant, Lia burst into tears and fled from the room, followed by Nefret. I sent Gargery away, since he was wreaking havoc with the Spode, and persuaded Evelyn that she had better go to her daughter. She gave me an appealing look, to which I responded with a smile and a nod; for indeed I understood the dear woman's dilemma. She would have risked her own safety to defend me from danger, but the safety of her child was another matter.

Not that I believed there was danger to me or anyone else. I managed to express this opinion once I had got the men to stop shouting at one another. My arguments were sensible and ought to have prevailed, but I found to my annoyance that he who ought to have been my strongest supporter had turned against me.

"Yes, well, I understand your viewpoint, Walter," Emerson said, with the affability that usually succeeds his fits of temper. "The child would not be in the slightest danger if she were with me—what did you say, Ramses?"

"I said 'with us,' Father. I beg your pardon for interrupting you, but I felt obliged to emphasize my willingness, and that of David, to lay down our lives if necessary—"

"Don't be so confounded melodramatic," Emerson snarled. "As I was saying, little Amelia would be perfectly safe with us, but perhaps this is for the best. I have decided to leave for Egypt as soon as possible. We will return to Kent tomorrow, pack our gear, and sail at the end of the week."

"Impossible, Emerson," I exclaimed. "I have not finished my shopping, and you have not finished your book, and—"

"The devil take your shopping, Peabody," Emerson said, with an affectionate look at me. "And the book as well. My dear, I intend to get you out of this bloody damned city at once. There are too many damned people here, including one of the bloodiest. If Sethos follows us to Egypt, so much the worse for him. Now come to bed. I want to get an early start."

Walter and Evelyn departed next morning with their unhappy child, leaving Mrs. Watson, their excellent housekeeper, in charge of shutting up the house and putting the servants on board wages. I expected Emerson would insist on driving the motorcar back to Kent, but to my surprise he gave in with scarcely a grumble when I said I preferred the comfort of the train. He ordered Ramses not to drive faster than ten miles per hour and presented Nefret with a preposterous motoring mask. Where he had found it, I cannot imagine. The tinted goggles were set in a frame of leather lined with silk, and it made her look like an apprehensive beetle.

From Manuscript H

"Take it off," Ramses said. "We're out of sight now."

Nefret, beside him in the front seat, gestured wildly. He couldn't decide whether the muffled noises that emerged from the narrow slit over her mouth were laughter, or an attempt at a reply, or the gasps of a woman who was unable to breathe. "Get it off her, David," he ordered in alarm.

David, who was in the tonneau, tugged at the straps until they gave way. There was no doubt about the nature of the noises he was making, and as soon as the hideous accoutrement came away from her face, Nefret joined him.

"Bless the dear man," she gasped, as soon as her laughter was under control. Her loosened hair blew around her face until she captured and hid it under a close-fitting bonnet.

Upon occasion—egged on by Nefret—Ramses had got the Daimler up to fifty miles per hour. Such speed was unachievable in the crowded city streets, but still the traffic noises made conversation impossible until they stopped for tea in a village on the outskirts of the city. Nefret made both of them try on the mask—to the amusement of the other customers—and then they got down to business. It was the first chance they had had for a private conference since the previous day.

"The situation has become serious," Nefret announced.

"Good Gad," said Ramses. "Do you really think so?"

"Ramses," David murmured.

"Oh, I don't mind him," Nefret said. "He's just trying to be frightfully, frightfully blasé. You were wrong, weren't you, dear boy? Sethos may not have known Aunt Amelia would be at the meeting, but we have not seen the last of him. He's after her again!"

She bit into a scone.

"It would appear that that is the case," Ramses admitted. "What I fail to understand is what prompted this renewed interest. It's been years since we heard from or about him. Unless . . ."

"Unless what?" David asked intently.

"Unless *she* has heard from him in the meantime. She wouldn't be likely to tell us about it."

"She never tells us anything," Nefret said indignantly.

"Why don't you ask her?"

"Why don't you? It's those eyes of hers," Nefret muttered theatrically, rolling her own. "That stormy gray shade is alarming even when she's in a pleasant mood, and when she's angry they look like—like polished steel balls." She gave an exaggerated shudder.

"It isn't funny," David said.

"No," Nefret agreed. "You didn't see the poor darling last night; she was covered with bruises. If the Professor gets his hands on Sethos he'll tear him to pieces, and I wouldn't mind joining in."

"Father has taken the necessary precautions," Ramses said. "Getting her out of London and away from England as soon as is possible."

"That's not enough," Nefret declared. "What if he follows her to Egypt?"

"He isn't likely to."

"So you say. What if he does? We need to know how to protect her! If she won't give us the necessary information, we must ferret it out! Well, Ramses?"

Ramses smiled ruefully. "Confound it, Nefret, I do wish you wouldn't read my mind. It's nothing to do with Sethos. I was thinking of something else. Did you know Mother once made a list of all the people who held a grudge against her and Father? There were fifteen names on it, and that was several years ago."

"Fifteen people who have wanted to murder her?" Nefret grinned. "How typical of her to make a neat, methodical list! Did she show it to you?"

"Not exactly."

Nefret chuckled. "Good for you, Ramses. I know, it's not *nice* to pry, but what other choice have we? Who were these people?"

Ramses prided himself on his memory, which he had cultivated (along with less acceptable skills) by hours of practice. He reeled off a list of names.

His companions followed him intently. They had not been with the Emersons during their earlier years in Egypt, but both of them knew the stories. "The Adventures of Aunt Amelia," as Nefret called them, had filled in many an idle hour.

"The majority of them are old enemies," David remarked, when Ramses had finished. "And some, surely, are out of the picture. Are you suggesting that it wasn't Sethos, but another former adversary, who attacked her yesterday?"

"No. I'm only considering all the possibilities. Most are, in fact, dead or in prison." Ramses added with a smile, "Mother made notes."

"What about the woman who kidnapped me during the hippopotamus affair?"* Nefret asked.

"We never knew her name, did we? Another of Mother's little omissions. However, there were only two women among the most recent additions to the list. Bertha was an ally of the villain in the case we were speaking of the other day, but she came over to Mother's and Father's side in the end. So, by a process of elimination, a female designated as Matilda must have been the villainess in the hippopotamus affair. There is no reason to suppose that she has turned up again, after so many years."

"There's no reason to suppose any of them have turned up again." Nefret picked up her gloves. "We must go, it's getting late. I commend your thoroughness, Ramses, but why look for other villains when we *know* who was responsible for the attack on Aunt Amelia? Sethos has returned! And if the Professor and Aunt Amelia won't tell us what we need to know to protect her, we are entitled to employ any underhanded method we like."

Kevin's informant at Scotland Yard served him well. The *Daily Yell* was the first to report my little adventure, which Kevin exaggerated in his usual journalistic fashion. I read the story that evening, after Emerson and I had boarded the train at Victoria. Gargery and his cudgel accompanied Emerson and me. He kept the cudgel concealed until after we had taken our seats, but it was not difficult for me to deduce its presence since he walked so close behind me the cursed thing kept jabbing me in the back. I am as democratic as the next man (or woman) and had no objection to sharing a first-class compartment with my butler, but the presence of Gargery (and the cudgel) had a sobering effect on me.

*The Hippopotamus Pool

For Emerson to accept any assistance whatever in looking after me was extraordinary. He was taking the business even more seriously than I had expected. I doubted that Sethos would be bold enough to try again, but if he were so inclined, we would certainly be safer in Egypt than in London. Our loyal men, all of whom had worked for us for many years, would have risked lives and limbs in our defense.

We were not able to leave England quite as soon as Emerson hoped, but in less than a fortnight we stood at the rail of the steamer waving and blowing kisses to the dear ones who had come to see us off. It did not rain, but the skies threatened, and a cold wind blew Evelyn's veils into gray streamers. Gargery had removed his hat, though I had strictly forbidden him to do so because of the inclement weather. He was looking particularly sulky, for I had refused to allow him to go with us "to look after you and Miss Nefret, madam." He made the same suggestion every year, and he always sulked when I refused.

Evelyn was trying to smile and Walter waved vigorously. Lia looked like a little effigy of grief, her face swollen with crying. Her distress had been so great Walter had promised that if nothing further occurred, he and Evelyn would bring her out with them after Christmas. As the ribbon of dark water between the ship and the dock widened, she covered her face with a handkerchief and turned into her mother's arms.

Her visible woe cast a damper over our spirits. Even Ramses seemed downcast. I had not realized he would miss his aunt and uncle so much.

However, by the time the boat approached Port Said, we had got back into our old routine, and anticipation had replaced melancholy. After suspiciously inspecting every passenger, particularly the ones who boarded at Gibraltar and Marseilles, Emerson had relaxed his vigilance, to the visible disappointment of several of the older ladies to whom he had been particularly charming. (The younger ladies were disappointed too, but he had not paid them so much attention because even he admitted Sethos would have some difficulty disguising himself as a five-foot-tall female with smooth cheeks and dainty feet.)

After the usual bustle and confusion on the quay we got our baggage sorted out and boarded the train for Cairo, where our dahabeeyah was moored. These charming houseboats, once the favorite means of Nile travel for wealthy tourists, had been largely replaced by steamers and the railroad, but Emerson had purchased one of them and named it after me because he knew how much I enjoy that means of travel. (And also because we could live on board instead of staying at a hotel while we were in Cairo. Emerson dislikes elegant hotels, tourists, and dressing for dinner.)

I approached the *Amelia* in a far happier frame of mind than I had ever enjoyed after such a prolonged absence. In previous years we had put Abdullah, our reis, in charge of making certain all was in readiness for our arrival. Abdullah was a man. Need I say more?

Among the crewmen waiting to greet us, standing modestly behind them all with her face veiled and her head bowed, was the individual who had replaced Abdullah—his daughter-in-law Fatima.

Fatima was the widow of Abdullah's son Feisal, who had passed on the previous year. One of his widows, I should say. The younger of his two wives, who had given him three children, had gone compliantly into the household of the man Abdullah selected for her, as custom decreed. Conceive of my amazement, therefore, when Fatima sought me out and asked for my help. She had loved her husband and he had loved her; he had taken a second wife only because she had begged him to, so that he might have the children she could not give him. She did not want another husband. She would work night and day to the limit of her strength at any position I could offer her so long as it enabled her to be independent.

The Reader can hardly doubt the nature of my response. To find a little flame of rebellion, a yearning for freedom—yes, and a marriage as tender and loving as any woman could wish—in an Egyptian woman thrilled me to the core. I consulted Abdullah, as a matter of courtesy, and was pleased to find that although he was far from enthusiastic, he did not forbid the scheme I had proposed.

"What else was to be expected?" he demanded rhetorically. "I do not know what the world is coming to, with the women learning to read and write, and the young men going to school instead of to work. I am glad I will not live to see it. Do as you like, Sitt Hakim, you always do."

And he went off, shaking his head and muttering about the good old days. Men always grumble, to make women believe they are reluctant about giving in, but I knew perfectly well Abdullah was delighted to be relieved of his housekeeping duties. He never did things the way I wanted them done and he always looked sour when I failed to register sufficient appreciation. Such encounters were very trying for both of us.

Fatima stayed in the background, as was proper, until we had greeted Reis Hassan and the other crewmen. Then I sent the men away so that Fatima could unveil.

She was a little woman, not as tall as I, with the fine, free carriage Egyptian women acquire from carrying heavy loads on their heads. I had taken her to be in her mid-forties, though she had looked older. The face she now displayed wore such a glow of happiness and welcome that her plain features were transformed.

"So, it is well?" I inquired.

"Yes, Sitt Hakim. All is very well." She spoke English, and my look of surprise made her beam even more broadly. "I study, Sitt, all the days I study, and I wash all thing, all thing, Sitt. Do you come and see, you and Nur Misur."

"Light of Egypt" was Nefret's Egyptian name. Knowing how much of a strain it is to carry on a prolonged conversation in a strange language, she said in Arabic, "Fatima, will you sometimes speak Arabic with me? I need the practice more than you need practice in English. How hard you have studied!"

She had done more than study. Every object on the boat that could sparkle or shine did so. The curtains had been washed so frequently they were wearing through in spots. She had sprinkled dried rose petals between the sheets (I looked forward to hearing Emerson's comments on that). There were vases of fresh flowers everywhere, and rosebuds floated in the water that filled the basins in each bedroom. My praise made her eyes shine, but as Fatima led the way to the saloon, Nefret said out of the corner of her mouth, "We are all going to smell like a bordello, Aunt Amelia."

"You are not supposed to know that word," I replied, as softly.

"I know others even less proper." With a sudden impulsive movement she threw her arms around Fatima, who had stopped to replace her veil, and gave her a hearty hug.

When we entered the saloon a muffled hiss of fury and dismay filtered through Fatima's veil. In less than a quarter of an hour the men had made a mess of the room. The boys were smoking cigarettes and letting the ashes fall onto the floor. Emerson had heaped papers and books on the table; and a vase (which had probably adorned that object of furniture) had been placed on the floor and kicked over, soaking the oriental rug. Emerson's coat was draped over the back of a chair. Ramses's coat lay on the floor.

Fatima darted forward and pushed ash receptacles up against assorted male elbows. Scooping up the battered blossoms she returned them to the vase, collected the discarded garments, and trotted toward the door.

"Oh, er, hmmm," said Emerson, watching the small black whirlwind warily. "Thank you, Fatima. Very good of you. Excellent job. The place looks . . . Is she annoyed about something, Peabody?"

Emerson's reaction to the rose petals was not quite what I had expected. He has a very poetic nature, though few besides myself are aware of it.

3

From Manuscript H

"**Y**ou look absolutely disgusting," Nefret said admiringly.

"Thank you." Ramses added another boil to his neck.

"I still don't see why you won't take me with you."

Ramses turned from the mirror and sat down on a stool in order to slip his feet into his shoes. Like his galabeeyah, they were of expensive workmanship but sadly scuffed and stained—the attire of a man who can afford the best, but whose personal habits leave a great deal to be desired. He stood up and adjusted the belt that held his heavy knife. "Are you ready, David?"

"Almost." David was also dirty, but not so afflicted with skin eruptions. An imposing black beard and mustache gave him a piratical air.

"It's not fair," Nefret grumbled.

She was sitting cross-legged on the bed in Ramses's room, stroking the cat whose sizable bulk filled her lap.

The cat in question, Horus by name, was the only one they had brought with them that season. Anubis, the patriarch of their tribe of Egyptian cats, was getting old, and none of the others had formed an attachment to a particular human. Horus was Nefret's—or, as Horus's behavior made clear, Nefret was his. Ramses suspected Horus felt the same about Nefret as he did about his harem of female cats; he abandoned her as cavalierly as Don Juan when he had other things on his mind; but when he was with her, no other male was allowed to approach—including Ramses and David.

Horus was the only cat Ramses had encountered whom he thoroughly disliked. Nefret accused him of being jealous. He was—but not because Horus preferred her. Since the death of his beloved Bastet, he had no desire to acquire another cat. Bastet could not be replaced; there would never be another like her. The reason why he was jealous of Horus was much simpler. Horus enjoyed favors he would have sold his soul to possess, and the furry egotist didn't even have the grace to appreciate them.

Years of painful experience had taught Ramses it was best to ignore Nefret's provocative speeches, but every now and then she got past his defenses, and the smirk on Horus's face didn't improve his temper.

"You are the one who is being unfair," he snapped. "I tried, Nefret—give me that. You know the result."

One night the previous winter he had spent two hours trying to turn her into a convincing imitation of an Egyptian tough. Beard, boils, skin paint, a carefully constructed squint—the more he did, the more absurd she looked. David had finally collapsed onto the bed, whooping with laughter. As Ramses struggled to keep his own face straight, Nefret had turned back to the mirror, inspected herself closely, and burst into a fit of the giggles. They had all laughed then, so hard that Nefret had to sit down on the floor holding her stomach and Ramses had to pour water over his head—to keep himself from snatching her up into his arms, beard, boils and all.

Seeing the corners of her mouth quiver in amused recollection he went on in the same brusque voice. "Mother will be back from that party at the Ministry before we return, and she may take a notion to look in on her dear children. If she finds *us* gone she'll lecture me long and loud in the morning, but if *you* are missing too, Father will skin me alive in the morning."

Nefret acknowledged defeat with a rueful grin. "One of these days I will convince him he mustn't hold you accountable for my actions, as if you were my nursemaid. You can't control me."

"No," Ramses said emphatically.

"Where are you going?"

"I'll tell you if you promise not to follow us."

"Confound you, Ramses, have you forgot our first law?"

David had proposed the rule: No one was to go off on his (or her) own without informing one of the others. Ramses had been in wholehearted agreement with the idea insofar as it pertained to Nefret, but she had made it clear that she would not conform unless they did too.

"I don't expect to run into any trouble tonight," he said grudgingly. "We are only making the rounds of the coffee shops in the old city to learn what has been going on since last spring. If Sethos is back in business, someone will have heard rumors of it."

"Oh, all right. But you are to report to me the instant you get home, is that understood?"

"You will be asleep by then," Ramses said.

"No, I won't."

The coffee shop was not far from the ruined Mosque of Murustan Kalaun. Its shutters were raised, leaving the interior open to the night air. Inside, the flames of small lamps twinkled in the gloom, and coils of blue smoke drifted like lazy djinn. The patrons sat on hassocks or stools around low tables, or on the divan at the rear of the room. Since this was an establishment favored by prosperous merchants, most of those present were well-dressed, their long kaftans silk-striped and their silver seal rings large and ornate. There were no women present.

A man at a table near the front looked up when Ramses and David entered. "Ah, so you have returned. The police have abandoned the search?"

"Very amusing," said Ramses, in the hoarse tones of Ali the Rat. "You know I always spend the summers at my palace in Alexandria."

A laugh acknowledged this witticism, and the speaker gestured them to join him. A waiter brought small cups of thick sweetened Turkish coffee and a narghileh. Ramses drew the smoke deep into his lungs and passed the mouthpiece to David. "So, how is business?" he inquired.

After a brief conversation their acquaintance bade them good night, and they were left alone at the table.

"Anything?" David asked. He spoke softly and without moving his lips—a trick Ramses had learned from one of his "less respectable acquaintances," a stage magician at the Alhambra Music Hall, and passed on to David.

Ramses shook his head. "Not yet. It will take time. But look over there."

The man he indicated was sitting alone on a bench at the back of the room. David narrowed his eyes. "I can't see . . . Surely it is not Yussuf Mahmud?"

"It is. Order two more coffees, I'll be right back."

He sidled up to a dignified bearded man at another table, who acknowledged his obsequious greeting with a curl of the lip. The conversation was rather one-sided; Ramses did most of the talking. He got only nods and curt answers for his pains, but when he came back he appeared pleased.

"Kyticas doesn't like me," he remarked. "But he dislikes Yussuf Mahmud even more. Kyticas thinks he's got something on his mind. He's been squatting on that bench every night for a week, but he hasn't tried to make any of his dirty little deals."

"Would the Master—uh—you know who I mean—deal with a second-rater like Yussuf Mahmud?"

"Who knows? He's one of the people I meant to talk with—and I'm beginning to suspect he wants to talk with me. He's carefully not looking at us. We'll take the hint and follow him when he leaves."

Yussuf Mahmud showed no sign of leaving. He sat stolidly drinking coffee and smoking. Unlike most of the others he was shabbily dressed, his feet bare, his turban tattered. His scanty beard did not conceal the scars of smallpox that covered his cheeks.

They passed another hour in not-so-idle gossip with various acquaintances. Ali the Rat was in a generous mood, paying for drinks and food with coins taken from a heavy purse. Yussuf Mahmud was one of the few who did not take advantage of his hospitality, though he was obviously fascinated by the purse. Ramses was about to suggest to David that they leave when a voice boomed out a hearty "Salaam aleikhum!"

Ramses almost fell off his stool, and David doubled over into an anonymous bundle, ducking his head. "Holy Sitt Miriam," he gasped. "It's—"

"—Abu Shitaim," said Ali the Rat, recovering himself in the nick of time. For good measure he added, "Curse the unbeliever!"

His father had advanced into the room with the asssurance of a man who is at home wherever he chooses to be. He glanced incuriously at Ali the Rat, dismissed him with a shrug, and went to join Kyticas. His sleeve over his face, David whispered, "Quick. Let's get out of here!"

"That would only attract his attention. Sit up, he's not looking at us."

"I thought he was at the reception!"

"So did I. He must have crept away while Mother wasn't looking. He hates those affairs."

"What's he doing here?"

"The same thing we are doing, I suspect," Ramses said thoughtfully. "All right, we can go now. Slowly!"

He tossed a few coins onto the table and rose. Out of the corner of his eye he saw Yussuf Mahmud get to his feet.

The following night they met by arrangement, and a short time later they were following Yussuf Mahmud into a part of the city which even Ali the Rat would have preferred to avoid. It bordered the infamous Fish Market, an innocuous name for a district where every variety of vice and perversion was for sale at all hours and, by European standards, at extremely reasonable prices. The narrow alley down which he led them was dark and silent, however, and the house they entered was obviously not his permanent address. The windows were tightly shuttered and the sole article of furniture was a rickety table. Yussuf Mahmud lit a lamp. Opening his robe, he loosened a leather strap.

Bound to his body by the strap was a bundle approximately sixteen inches long and four inches in diameter, wrapped in cloth and supported by splintlike lengths of rough wood.

Ramses knew what it was, and he knew what was going to happen. He dared not protest. Fearing David would let out an involuntary and betraying exclamation, he stamped heavily on his friend's foot as Yussuf Mahmud removed the wrappings and unrolled the object they had concealed. A few yellowed, brittle flakes sifted onto the table.

It was a funerary papyrus, the collection of magical spells and prayers popularly known as "The Book of the Dead." The section now visible showed several vertical columns of hieroglyphic writing and a painted vignette that depicted a woman clad in a transparent linen gown hand in hand with the jackal-headed god of cemeteries. Before he could see more, Yussuf Mahmud drew a piece of cloth over the roll.

"Well?" he said in a whisper. "You must decide now. I have other buyers."

Ramses scratched his ear, detaching a few flakes of a substance that had been designed to resemble encrusted dirt. "Impossible," he said. "I must know more before I consult my customers. Where did it come from?"

The other man smiled tightly and shook his head.

It was the first stage of a process that often took hours, and few Europeans had the patience to go through the intricate pattern of offer and counteroffer, question and ambiguous answer. In this case Ramses knew he must play the game to the best of his skill. He wanted that papyrus. It was one of the largest he had ever seen, and even that brief glimpse had suggested its quality and condition were extraordinary. How the devil, he wondered, had a petty criminal like Yussuf Mahmud come by something so remarkable?

Feigning disinterest, he turned away from the table. "It is too perfect," he said. "My buyer is a man of learning. He will know it is a fake. I could get, perhaps, twenty English pounds . . ."

When he and David left after another hour of bargaining, they did not have the papyrus. Ramses had not expected they would. No dealer or thief would part with the merchandise until the payment was in his hand. But they had come to an agreement. They were to meet again the following night.

David had not spoken at all during the discussion. He was not skilled at disguising his voice, so his role was to look large, loyal, and threatening. He was fairly bursting with excitement, however, and as soon as the door of the house closed behind them he exclaimed, "Good God! Did you—"

Ramses cut him off with a curt Arabic expletive, and neither of them spoke again until they reached the river. The small skiff was moored where they had left it. David took first turn at the oars. They were some distance from the shore, hidden by darkness, before Ramses had finished the process that transformed him from a shady-looking Cairene to a comparatively well-groomed young Englishman.

"Your turn," he said. They changed places. David peeled off his beard and removed his turban.

"Sorry," he said. "I should not have spoken when I did."

"Speaking educated English in that part of Cairo at that hour is not a sensible thing to do," Ramses said dryly. "There's more to this than meets the eye, David. Yussuf Mahmud doesn't deal in antiquities of that quality. Either he is acting as middle man for someone who doesn't want his identity known, or he stole the papyrus from a bigger thief. The original owner may be after him."

"Ah," David said. "I thought he was uncommonly edgy."

"I think you thought right. Marketing stolen antiquities is against the law, but it wasn't fear of the police that made the sweat pour off him."

David bundled up his disguise and tucked it away under the seat, then bent over the side to splash water on his face. "The papyrus was genuine, Ramses. I've never seen one as beautiful."

"I thought so too, but I'm glad to have you confirm my opinion. You know more of these things than I. You missed a wart."

"Where? Oh." David's fingers found the protuberance. Softened by water, it peeled off. "The Egyptians are right when they say you can see in the dark, like a cat," he remarked. "Are you going to tell the Professor about the papyrus?"

"You know how he feels about buying from dealers. I admire his principles, just as I admire the principles of pacifism, but I fear they are equally impractical. In the one case you end up dead. In the other, you lose valuable historical documents to idle collectors who take them home and forget about them. How can the trade be stopped when even the Service des Antiquités buys from such people?"

The little boat came gently to rest against the muddy bank. Ramses shipped the oars and went on, "In this case I can't see any other way out of what my mother would call a moral dilemma. I want that damned papyrus, and I want to know how Yussuf Mahmud got hold of it. How much money have you?"

"I—er—I'm a bit short," David admitted.

"So am I. As usual."

"What about the Professor?"

Ramses shifted uncomfortably. "There's no use asking him for the money, he wouldn't give it to me. He'd give me a fatherly lecture instead. I can't stand it when he does that."

"Then you'll have to ask Nefret."

"Damned if I will."

"That's stupid," David said. "She has more money than she knows what to do with, and she's eager to share. If she were as good a friend and a *man*, you wouldn't hesitate."

"It isn't that," Ramses said, knowing he was a liar and knowing that David knew it. "We'd have to tell her why we want the money, and then she'd want to come with us tomorrow night."

"Well?"

"Take Nefret to el Was'a? Have you lost your mind? Not under any circumstances whatever."

From Letter Collection B

It surely won't surprise you to learn I had the devil of a time *persuading* Ramses to let me go with them. The methods I use on the Professor—quivering lips, tear-filled eyes—haven't the *slightest* effect on that cold-blooded creature; he simply stalks out of the room, radiating disgust. So I was forced to resort to blackmail and intimidation, irrefutable female logic, *and* a gentle reminder that without my signature they couldn't get the money. (I suppose that's another form of blackmail, isn't it? How shocking!)

If I do say so, I made a very pretty boy! We bought the clothing that afternoon, after we had stopped by the banker's—an elegant pale blue wool galabeeyah, gold embroidered slippers, and a long scarf that covered my head and shadowed my face. Ramses darkened my eyebrows and lashes and painted kohl round my eyes. I thought it altered my appearance amazingly, but Ramses wasn't pleased.

"There's no way of changing *that* color," he muttered. "Keep your head bowed, Nefret, and your eyes modestly lowered. If you look directly at Mahmud or utter a single syllable while we are with him, I will—I will do something both of us might regret." A fascinating threat, wasn't it? I was tempted to disobey just to see what he had in mind, but decided not to risk it.

I had never been in that part of the Old City at night. I don't recommend that you venture there, darling; you are so fastidious you would be put off by the stench of rotting garbage and the rats scuttling past and the intense darkness. The darkness of the countryside is nothing to it; in Upper Egypt there is always starlight, even when the moon is down. Nothing so clean and pure as a star would dare show itself in that place. The tall old houses seemed to lean toward one another, whispering ugly secrets, and their balconies cut off even the clouded night sky. My heart was beating faster than usual, but I wasn't afraid. I am never frightened when we three are together. It's when they go off on some harebrained adventure without me that I get into a state of abject panic.

Ramses led the way. He knows every foot of the Old City, including some parts which respectable Egyptians avoid. When we got near the house, Ramses made me stay with him while David went ahead to reconnoiter. When he came back he didn't speak, but gestured us to go on.

It was a tenement or rooming house of the meanest kind. The hallway smelled of decaying food and hashish and the sweat of too many bodies confined in too small a space. We had to feel our way up the sagging stairs, keeping close to the wall. I couldn't see a cursed thing, so I followed David as I had been directed to do, my hand on his shoulder for guidance. Ramses was close behind me, gripping my elbow to keep me from falling when I stumbled— which I did do once or twice, because the curly toes of my bee-yootiful slippers kept catching on the splintered boards. I hated this part of it. I could *feel* crawly, slimy things all around me.

Our destination was a room on the first floor, distinguishable only by the slit of pale light at the bottom of the door. Ramses scratched at the panel. It opened at once.

Yussuf Mahmud gestured us to come in and then barred the door behind us. I supposed it was Yussuf Mahmud, though no one introduced us. He gave me a long look and said something in Arabic I didn't understand. It must have been something *very* rude, because

David made growling sounds and drew his knife. Ramses just squinted at the fellow and said something else I didn't understand. He and the man laughed. David didn't laugh, but he put the knife back in his belt.

The only light in the room came from a lamp on the table, dangerously close to the papyrus, which had been partially unrolled to display a painted vignette. I edged closer. The sheer size of it was enough to take one's breath away; I could tell, from the thickness of the unrolled portions, that it must be very long. The miniature scene depicted the weighing of the heart.

Before I saw more than that, Ramses grabbed hold of me and turned me round to face him. He must have thought I was about to exclaim aloud or move closer to the light—which I never would have done! I scowled at him and he leered at me. You have no idea how horrible Ali the Rat looks close up, even when he *isn't* leering.

The man said, "A new one, is he? You are a besotted fool to bring him here."

"He is such a pretty thing I cannot bear to be parted from him," Ramses muttered, leering even more hideously. "Go stand in the corner, my little gazelle, until we complete our business."

They had reached an agreement on the price the night before, but knowing the way these people operate I fully expected Yussuf Mahmud would demand more. Instead Yussuf Mahmud shoved the ragged bundle at Ramses—keeping one hand firmly on it—and said brusquely, "You have the money?"

Ramses stared at him. Then he said—squeaked, rather—"Why such haste, my friend? I hope you are not expecting anyone else this evening. I would be . . . displeased to share your company with others."

"Not so displeased as I," the fellow said, with a certain air of bravado. "But none of us will linger if we are wise. There are those who can hear words that are not uttered and see through windowless walls."

"Is it so? Who are these magicians?" Ramses leaned forward, smiling Ali's distorted smile.

"I cannot—"

"No?" Ramses took a heavy sack from the folds of his robe and poured a rain of shining gold coins onto the table. We had agreed they would make a more impressive show than banknotes, and they certainly had the desired effect on Yussuf Mahmud. His eyes practically popped out of his head.

"Information is part of the bargain," Ramses went on. "You have not told me where this came from, or through what channels it passed. How many people did you cheat or murder or rob to get it? How many of them will transfer their attentions to me once I have possession of it?"

He gestured unobtrusively to David, who took the papyrus and laid it carefully in the wooden case we had brought with us. The man paid no attention; his greedy eyes were fixed on that shining golden heap. Ramses glanced quickly from the shuttered window to the barred door. He didn't look at me. He didn't have to; the room was so small that the shadowy corner to which he had directed me was within the range of his vision. I didn't see or hear anything out of the way, but he must have done, for he jumped up and reached for me as the flimsy wooden shutters gave way under the impact of a heavy body.

The body was that of a man, his face covered by a tightly wound scarf that left only his eyes exposed. He hit the floor and rolled upright, agile as an acrobat. I thought there was another one behind him, but before I could be sure Ramses tucked me under one arm and sprang toward the door. David was already there, the case that held the papyrus in one hand, his knife in the other. He flattened himself against the wall on one side of the door; Ramses pulled the bar back and jumped out of the way. The door flew open, and the man who had hurled himself against it stumbled into the room.

David kicked him in the ribs and he fell flat. I was tempted to kick Ramses, for handling me like a bundle of laundry instead of letting me join in the defense, but I decided I hadn't better; he and David were operating quite efficiently and it would have been stupid (and possibly fatal) to break their rhythm. The whole business had taken only a few seconds.

That heap of gold was our second line of defense. Over Ramses's shoulder I saw a writhing tangle of limbs as the newcomers and Yussuf Mahmud fought with teeth and knives and bodies to possess their prize. They fought on a carpet of gold; coins spilled from the table and rolled across the floor.

David had gone out the door. Another body fell into the room and David called out to us to come ahead. Ramses pulled the door shut behind us.

"I hope you didn't hit him with the papyrus box," he remarked in Arabic.

"What do you take me for?" David's voice was breathless but amused.

"Was he the last?"

"Yes. Lock the door and come on."

Ramses set me on my feet. The stairwell was dark as pitch, but I heard the click of a key turning. I doubted it would hold the men inside for long, for the door was a flimsy thing; but by the time they finished fighting over the gold, there might not be anyone left to follow.

We pelted down the creaking stairs—first David, then me, then Ramses. When we emerged onto the narrow street I realized that there was light where there had been none before. A door opposite stood open. The form silhouetted in the opening was definitely female; I could see every voluptuous curve through the thin fabric that draped her body. The light glimmered off twists of gold in her hair and on her arms.

David had come to an abrupt halt. Seeing the woman, he let out a sigh of relief. I will not repeat what she said, dear, for fear of shocking you; but I am happy to report that David refused the invitation in terms as blunt as those in which it had been couched. He started to turn away. The street was very narrow; a single step brought her close to him. She threw her arms around him—and I hit her behind her ear with my joined fists, the way Aunt Amelia taught me.

As that dear lady would say, the result was most satisfactory. The woman dropped the knife and fell to the ground. Another silhouetted shape appeared in the open doorway—a man this time. There were others behind him. In their haste they blocked one another trying to get through the narrow aperture, which was lucky for us, since both my valiant escorts appeared to be momentarily paralyzed. I gave Ramses a shove.

"Run!" I said.

It isn't difficult to lose pursuers in that maze of filthy alleyways and dark streets, if one knows the area. I didn't, but once Ramses had got his wits back he took the lead, and the sounds of pursuit died away. We were all tired and out of breath, and *very* dirty, by the time we reached the river, but Ramses wouldn't let me take off my stained, smelly robe until we were in the boat and underway. In case I neglected to mention it, I was wearing my own shirt and trousers under my disguise. The boys weren't, and they made me turn my back while they changed. Men are sometimes very silly.

When we reached the other side and the little boat had come to rest, I waited for someone to clap me on the shoulder and say "Well done!" or "Jolly good show!" or some such thing. Neither of them spoke. They sat motionless, like a pair of twin statues, gaping at me. The cut at the base of David's throat had stopped bleeding. It looked like a thin dark cord.

"Don't just sit there," I said in exasperation. "Let's go back to the dahabeeyah where we can talk in comfort. I want a drink of water and a cigarette and a change of clothing and a nice soft chair and—"

"You'll have to settle for one out of four," Ramses said, rummaging under the seat. He handed me a flask. "We must finish our discussion before we go back to the dahabeeyah. Mother is always hanging about, and this is one conversation I don't want her to overhear."

I drank deeply of the lukewarm water, wishing it were something stronger. Then I wiped my mouth on my sleeve and handed the bottle to David. "Yussuf Mahmud betrayed us," I said. "It was an ambush. You expected it."

"Don't be an idiot," Ramses said rudely. "If I had anticipated an ambush I would not have allowed . . . That is, I would have acted differently."

"I don't see how you could have acted any more effectively," I admitted. "You and David must have worked out in advance what to do if things went wrong."

"We always do," Ramses said. "Never mind the flattery, Nefret; the fact is, I miscalculated rather badly. We were lucky to get away unhurt."

"Lucky!" I said indignantly.

Ramses started to speak, but for once David beat him to it. "It wasn't luck that saved my life tonight, it was Nefret's quick wits and courage. Thank you, my sister. I didn't see the knife until it was at my throat."

Ramses shifted position slightly. "I didn't see it until it fell from her hand."

It had taken them long enough to admit it. I couldn't resist. "That," I said, "is because neither of you knows—"

"Anything about women?" Ramses finished.

The moon was high and bright. I could see his face clearly. It was what I call his stone-pharaoh face, stiff and remote as the statue of Khafre in the Museum. I thought he was angry until he leaned forward and pulled me off the bench and hugged me so hard I could feel my ribs creaking. "One of these days," he said in a choked voice, "you are going to make me forget I am supposed to be an English gentleman."

Well, my dear, I *was* pleased! For years I've been trying to shatter that shell of his and get him to act like a human being. Occasionally I succeed—usually by stirring up his temper!—but the moment never lasts long. Making the most of that *particular* moment, I held on to him when he would have drawn away.

"You're trembling," I said suspiciously. "Are you laughing at me, curse you?"

"I am not laughing at you. I'm shaking with terror." I thought I felt his lips brush my hair, but I must have been mistaken, because he returned me to the hard seat with a thump that rattled my teeth. Ramses has the most formidable eyebrows of anyone I know, including the Professor. At that moment they met in the middle of his forehead like lifting black wings. I had been right the first time. He was absolutely furious!

"Hell and damnation, Nefret! Will you never learn to stop and think before you act? You were quick and brave and clever and all that rot, but you were also bloody lucky. One of these days you are going to get yourself in serious trouble if you rush headlong into action without—"

"You're a fine one to talk!"

"I never act without premeditation."

"Oh, no, not you! You have no more feelings than a—"

"Make up your mind," said Ramses, between his teeth. "I can't be both impetuous and unfeeling."

David reached out and took my hand (fist, rather; I admit it was clenched and raised). "Nefret, he's scolding because he was frightened for you. Tell her, Ramses. Tell her you aren't angry."

"I am angry. I . . ." He stopped speaking, drew a long breath and slowly let it out. The eyebrows slipped back into their normal position. "Angry with myself. I failed you, my brother. I failed Nefret too. She wouldn't have had to take such a hideous risk if I had been more alert."

David took Ramses's outstretched hand. His eyes shone bright with tears. David is as sentimental as Ramses is *not*. I am all in favor of sentiment—as *you* know—but the reaction had hit me and *I* was starting to shake too.

"None of that," I said sternly. "As usual, you are taking too much on yourself, Ramses. An exaggerated sense of responsibility is a sign of excessive egotism."

"Is that one of Mother's famous aphorisms?" Ramses was himself again. He released David's hand and smiled sardonically at me.

"No, I made it up myself. You were both at fault this time. You'd have seen the knife, as I did, if your masculine conceit hadn't assumed that there was nothing to be feared from a woman. My suspicions were aroused the instant she appeared; it was too much of a coincidence that a lady of the evening should present herself at that precise moment, when we'd seen no sign of activity in the house earlier. Establishments of that sort aren't so discreet as to—"

"You have made your point," Ramses said, looking down his nose at me.

Something rustled through the reeds along the bank. None of us started; even I have learned to know the difference between the movements of a rat and those of a man. I do not much like rats, though, and I wanted to go home.

"Be damned to that," I said, trying to look down my nose at him (that's not easy when the other person is almost a foot taller). "Thanks to our *combined* quick wits and daring we got away unscathed, with the papyrus, but we haven't settled the vital question of how to *remain* unscathed. What went wrong tonight?"

Ramses settled back on the seat and rubbed his neck. (The adhesive itches, even after it has been washed off.) "There was always a possibility that Yussuf Mahmud meant to cheat us—to keep the money as well as the papyrus. But he couldn't hope to pull off a swindle like that without murdering both of us, and I doubted he would risk it. Ali the Rat and his taciturn friend have a certain . . . reputation in Cairo."

"A fictitious reputation, I hope," I said.

The two of them exchanged glances. "For the most part," Ramses said. "Anyhow, I decided the risk was negligible. Yussuf Mahmud has a certain reputation too. He deals in stolen antiquities, and he would cheat his own mother, but he is no killer."

"Then he must have swindled some other thief to get his hands on the papyrus," I said. "That would mean that the men who broke in were after it—and him. Not us."

"I would love to be able to believe that," Ramses muttered. "The alternative is decidedly unpleasant. Let us suppose that Yussuf Mahmud and his employers, whoever they may be, have worked out an ingenious method of robbery. They offer the papyrus for sale, lure prospective buyers to the house, knock them over the head, steal the money, and walk away with the papyrus. They can repeat the process over and over, since the victims aren't likely to admit participating in an illegal transaction. This time Yussuf Mahmud decided to go into business for himself. He was expecting the others, but not so soon. He hoped to conclude the deal and get away with the money before they arrived. He'd have locked us in—I noticed he'd left the key on the outside of the door, which ought to have made me more suspicious than it did—and left us to the tender mercies of the lads. They came early because *they* didn't trust *him*. Instead of joining forces against us, the fools let greed get the better of them. Gold, I have been informed, has a demoralizing effect on those of weak character."

"Must you be so cursed long-winded?" I demanded. "Do you think that's the explanation for the ambush? A simple swindle?"

"No," Ramses said. "The second part of the theory holds, I think—Yussuf Mahmud hoped to get away with the money before the others came—but I'm afraid we must consider that unpleasant alternative I mentioned. The woman had every intention of slitting David's throat. And is it only a coincidence that they held off attacking until you were with us?"

"I hope so," I said honestly.

"So do I, my girl. They couldn't have known you would be there, but they were definitely expecting David and me, and they took extraordinary measures to ensure we would be caught or killed. It can't be a coincidence that Yussuf Mahmud offered the papyrus to us. There are too many other dealers in Cairo who would have snapped it up at the price we paid. I'm afraid we must face the possibility that somehow, some way, someone has discovered our real identities."

"How could they?" David demanded.

Poor boy, he had been so proud of his clever disguise! Ramses wasn't keen on admitting failure either. He tightened his mouth up in that way he has. When he answered, the words sounded as if they were being squeezed through a crack.

"No scheme is completely foolproof. Several possibilities occur to me . . . But why waste time in conjecture? It's late, and Nefret should be in bed."

The reeds rustled eerily. I shivered. The night wind was cold.

David leaned forward and took my hand. He is such a dear! That sweet smile of his softened his face (and a handsome face it is, too). "Quite right. Come, little sister, you've had a busy night."

I let him help me out of the boat and up the bank. We went single file, with David leading, finding the easiest and least-littered path. The mud squelched under my boots.

"Coincidences do happen," David said. "We may be starting at shadows."

"It's always safest to expect the worst," said a sour voice behind me. "What a damned nuisance. We spent three years building up those personae."

I slipped on something that squashed and gave off a horrible smell. A hand grabbed my shirttail and steadied me.

"Thank you," I said. "Ugh! What *was* that? No, don't tell me. Ramses is right, you can't be Ali and Achmet again. If they do know who you really are, the papyrus could have been a means of luring you into that awful neighborhood. A would-be killer or kidnapper couldn't easily get at you when you're on the dahabeeyah with us and the crew, or in the respectable parts of Cairo, with lots of other people around."

"There's one positive aspect to this," Ramses admitted. (He much prefers to look on the dark side.) "We got the papyrus. That wasn't supposed to happen."

"All the more reason to stay away from the Old City," I said. "Give me your word, Ramses, that you and David won't go back there at night."

"What? Oh, yes, certainly."

So that was the end of *that*. None of us had to point out that we would soon know the answer to our question. We had got away—with the papyrus—and if Whoever-They-Were knew who Ramses and David were, they might come after it. But don't worry, darling, we know how to take care of ourselves—and each other.

"My dear Emerson," I said. "We must call on M. Maspero before we leave Cairo."

"Damned if I will," snarled Emerson.

We were breakfasting upon the upper deck, as is our pleasant custom—though not as pleasant as it had been before motorized barges and steamers invaded the area. How I yearned to retreat to the bucolic shores of Luxor, where the sunrise colors were undimmed by smoke and the fresh morning breeze was untainted by the stench of petrol and oil!

Emerson had already expressed the same opinion and proposed that we sail that day. That is so like a man! They assume that they need only express a desire to have it immediately fulfilled. As I pointed out to him, a number of matters remained to be done before we could depart—such as giving Reis Hassan time to collect the crew and get the necessary supplies on board. Calling on M. Maspero was, in my opinion, almost as important. The goodwill of the Director of the Department of Antiquities is essential for anyone who wishes to excavate in Egypt. Emerson did not have it.

For the past several seasons we had been working on a particularly boring collection of tombs. In all fairness to Maspero it must be admitted that Emerson's stubbornness was chiefly responsible. He had infuriated Maspero by refusing to open the tomb of Tetisheri—our great discovery—to tourists. This refusal had been couched in terms that were remarkably rude even for Emerson. Maspero had retaliated by rejecting Emerson's request to search for new tombs in the Valley of the Kings, adding insult to injury by suggesting that he finish clearing the smaller, nonroyal tombs, of which there were quite a number in the Valley. Most of these sepulchres had been discovered by other archaeologists and were known to contain absolutely nothing of interest.

In all fairness to Emerson, we had every right to expect special consideration from Maspero, since, for reasons that have no bearing on the present narrative, we had handed over the entire contents of the tomb to the Cairo Museum, without claiming the usual finder's share. (This had also had a deleterious effect on our relations with the British Museum, whose officials had expected we would donate our share to them. Emerson cared no more for the opinion of the British Museum than he did for that of M. Maspero.)

A sensible man would have backed off and asked for permission to work elsewhere. Emerson is not a sensible man. With grim determination, and a good deal of bad language, he had accepted the project and kept at it until we were all ready to scream with boredom. Over the past years he had investigated a dozen of the tombs in question. There were, I calculated, a dozen more to go.

"I will go alone, then," I said.

"No, you will not!"

I was pleased to observe that our little disagreement (together with several cups of strong coffee) had roused Emerson from his habitual morning lethargy. He sat up, shoulders squared and fists clenched. A handsome flush of temper warmed his cheeks, and the cleft in his strong chin quivered.

It is a waste of time to argue with Emerson. I turned to the children. "And what are your plans for the day, my dears?"

Ramses, sprawled on the settee in a position as languorous as Emerson's had been before I stirred him up, started and straightened. "I beg your pardon, Mother?"

"How lazy you are this morning," I said disapprovingly. "And Nefret looks as if she had not slept either. Was it one of your bad dreams that kept you awake, my dear girl?"

"No, Aunt Amelia." She covered her mouth with her hand to hide a yawn. "I was up late. Studying."

"Very commendable. But you need your sleep, and I would like to see you take a little more trouble over your morning toilette. You ought to have put your hair up, the wind is blowing it all over your face. Ramses, finish doing up your shirt buttons. David at least is . . . What is that mark on your neck, David? Did you cut yourself?"

He had buttoned his shirt as high as it would go, but eyes as keen as mine cannot be deceived. His hand went to his throat.

"The razor slipped, Aunt Amelia."

"Now that is just what I mean. Lack of sleep makes one clumsy and careless. Those straight razors are dangerous implements, and you—"

The engines of a passing tourist steamer made me break off, for it was impossible for me to make myself heard over the racket. Emerson managed to make himself heard, however.

"Damnation! The sooner we leave this cacophonous chaos, the better! I am going to speak with Reis Hassan."

Hassan informed him we could not possibly get off before the Thursday, two days hence, and Emerson had to be content with that. He was still muttering profanely when we started for the museum, where he proposed to spend the morning examining the most recent exhibits.

His refusal to call on Maspero suited me quite well, in fact, since an encounter between them was sure to make matters worse. I decided to take Nefret with me. She and M. Maspero were on excellent terms. French gentlemen are usually on excellent terms with pretty young women.

We left Emerson and the boys in the Salle d'Honneur and proceeded to the administrative offices on the north side of the building. Maspero was expecting us. He kissed our hands and paid us his usual extravagant compliments—which were, honesty compels me to admit, not undeserved. Nefret looked quite the lady in her spotless white gloves and beribboned hat; her elegant frock of green muslin set off her slim figure and golden-red hair. My own frock was a new one and I had put aside my heavy working parasol for one that matched the dress. Like all my parasols it had a stout steel shaft and a rather sharp point, but ruffles and lace concealed its utility.

After a servant had served tea, I began by making Emerson's apologies. "We are to leave Cairo in two days, Monsieur, and he has a great deal of work to do. He asked me to present his compliments."

Maspero was too intelligent to believe this and too suave to say so. "You will, I hope, present my compliments to the Professor."

Frenchmen are almost as fond as Arabs of prolonged and formal courtesies. It took me a while to get to the reason for my visit. I had not counted on a positive answer, so I was not surprised—though I was disappointed—when Maspero's face lost its smile.

"Alas, chère Madame, I would do anything in my power to please you, but you must see that it is impossible for me to give the Professor permission to carry out new excavations in the Valley of the Kings. Mr. Theodore Davis has the concession and I cannot arbitrarily take it from him, particularly when he has had such remarkable luck in finding new tombs. Have you seen the display of the materials he discovered last year in the tomb of the parents of Queen Tiyi?"

"Yes," I said.

"But, Monsieur Maspero, it is such a pity." Nefret leaned forward. "The Professor is the finest excavator in Egypt. He is wasting his talents on those boring little tombs."

Maspero gazed admiringly at her wide blue eyes and prettily flushed cheeks—but he shook his head. "Mademoiselle, no one regrets this more than I. No one respects the abilities of M. Emerson more than I. It is entirely his decision. There are hundreds of other sites in Egypt. They are at his disposal—except for the Valley of the Kings."

After chatting a little longer we took our leave, and had our hands kissed again.

"Curse it," said Nefret, as we made our way toward the Mummy Room, where we had arranged to meet the others.

"Don't swear," I said automatically.

"That was not swearing. What an obdurate old man Maspero is!"

"It is not altogether his fault," I admitted. "He exaggerated, of course, when he said Emerson could have any other site in Egypt. A good many of them have already been assigned, but there are others, even in the Theban area. It is only Emerson's confounded stubbornness that keeps us chained to our boring task. Where the devil has he got to?"

We finally tracked him down where I might have expected he would be—brooding gloomily over the exhibit Maspero had referred to. Mr. Davis's discovery—or, to be more accurate, the discovery of Mr. Quibell, who had been supervising the excavations at that time—was that of a tomb that had survived until modern times with its contents almost untouched. The objects were not as fine as the ones WE had found in Queen Tetisheri's tomb, of course. Yuya and Thuya had been commoners, but their daughter was a queen, the chief wife of the great Amenhotep III, and their mortuary equipment included several gifts from the royal family.

"Ah, there you are, my dear," I said. "I hope we did not keep you waiting."

Emerson was in such an evil temper that my sarcasm went unremarked. "Do you know how long it took Davis to clear this tomb? Three weeks! We spent three years with Tetisheri! One can only wonder—"

I cut his fulminations short. "Yes, my dear, I am in complete agreement, but I am ready for lunch. Where are Ramses and David?"

"They went to look at papyri," Emerson said. He waved his hand vaguely in the direction of the doorway.

Though M. Maspero's methods of organization left a great deal to be desired, he had gathered most of the papyri together in a single room. Ramses and David were in rapt contemplation of one of the finest—a funerary papyrus that had been made for a queen of the Twenty-first Dynasty.

The Book of the Dead is a modern term; ancient collections of spells designed to ward off the perils of the Underworld and lead the dead man or woman triumphantly into everlasting life bore various names: the Book of That Which Is in the Underworld, the Book of Gates, the Book of Coming Forth by Day, and so on. At certain periods these protective spells were written on the wooden coffins or on the walls of the tomb. Later, they were inscribed on papyri and illustrated by charming little paintings showing the various stages through which the deceased passed on his way to paradise. The length of the papyrus and, by extension, its efficacy, depended on the price the purchaser was able to pay. Yes; even immortality could be bought, but let us not sneer at these innocent pagans, dear Reader. The medieval Christian church sold pardons and prayers for the dead, and are there not those still among us who endow religious institutions in the expectation of being "let off" punishment for their sins?

But I digress. More relevant to the tale I am about to unfold is the origin of certain of these papyri. They were buried with the dead, sometimes at the side or between the legs of the mummy. The particular roll the boys were inspecting had come from the royal cache at Deir el Bahri. The mummies of a miscellaneous lot of royal personages had been rescued from their despoiled tombs and hidden in a cleft in the Theban hills, where they had escaped discovery until the 1880s of the present era. The discoverers were tomb robbers from the village of Gurneh on the West Bank. For several years they had sold objects such as papyri to illegal dealers, but finally the Antiquities Department got wind of their activities and forced them to disclose the location of the tomb. The battered, abused mummies and the remains of their funerary equipment had been removed to the Museum.

Nefret went at once to join the lads. She had to nudge Ramses before he moved aside, whereupon she bent over the case and stared as fixedly as he had done.

"It is much darker than . . . than some I have seen," she murmured.

"They always darken when they are exposed to the light, especially under conditions like these," Emerson grumbled. "The inside of the case is as filthy as the outside. That idiot Maspero—"

"It is Twenty-first Dynasty," said David. "They are generally darker than the earlier versions."

He spoke with the quiet authority he displayed only when he was talking about his specialty, and we listened with the respect he commanded at such times. He politely made way for me as I approached the case.

"It is very handsome, though," I said. "These papyri always remind me of medieval manuscripts, with the long rows of elegantly written text and the little paintings. This scene is the weighing of the heart against the symbol of truth—such a charmingly naive concept! The queen, crowned and dressed in her finest robes, is led by Anubis into the chamber where Osiris sits enthroned. Thoth, the ibis-headed divine scribe, stands with pen poised, ready to record the judgment. Behind him the hideous monster Amnet waits, ready to devour the soul should it fail the test."

"To whom are you addressing your lecture, Peabody?" Emerson inquired disagreeably. "There are no tourists here, only those who are as familiar with the subject as you."

Nefret made a tactful attempt to soften this criticism—unnecessarily, since I never take Emerson's sarcasm to heart. "This adorable little baboon, perched atop the scales—that is Thoth too, isn't it? Why does he appear twice in the same scene?"

"Ah well, my dear, the theology of the ancient Egyptians is

something of a hodgepodge," I replied. "The ape atop the balance, or, as in some cases, beside it, is one of the symbols of Thoth, but I defy even my learned husband to explain what he is doing there."

Emerson made a growling noise, and Nefret went quickly to take his arm. "I am very hungry," she announced. "Can we go to lunch now?"

She drew him away, and I followed with the boys. Ramses offered me his arm, a courtesy he seldom remembered to pay. "That was neatly done," he remarked. "I believe he would jump into the jaws of a crocodile if she proposed it. Mother, you really ought not provoke him when he is in a state of aggravation."

"He started it," I replied, and then laughed a little because the statement sounded so childish. "He is always in a state of aggravation when he visits the museum."

"What did Maspero say?" Ramses asked. "For I feel certain you and Nefret tried to persuade him to change his mind."

"He said no. He is in the right, I suppose. Having given the firman to Mr. Davis, he cannot cancel it without an excellent reason. I cannot imagine why your father insists on remaining in the Valley. It is tantamount to rubbing salt in his wounds. Every time Mr. Davis finds another tomb, Emerson's blood pressure soars. Tetisheri's tomb was accomplishment enough for any archaeologist, but you know your father; it has been quite some time since we came across anything interesting, and he would dearly love another remarkable discovery."

"Hmmmm," said Ramses, looking thoughtful.

4

I of course reported Maspero's offer to Emerson. "What about Abusir, Emerson? Or Medum? And there are large areas of Sakkara that cry out for excavation."

"Are you so ready to abandon our home in Luxor, Peabody? We built the house because we planned to concentrate on that area for years to come. Curse it, I swore I would finish the job, and I resent your attempts . . ." But then his face softened and he said gruffly, "I know you still yearn for pyramids, my dear. Just allow me one more season in the Valley, and . . . Well, then we will see. Is that a satisfactory compromise?"

In my opinion it was not a compromise at all, for he had promised nothing. However, the affectionate demonstrations that accompanied his speech *were* satisfactory. I responded with my customary appreciation, and the subject was dropped—for the time being.

We were staying at Shepheard's, my favorite hotel in Cairo, when this conversation took place. Emerson had graciously agreed to my suggestion that we spend a few days there before leaving the city. My excuse for removing to the hotel was that it would be more convenient for making arrangements for my annual dinner party; but though I was loath to admit the fact, the dear old dahabeeyah was inconveniently small for our enlarged family. It had only four staterooms and a single bath chamber, and with all of us engaged in professional pursuits the saloon was so full of desks and books and reference materials there was no room for a dining table. Fatima could not be expected to sleep on the lower deck with the crewmen, which meant that one of the staterooms had to be given to her. (She had proposed sleeping on a pallet in the corridor, or on the floor in Nefret's room—both out of the question.) So David and Ramses had to share a bedroom, and I believe I need not describe the condition of that room to any mother of young male persons. One had to wade through books and discarded garments to reach the beds.

With a mournful sigh I admitted the truth, to myself if not to Emerson (who, being a man, did not even notice the inconveniences I have reported). While the children were with us, the *Amelia* did not offer adequate living quarters. That state of affairs would not continue indefinitely, though, I reminded myself. David was twenty-one, and already establishing a reputation as an artist and designer. He would strike out on his own one day, as was only proper. Nefret would certainly marry; I was only surprised she had not yet accepted one of the numerous suitors who constantly besieged her. Ramses . . . It was impossible for any normal human being to predict what Ramses would do. I was fairly certain it was something I would not like, but at least he would eventually go off and do it somewhere else. The prospect ought to have been pleasing. To be alone again with Emerson, without those dear but distracting young persons, would once have been my fondest dream. It still was, of course . . .

After a useful conversation with M. Baehler making arrangements for my dinner party, I had retired to the terrace to wait for Emerson and Nefret to join me for tea. The sun shone from a cloudless sky, brightening the flamboyant tarbooshes and gold-trimmed vests of the dragomen gathered round the steps of the hotel; the scent of roses and jasmine on the carts of the flower vendors was wafted to my appreciative nostrils by a soft breeze. Even the rolling of wheels and the shouts of the cabdrivers, the braying of donkeys and bellowing of camels fell pleasantly on my ears because they were the sounds of Egypt, hallowed by familiarity and affection. Emerson had *said* he was going to the French Institute. Nefret had *said* she meant to do some shopping. In deference to what she was pleased to call my old-fashioned principles, she had taken Fatima with her. The boys had gone off somewhere; they no longer accounted to me for their activities, but I had no reason to suppose they were doing anything they ought not. Why then did vague forebodings trouble a mind that ought to have been at ease?

Those forebodings were not prompted by my old adversary and (as he claimed) admirer, the Master Criminal. Emerson had got in the habit of assuming that Sethos was behind every threatening incident or mysterious event. The fact that he was usually wrong had not lessened his suspicions, and I knew (though he had tried to conceal it from me) that he had been prowling the suks and the coffee shops looking for evidence that Sethos had followed us to Egypt.

I had my own reasons for feeling certain this was not the case—and this certainty, to be entirely candid, was one cause of my discontent. For the first time in many years there was no prospect of an interesting adventure, not even a threatening letter from villains unknown! I hadn't realized how accustomed I had become to that sort of thing. Admittedly our adventures were often more enjoyable in retrospect than in actuality, but if I must choose between danger and boredom I will always choose the former. It was cursed discouraging, especially since our excavations offered no prospect of excitement.

I glanced at my lapel watch. Nefret was not really late, since we had not specified a time, but she ought to have been here by now. I decided to go in search of her.

When I knocked at her door I did not receive an immediate reply, and concluded she had not yet returned, but as I was about to turn away the door opened a few inches and Nefret's face appeared. She looked a trifle fussed.

"Oh, it is you, Aunt Amelia. Are you ready for tea?"

"Yes, and have been this past quarter hour," I replied, standing on tiptoe and trying to see past her into the room, from which I could hear surreptitious sounds. "Is someone with you? Fatima?"

"Er—no." She tried to outstare me, but of course did not succeed. With a little smile she stepped back and opened the door. "It is only Ramses and David."

"I don't know why you were making such a mystery of it," I remarked. "Good afternoon, boys. Are you joining us for tea?"

They were standing, but one of them must have been sprawled on the bed, for the spread was crumpled. I forbore comment, however, since they were both properly attired, except for Ramses's tie, which was not around his neck or anyplace else that I could see.

"Good afternoon, Mother," said Ramses. "Yes, we intend to take tea with you, if that is agreeable."

"Certainly. Where is your tie? Find it and put it on before you come downstairs."

"Yes, Mother."

"We will meet you on the terrace, then."

"Yes, Mother."

"In half an hour."

"Yes, Mother."

From Manuscript H

Nefret closed the door, waited for thirty seconds, and eased it open again just far enough to peer out.

"She's gone."

"Did you think she would be listening at the door?" David asked.

Neither of the others bothered to answer. Ramses carefully drew back the rumpled counterpane and let out a breath of relief. "No damage," he reported. "But we cannot go on doing this sort of thing."

"We won't do it again," Nefret said. "But we had to have a closer look, and we couldn't risk it while we were on the boat. Our quarters are too cramped and Fatima was always popping in to see if I wanted anything. It was clever of you to persuade Aunt Amelia to book rooms at the hotel."

"She thinks it was her idea," Ramses said.

David had designed and built a container that displayed one twelve-inch panel at a time, with compartments at either end to hold the unrolled and re-rolled sections. The panel now visible showed the same subject depicted on the papyrus in the museum—the weighing of the soul—but this rendering was even surer and more delicate. The suppliant's slender form showed through her robe of sheer white linen. Before her stood the balance, with her heart—the seat of understanding and conscience—in one pan, and in the other the feather of Maat, representing truth, justice and order. The fate that followed a guilty verdict was dreadful indeed: to be devoured by Amnet, Eater of Souls, a monster with the head of a crocodile, the body of a lion, and the hind quarters of a hippopotamus.

"Of course that never happened," Ramses said. "The papyrus itself assured a successful outcome, not only by affirming it but by—"

"I don't want to hear a lecture on Egyptian religion," Nefret said. "This is like the queen's papyrus, but it's much longer and the workmanship is even finer."

"It is two hundred years older," David said. "Nineteenth Dynasty. Papyri of that period are lighter in color and less brittle than later examples. I don't think we've damaged it but Ramses is right, we must keep it covered and not unroll any more of it."

"I wonder," Ramses said.

"What do you mean?"

"Ordinarily I would agree that it ought to be handled as little as possible. I have a feeling, though, that somebody wants it back. We ought to have a copy in case he succeeds."

"Nonsense," Nefret scoffed. "It's been three days and no one has bothered us."

"Except for the swimmer Mohammed saw night before last."

"Mohammed imagined it. Or invented it, to prove he was alert and wakeful, after the Professor caught him sleeping on duty."

"Possibly. All the same, I think we will have to risk it. David, how long would it take you to photograph the thing?"

David stared at him in consternation. "Hours! Days, if I do a proper job. What would I use for a darkroom? How do we keep Aunt Amelia from finding out? What if I damage it? How—"

"We'll work out the details," Nefret said, brushing these difficulties aside with her usual nonchalance. "I'll help you. Where do you suppose it came from? Originally, I mean."

"Thebes," Ramses said. "She was a princess—one of the daughters of Ramses the Second. Precisely where in Thebes is the question."

"The Royal Cache?" David suggested.

"Deir el Bahri?" Nefret stared at him. "But that tomb was cleared out years ago. The mummies and other objects are in the museum."

"Not all of them." David replaced the cover of the container. "You know the story, Nefret. Before they were caught, the Abd er

Rassul family sold a number of objects to dealers and collectors. It's possible not all of those objects were reported."

"It's a virtual certainty that some of them were not," Ramses said.

There was a brief silence. Then Nefret said in exasperation, "Why don't you say what you're thinking? Sethos was in the business when the Abd er Rassuls were clandestinely marketing the objects from the Royal Cache. Let's suppose one of the things he bought was the princess's papyrus—"

"The possibility had occurred to me, of course," said Ramses.

"Of course!" Nefret's voice was rich with sarcasm. "Did you think I'd cower and scream at the mention of that dread name?"

"It was a possibility, nothing more. We've fahddled with every dealer in Cairo and found not the slightest hint that the Master, as they called him, has returned. Things like that can't be kept secret; you may not know where the body is hidden, but you can't miss the smell."

"What an elegant metaphor," Nefret remarked.

"We couldn't have missed it," Ramses insisted. "And yet there is the fact that the papyrus was used to lure us into a trap. If Sethos was responsible, that would mean we weren't his main object. The one he wants is Mother. His attempt to abduct her in London failed, so he tried to get his hands on one or all of us as a means of reaching her."

Nefret nodded. "That possibility had occurred to me, too, believe it or not. The Professor hasn't let her out of his sight since the attack in London, and even *she* would have better sense than to go into the Old City alone at night."

"Unlike us," Ramses said wryly. "But she'd march into the fires of hell brandishing that parasol of hers if she thought one of us was in danger."

"Yes," David said softly. "She would."

A sound outside the door made him start nervously. Nefret laughed and patted his hand. "It's only the German count who has rooms farther along the corridor; he bellows like a hippopotamus. Were you afraid it was Aunt Amelia come back?"

"She will come back if we don't hurry down," Ramses said. "Here, Nefret, give me the box."

"Put it under the bed. The suffragi never sweeps there." Nefret went to the mirror and began tucking in strands of loosened hair.

"I'd rather not leave it with you. If someone comes looking for it—"

"They'd look for it in your room, or David's," Nefret said. "Even if they had identified you two, they couldn't possibly have known I was your . . . What was that interesting word?"

"Little gazelle," said Ramses, unable to repress a smile. "Never mind the other one."

"Hmph. Need I change, do you think?"

She straightened her blouse and smoothed her skirt over her hips, frowning critically at her reflection in the mirror. After a moment Ramses said, "In my opinion you are properly attired."

"Thank you. Where is your tie?"

They found it under the bed, when Ramses knelt to hide the papyrus there. He refused her offer to tie it for him, and after she had put on her hat David opened the door.

"When are you going to tell the Professor and Aunt Amelia?" he asked in a worried voice. "Strictly speaking, the papyrus is the property of the Foundation, and they are members of the Board. They are going to be furious when they learn we kept this from them."

"They keep things from us, don't they?" Ramses had fallen behind the other two so that he could indulge himself in the pleasure of watching Nefret walk. She claimed it made her nervous when he stared at her as he sometimes did—like a specimen under a microscope, as she described it. She'd have been even more unnerved if she had known why he stared. From any angle and in every detail she was beautiful—the tilt of her head under that absurdly becoming hat, the curls that brushed her neck, the square little shoulders and trim waist and rounded hips and . . . Good God, it's getting worse every day, he thought in disgust, and forced himself to listen to what David was saying.

"I don't feel right about deceiving them. I owe them so much—"

"Stop feeling guilty," Ramses said. "They'll blame me in any case, they always do. Let's not say anything until after we've left Cairo. Father will raise bloody hell with Maspero for failing to shut down the black market in antiquities, and Mother will snatch up her parasol and go looking for Yussuf Mahmud."

"You haven't been looking for him, have you?" Nefret asked.

"Not as Ali the Rat, no. We agreed it would be advisable for that engaging character to lie low for a time."

Nefret pulled away from David and turned on Ramses. "Not as Ali? As who, then? Confound it, Ramses, you gave me your word."

"I've not broken it. But you know perfectly well our only chance of finding out where the papyrus came from is to start with Yussuf Mahmud."

"Stop goading her, Ramses," David said. He took Nefret's arm. "Honestly, you two are enough to drive a sensible person wild. Shouting at one another in a public place!"

"I wasn't shouting," Nefret said sullenly. She let him lead her on. "Ramses would try the patience of a saint. And I'm no saint. What have you been up to?"

"Trying to buy antiquities," David said. "Ramses as a very rich, very stupid tourist and I as his faithful dragoman."

"Tourist," Nefret repeated. Again she stopped and whirled round, so suddenly that Ramses had to rock back on his heels to avoid running into her. She shook her finger under his nose. "Not the silly-looking Englishman with straw-colored hair who ogled me through his monocle and said—"

" 'By Jove, but that's a dashed handsome gel,' " Ramses agreed, in the silly-looking Englishman's affected drawl.

Nefret shook her head, but could not help smiling. "What did you find out?"

"That a tourist with plenty of money and no scruples can find all the antiquities he wants. We've not been offered anything of the same quality as the papyrus, though, despite the fact that I sneered at everything I was shown and kept on demanding something better. Yussuf Mahmud never showed his face. He is usually one of the first to prey on gullible tourists."

"They murdered him," Nefret breathed.

"Or he has gone into hiding," said Ramses. "Do shut up, Nefret, there is Mother. She can hear a word like 'murder' a mile away."

Though the arrangements were all that could be desired, I did not enjoy our annual dinner party as much as usual. So many old friends were gone, into the shadows of eternity or less permanent exile. Howard Carter was not there, nor Cyrus Vandergelt and his wife; the knowledge that we would meet all three in Luxor did not entirely compensate for their absence. As for M. Maspero, I had of course invited him, but was secretly relieved when he pleaded a previous engagement. Though I knew resentment was unreasonable, I could not help feeling that emotion, and listening to the others wax enthusiastic about their pyramids and mastabas and rich cemetery sites, while we contemplated another tedious season among the lesser tombs of the Valley, only increased my vexation with the Director.

Mr. Reisner very kindly invited me to visit Giza, where he held the concession for the Second and Third Pyramids, but I declined, with the excuse that we were to sail on the next day but one. In fact, I saw no point in tantalizing myself by looking at other people's pyramids when I had none of my own. Emerson, who had overheard the offer, gave me a self-conscious look, but he did not refer to the subject then or later. His demonstrations of affection were particularly engaging that night. I responded with the enthusiasm Emerson's demonstrations always evoke, but a small seed of annoyance prickled my mind. It is so like a man to suppose that kisses and caresses will distract a woman from more serious matters.

The day after our dinner party Nefret joined us for luncheon at one of the new restaurants. She had been to the dahabeeyah that morning to get some of her things.

"Was that Ramses?" I asked, turning to peer at a familiar form that was retreating at a speed that suggested the individual in question did not wish to be detained. "Why is he not joining us?"

"He went with me," Nefret said. "But he had an appointment, so could not stay."

"With some young woman, I suppose," I said disapprovingly. "There is always *some* young woman, though I cannot imagine why they follow after him. It isn't Miss Verinder, I hope. She has not a brain in her head."

"Miss Verinder is no longer in the running," Nefret said. "I have taken care of her." Seeing my expression, she went on quickly, "Have you seen this, Aunt Amelia?"

The object she proffered was a newspaper, though not a particularly impressive example of that form. The type was smudged, the paper was thin enough to crumple at a touch, and there were only a few pages. I do not read Arabic as easily as I speak it, but I had no difficulty in translating the name of the newspaper.

"*The Young Woman.* Where did you get this?"

"From Fatima." Nefret stripped off her gloves and accepted the menu the waiter handed her. "I always take time to talk with her and help her with her English."

"I know, my dear," I said affectionately. "It is good of you."

Nefret shook her head so vigorously the flowers on her hat wobbled. "I don't do it out of kindness, Aunt Amelia, but out of a strong sense of guilt. When I see how Fatima's face lights up when she pronounces a new word—when I think of the thousands of other women whose aspirations are as high and who have not even *her* opportunities—I despise myself for not doing more."

Emerson patted the little hand that rested on the table. It was clenched into a fist, as if anticipating battle. "You feel what all decent individuals feel when they contemplate the unfairness of the universe," he said gruffly. "You are one of the few who cares enough to act on your feelings."

"That is right," I said. "If you cannot light a lamp, light a little candle! Thousands of little candles can illumine a—er—a large space!"

Emerson, regretting his descent into sentimentality, shot me a critical look. "I do wish you would not spout those banal aphorisms, Peabody. What is this paper?"

"A journal written for and by women," Nefret explained. "Isn't it exciting? I had no idea such things were done in Egypt."

"There have been quite a number of them," I said.

Nefret's face fell. People who relate what they believe to be new and startling information like to have such information received with exclamations of astonishment and admiration. It is a natural human tendency, and I regretted having spoiled the effect.

"It is not surprising that you should not know of them," I explained. "Few people do. Most, unfortunately, were short-lived. This one is new to me, though the same name—*al-Fatah*—was employed by a journal published some years ago."

"Hmph," said Emerson, who had been perusing the first page.

"The rhetoric is not precisely revolutionary, is it? 'The veil is not a disease that holds us back. Rather, it is the cause of our happiness.' Bah."

"One does not reach the mountaintop in a single bound, Emerson. A series of small steps can . . . er, well, you catch my meaning."

"Quite," said Emerson shortly.

I deemed it advisable to change the direction of the discussion. "How did Fatima come by this, Nefret?"

"It was given to her and the other students at her reading class," Nefret explained. "Did you know she has been attending classes every night, Aunt Amelia, after she finishes her duties?"

"No," I admitted. "I am ashamed to say I did not know. I ought to have inquired. Where are the classes, at one of the missions?"

"They are conducted by a Madame Hashim, a Syrian lady; she is a wealthy widow who does this out of pure benevolence and a desire to improve the lot of women."

"I would like to meet her."

"Would you?" Nefret asked eagerly. "Fatima did not want to ask, she is in such awe of you, but I know she would be pleased if we would attend one of the classes."

"I fear there will not be time before we leave. This is our last night in Cairo, you know, and I have asked the Rutherfords to dine with us here. I will try to call on the lady next time I am in the city, for as you know I am extremely supportive of such enterprises. Literacy is the first step toward emancipation, and I have heard of other ladies who conduct such small private classes, without encouragement or government support. They are lighting the—"

"You are lecturing again, Peabody," said my husband.

"Would you mind if I went with Fatima this evening, then?" Nefret asked. "I would like to encourage her, and find out how the classes are conducted."

"I suppose it would be all right. Emerson, what do you think?"

"Certainly," said Emerson. "In fact, I will indicate my support for the cause of emancipation by accompanying her."

I knew perfectly well what Emerson was up to. He loathes formal dinner parties and the Rutherfords. The ensuing discussion involved quite a lot of shouting (by Emerson) and I insisted we retire to our sitting room, where Nefret settled the matter by perching on the arm of Emerson's chair and putting her arm around his neck.

"Professor darling, it is sweet of you to offer, but your presence would only make everyone uncomfortable. The classes are for women only; the students would be struck dumb with awe of the Father of Curses, and Madame would have to veil herself."

"Hmph," said Emerson.

"You might send a messenger to Madame, telling her you are coming, Nefret," I said. "That is only courteous."

From Letter Collection B

I had told Ramses and David where I was going. It was unnecessary in this case, but I make a point of conforming to our agreement so *they* won't have any excuse to squirm out of it. Ramses is getting to be as nervous as a little old maiden aunt; he tried to persuade me to abandon the scheme, and when I laughed at him he said he and David would go with me. Really, men can be very exasperating! Between Ramses and the Professor I thought we would never get away.

The Professor is a dear, though. He sent a cab to fetch Fatima from the dahabeeyah and take us on to her class. The poor little woman was absolutely overcome; when she joined us in the sitting room she could hardly speak coherently as she attempted to thank him.

The Professor went rather red in the face. He grunted at her the way he does when he is embarrassed or trying to hide his feelings. "Hmph. If I had known you were coming into the city to attend these classes I would have made arrangements for transportation. You ought to know better than to wander round by yourself."

Someone who didn't know him would have thought he was angry. Fatima knows him. Her eyes shone like stars over the black of her veil.

"Yes, Father of Curses," she murmured. "I hear and will obey."

He escorted us down to the street and put us in the cab and threatened the driver with a number of unpleasant things if he drove too fast or ran into another vehicle or got lost. There was no danger of his losing his way, for Fatima was able to give precise directions.

The house was on Sharia Kasr el Eini—a pretty little mansion with a small garden shaded by pepper trees and palms. A servant dressed in galabeeyah and tarboosh opened the door for us and bowed us into a room on the right.

It was a small room, unoccupied and rather shabbily furnished. We waited for what seemed like a long time before the door opened and Madame entered, with fulsome apologies for having kept us waiting.

She must have been very beautiful when she was young. Like many Syrians she was fair-skinned, with soft brown eyes and delicately shaped brows. She wore a black silk robe and a habara, or head covering, of the same fabric; but modish strap sandals showed under the ankle-length robe and her white chiffon veil had been lowered so that it framed her face like the wimple of a medieval nun. (I may take to wearing one myself when I reach middle age; it looks very romantic, and hides little difficulties like sagging chins and wrinkled necks.)

She greeted me in French. "C'est un honneur, mademoiselle. But I had hoped that the so distinguished Madame Emerson would be with you."

I explained, in my rather stumbling French, that the distinguished Madame Emerson had had a previous engagement, but that she sent her compliments and hoped for a meeting in the future.

"I share that hope," Madame said politely. "It is a small thing I do here; the support of Madame Emerson would be invaluable to our cause." Opening another door, she preceded us into an adjoining room, where several women were seated on the floor. There were only eight of them, including Fatima; they ranged in age from girls of ten or twelve to a wrinkled old lady.

I took the chair Madame indicated and listened with considerable interest while the class proceeded. The textbook was the Koran. The women took turns reading, and I was pleased to find that Fatima was one of the most fluent. Some of the others spoke so low they could scarcely be heard; I suppose the presence of a visitor made them nervous. The elderly woman found the business heavy going, but she persisted, irritably refusing the attempts of the others to help her; and when she got through her verse she gave me a toothless, triumphant grin. I smiled back at her, and I am not ashamed to admit there were tears in my eyes.

The class lasted only forty minutes. After the students had filed out, I tried to express my admiration. My French ran out, as it does when I am moved; I thanked her for letting me come, and bade her good evening.

"You must not go so soon," Madame exclaimed. "You will have a glass of tea and we will talk."

She clapped her hands. The servant who entered was a man. Since Madame did not veil herself, I wondered if the poor fellow had been—how would Aunt Amelia put it?—rendered incapable of a particular physical function. Such things are now forbidden by law, but they were common enough in the past. He looked to be no older than forty, and there was more muscle than fat on his tall frame.

Madame turned to him and was about to speak when I heard a thunderous knocking at the door of the house. There was no mistaking that knock—or so I thought.

"Curse—" I began. "Er—mille pardons, Madame. I am afraid that is Professor Emerson, come to get me. He is not a patient man."

Madame smiled. "Yes, I have heard this about Professor Emerson. He is welcome, of course."

She gestured at the servant, who bowed and backed out. The white chiffon boukra had golden loops that hooked over the ears. Madame adjusted hers, and the door of the sitting room opened to admit, not the Professor, but Ramses and David.

I wanted to murder them, but I could not help feeling a little proud of my menfolk. They were looking particularly smart. David is always neat and well-groomed, and Ramses was wearing his best tweed suit. I supposed he had forgotten his hat, since his hair was somewhat windblown; it is very wavy and usually too long, since he dislikes taking the time to have it cut. I could tell Madame was favorably impressed, despite the veil that concealed most of her features. She looked them over, slowly and deliberately, and then gestured to Ramses to take a seat beside her on the divan.

Ramses shook his head. "Ma chère Madame, we would not dream of taking up your time. My sister is expected at the hotel for a dinner engagement. I am only pleased to be able to express my admiration and that of my parents for your encouragement of a cause we all support."

Ramses speaks French, as he does many languages, fluently and idiomatically. When Madame replied, I thought she sounded amused. "Ah. So you too are a believer in the emancipation of women?"

"It could hardly be otherwise, Madame."

"Naturellement. I had hoped I might persuade your mother to write a little article for our journal. Have you perhaps seen it?"

"Not yet, but I look forward to doing so. I will pass your request on to my mother. I am sure she would be pleased to assist in any way. Now, if you will excuse us . . ."

"Un moment, s'il vous plaît." Her hands went to the back of her neck. After a moment she lowered them and displayed a gold chain from which depended a small carved pendant. "A small token of esteem for your distinguished mother," she said. "It is the insignia of our organization."

Ramses bowed. "You are most gracious, Madame. Surely this is of ancient Egyptian origin—the baboon, one of the symbols of Thoth."

"It is appropriate, n'est-ce pas? The ape who sits beside the balance that weighs the heart. It might be considered a symbol of justice."

"It might," said Ramses.

It was an ungracious response, I thought, and anyhow Ramses had been monopolizing the conversation too long. I reached for the little trinket. "The justice women deserve, and that they will attain one day! I will give it to her, Madame. I know she will treasure it."

"Let me put it round your neck so you won't lose it."

She insisted on fastening it with her own hands. The pendant was carved of a red-brown stone. It was surprisingly heavy.

She did not see us to the door. The little garden was a magical place in the night shadows, redolent with the sweet smell of jasmine, but I was not allowed to linger; Ramses had me by the arm, and he shoved me into the carriage with more energy than courtesy. David helped Fatima in and we started off.

"What was the point of that performance?" I demanded.

"I wanted to have a look at the lady," Ramses replied coolly.

"So I deduced. And what did you think of her?"

"I concluded," said Ramses, "that she was no one I had met before."

I hadn't expected *that*; I had assumed that Ramses was playing big brother on general principles. "Good Gad!" I exclaimed. "Sethos? Ramses, that is the most far-fetched hypothesis—"

"Not so far-fetched. However, it appears my theory was unfounded. Sethos is a master of disguise, but not even he could take eight inches off his height or reduce the size of that prominent aquiline nose. The lady's veil was thin enough for me to make out the outline of her features."

"And I saw those features unveiled," I reminded him. "There can be no doubt of her gender. Her cheeks were smooth, her countenance benevolent and kind."

"Kind," said Fatima, who had been following the conversation intently and who had understood that word, at least. "Kind, good teacher."

Ramses said in Arabic, "Yes. We will get another teacher for you when we reach Luxor, Fatima. Won't we, Nefret?"

"You mean me, I suppose. By all means, if we can't find someone better than I. Curse it, Ramses, what on earth put it into your head that Sethos might have taken up a teaching career?"

Ramses looked a little sheepish. It's hard to tell, I admit, but I have been making a study of his expressions, such as they are. "Sheepish" is two quick blinks and a slight compression of his lips.

"Father put it into my head. Admittedly he is not entirely reasonable about Sethos, but once he inserted the idea it found fertile ground. You've never seen Sethos in action. The man is a confounded genius, Nefret."

"Well, you and the Professor were wrong this time."

"You aren't angry that we came after you, are you?" David asked.

I *was* annoyed, but not with him. I knew perfectly well whose idea that "rescue" expedition had been. I leaned forward and brushed the curls back from Ramses's forehead. He hates it when I do that.

"You meant well," I admitted. "But I find it difficult to forgive you for bringing me back in time to dine with those boring people."

It took us almost two weeks to reach Luxor, despite the assistance of the motorized tug that accompanied us. The delays were only the usual sort of thing, but my intuition, which is seldom in error, assured me that everyone seemed preoccupied and on edge. The boys were particularly restless, prowling the deck all day and half the night. There was no doubt about it, the dear old dahabeeyah was too cramped for such energetic individuals, though Fatima had gone on ahead by train to get the house in order and David was able to reclaim his room.

I attempted to distract my mind with scholarly work, but even I, well disciplined though I am, was unable to settle down to anything. In past years I had made something of a reputation with my translations of little Egyptian fairy tales, but when I looked over the material at hand I could not find anything that caught my interest. I had already done the most entertaining of them: The Tales of the Doomed Prince and the Two Brothers, the Adventures of Sinuhe, the Shipwrecked Sailor. When I voiced my difficulty to Emerson he suggested I turn my attention to historical documents.

"Breasted has published the first volume of his texts," he added. "You could correct his translations."

Emerson was making one of his little jokes. Mr. Breasted of Chicago was a linguist whom even Walter respected, and Volume One of his *Ancient Records of Egypt* had appeared that spring to universal acclamation. I smiled politely.

"I have no intention of treading on Mr. Breasted's toes, Emerson."

"Tread on Budge's toes, then. His translation of the Book of the Dead is riddled with errors."

"Ramses appears to be working on that," I said. I had seen the photographs on Ramses's desk and wondered when and where he had acquired them.

"That must be another version, not the one Budge mangled. His is in the British Museum, as you ought to know—one of Budge's contemptible violations of the laws against purchasing antiquities from dealers. Why the authorities at the Museum continue to countenance that villain . . ."

I left the room. Emerson's opinions of Mr. Budge were only too familiar to me.

What with one aggravation or another, I was even more pleased than usual to round the curve in the river and see before me the monumental ruins of the temples of Luxor and Karnak and the buildings of the modern village of Luxor. The village was rapidly becoming a town, with new hotels and government buildings rising

everywhere. Tourist steamers lined the bank. There were a few da-
habeeyahs among them; certain wealthy visitors, especially those
who returned to Egypt every season, preferred the comfort of a private boat.

Our friend Cyrus Vandergelt was one of them. His boat, the
Valley of the Kings, was moored on the West Bank, across from Luxor.
He was good enough to share his private dock with us, and as the
Amelia glided in under the skillful hands of Reis Hassan, I saw the
usual reception party awaiting us. Abdullah was there, stately as a
high priest in the snowy robes he preferred, and Selim, his beloved
youngest son, and Daoud and Ibrahim and Mohammed—the men
who had worked for us so long and who had become friends as well
as valued employees.

Over the years Abdullah's once-formal manner toward me had
gradually softened; now he took my outstretched hand in both of
his and pressed it warmly.

"You look well, Abdullah," I said. It was true, and I was relieved
to see it, for he had suffered a mild heart attack the previous year.
Precisely how old he was I did not know, but his beard had been
grizzled when I first met him, and that had been over twenty years
ago. We had given up trying to persuade him to retire with a well-
deserved pension; it would have broken his heart to leave us and
the work he loved as much as we did.

Abdullah straightened his shoulders. "I am well, Sitt. And you—
you do not change. You will always be young."

"Why, Abdullah," I said, laughing. "I believe that is the first
compliment you have ever paid me."

I passed him over to the respectful embrace of his grandson David, and went to Ramses, who was embracing his horse. The beautiful Arabian stallion had been a gift from our old friend Sheikh
Mohammed, with whom Ramses and David had lived for a time
learning to ride and shoot—and, I suspected, learning other things
they had never admitted to me. High-spirited yet gentle, as intelligent as he was handsome, Risha had won all our hearts, as had his
consort Asfur, who belonged to David.

Emerson's amiable curses ended the demonstration and we proceeded to the house. Fatima was waiting for us on the verandah,
and I was delighted to see that the vines I had planted the previous
year were flourishing. Abdullah had never bothered to water them.

Now they twined green arms up the trellises that framed the open window apertures, and blooming roses scattered crimson petals onto the dusty ground.

The young people immediately went off to the stables, accompanied by Selim; he was an excitable young fellow, and even Ramses was unable to get a word in as Selim reported on the livestock that had been left in his charge. The donkeys had been washed, the goat Tetisheri was fatter than ever, and the filly . . .

Asfur and Risha had become proud parents the previous year. Nefret, whose claim to the beautiful little creature no one denied, had named her Moonlight; she was a gray, like her sire, but of a paler shade that glowed with a pearl-like luster. Nefret had a well-nigh uncanny rapport with animals of all kinds; by the time we left Egypt in the spring the filly had taken to following her like a puppy. She had, of course, never known the touch of saddle or bridle.

When Nefret came back, her face was alight with pleasure. "She remembers me!"

"She certainly does," I said, for Moonlight was at her heels, quite prepared, as it appeared, to join us for luncheon. Frustrated in this purpose she went round to the window opening and poked an inquiring nose at Horus, who was sitting on the ledge. Horus was accustomed to horses, but not on his territory. He sprang up with a hiss, his fur bristling, and the filly began to browse on my roses.

Nefret finally persuaded her to go with Selim, and the rest of us sat down to eat. This sort of fraternization, which had become a custom with us, was a source of scandalized gossip among the European community of Luxor. The more "liberal" of them condescended from time to time to entertain Egyptians of the wealthy, educated class, but none of them would have sat at table with their own workers. Our people were of a superior sort, of course.

Naturally I did not invite Fatima to join us. She would have been as horrified at the idea of sitting with a group of men as the men themselves would have been. She bustled back and forth, superintending the service of the food and drink.

When we had caught up on the gossip—marriages, deaths, illness, new babies—Emerson pushed his chair back and took out his pipe.

"So, Selim," he said genially. "What have your rascally relations in Gurneh been up to lately? Any new tombs?"

A shadow of vexation crossed the imperturbable countenance of my son, who had taken up his favorite position on the window ledge, with his back against a pillar. I thought I understood its cause, for I shared the emotion. Emerson is so direct and forthright he does not understand that inquiries of that sort should not be pursued so directly. Selim was related by blood or marriage to a good many of the Gurnawis, and a good many of the Gurnawis were accomplished tomb robbers. A direct question put all our men, especially Abdullah, in a difficult position; they had to choose between informing on their kin or lying to us.

Selim, sitting on the ledge next to Ramses and David, looked uncomfortable. He was a handsome young man, with the big dark eyes and well-cut features of his handsome family, and he bore a strong resemblance to his nephew David, who was only a few years younger than he. With an apologetic glance at Abdullah, he said, "No new tombs, Father of Curses. Nothing. Rumors only. The usual rumors . . ."

"What rumors?" Emerson demanded.

"Now, Emerson, this is not the time for that sort of discussion," I said, taking pity on the afflicted youth. I knew Emerson had already quizzed Abdullah, but Abdullah had been away from Luxor most of the summer, visiting family in Atiyah near Cairo, so he could not be expected to know as much as Selim about what had been going on in Thebes. At least he had a good excuse for claiming not to know.

"What about the antiquities dealers?" I went on. "Has anything of unusual interest turned up?"

That was safer ground, for once a stolen or looted object reached the hands of the dealers it became public knowledge. Brightening, Selim rattled off a list of artifacts which had come onto the market. Even Emerson could find nothing of particular significance among them. It annoyed him a great deal; he had hoped there would be evidence that the Gurnawis had discovered a rich new tomb, which would give him an excuse to look for it.

The morning after our arrival I tried once again to persuade Emerson to a more sensible course of action. My approach was, as always, subtle and oblique.

"Cyrus and Katherine Vandergelt have asked us to dine this evening," I remarked, looking through the messages that had awaited us.

Emerson grunted. He had covered half the breakfast table with his notebooks and was looking through them. I removed one of them from his plate, wiped off the buttery crumbs, and tried again. "Cyrus is planning to excavate in the Asasif this year. I am sure he would appreciate assistance. His staff—"

". . . is adequate for the purpose." Emerson looked up, scowling spectacularly. "Are you at it again, Amelia? We will start work today on the tombs in that small side valley—if I can locate the sketch map I made last year. Ramses, have you been borrowing my notes again?"

Ramses swallowed—he had just filled his mouth with the last bite of his porridge—and shook his head. "No, Father. Not those notes. I took the liberty—"

"Never mind." Emerson sighed. "I suppose you and David won't be joining us."

"As I told you, sir, we intend to begin copying the inscriptions at the Seti I temple. But if you want us . . ."

"No, no." Another deep sigh expanded Emerson's muscular chest. "Your publication on the Colonnade Hall of the Luxor Temple was a splendid piece of work. You must continue with your copying. A series of such volumes will make your reputations and be an invaluable record."

"If the boys were to help us we would be done sooner," I remarked.

"No, Peabody, I will not allow it. Ramses is right, you know."

"Ramses right?" I exclaimed. "What about?"

"About the importance of preservation over excavation. As soon as a monument, a temple or a tomb, is uncovered, it begins to deteriorate. There will come a time, in the not too distant future, when the only remainders of vital historical data are copies like the ones the boys are making. What Ramses and David are doing is of greater value to Egyptology than the totality of my work."

His voice was low and broken, his brow furrowed. He bowed his head.

"Good Gad, Emerson!" I cried in alarm. "I have never heard you speak like this. What is wrong with you?"

"I am waiting for someone to contradict me," said Emerson in his normal tones.

After Emerson had enjoyed his little joke at our expense, he admitted his earlier announcement had also been in the nature of a jest.

"We need not begin work for another day or two. I would like to have a general look round the Valley before I decide where to begin. The rest of you may do as you like, of course."

Not surprisingly, everyone decided that a visit to the Valley was precisely what would suit them. As was our habit, we followed the path that led up the cliffs behind Deir el Bahri and across the plateau. Emerson forged ahead, holding my hand, and the children fell behind. Nefret was encumbered with the cat, who had indicated a desire to accompany her. She treated him like a kitten, which he was not (by a good fifteen pounds), and he took ruthless advantage of her.

The slanting sunlight of early morning outlined rocks and ridges with blue-black shadows. In a few hours, when the sun was directly overhead, the barren ground would be bleached to pale cream. Blistering hot by day, bitter cold in the winter nights, the desert plateau would have been considered forbidding, even terrifying, by most people. To us it was one of the most exciting places on earth—and beautiful, in its own fashion. The only signs of life were the marks on the white dust of the path we followed: the footprints of bare and booted feet, the hoofprints of donkey and goat, the slithering curves that marked the passage of snakes. Some of the more energetic tourists came this way, but from the other direction, after visiting the Valley. The only persons we met were Egyptians, all of whom greeted us with the smiling courtesy of their race. The graceful (if tattered) folds of their dusty robes suited the scene.

As did my spouse. Striding briskly, tall form erect and face alight with anticipation, Emerson was in his natural element here, and his casual attire set off his muscular frame far better than the formal garments convention forced upon him in civilized regions. Bronzed throat and arms bared, black hair blowing in the breeze, he was a sight to thrill the heart of any female.

"You were joking, Emerson, weren't you? I agree with you about the importance of copying the records, but what you are doing is a kind of preservation too. If you had not found Tetisheri's tomb, those wonderful objects would have been stolen or destroyed."

Emerson looked at me in surprise. Then his well-cut lips curved in a smile. "My darling Peabody, it is like you to be concerned, but quite unnecessary, I assure you. When have you ever known me to suffer from a deficiency of self-assurance?"

"Never," I said, returning his smile.

"I am the most fortunate of men, Peabody."

"Yes, my dear. What do a few boring tombs matter? We are here, where we love to be, with those we love best." I looked back over my shoulder. "What a handsome trio they are, to be sure, and how friendly with one another! I always said, Emerson, that they would turn out well."

From Manuscript H

Nefret was lecturing again. "You said we would tell them after we left Cairo. Then you put it off until we reached Luxor. What are we waiting for? I agree with David, if we're going to be scolded—"

"There's no if about it," Ramses said dourly.

"Then let's get it over with! Anticipation is always worse than actuality."

"Not always."

"It is for me. When I looked in the mirror this morning I found two new wrinkles! Haven't you noticed how pale and drawn I have become?"

Ramses looked down at the golden head near his shoulder. She was absolutely irresistible when she was in this mood, stamping along like a sulky child and scolding him in a voice that always held an undercurrent of laughter.

"No, I hadn't noticed," he said.

"You wouldn't. I know what it is. You want to prove to the Professor and Aunt Amelia that you can handle a mess like this one with no help from them. You don't want to show them the papyrus until you can tell them where it came from and hand over the thief, dead or alive—"

He was sure he had not reacted except by a slight break in his stride, but Nefret caught herself with a gasp and turned her head to look up into his face.

"I didn't mean it. I'm sorry. I thought you'd got over it."

"Over what?"

He began walking faster. She broke into a trot, keeping pace with him. "Damn it, Ramses—"

"And don't swear. Mother doesn't like it."

Nefret stopped. "Hell and damnation!" she shouted.

"Now she's looking back," Ramses said apprehensively. "And Father is glowering at me over his shoulder. Could you please stop yelling and try to look pleasant before you get me in serious trouble?"

Nefret gave him a calculating look. Then she threw her head back and let out a piercing soprano peal of laughter. It rose to an even more piercing shriek as Horus stuck all his claws into her. He didn't like people to yell in his ear.

"And put the damned cat down!" Ramses's fingers itched with the urge to remove the beast from her arms and find out whether a cat always lands on its feet when it is dropped from a height. He knew better than to try it, though. "You can't carry him all the way to the Valley, he weighs almost twenty pounds."

"Would you . . ." Nefret began.

"I would gladly die to please you, but I draw the line at carrying that lazy carnivore."

Nefret glanced at David, who was staring fixedly at the horizon. He didn't care for Horus either. With a martyred sigh, she lowered Horus gently to the ground. The cat gave Ramses a malevolent look. He knew who was responsible for this indignity, but he had discovered early on that heavy boots were impervious to teeth and claws.

They went on, with the cat stalking after them. Ramses knew Nefret was angry with herself for probing that old wound, and with him for refusing to talk about it. No doubt she was right, it would have been better to get his feelings out into the open and accept the consolation she was aching to offer; but reticence was an old habit that was hard for him to overcome. A damned annoying habit too, he supposed, to Nefret, who never left anyone in doubt as to how she felt about anything. A little moderation wouldn't do either of them any harm.

She hadn't meant to upset him. How could she have known it would hurt so much, when he himself had been caught unawares? He seldom thought about that ugly business now, except on the rare occasions when a bad dream brought back every grisly detail of the desperate struggle in the dark and its unspeakable ending—the sound of bone and brain spattering against stone.

She remained silent, her face averted, and Ramses took up the conversation at the point it had reached before her unwitting blunder.

"I admit I wouldn't mind showing off a bit, but there's not much hope of our succeeding. We're working in the dark, and in part it's because Mother and Father still treat us like helpless infants who require to be protected—especially you, Nefret."

Ramses kicked a stone. It missed Horus by a good two feet, but the cat howled and rolled over onto his back. Nefret picked him up, cuddled him, and crooned endearments. Ramses scowled at Horus, who sneered back at him over Nefret's shoulder. One way or another Horus would get what he wanted.

They were approaching the end of the path and the steep descent from the plateau into the eastern Valley. Nefret's shoulders sagged, probably from the dead weight of Horus, since she sounded quite her old self when she spoke.

"You're right about that, and I intend to take steps to change it. I adore both of them, but they do infuriate me at times! How can they expect us to take them into our confidence when they won't tell us what we need to know?"

The path leading down into the Valley is steep but not difficult if one is in fit condition, which all of us were. I persuaded Nefret to put the cat down and put her hat on. Horus complained, but even Nefret had better sense than to attempt the descent with her arms full of cat. The tourists were out in full force; this was the height of the season and the tombs closed at one P.M. Some of them stared impertinently at our party, especially at Horus. Emerson scowled.

"It gets worse every year," he grumbled. "They are all over the place, buzzing like flies. Impossible to find a spot remote enough where one can work in peace without being gaped at and subjected to impertinent questions."

"The side wadi where we worked last year is relatively remote," I reminded him. "We were not often interrupted by tourists."

"That is because we were not finding anything that was worth a damn," said Emerson. Tourists always put him in an evil humor. Without further ado or further comment, he stamped off along the cleared path that led, not to the rocky ravine I had mentioned, but toward the main entrance to the Valley and the donkey park.

"Where is he going?" Nefret asked.

I knew the answer, and—of course—so did Ramses. He has superb breath control and always gets in ahead of me. "He wants to have a look at numbers Three, Four and Five. He has not given up hope of being allowed to excavate them, especially number Five."

Not even I can claim to be able to identify all the tombs in the Valley by number, but all of us knew these particular tombs. We had heard Emerson rant about them only too often. All had been known to earlier archaeologists; none had been properly cleared or recorded; no one particularly wanted to clear them; but the terms of Emerson's firman did not permit HIM to investigate them, because they were considered to be royal tombs. Cartouches of Ramses III had been noted in number Three, though that monarch had actually been buried in another, far more elaborate, tomb elsewhere in the Valley. Number Four, attributed to Ramses XI, had been used as a stable by Christian Arabs and was assumed to have been thoroughly ransacked. The name of Ramses II had been seen in number Five, but he also had a tomb elsewhere, and attempts to investigate this tomb—the latest by our friend Howard Carter five years earlier—had been frustrated by the hard-packed rubble that filled the chambers.

Emerson would have been the first to admit that the possibility of discovering anything of unusual interest was slight, but it infuriated him to be prevented from making the attempt because of an arbitrary, unfair decree. The firman granting permission to look for new tombs in the Valley of the Kings was held by Mr. Theodore Davis and it was strictly enforced, not only by M. Maspero, but by the local inspector, Mr. Arthur Weigall.

"We had better catch him up," I said uneasily. "If he should encounter Mr. Weigall he is sure to say something rude."

"Or do something rude," said Nefret with a grin. "The last time he met Mr. Weigall he threatened to—"

"Hurry," I begged.

Most of the tourists were going in the opposite direction from ours, so our progress was slower than I would have liked. I had to agree with Emerson's assessment; in general they were a silly-looking lot, unsuitably attired and vacantly gaping. The men had the advantage, since they were unencumbered by high-heeled shoes and corsets. Men and women alike stared at Nefret, who strode as easily as a slender boy in her sensible boots and trousers. At my insistence she wore a coat, but her shirt was open at the neck and golden-red locks had escaped from her pith helmet and curled round her face. She paid no heed to the impertinent stares—critical on the part of the women, quite otherwise on the part of the gentlemen.

As I had expected, we found Emerson planted firmly in front of tomb number Five. Only those tombs containing painted reliefs had been provided with locked gates. The barrier that prevented entrance to this one was equally effective—heaped-up rubble and miscellaneous trash that concealed all but the outline of a door.

I was sorry to see that my premonition had been accurate. Facing Emerson, his back to the tomb, was a young man wearing a neat tweed suit and a very large pith helmet—Mr. Weigall, who now held our friend Howard's former position of Inspector for Upper Egypt. Neither their postures nor their expressions were combative, and I was about to dismiss my forebodings when Emerson swung his arm and struck Mr. Weigall full in the chest. Weigall toppled over backwards, into the half-filled opening.

5

We celebrated Christmas in the good old-fashioned way, with a tree and carols and friends gathered round. To be sure, the setting was a trifle unusual—golden sand instead of snow, a balmy breeze wafting through the open windows instead of sleety rain pounding at the closed panes, a spindly tamarisk branch instead of an evergreen—but we had spent so many festal seasons in Egypt that it seemed entirely natural to us. Even the spindly tamarisk made a brave show, thanks to David's ingenious decorations. Comical camels, garlands of delicate silvery stars, and innumerable other designs cut from tin or shaped of baked clay filled in the empty spaces and twinkled in the lights of the candles.

Mr. Weigall and his wife had declined our invitation. They appeared to harbor a grudge, though I could not imagine why; Emerson's prompt action had saved the young man from far more serious injuries than he received when he landed (rather heavily, I admit) on the hard surface, and my heroic husband was still favoring his left leg, which had been badly bruised by the shower of stones dislodged by idiot tourists trying to climb the rocks above the tomb.

"Perhaps," I had remarked, following the event, "you need not have pushed him quite so hard, Emerson."

Emerson gave me a look of hurt reproach. "There was no time to calculate, Peabody. Do you suppose I would deliberately set out to injure an official of the Antiquities Service?"

No one could possibly have proved that he had, but I feared relations between ourselves and the Weigalls had not become any warmer. However, the presence of older and better friends made their absence unimportant. Cyrus and Katherine Vandergelt were there, of course; Cyrus was one of our dearest friends, and we had become very fond of the lady he had espoused a few years earlier, despite her somewhat questionable past.

When we first met her, Katherine was busily bilking a gullible acquaintance of ours in her then-capacity as a spiritualist medium. She had come round to a right way of thinking and had been on the verge of honorably refusing Cyrus's offer of marriage when I persuaded her to reconsider. I had never regretted my intervention (I seldom do), for they were very happy together, and Katherine's caustic wit and cynical view of humanity made her a most entertaining companion.

Prices had gone up shockingly since my early days in Egypt; despite Fatima's skills in bargaining, the turkey cost almost sixty piastres, four times what it would have cost twenty years ago. After dinner—including a splendid plum pudding in a blaze of brandy, borne in by Fatima—we retired to the verandah to watch the sunset. As Katherine sank gratefully into a chair she cast an envious eye upon Nefret, who was wearing one of her loose, elaborately embroidered robes, and declared her intention of acquiring a similar garment herself.

"I ate far too much," she declared. "And my corsets are killing me. I ought to have followed your advice, Amelia, and left them off, but I am a good deal stouter than you."

"You are just right as you are," Cyrus declared, looking fondly at her.

The others hastened to express their agreement. We had only two other guests—Howard Carter and Edward Ayrton, with whom Ramses had struck up a friendship the previous year. Ned, as he had invited me to call him, was the archaeologist in charge of Mr. Davis's excavations. He got little credit from Davis, who referred to his discoveries in the first person singular, but since the American was completely ignorant of excavation procedures and disinclined to follow them anyhow, Maspero had required him to employ a qualified person. Ned was a slight young fellow, pleasant-looking rather than handsome. I thought he seemed a little shy with us, so I put myself out to include him in the conversation.

"Your official season begins, I believe, on January the first. You have had remarkable good fortune thus far in finding interesting tombs for Mr. Davis. Not that I mean to disparage the archaeological skills which have contributed to your success."

"You are too kind, Mrs. Emerson," the young man replied in a soft, well-bred voice. "In fact, we didn't find anything last year that measured up to Yuya and Thuya."

"Good Gad, how many unrobbed tombs does the bas—er—man expect to find in one lifetime?" Emerson demanded.

"He has rather got into the habit of expecting at least one a year." The comment came from Howard, who had taken a seat a little distance from the rest of us. "I don't envy you your job, Ayrton."

There was a brief, embarrassed silence. Howard had once supervised Davis's excavations, in addition to holding down the post of Inspector for Upper Egypt. Now he had lost both positions, and the bitterness in his voice belied his claim of indifference.

In the spring of 1905 Howard had been transferred to Lower Egypt in place of Mr. Quibell, who had taken over Howard's position as Inspector for Upper Egypt. Not long after Howard moved to Sakkara, a group of drunken French tourists had tried to enter the Serapeum without the necessary tickets. When they were refused entry, they attacked the guards with fists and sticks. Upon being summoned to the scene, Howard ordered his men to defend themselves, and a Frenchman was knocked down.

Since the inebriated individuals had also invaded the house of Mrs. Petrie that same morning and behaved rudely to her, there was no doubt that they had been in the wrong—but for a "native" to strike a foreigner, even in self-defense, was a greater wrong in the eyes of the pompous officials who controlled the Egyptian government. The French demanded an official apology. Howard refused to give it. Maspero transferred him to a remote site in the Delta, and after several months of brooding Howard resigned. Since then he had been scraping a dubious living by selling his paintings and acting as a guide to distinguished tourists. He had no private means, and the career which had been so promising was now cut short.

It was Emerson who broke the silence, with the sort of comment he had promised me he would not make. The previous year he had

had a major falling-out with Mr. Davis—as opposed to his minor fallings-out with other people. He had sworn he would not disturb the felicity of the day by cursing Davis, but I might have known he would be unable to resist.

"You're well out of it, Carter," he growled. "Quibell couldn't stick working with Davis, that's why he got himself transferred back north, and after Weigall took over the inspectorate he persuaded Davis to hire Ayrton because *he* couldn't stand the old idiot either."

Emerson's fulminations had a better effect than my attempts at tact. They broke the ice as emphatically as a boulder crashing onto a frozen stream. Everybody relaxed, and even Howard grinned sympathetically at Ned Ayrton. Nevertheless, I felt obliged to utter a gentle remonstrance.

"Really, Emerson, you are the most tactless man alive. I had hoped that on this day of all times we might avoid topics that lead to cursing and controversy."

Cyrus chuckled. "That would be doggone dull, Amelia dear."

Nefret went to sit on the arm of Emerson's chair. "Quite right. The Professor only said what we were all thinking, Aunt Amelia. Allow us the pleasure of a little malicious gossip."

"I never gossip," said Emerson loftily. "I am only stating facts. Where are you planning to work this season, Ayrton?"

This sounded to Ned like a relatively innocent question, and he was quick to answer. "The area south of the tomb of Ramses IX was what I had in mind, sir. The heaped-up rubble doesn't appear to have been disturbed since . . ."

After a while Cyrus drew up a chair and joined in, so I went to sit beside Katherine, who had been listening with considerable amusement.

"Poor Cyrus," she said. "It is no wonder he resents Mr. Davis, after all those unproductive years he spent digging in the Valley."

"He might not be so resentful if Davis didn't swagger and gloat whenever they chance to meet. It really isn't fair. Cyrus was at his dig every day, supervising and assisting; Davis only turns up after his archaeologist has found something interesting."

A burst of laughter drew our attention back to the group. Ramses must have said something particularly rude (or possibly witty), for they had all turned to him, and Nefret went to sit beside her brother on the ledge. The rays of the setting sun gilded her luxuriant golden-red hair and flushed, laughing face. Katherine drew in her breath.

"She is frighteningly beautiful, isn't she? I know, Amelia, I know—beauty is only skin-deep, and vanity is a sin, and nobility of character is more important than appearance—but most women would sell their souls to look like that. I had better go and remind Cyrus that he is a happily married man. Only see how he is staring."

"They are all staring," I said, with a smile. "But Nefret is completely without vanity, thank heaven, and it is the qualities within that render her beautiful. Without them she would be only a pretty little doll. She is in tearing high spirits today."

"There is certainly a glow about her," Katherine said thoughtfully. "The sort of glow one sees on the face of a girl who is in the company of an individual who has engaged her affections."

"It is not like you to employ circumlocutions, Katherine. If you mean that Nefret has fallen in love, I fear your instincts have, for once, led you astray. Her feelings for Howard and Ned Ayrton are friendly at best, and I assure you she would never set her cap for a married man."

My little jest brought a smile to Katherine's lips. "No doubt I am mistaken. I often am."

The first star of evening had appeared in the sky over Luxor and I was about to suggest we retire to the parlor when Ramses turned his head. "Someone is coming," he said, interrupting his father in mid-expletive.

The Egyptians call Ramses "the brother of Demons," and some of them believe he can see in the dark, like an afreet or a cat. I would not deny that his vision is excellent. Several seconds had passed before I made out the shadowy form of a man on horseback. He dismounted and advanced toward us, and when the dying light illumined his well-cut features I let out an exclamation.

"Good Gad! Is it—can it be—Sir Edward? What are you doing here?"

Sir Edward Washington—for it was indeed he—removed his hat and bowed. "I am flattered that you remember me, Mrs. Emerson. It has been several years since we last met."

It had been over six years, to be precise. He had not changed appreciably; his tall form was as trim, his fair hair as thick, and his blue eyes met mine with the same look of lazy amusement. I remembered my manners, which astonishment had made me forget. Astonishment—and a certain degree of uneasiness. At that last meeting I had bluntly informed Sir Edward that he must give up any hope of winning Nefret and he had informed me, less bluntly but just as unequivocally, that he intended to try again. And here he was, and there was Nefret, smiling and dimpling in a particularly suspicious manner.

I rose and went to meet him. "It is unlikely that I would forget an individual who worked so diligently with us on Tetisheri's tomb, and who was, moveover, responsible for rescuing me from a particularly awkward situation."

This reference reminded Emerson of *his* manners. At their best they were far from perfect, and he had never been very fond of Sir Edward; but gratitude won out over dislike. "I suppose being strangled could be described as an awkward situation," he said dryly. "Good evening, Sir Edward. I had not expected to see you again, but so long as you are here you may as well sit down."

Sir Edward appeared to be amused rather than offended by this less-than-effusive invitation. His own manners were admirable. His greeting to Nefret was warm but in no way familiar; his comments on how Ramses and David had grown since he had last seen them were only a little condescending. Ramses's reaction was to rise to his full height, an inch or two greater than that of Sir Edward, and shake hands rather more vigorously than courtesy demanded.

As it turned out, Sir Edward was acquainted with all the others except Katherine.

"I had heard of Mr. Vandergelt's good fortune, and am delighted to make the acquaintance of a lady who has been so widely praised," he said with a graceful bow.

"How very kind," Katherine replied. "I had heard of you too, Sir Edward, but was not aware of the remarkable incident to which the Professor referred. Is it a secret, or will you tell us about it?"

Sir Edward remained modestly silent, and I said, "It is no longer a secret. Is it, Emerson?"

Emerson glowered at me. "People are not infrequently moved to strangle you, Amelia. This—er—incident occurred a few years ago, Katherine, when my discreet, prudent wife took a notion to go haring off to confront a suspect without bothering to inform me of her intentions. Had not Sir Edward followed her—for reasons which were never explained to my entire satisfaction—she might have been efficiently murdered by—"

"Emerson!" I exclaimed. "Enough of this morbidity. We were just about to retire to the parlor for refreshment and a bit of carol singing, Sir Edward. You will join us, I hope?"

"I had no intention of intruding," the gentleman in question exclaimed. "I came only to wish you the felicitations of the season, and to present you with a small token of my esteem." He took a small box from his coat pocket and offered it to me. "It is nothing, really," he went on, overriding my thanks. "I happened to come across it in an antiquities shop the other day, and I thought it might appeal to you."

Inside the box was an amulet of blue faience, approximately two inches long. The molded loop showed that it had been worn on a cord or string as a protective amulet—almost certainly by a woman, since the protruding muzzle and swollen belly were those of the hippopotamus goddess Taueret, who watched over mothers and children.

"How charming," I murmured.

"A memento of our last meeting?" Brows elevated, voice harsh, Emerson addressed Sir Edward. "You exhibit less than your usual tact, Sir Edward; Taueret was for us a symbol of danger and bad luck."

"But you triumphed over both," Sir Edward said winsomely. "I thought it might be a reminder of your success, but if Mrs. Emerson does not care for it she must feel free to discard it. It is probably a forgery; some of the Gurnawis produce excellent fakes."

He carefully avoided looking at David, but I could not help wondering if the reference had been accidental. Sir Edward had been with us the year we met David, who had been working for one of the best forgers in Gurneh.

"Not at all," I said quickly. "That is—thank you, Sir Edward. I am acquiring quite a collection of nice little amulets; yours will be a welcome addition to the Bastet Ramses gave me some years ago, and this one, which I received only recently."

I had had the little statue of the baboon added to the chain on which I wore Ramses's cat and the scarab of Thutmose III, which had been Emerson's bridal gift. Sir Edward leaned forward to examine them.

"The baboon is a symbol of the god Thoth, is it not? A handsome piece, Mrs. Emerson. What special significance does this amulet have, if I may ask?"

"It symbolizes a cause dear to my heart, Sir Edward—that of equal rights for women. 'Huquq al ma'ra,' as they say here. It was given me by a lady who is taking an active part in the movement."

"I am not surprised that you should wear it, then. But is there really such a movement in Egypt, of all places?"

"The flame of freedom burns in the hearts of all women, Sir Edward."

Emerson snorted—not, I felt sure, at the sentiment, but at my manner of expressing it. I took my revenge by delivering a little lecture (or, to be accurate, rather a long lecture) on the history of the women's movement in Egypt, mentioning the periodical we had seen and the literacy classes. Sir Edward was too well-bred to appear bored, but in fact I felt certain he was genuinely interested, as his occasional questions indicated.

Emerson was bored, and soon said so.

As I had expected, Sir Edward's reluctance to intrude was readily overcome; I led the way into the house and we gathered round the pianoforte. Sir Edward's mellow baritone swelled the chorus and after a while Emerson stopped scowling at him and joined in. Emerson always suspects men of having designs on me. It is a flattering but inconvenient delusion of his, and in this case it was completely without foundation. If Sir Edward had designs on anyone, it was on another; seeing his face soften as he watched Nefret I knew he had not abandoned his hopes. She was careful to avoid his eyes, which was even more suspicious.

The only one who did not participate was Ramses. As a child he had been prone to croon in a wordless, tuneless fashion that was particularly annoying to my ears. He had abandoned the habit, at my request, and it had taken considerable persuasion by Nefret before he would condescend to join in our little family concerts. To my surprise, I found that his singing voice was not unpleasing, and that in some manner (not from his father) he had learned to carry a tune.

He excused himself that evening on the grounds that his throat was a trifle sore. Nefret did not urge him.

From Manuscript H

"It's him!" Careless of grammar and the legs of the furniture, Ramses flung himself into a wicker armchair. "He's the one she was meeting in London."

"What makes you think that? She always has followers." David closed the door of Ramses's room and settled himself in another chair.

"She met that fellow on the sly, and lied about it. That isn't like her."

"Perhaps she's tired of hearing you ridicule her admirers."

"Most of the victims have made sufficient fools of themselves without any help from me. Well—not much help."

"Why don't you tell her how you feel? I know, by your Western standards you are still too young to think of marriage, but if she agreed to an engagement you would at least be sure of her."

"Oh, yes," Ramses said bitterly. "She might just be soft-hearted and soft-headed enough to accept my proposal out of sheer pity, and if once she gave her word she wouldn't break it. Are you suggesting I take advantage of her kindness and affection, and then ask her to remain true to me for four or five years?"

"I hadn't thought of it that way," David said quietly.

"You aren't fool enough to fall in love with a girl who doesn't love you. I will not admit my feelings until she shows some sign of returning them. So far I don't seem to be making much progress."

"Someone has to take the first step," David said sensibly. "Perhaps she would respond if you took the trouble to demonstrate your feelings."

"How? Nefret would fall over laughing if I turned up with flowers in my hand and flowery speeches on my lips."

"She probably would," David agreed. "You don't seem to have any difficulty making other women fall in love with you. How many of them have you—"

"That is a question no gentleman should ask, much less answer," Ramses said, in the same repressive tone his mother would have used, but with a faint smile. "I wouldn't blame Nefret for—er—amusing herself with other men. I'd hate it, but I'm not hypocrite enough to condemn her for it. And I would never stand in her way if she truly cared for a man who was worthy of her."

"Wouldn't you?"

Only lovers and deadly enemies look directly into one another's eyes.

Was that one of his mother's famous aphorisms? It sounded like the sort of thing she would say; and as his eyes met those of his friend in a direct unblinking gaze, Ramses felt a chill run through him. David looked away, clasping his arms around his body as if he too felt suddenly cold.

After a moment Ramses said, "You must be getting frightfully bored with my histrionics."

"Anything that is important to you is important to me, Ramses. You know that. I only wish I could . . ."

"You look tired. Go to bed, why don't you?"

"I'm not tired. But if you don't want to talk any longer—"

"You've heard it all before. To the point of tedium, I expect." He forced a smile. "Good night, David."

The door closed softly. Ramses sat without moving for a long time. The suspicion that had entered his mind was despicable and baseless. A single meeting of eyes, an altered note in the voice that had responded to his statement: "I would never stand in her way if she cared for someone who was truly worthy of her . . ." David *was* worthy of her. Not by the false standards of the modern world, perhaps, but Nefret's formative years had been spent in quite a different world. The strange culture of the oasis had not been free of bigotry and cruelty, but its prejudices were based on caste rather than race or nationality. Nefret didn't think of David as an inferior. Neither did Ramses. David was—might be—a rival more dangerous than any he had yet encountered. And David, being the sort of man he was, would feel guilty and ashamed at coming between his best friend and the girl his friend wanted.

We resumed work the following morning. Others of the English community in Luxor might make a festival of Boxing Day, but I had had a hard enough time persuading Emerson to celebrate Christmas, which he considered a heathen festival. "Why don't we just wreathe mistletoe around our brows and sacrifice someone to the sun?" he had inquired sarcastically. "That is all it is, you know, the ancient celebration of the winter solstice. Nobody knows what year the fellow was born, much less what day, and furthermore . . ."

But I cannot in conscience reproduce Emerson's heretical remarks on Christian dogma.

When we started for the Valley Abdullah walked with me, as he often did. He honestly believed he was helping me, so I gave him my hand on the steeper slopes; and when we reached the top I tactfully suggested we rest for a moment before following the others.

"We are not so young as we once were, Sitt," said Abdullah, subsiding rather heavily onto a rock.

"None of us is. But what does it matter? It may take us a little longer to reach the summit, but never fear, we will get there!"

The corners of Abdullah's mouth twitched. "Yours are words of wisdom, as always, Sitt."

He did not appear in any hurry to go on, so we sat for a time in silence. The air was cool and clean. The sun had just risen above the eastern cliffs and the morning light spread slowly across the landscape like a wash of watercolor, turning the gray stone to silver-gold, the pale river to sparkling blue, the dull-green fields to vivid emerald. After a while Abdullah spoke.

"Do you believe, Sitt, that we have lived other lives on this earth and will come back to live again?"

The question startled me, not only because philosophical speculation was not a habit of Abdullah's, but because it was an uncanny reflection of my own thoughts. I had been thinking that the golden palaces of heaven could be no more beautiful than the morning light on the cliffs of Thebes, and that my definition of Paradise would be a continuation of the life I loved with those I loved beside me.

"I do not know, Abdullah. Sometimes I have wondered . . . But no; our Christian faith does not hold with that idea."

Neither did the faith of Islam. Abdullah did not mention this. "I have wondered too. But there is only one way to know for certain, and I am not eager to explore that path."

"Nor I," I said, smiling. "This life holds pleasure enough for me. But I fear we will have a dull season, Abdullah. Emerson is very bored with his little tombs."

"So am I," said Abdullah.

With a grunt he got to his feet and offered a hand to help me rise. We tramped on together in silence and in perfect amity. He was bored, I was bored, Emerson was bored. We were all bored to distraction, and there was nothing I could do about it. Glumly I followed the familiar path into the small side wadi in which we were working.

The tomb of Amenhotep II was at its far end, and we had been investigating the small pit tombs along the way that led toward the main valley. Most of them had been found by Ned Ayrton in his previous seasons with Mr. Davis. He had removed the only objects of interest, and there had not been many of those. Three of the miserable little tombs had contained animal burials. They were certainly curious—a yellow dog, standing upright, with its tail curled over its back, nose to nose with a mummified monkey, and a squatting ape wearing a pretty little necklace of blue beads—but I could understand why Ned's patron had not been thrilled by the discoveries of that season.

Emerson of course found objects Ned had overlooked. He always does find things other archaeologists overlook. There were several interesting graffiti (described and translated in our forthcoming publication) and a number of beads and pottery fragments which were to lead Emerson to a remarkable theory concerning the length of the reign of Amenhotep II. These details will be of even less interest to my Reader than they were (candor compels me to admit) to me.

From Manuscript H

Ramses sat up with a start. At first he couldn't think what had waked him. The room was quite dark, for vines covered part of the single window, but his night vision was good—if not as uncannily acute as some of the Egyptians believed—and he saw only the dim shapes that ought to have been there—table and chairs, chest of drawers, and the garments hanging on hooks along the wall.

He threw back the thin sheet. Ever since an embarrassing incident a few years ago he had taken to wearing a pair of loose Egyptian-style drawers to bed. They did not encumber his movements as he went to the door, noiseless on bare feet, and eased it open.

Like the other bedchambers his opened onto a walled courtyard. Nothing moved in the starlight; a spindly palm tree and the potted plants his mother nurtured cast dim, oddly shaped shadows. No lights showed at the windows. His parents' room was at the far end of the wing, then David's, then his, with Nefret's at this end. Like his parents' room, hers had windows on an outer wall as well as the courtyard.

He took in the peaceful scene without pausing, drawn on by the same indefinable sense of uneasiness that had waked him. He had reached Nefret's door before he heard her cry out—not a scream, a soft, muffled sound that would have been inaudible a few feet away.

She hadn't locked her door. It would not have mattered; the hinges gave way when his shoulder hit the panel, and he pushed the door aside. The room was as dark as his had been; something was blocking the outer window, cutting off the starlight. Then the obstruction disappeared and he saw the glimmer of Nefret's white nightdress, motionless on the floor between the bed and the window.

"Curse it!" she gasped, raising herself to a sitting position. "He got away! Go after him!"

The full sleeve of her gown fell back as she flung out her arm. It had been slit from elbow to wrist, and the fabric was no longer white.

"Too late," Ramses said. At least that was what he intended to say. His heart was pounding, trying to compensate for the beats it had skipped before she moved and spoke, and the words caught in his throat. She was wriggling around, trying to stand up, but her movements were slow and unsteady and her long skirts were twisted around her legs. He dropped to his knees and took her by the shoulders. "Stay still. He's long gone, whoever he was, and you're going to faint."

Nefret said indignantly, "I've never fainted in my . . ." Her head fell back, and he gathered her limp body into his arms.

He was still holding her when a light appeared in the doorway and he looked up to see David, a lamp in one hand, his knife in the other.

"Good Lord! Is she—"

"Half-smothered," said Nefret in a muffled voice.

She probably was at that, Ramses thought. He relaxed his grip enough for her to turn her head away from his shoulder, and she gave him a cheerful grin. "That's better. Close the door, David, and bring the lamp over here. Put me down, Ramses. No, not on the bed, there's no sense in getting blood on the sheets."

Wordlessly Ramses lowered her onto the rug.

"You look as if *you* are about to faint," she remarked. "Sit down and put your head between your knees."

Ramses sat down. He did not put his head between his knees, but he left it to David to clean and bandage the cut. By the time the job was done, his hands and his voice were fairly steady.

"All right," he said harshly. "What happened?"

Nefret let David help her to her feet and lead her to a chair. "A man climbed in through the window," she explained. "I didn't wake up until he was already in the room. He was after the papyrus."

"How do you know?" Ramses demanded.

"Because that was when I woke up, when he dragged the case out from under the bed. He let out a sort of hiss, and—"

"And you tried to stop him?" Fury roughened his voice, and Nefret glared back at him.

"I did stop him. He didn't get it. I'd have caught him, too, if you hadn't burst in."

"Oh, yes, right," Ramses said. "What with, a hair ribbon?"

"I had my knife. I always sleep with it under my pillow." She gestured at the puddle of blood on the floor. "That's not all mine. I slashed at his arm, to keep him from picking up the case, you know—I was afraid he'd drop it once we got to fighting—and then he backed away, and I got out of bed and went after him, and he—"

"Got to fighting?" David stared at her in horror. "Went after him? For the love of heaven, Nefret! Ramses is right, you are too damned impulsive. Why didn't you call for help?"

"There wasn't time. I blocked his blow, the way Ramses taught me, but I guess I wasn't quite quick enough. It was only a little cut," she added defensively. "But I slipped in the blood on the floor. Then Ramses broke the door down, and the man got away."

"You didn't recognize him?" Ramses asked, ignoring the implied reproof.

"I didn't get a good look at him, it was dark, and he had a scarf wound round his head. It might have been Yussuf Mahmud; his height and build were the same."

"An ordinary thief," David began.

"No," Ramses said. "Sneak thieves don't carry knives, or use them—especially on the family of the dread Father of Curses. He went straight for the papyrus. That's another interesting point. How did he know Nefret had it? No proper gentleman would leave such a potentially dangerous object in the hands of a poor little weak woman."

"Ha," said Nefret.

"Ha indeed. Nefret, are you sure you didn't tell anyone? Or let slip . . . No, of course not."

"Damn right."

She might have let something slip, though, without being aware of it—to a man who asked the right questions. She'd been seeing a lot of Sir Edward the past few days . . .

He knew better than to hint at that theory. "Get some rest, Nefret. We'll have a look round in the morning."

"I'll wipe up the blood," David offered. "We don't want Aunt Amelia to see it, do we."

"Don't bother," Ramses said. "I cannot imagine why Mother is not already on the scene—she usually is—but she'll certainly notice the door being off its hinges and Nefret favoring her arm, and . . . And we've no right to keep silent, not now."

"Oh dear," Nefret murmured. "The Professor is going to roar."

"Undoubtedly. And Mother will lecture. On the whole, I prefer Father's roars."

"We'll confess tomorrow, then." Nefret stood up. "Good night."

She waved away David's supporting arm and followed them to the door. "Ramses," she said.

"Yes?"

"How did you get here so quickly? I didn't cry out until he cut my arm, and you must have been already outside my door."

"Something woke me. Perhaps he made a sound climbing in the window."

A window on the opposite wall of her room, with a mud-brick partition between. Luckily she didn't notice the illogic of that. "I'm sorry if I was rude," she said.

"No more than usual."

"Thank you for being there when I needed you, my boy." She put an affectionate hand on his arm and smiled at him. Ramses stepped back.

"Not at all."

"Don't be angry. I said I was sorry."

"I'm not angry. Good night, Nefret."

Leaving David to deal with the damaged door, he strode toward the back gate and went out. It would have been more in keeping with the Byronic tradition to pace back and forth under her window—groaning and clutching his brow—but he didn't want to risk disturbing footprints or other clues; so he sat down with his back against the wall of the house and hugged his knees for warmth, and damned himself for a sentimental fool. The intruder, whoever he had been, would not return that night, and the air was cold. There was no point in going to bed, though. He wouldn't sleep.

Sometime later he became aware of movement. The moon had set, but the stars were bright. A form emerged from the shadows. It moved with a swagger, ears pricked and tail swinging. Seeing him, it stopped several feet away and stared at him.

Ramses stared back.

Some of the Egyptians believed he could communicate with animals. It required no extrasensory perception to know where Horus had been and what he had been doing. He had been doing it every night since they arrived in Luxor. Having a vile temper, a well-muscled, well-fed body, and an ego the size of a lion's, he had no difficulty in running off rivals for the affections of the local female felines. The cat Bastet would never have allowed an intruder to get within six feet of Nefret, but this selfish, single-minded beast had been too busy satisfying his appetites to guard her.

He had a feeling Horus knew exactly what he was thinking, and that Horus didn't give a damn. After a long, silent, supercilious survey, the cat proceeded on his way. He sprang onto Nefret's windowsill and turned for a final contemptuous look before vanishing inside.

For the first time in his life Ramses was tempted to throw something at an animal. Something hard and heavy.

117

"**W**here did this come from?" Emerson asked.

He spoke in the soft, purring voice his acquaintances had come to know and dread. Nefret met his keen blue eyes without flinching, but I saw her brace herself.

"It is the property of the Foundation," she replied.

"Ah, yes. The Foundation for the Exploration and Preservation of Egyptian Antiquities." Emerson sat back, fingering the cleft in his chin. In the same mild voice he added, "Your Foundation."

"Ours," Nefret corrected. "You are on the Board; so are Ramses and David and Aunt Amelia."

"Good Gad," Emerson exclaimed. "The fact must have slipped my mind. Or is it the fact that the Board gave its approval for this particular purchase? Dear me, I am getting old and forgetful."

"Enough, Emerson," I said sharply.

Emerson might have ignored my suggestion, for he really was in a considerable rage. It was the sight of Nefret's face that stopped him. Her rounded chin was quivering and her eyes were luminous with tears. When one crystal drop overflowed the cornflower-blue depths and slid down her cheek, Emerson let out a roar.

"Stop that immediately, Nefret! You are taking unfair advantage, curse it."

Nefret's trembling lips curved into a broad, relieved smile. No one minded Emerson's bellows. She sat down on the arm of his chair and ruffled his hair. "Professor darling, you let me set up the Foundation when I came into my money—in fact, you encouraged the idea—but you have never accepted a penny or allowed anyone else in the family to do so. It has hurt me deeply, though of course I have never complained."

"You may as well give in, Father," said Ramses. "If you don't, she'll start crying again."

"Hmph," said Emerson. "I see she has already got round you and David. If I remember correctly, any major expenditure requires the consent of a simple majority of the Board. You three are a majority. Amelia, why the devil didn't you point this out to me when the papers were drawn up?"

"I didn't think of it either," I admitted. I had always considered his refusal to accept financial assistance from Nefret absurd—another example of masculine pride. Why shouldn't she use her money as she liked? And what worthier recipient could there be than the greatest Egyptologist of this or any other age—Radcliffe Emerson, to be precise?

Tactfully I turned Emerson's attention back to the papyrus. "It is one of the finest I have ever seen," I said. "A worthy purchase for the Foundation, for if you had not acquired it—illegally, I suppose?—it would have been sold to a private collector and lost to science. Now, Emerson, don't start ranting about the iniquities of buying from the dealers, we have all heard that lecture a thousand times. In this case it had to be done. You do grasp the subtler implications of this discovery, I suppose?"

Emerson glared at me. I was pleased to see that my question had taken his attention away from the children.

"Do you take me for a fool, Peabody? Of course I grasp them. However, I refuse to allow you to waste time in idle speculation until we have ascertained the facts. Pray allow me to conduct this interrogation. I repeat: Where did you get this?"

His ice-blue gaze swept over the three young persons. Nefret's smile faded; David flinched; and both looked hopefully at Ramses, who was, as I had expected, not unwilling to do the talking.

"From Yussuf Mahmud in Cairo. David and I were—"

"Impossible," Emerson said. "Yussuf Mahmud deals in forgeries and second-rate antiquities. How could he lay his hands on something like this?"

"It is a pertinent question," said Ramses. "Father, if you will allow me to complete my narrative without interruption . . ."

Emerson folded his hands. "That goes for you too, Peabody. Proceed, Ramses."

As Ramses's narrative unfolded I found it difficult to repress exclamations of horror, surprise, and consternation. I must do Ramses the justice of believing that on this occasion he told not only the truth, but the whole truth. It had to be the whole truth because nothing could have been worse. Emerson's countenance did not change; but his hands gripped one another until the fingers turned white and the tendons stood out like cords.

"We made it back to the boat without further incident," Ramses concluded.

"Further incident," Emerson repeated. "Hmmm, yes. There had been incidents enough. Well, well. It is not the first time you have behaved recklessly, and it will probably not be the last. There is only one thing I fail to understand."

"Yes, sir?" Ramses said warily. He was not deceived by Emerson's mild tone.

"I do not understand why . . ." Emerson's voice broke with sheer fury and then rose to a roar that rattled the cups in their saucers. "Why in the name of God you took your sister with you!"

The cat Horus shot out from under the table and headed for the door, his ears flattened and his tail straight out. There he encountered Abdullah, who had been waiting for us on the verandah and who had, I supposed, been alarmed by Emerson's shouts and hurried to discover what disaster had prompted them. The cat got entangled in Abdullah's skirts and a brief interval of staggering (by Abdullah), scratching (by Horus) and swearing (by both parties) ensued before Horus freed himself and departed.

So Ramses had to go over it again, while I applied iodine to Abdullah's shins. Ordinarily he would have objected to this procedure, but the interest of the narrative distracted him; his eyes got rounder and rounder and when Ramses finished he gasped, "You took Nur Misur with you?"

"They didn't take me," Nefret said. "We went together. Abdullah, please don't get excited. It is not good for you."

"But—but—Yussuf Mahmud," Abdullah exclaimed. "That crawling snake . . . Into el Was'a. . . . At night . . ."

"If you don't calm down I am going to get my stethoscope and listen to your heart." She pressed him back into his chair with one small brown hand and offered him a glass of water with the other.

The threat was sufficient. Abdullah viewed modern medical procedures with deep suspicion, and the very idea of being examined by a young woman filled him with horror.

"If she had not been with us, I might not be here with you now, Grandfather," David said. "She is as quick as a cat and as brave as a lion."

I decided it was time for me to take charge of the discussion, which had degenerated into a series of emotional exchanges. This is often the case when men carry on a conversation.

"Let us hear the rest of it, Ramses," I said.

Emerson, who had begun to relax, came to attention with an audible snap of muscles. "There is more?"

"I rather think so. We will have to call Ibrahim to repair the hinges of Nefret's door. Well, Ramses?"

"I'll tell it," Nefret said.

Emerson must already have reached the pinnacle of outrage, for his only reaction was to twitch a bit. Abdullah sipped his water, watching Nefret suspiciously over the rim of the glass. Nefret did not give either of them the opportunity to comment.

"I admit we ought to have told you about the papyrus earlier," she said. "But that's over and done with, and we know how you feel, and you know how we feel, so let us not waste time shouting at one another."

"Now see here, young lady," Emerson began.

"Yes, Professor darling, we all know you never shout. The question is, what are we to do now? As I see it," she continued, without waiting for a reply, "there are two questions to be answered. First, who was the man who entered my room last night? Second, where did the papyrus originate? Has a new tomb been discovered?"

"Well-reasoned," I said approvingly. "I was about to put the same questions myself. You think the intruder was Yussuf Mahmud?"

"It was not an ordinary thief," Abdullah grunted. "No man of Thebes would risk the anger of the Father of Curses."

Emerson growled agreement. "He left no clue?"

It was Ramses who answered. "I searched the area under Nefret's window this morning. The sand had been disturbed, but it does not take footprints. He was not so considerate as to lose an article of clothing or—"

"Yes, yes," said Emerson, who recognized the start of one of Ramses's lectures. "I find it difficult to believe that Yussuf Mahmud would have the intestinal fortitude to break into the house. He's a second-rater in every way."

"He might have summoned up the intestinal fortitude if he feared someone else more than he did us," Ramses said.

"Hmmm." Emerson rubbed his chin. "The individual from whom he got the papyrus, you mean. He was sent here to retrieve it, with the promise that his worthless life would be spared if he succeeded? Possible. Curse it, Ramses, why didn't you tell me this before we left Cairo? I can think of several people who deal in antiquities of exceptional quality and whose scruples are questionable."

"So can I, Father. I saw no point in pursuing that line of inquiry, however. The guilty person would not admit anything, and questioning the others would only arouse speculation of the sort we want to avoid."

"I suppose so." The admission came grudgingly. Emerson would have preferred to call on all his suspects and bully one of them into a confession.

His eyes returned to the papyrus, which lay on the table in David's ingeniously designed case. One of the charming little painted vignettes had been exposed; it showed the mummy case of the princess being drawn to the tomb by a pair of oxen. Emerson fingered the cleft in his chin, as was his habit when perplexed or in deep thought. Half to himself, he said, "It's odd, though. The papyrus is very fine, no question of that; but I would not have believed any of the persons I had in mind would go to such lengths to get it back. Attacking a scruffy fellow swindler like Ali the Rat is one thing. Attempting to rob ME requires more audacity than I would have supposed them to possess."

"Have you any ideas about who such an audacious person might be, sir?" Nefret inquired politely.

Emerson shot her a wary look. "No. How should I? The question of the origin of this object is equally mysterious. It came from Thebes, obviously, but where in Thebes?"

"It occurred to David," Ramses said, "that this papyrus might have come from the Royal Cache. The Abd er Rassul brothers had been looting the tomb of small objects for years before they were—er—persuaded to lead Herr Brugsch to the site. Some things were sold to collectors—"

"And other things they concealed in their house in Gurneh," said Abdullah. "There were papyri among those things."

Emerson was smoking furiously. "There is another possibility. Brugsch could easily have overlooked something, he bundled everything out of the place in such a cursed hurry."

"Surely it is unlikely that he and the Abd er Rassuls would both overlook something as valuable as this," I mused. "However, a proper excavation might yield interesting results."

Emerson gave me a critical look. "Bored with our tombs, are you,

Peabody? Don't suppose you can distract me from my duty with your tempting suggestions. What we are endeavoring to determine is how the papyrus got to Cairo and where it originated. I see four possibilities. The first, that it came from the undiscovered tomb of the princess, is cursed unlikely. Other objects from that tomb would have surfaced. The second, third, and fourth theories assume it was part of the Deir el Bahri cache. It was sold by the thieves either shortly after they discovered the tomb, or later, after having been concealed in their house for an undetermined number of years; or it was found and marketed only recently."

I opened my mouth to speak. Emerson said in a loud voice, "Don't begin theorizing, Peabody, I am having difficulty enough controlling my temper. We have not sufficient evidence to construct a theory as yet. Unless our dear dutiful children are concealing evidence from us?"

"*We* aren't concealing anything," Nefret said. "Ramses held nothing back. If I had been telling the story I would have been strongly tempted to omit a few of the more—um—interesting details."

"I suppose I must give him that," Emerson said. "Confound it, Ramses, for how long have you and David been prowling the streets of Cairo in those disgusting disguises? 'Curse the unbeliever' indeed!"

"We established those identities three years ago, Father."

"Well, you had better dis-establish them. It has occurred to you, I trust, that someone more acute than your father must have penetrated your disguises? I confess," Emerson added with grudging admiration, "that you took me in completely."

"The events of last night confirm that assumption, sir. Though I cannot explain how. We were very careful."

"Hmph. Well, if we can find Yussuf Mahmud he can answer all our questions. Our first move should be to learn whether he has shown himself in Luxor. I will just have some little chats with the antiquities dealers. Abdullah, you will question your friends and relatives in Gurneh?"

Abdullah nodded. He looked so grim I felt sorry for the friends and relatives. "It must be made known that the object the thief sought is no longer in Nur Misur's room."

"It is a good thought, my father." Ramses switched from English to Arabic. "But after today it will be my room, and she will occupy mine. Do not speak of this, or of the papyrus. I would be very glad if the man would come back."

Clipping from *Al Ahram*, December 29, 1906:

The body of a man was drawn from the Nile yesterday at Luxor, under strange circumstances. The hands and feet had been bound, and the remains were horribly mutilated, apparently by the jaws of a large animal such as a crocodile. There are no longer any crocodiles in the Luxor area.

6

The news was all over Luxor next morning. We heard of it from Abdullah, who had heard of it from his cousin Mohammed, who had been told of it by his son Raschid, who had spoken with one of the unfortunate boatmen who had found the remains. I did not doubt that the discovery had been unpleasant enough, but by the time it reached us it had been magnified and exaggerated to an astonishing degree.

"A crocodile," Abdullah insisted. "Raschid said Sayed said it could have been nothing else."

"Nonsense, Abdullah. You know there have been no crocodiles in Egypt since . . . well, not in our lifetimes."

Abdullah rolled his eyes. "Let us hope it was a crocodile, Sitt. For if it was not, it was something worse."

"What could be worse?" I demanded.

Abdullah leaned forward and planted his hands on his knees. "There are men who believe the old gods are not dead, but only sleeping. Those who violate the tombs of the dead—"

"Some believe that," I agreed. "Surely you are not one of them, Abdullah?"

"Not believing is not the same as not knowing, Sitt."

"Hmm," I said, after I had worked my way through the string of negatives. "Well, Abdullah, if it is true that the old gods resent those who enter the tombs we are all in trouble—you and I and Emerson. So let us hope it is not true."

"Yes, Sitt. But there is no harm in protecting oneself against that which is not true." He gestured at the amulets on the chain round my neck, and then reached into the breast of his robe. "I have brought you another one."

Like most of the amulets found in Egypt, it was of blue-green faience, and it had been molded with a loop on the back so that it could be hung on a cord. I didn't doubt it was genuine. Abdullah had his connections. Smiling, I took the trinket from his hand.

"Thank you," I said. "But what of Emerson? Have you brought amulets for him too?"

"He would not wear them, Sitt."

"No. Abdullah, are you sure that is the reason why you gave this to me and not to Emerson? It couldn't be, could it, that you consider me more in need of protection than he?"

Abdullah's face remained grave, but there was a glint in his black eyes that I had learned to recognize. Had he been teasing me the whole time? He was certainly laughing at me now. "You are not careful, Sitt. You do foolish things."

"If I do, you and Emerson will watch over me," I said cheerfully. "And now I will have Sobek to protect me too."

I unfastened the chain and added the little figure of the crocodile god to the others.

Ramses went to view the body. The rest of us declined the treat, even Emerson, who remarked—ostentatiously not looking at Ramses—that he did not need to prove *his* manhood by inspecting mangled corpses.

Emerson was out of temper with Ramses. I knew why, of course. He blamed the boy for allowing Nefret to accompany him and David on their midnight foray into the Old City. To be sure, Emerson had taken me into areas of Cairo almost as dirty and dangerous, but he still thought of his adopted daughter as a sweet-faced, golden-haired child. She was no longer a child, as a number of young gentlemen could testify, but fathers are absurdly sentimental about their daughters. (I have been informed that some mothers are just as silly about their sons. This has never been a failing of mine.)

I did not hold Ramses accountable for Nefret's behavior on that occasion. However, when I found that he had let her go with him to examine the corpse, I discovered I was not so broad-minded as I had believed.

The rest of us were on the verandah taking tea when she and Ramses rode up, and one look at her face told me she had been doing something other than paying calls in Luxor, as she had said she intended. Ramses's face was set like stone, a certain indication of some strong emotion rigidly controlled. Ignoring his attempt to help her dismount, she slipped out of the saddle, tossed the reins to the stableman, and joined us round the tea table.

"Will you have a slice of cake?" I inquired, offering the plate. The cake was especially rich, stuffed with nuts and dates and thickly iced.

Nefret swallowed and turned her head away. "No, thank you."

"Ah," I said. "So you did go with Ramses. Nefret, I strictly forbade you—"

"No, Aunt Amelia, you didn't. No doubt you would have done if you had thought of it, but you didn't." She gave me a rather strained smile and reached out a hand to pat Emerson's rigid arm. "Professor darling, stop sputtering. Recall, if you please, that I am the only one of us who has had medical training."

"She was sick," said Ramses. Arms folded, he leaned against the wall and fixed a critical look on his sister.

"Not until afterwards! You were a bit green around the mouth yourself." She snatched up a bit of cake and thrust it at him. "Here, have a bite."

"No, thank you," said Ramses, averting his eyes.

"That bad, was it?" I inquired.

"Yes." Nefret replaced the sticky morsel on the plate and wiped her fingers on a serviette.

"Yes." Ramses had gone to the side table. He came back with two glasses of whiskey and soda and handed one to Nefret. "I trust you do not object, Mother. As you have often said, the medicinal effects of good whiskey—"

"Quite," I agreed.

Ramses raised his glass in a salute to Nefret before drinking quite a quantity himself. He settled himself in his favorite place on the ledge and remarked, "She made a closer examination of the wounds than I would have cared to do. They appeared to be consistent with the assumption that has been made."

"What, a crocodile?" I exclaimed. "Ramses, you know perfectly well—"

"Peabody." Emerson had recovered himself. His tone was calm, his face composed—except for a certain glitter in his blue eyes. "Does this strike you as suitable conversation for the tea table?"

"Many of our conversations would not be considered suitable for polite society," I replied. "If the young people can put themselves through the discomfort of actually viewing the remains, we can do no less than listen to their description. Er—you might just get me a whiskey and soda too, if you will be so good."

"Bah," said Emerson. But he complied with my request and filled a glass for himself. David declined the offer. Except for an occasional glass of wine he did not imbibe. At least not in my presence.

Stroking Horus, who had settled himself solidly across her lap, Nefret said, "I won't go into lurid detail, Professor dear. The wounds were consistent with those that might have been made by the large jaws of an animal with long sharp teeth. Since we know that no such animal is to be found in this area, we must conclude that they were made by some man-made tool. I was reminded of the Iron Maiden we saw in the museum in Nuremberg."

"Good Gad," I cried. "Are you suggesting that someone has imported an instrument of medieval torture?"

"Stop that, Peabody," said Emerson, who had forgot his qualms and was listening with intense interest. "The Iron Maiden, so called because it was the size and shape of a human body, had spikes protruding from the interior of the back and the lid. When the lid was closed the spikes penetrated the victim's body. The same effect could be produced by a less complex mechanism—long nails driven into a heavy wooden plank, for instance."

"Exactly," said Nefret, finishing her whiskey. "The wounds were confined to the head and torso, and I distinctly saw the gleam of metal in one of them. It was, as I suspected, the broken-off point of a spike or nail."

"You—you extracted it?" David asked, swallowing.

"Yes. It is evidence, you know." She touched her shirt pocket. "I brought it back with me, since no one at the zabtiyeh seemed to want it. There was only one other extraneous object on the body—a piece of cord deeply imbedded in his neck."

"A strangling cord," I breathed. "The devotees of the goddess Kali—"

An odd sound from Ramses interrupted me. His lips were so tightly compressed they formed a single narrow line.

"The poor fellow wasn't strangled, Aunt Amelia," Nefret said. "The fragment was at the back of his neck, not his throat. It seems more likely that he was wearing a crucifix or amulet round his neck, and that someone or something pulled at the cord until it snapped."

"I suppose you—er—extracted that, too," Emerson said resignedly.

"Yes. The question is, why would anyone go to such elaborate lengths to kill someone?"

"A new murder cult," I exclaimed. "Like the cult of Kali in India. A revival, by insane fanatics, of the worship of the crocodile god, Sobek—"

"Kindly control your rampageous imagination, Peabody," Emerson snarled. "The metal jaws of some machine, such as—er—some machine or other could cause similar wounds. If he was drunk and stumbled into something of the sort—"

"Headfirst?" I inquired with, I believe, pardonable sarcasm. "And the operator of the machine, not noticing a pair of protruding legs, started it up?"

David, gentle soul that he was, turned a shade paler.

Since the hypothesis was obviously absurd, Emerson did not try to defend it. "A more important question is: Who was the dead man?"

"The face was unrecognizable," said Ramses. "However, Ali Yussuf was missing the first two joints of the third finger of his left hand. The extremities had been nibbled at by smaller predators, but only the ends of the fingers and toes were gone, and that particular finger—"

David rose precipitately and hurried away.

"I believe I will just have another whiskey and soda, Emerson," I said.

On the face of it, the news was cursed discouraging. One cannot interrogate a dead man. To look at it another way—and I am always in favor of looking on the bright side—Yussuf Mahmud's murder confirmed our theory that another group of villains was involved, villains more interesting than a seller of second-rate antiquities. Emerson could (and did) jeer all he liked at my theories of mysterious and deadly cults, but I remained convinced that Yussuf Mahmud's death had all the hallmarks of ritual murder—execution, even. In some way he had betrayed the others, and he had paid a hideous price. But in what way had he betrayed them?

The answer was obvious. Yussuf Mahmud's desperate attempt to retrieve the papyrus—for only a desperate man would risk invading the house of the Father of Curses—was his last hope of saving himself from the vengeance of the cult. I did not doubt that the Followers of Sobek (as I termed them) employed valuable antiquities like the papyrus to lure prospective victims into their murderous hands. Not only had Yussuf Mahmud allowed the victims and the valuable to slip through his hands, but he had selected for the slaughter, not a naive tourist, but the members of a family known the length and breadth of Egypt for its success in tracking down evildoers.

Yussuf Mahmud could not have known who Ali the Rat was, or he would not have approached him. Someone undoubtedly was cognizant of the fact now, however. I concluded that the children must have betrayed themselves in some manner during the struggle and ensuing flight. Yussuf Mahmud had been given one last chance to compensate for his fatal error. He had failed—and he had paid the price.

My solution was the only one possible, but Emerson dismissed it with an emphatic "Balderdash, Peabody!" and did not even allow me to finish my explanation.

Of course I knew why. Though he would not admit it, Emerson was still obsessed with Sethos. This was patently ridiculous. Sethos would never become involved with anything so crude as a murder cult.

Ramses and Nefret had changed rooms, and I knew my son was bitterly disappointed when no further intrusion took place. I was disappointed too, although I had not expected the cult would risk another man. Our interrogations of the antiquities dealers and the men of Gurneh, though time-consuming, were unproductive. No one had seen Yussuf Mahmud; no one admitted to being a member of a murder cult. I had not really expected that anyone would.

The week between Christmas and New Year's Day continued to be filled with social activities, and we received a number of invitations from what Emerson referred to as "the dahabeeyah dining society"—an increasingly inaccurate term, since the majority of the individuals concerned stayed at the hotels, particularly the elegant new Winter Palace. In social terms they were a glittering group, some titled, all wealthy. In intellectual terms they were deadly bores, and I did not object to Emerson's insistence that we refuse most of the invitations. However, *I* insisted that we behave civilly to archaeological friends and old acquaintances.

Among the latter I had to include Mr. Davis, who had arrived in Luxor on board his dahabeeyah. Emerson might and did despise the man, but he had become a prominent figure in Egyptological circles and he had always been civil to me. His cousin, Mrs. Andrews, who always traveled with him, was an amiable individual. (I will not repeat Emerson's rude speculations concerning the relationship between her and Mr. Davis.)

In point of fact, we did not receive an invitation from Mr. Davis. He and Mrs. Andrews (his cousin, as I kept telling Emerson) were among the most enthusiastic members of the dining society, hobnobbing not only with favored archaeologists but with any tourist who had the slightest pretension to social status or distinction. Apparently we were not in either category. This fact did not disturb me; it relieved my mind, rather, for Emerson could not be counted upon to behave properly when he was in the company of Mr. Davis. It was inevitable that we should meet, however, and when I received an invitation to a particularly elegant affair at the Winter Palace Hotel, hosted by the manager in honor of several members of the British nobility, I did not press Emerson to accompany the rest of us. I knew Davis would be there, because he doted on the nobility.

To my surprise and annoyance, Emerson volunteered. Not only that, but he got himself into his evening clothes without argument and with a minimum of grumbling. A strong sense of foreboding filled me.

Everyone who was anyone in Luxor had been invited. We were late in arriving, but though the room was crowded with people, our entrance drew all eyes to us. Emerson, of course, looked magnificent. I cannot complain about the appearance of the boys.

It had proved impossible to remove all the cat hairs from Nefret's skirt, but they did not show too much against the satin-striped ivory chiffon. The soft shade set off the golden tan of her skin—a little too much of it, in my opinion. Between leaving the house and arriving at the hotel she must have done something to the neckline, for it looked a good deal lower than it had. At least her elbow-length gloves hid the unladylike scab on her forearm.

Emerson headed straight as a bullet for Mr. Davis. He was a little man with a large mustache who thought he was tall. (That was another of the reasons why he and Emerson did not get on; it is difficult to think of yourself as tall when Emerson is looming over you.) I managed to pull Emerson away before he could say anything except, "Hmph. So you're back, are you?"

The rest of Davis's party was with him: Mrs. Andrews, resplendent in jet-beaded black satin; several young ladies who were introduced as her nieces; and an American couple named Smith, who were staying with the Weigalls. Mr. Smith was a painter who had spent a number of seasons in Egypt and had copied for Davis and other archaeologists—a sprightly, convivial man in his mid-forties.

As soon as she had passed through the receiving line, every young (and not so young) man in the room converged on Nefret, leaving a number of ladies abandoned and forlorn. I saw my ward led onto the dance floor by the gentleman she had accepted, and turned toward Emerson. However, he had wandered off.

"Would you care to dance, Mother?" Ramses asked.

"Hmmm," I said.

"I will try not to tread on your feet."

I presumed he was making one of his peculiar jokes. Truth compels me to admit he is a better dancer than his father. No one waltzes more magnificently than Emerson; the only problem is that he insists on waltzing no matter what sort of music is being played.

I gave Ramses my hand, and as he guided me respectfully around the floor, I explained, "My momentary hesitation was not occasioned by concern for my feet, but by concern about your father. Someone ought to be with him. He is going to start an argument with someone; I know the signs."

"We are taking him in turn," Ramses replied. "David has the first dance."

Glancing around the room I saw Emerson near the buffet table, talking with M. Naville. David stood next to them. He looked very handsome in his evening clothes, but he also looked, I thought, a trifle apprehensive.

"My dear boy, David cannot possibly stop your father once he gets to ranting," I said. "I had better go and—"

"It's my turn next." The music stopped, and Ramses offered me his arm to lead me from the floor. He was showing off again, and I wondered which of the young ladies present he was trying to impress with his fine manners.

Before we reached the chairs along the wall we were intercepted. "May I beg the honor of the next dance, Mrs. Emerson?" said Sir Edward Washington, with an elegant bow.

I had not seen him since Christmas Day, but I suspected Nefret had. We circled the floor in silence for a time. Then he said, "I suppose, Mrs. Emerson, that your detectival talents are busy at work on our latest mystery."

"Which mystery did you have in mind, Sir Edward?" I countered.

"Is there more than one? I was referring to the mangled body pulled from the Nile recently. The murderer cannot have been a crocodile."

"No," I admitted.

"I was informed that you allowed Miss Forth to examine the remains."

"Good heavens, how gossip spreads in this village! I do not allow Miss Forth to do a good many things, Sir Edward. She does them anyhow."

"A very spirited young lady," Sir Edward murmured. His eyes moved to Nefret, who was talking with Mr. Davis. Both of them appeared to be enjoying themselves immensely, and it seemed to me her neckline had slipped even lower.

"But what of the murder, Mrs. Emerson?" Sir Edward resumed. "You must have a theory."

"I always have a theory," I replied. "But I will not tell you this one, Sir Edward. You would only laugh at me. Emerson has already informed me that it is balderdash."

"I would never laugh at you, Mrs. Emerson. Please."

"Well . . ."

Naturally I omitted any reference to those aspects of the case that concerned us personally. "What the man was doing here in Luxor we will never know," I concluded.

"Was he not a Luxor man, then?"

Curse it, I thought. The slip had been so slight, only a very astute individual would have caught it. I kept forgetting that Sir Edward was a very astute individual. Fortunately the music stopped and I sought an excuse to end the discussion.

"I can't recall where I got that impression," I replied evasively. "No doubt I misinterpreted some bit of gossip. If you will excuse me, Sir Edward, I must head Emerson off before he—"

"One other question, Mrs. Emerson, if I may." I stopped, perforce. He had taken my arm in quite a firm grip preparatory to escorting me to a chair.

"Once again I am seeking employment," he went on, and his courteous social smile broadened as he saw my look of surprise. "Not because I am in need of it—that little inheritance I mentioned has made me financially independent—but because I want something to occupy me. Mine is not the sort of temperament that enjoys idleness, and I have always been keen on archaeology. I don't suppose your husband is in need of a photographer, or any other sort of assistant?"

I was not taken in by this disingenuous explanation. Sir Edward was about to make his move! He would get no help from me. I explained, with perfect truth, that we had all the staff we needed at present.

"Yes, I understand." His raised eyebrow and half-smile made it clear that he did understand. "If he should change his mind, please let me know."

I had observed Emerson talking with a lady who was unfamiliar to me. His handsome head was bent attentively and his well-cut lips were wreathed in a smile. The lady was elegantly dressed and extravagantly bejeweled. A diamond ornament as big as my hand crowned the coils of her dark hair. It was shaped like a cluster of roses with the flowers and leaves set en tremblant, so that the slightest movement of her head made the roses sway on the thin wires. They sent off sparks of diamond fire as she tilted her head to gaze up at Emerson.

"Ah," said Emerson. "Here is my wife now. Peabody, allow me to introduce Mrs. Marija Stephenson. We were talking about cats."

"A fascinating subject," I said, bowing politely to the lady. She bowed politely to me. Rainbow fire glittered atop her head. A diamond necklace and matching bracelets glittered too, if not as extravagantly. I blinked.

"Quite," said Emerson. "She has one. A cat. Its name is Astrolabe."

"An unusual name."

"Your husband tells me you favor Egyptian names for your cats," said Mrs. Stephenson. She had a pleasant voice, marred only by an unfortunate American accent.

We exchanged conventional questions—"Is this your first visit to Egypt? How long are you planning to stay? Is your husband with you?"—and conventional answers—"Yes, I am enjoying it excessively; two weeks longer in Luxor and then back to Cairo; unfortunately he was unable to get away from his business." I was conscious throughout this exchange of the lady's dark eyes examining my own simple ornaments. The faience and carved stone amulets did not make much of a show compared with that galaxy of diamonds.

After introducing Mrs. Stephenson to someone else—for I hope I have better manners than to leave a stranger alone—I drew Emerson away.

" 'Pon my word, Peabody, you were cursed inquisitive," Emerson remarked. "Did you have one of your famous premonitions about the lady? I thought her very pleasant."

"So I observed. You haven't asked me to dance, Emerson. They are playing a waltz."

"Certainly, my dear." His strong arm caught me to him and swung me onto the floor.

I looked round for Nefret. I had been pleased to note that the boys had rather monopolized her that evening, taking most of her dances and preventing her from stealing out into the gardens unchaperoned. She was now dancing with Ramses, who was demonstrating more panache than he had with me. Her full skirts swung out as he spun her in a sweeping turn, and she smiled up at him.

Emerson was deep in thought, his manly brow furrowed.

"You are uncommonly taciturn, Peabody. Was it the diamonds? I saw you staring at them. You can have all you want, you know. I didn't think you cared for such things."

His sensitive perception and generous offer made me feel ashamed of myself. "Oh, Emerson," I murmured. "You are so good to me."

"Well, I try to be, curse it. But if you won't tell me what you would like, how am I supposed to know?"

"I don't want diamonds, my dear. You have given me everything I want and more."

"Ah," said Emerson. "Shall we go home, Peabody, so that I can give you—"

"That would be very agreeable, Emerson."

You may be certain, dear Reader, that Emerson had not allowed us to neglect our professional activities. I have not reported on them in detail because they produced nothing of interest. While the rest of us toiled in the remote corners of the Valley, Ramses and David worked at the Seti I temple copying inscriptions.

The weather had turned unusually warm, which did not lighten our labors. Under the burning rays of the solar orb the bare rock walls of the Valley absorb heat as a sponge soaks up water—a commodity, I might add, that is in exceedingly short supply there. We all felt it excepting Emerson, who appears to be impervious to temperatures hot or cold.

I attempted to find little tasks for Abdullah that would keep him from overexertion, but eventually he saw through my schemes and went at it harder than ever, his aristocratic nose pinched with indignation. I kept a close eye on him, therefore, and so was the first to see him fall.

He sat up when I ran to him and tried to tell me there was nothing wrong, but he could not summon up enough breath to speak. Nefret was at his side almost as soon as I. From her shirt pocket she took an envelope and reached into it.

"Hold his mouth open," she ordered, in the tone she would have used to a servant. Naturally I obeyed at once. In went her fingers and out they came; she clamped her small brown hands around Abdullah's bearded jaws and brought her face so close to his that their noses were almost touching.

Abdullah stared as if mesmerized into her intent blue orbs. Gradually his breathing slowed and deepened, and Nefret released her grasp and sat back on her heels. Abdullah blinked. Then he looked at me.

I gave him a reassuring nod. "It is well, Abdullah. Nefret, go and tell the Professor we are stopping work."

So she did, and as soon as Emerson learned what had happened he came out of the tomb and lectured Abdullah, which made him sulk, and sent Selim to ask Cyrus for the loan of his carriage, which made Abdullah swear.

"We are finished for the day," Emerson said, in the voice that brooked no argument. "Go home and rest, you stubborn old villain."

"Why not?" Abdullah said tragically. "I am old and of no use to anyone. It is a sad way to end, sitting in the sun like a toothless infant . . ."

Daoud took him by the arm. We watched them walk slowly away, Abdullah irritably swatting at Daoud.

"What the devil am I going to do with him?" Emerson demanded. "He will drop dead in his tracks one day and it will be my fault."

"Perhaps he would prefer it that way," Nefret said. "Wouldn't you?"

Emerson's worried face softened, and he put an affectionate arm around her. "You are very wise for such a young creature, my dear. What was it you gave him?"

"I knew he would lose or throw away those nitroglycerine tablets I gave him, so I brought a fresh supply. I always carry them with me."

The boys had returned to the house by the time we got there, and when Nefret said she wanted to ride to Gurneh and make sure Abdullah was all right, they went with her.

From Manuscript H

The house, one of the largest in Gurneh, was midway up the hill, near the tomb of Ramose. Abdullah shared it with his nephew Daoud and Daoud's wife Kadija, a tall, gray-haired woman with dark brown skin and muscles almost as impressive as Daoud's. Nefret claimed she was a very entertaining conversationalist, with a delightful sense of humor, but Ramses had to take her word for it since Kadija never unveiled in his presence or spoke more than a murmured greeting.

They had to pretend they had dropped in for a social call while exercising the horses. Kadija served them with cups of dark sweet tea and then retired to a corner. After Nefret had watched Abdullah for a while without seeming to, she joined Kadija and a murmured undercurrent of conversation began, broken at intervals by Nefret's musical chuckles.

They took their leave without the unpleasant subject of Abdullah's health ever being mentioned. Once outside, David said anxiously, "He looks better, but he is bound to have more of these attacks. What will happen if you aren't there with your medicine?"

"I gave Kadija a supply and told her what to watch out for. She'll make certain he takes it."

"She has the strength to do it," Ramses said. "But has she the will?"

"Of course. She is a very intelligent woman. She told me the most amusing story, about . . ." Nefret laughed. "Well, perhaps it is not suitable for delicate masculine ears."

It was still early, so at David's suggestion they took a stroll through the village—"revisiting the scenes of my youth," as he put it with uncharacteristic irony. The house where he had spent so many miserable years as the apprentice of a forger of antiquities had passed into the hands of Abd el Hamed's cousin, who was carrying on the same trade. In theory the workshop turned out copies which were sold as such, but everyone knew that business was only a cover for the production of fakes.

"He's not as good as my late and unlamented master," David said. "I've seen some of his fakes in the antiquities shops, and they are so poor only the most gullible tourist would buy them. I'll wager half the great museums of the world have Abd el Hamed's reproductions."

"You sound as if you regret his death," Nefret exclaimed. "After the way he treated you!"

"It's a pity talent and moral worth don't go together," David said. A shiver passed through his tall frame and he turned abruptly away from the house. "Abd el Hamed was a sadistic swine, but he was also a genius. And it was through him that I met you. Come, let's go. I've had enough of nostalgia."

They had left the horses at the bottom of the slope. As they made their way down the path single file, Ramses fell behind. The rays of the setting sun did remarkable things to Nefret's hair.

Something dropped onto the path in front of him with a soft plop. Startled out of his dreamy state, he jumped back and then relaxed when he saw it was only a flower—a hibiscus blossom, velvety-petaled and bright orange red. He heard a soft laugh. The door of the house he was passing had opened. A woman stood there, leaning against the frame. He knew her at once for what she was; her face was unveiled and she wore only a vest and a pair of diaphanous trousers. Such clothing was worn in the privacy of the harem, but no respectable woman would have appeared in public without an enveloping robe.

Over one ear she had pinned a matching blossom; the vivid color set off her dark hair. It was difficult to judge her age. She had the body of a young woman but there were threads of silver in her hair and a certain tightness around her full lips.

Ramses stooped and picked up the flower. It seemed rude not to do so, though he suspected the gesture might have another significance. "Thank you, Sitt. May you be well."

"An offering," she said, in a low, intimate voice. "Did not the ancients offer flowers to the king?"

"Alas, Sitt, I am no king."

"But you bear a royal name. It is not for a humble servant like myself to use it; shall I call you 'my lord?' "

Her eyes were not brown or black but an unusual shade between green and hazel. She had framed them with powdered malachite.

Ramses was rather enjoying the banter—it was a different approach, at least—but Nefret and David had stopped to wait for him, and he was reasonably certain that Nefret would not wait long. He saluted the woman and started to turn away.

"You are very like your father."

She had spoken English. That, and the astonishing statement, roused his curiosity. "Not many people think so," he said.

She struck a match against the doorframe and lit the cigarette she had taken from somewhere in the folds of the voluminous trousers. Her eyes moved slowly from his face to his feet and then back, even more deliberately. "Your body is not so heavy as his, but it is strong and tall, and you move in the same way, light as a panther. Your eyes and skin are darker; in that you might almost be one of us, young lord! But the shape of your face, and your mouth . . ."

Ramses felt himself blushing—something he had not done for years. But then no woman had ever talked to him this way, or examined him as a buyer would examine a horse.

Or as some men examined women.

Sauce for the gander, as his mother would say. Wry amusement replaced embarrassment, and he cut off the catalog of his charms with a compliment on her English. Her vocabulary was certainly extensive.

"It is the new way for women" was the reply. "We go to school like obedient children, so that one day we will no longer be children but the rulers of men. Have you not heard of it, young lord? Your lady mother knows. Ask her whether women cannot be as dangerous as men when they—"

"Ramses!"

He started. Nefret's voice held a note that was unpleasantly reminiscent of his mother's. "I must go," he said.

Her closed-lipped smile reminded him of one of the statues in the museum—the painted limestone bust called "the White Queen." This woman's skin was not alabaster pale, but a soft deep brown, lustrous as satin. "You obey when she summons you? You are more like your father than I thought. My name is Layla, young lord. I will be here, waiting, if you come."

When he joined the others, he realized he was still holding the flower. Offering it to Nefret would probably not be a wise move. He did not toss it away until after they were out of the woman's sight.

Nefret waited until they had reached the bottom of the hill. She let him lift her into the saddle and then said coolly, "Wait a moment. Stand still. I want to look at you."

"Nefret—"

"I suppose you don't do it deliberately. Or do you?"

"Do what?" He knew why she had mounted before she started on him. Her pose and manner were those of a highborn lady addressing a groom, and it cost him something of an effort to throw his shoulders back and meet her eyes squarely.

Nefret nodded. "Yes. It's very interesting. The Professor has it too, in a different sort of way. David doesn't, though you and he look enough alike to be brothers."

David, already in the saddle, said lightly, "Is that an insult or a compliment, Nefret?"

"I'm not sure." She turned back to Ramses, who had taken advantage of her momentary distraction to mount Risha. He knew she wasn't going to let him off so easily, though.

"Who is she?"

"She said her name is Layla. That's all I know."

"Layla!" David exclaimed. "I thought she looked familiar. I haven't seen her for five years or more."

"You knew her, David?" Nefret asked in surprise.

"Not—not to say know. Not in that way."

"I don't suppose you could have afforded her," Nefret conceded.

David let out a sputter of laughter. "Really, Nefret, you ought not say such things."

"It's true, though, isn't it?"

"Oh, quite." They had left the village behind and were riding side by side at an easy walk. David went on, "Don't you remember her? She was the third wife of Abd el Hamed, my former employer. Hers was rather a remarkable career. They say she started out in the House of the Doves in Luxor—"

"The house of what?" Nefret exclaimed.

"One must assume the name is either euphemistic or ironic," Ramses murmured. "I wouldn't care to say which. Would you prefer to drop the subject? Mother would certainly disapprove of our discussing it."

"Go on," Nefret said grimly.

"You understand, I am only repeating what I overheard when I was living in Gurneh," David insisted. "The place is the best—uh—

place in Luxor, which isn't saying a great deal. The girls are reasonably well paid, and some of them marry after they—um—after a certain time. Layla was one of these. With her help, her husband began dealing in antiquities and stolen goods, and acquired a small fortune. Then he died—rather suddenly, it was said—which left Layla a wealthy widow. Later she married that old swine Abd el Hamed, I never understood why. She refused to live in his house, so perhaps you never met her."

"She had met Father," Ramses said thoughtfully. "She commented on the resemblance between us."

Nefret gave him an enigmatic look, but before she could comment, David said in a shocked voice, "Everyone in Egypt knows the Father of Curses, Ramses. He would never have had anything to do with a—with a woman like that."

"No," Nefret said. "No decent man would." She must have seen them exchange glances, for she went on in a voice shaking with indignation. "Oh, yes, I know some eminently respectable 'gentlemen' go to prostitutes. At least they call themselves gentlemen! Their *gentlemen's* laws forbid women to earn a decent living at a respectable profession, and when the poor creatures are forced into a life of disease and poverty and degradation the pious hypocrites visit them and then punish the *women* for immorality!"

Her eyes swam with tears. David reached out and patted her hand. "I know, Nefret. I'm sorry. Don't cry."

"You can't reform the world overnight, Nefret. Don't break your heart about things you can't help." Ramses knew his voice sounded hard and uncaring, but it tore him apart to see her cry when he couldn't comfort her as he ached to do. If he ever dared hold her close he would give himself away.

Anyhow, he thought, dragging a girl out of her saddle and dumping her onto his would probably be more painful than romantic.

She wiped her eyes with the back of her hand and gave him a watery but defiant smile. "I *can* help. And I will one day, just wait and see."

Seeing her chin jut out and her mouth set tightly, Ramses understood what his mother meant when she talked about forebodings and premonitions. He was in complete sympathy with Nefret's sentiments, but she had a dangerous habit of rushing in where angels feared to tread, and this particular cause could lead her into real trouble. Somehow, God only knew how, he would have to keep her away from the House of the Doves—and Layla. Two of Layla's husbands had died suddenly and violently. If he'd ever seen a woman who did not need help and sympathy, it was that one.

We were dining with Cyrus and Katherine one evening that same week when a casual remark of the latter reminded me of a promise I had not kept. Katherine had asked when we expected the younger Emersons and Lia, and Cyrus had offered to put them up at the Castle. He was a sociable individual and enjoyed company, but though his residence was far more commodious and elegant than our humble abode, I declined the invitation with proper expressions of appreciation.

"They are due to arrive in Alexandria on Monday next, but I don't know how long they will remain in Cairo before coming on."

"Not long, I expect," Katherine said. "They will be anxious to be with you. We hope to see a great deal of them. I believe you mentioned that little Miss Emerson is determined to go to university next autumn. If she wants to keep up her studies this winter, remember that I am a former governess and teacher."

"Good gracious," I exclaimed. "That reminds me—Fatima! We promised we would find a teacher for her. She is so timid she would not venture to ask again."

"She has more enterprise than you suppose, Aunt Amelia," Nefret replied. "She has already made her own arrangements. It seems there is a lady in Luxor who holds private classes."

The reference was of course lost on Katherine, who requested elucidation. She responded to my explanation with the sympathetic enthusiasm I had come to expect of her.

"To think of that humble little woman harboring such aspirations! She makes me feel thoroughly ashamed of myself. I ought to be conducting such classes myself."

"Why not start a school?" Cyrus suggested. "Find a suitable building and hire teachers."

"Do you mean it?" Her face lit up. Katherine had always reminded me of a pleasant tabby cat, with her gray-streaked hair and rounded cheeks and green eyes. One would never have called her beautiful, but when she looked at her husband as she was looking now, she appeared quite beautiful to my eyes—and, it was clear, to his. "Do you mean it, Cyrus? In addition to reading and writing, we could instruct the girls in household management and child care, train those who show ability in a particular area such as typewriting and—"

Cyrus burst out laughing. "And provide college scholarships for the lot! My dear, you may start a dozen schools if it will make you happy."

After dinner we retired to the drawing room, where we were affectionately greeted by the Vandergelts' cat, Sekhmet. She had belonged to us originally; we had brought her to Egypt in the hope that she would compensate Ramses for the loss of his longtime companion, the cat Bastet. He had not taken to Sekhmet, referring to her contemptuously as "the furry slug." It is true that Sekhmet was so fatuously and indiscriminately affectionate she did not care whose lap she occupied, but this very trait had endeared her to Cyrus. She now lived like a princess in "the Castle," fed on cream and filleted fish by the majordomo when the Vandergelts were in America, and never leaving the walled borders of the estate—for Cyrus would not allow her to mingle with common cats.

She settled down on David's knee, purring hysterically, and Nefret went to the pianoforte. Cyrus took me aside.

"Thank you, Amelia, my dear," he said warmly. "You have given Katherine a new interest. She was moping a bit before you arrived; missed the kiddies, you know."

"And so did you, I daresay."

Katherine's children by her first, unhappy marriage were at school in England. I had not met them, since they spent their holidays in America with their mother and stepfather; but Cyrus, who had always wanted a family of his own, had taken them to his generous heart. He sighed wistfully.

"Yes, my dear, I did. I wish you could persuade Katherine to let them come out with us next season. I've offered to hire tutors, teachers, anything she wants."

"I will talk to her, Cyrus. It strikes me as an excellent idea. There is no climate so salubrious as that of Luxor in winter, and the experience would be extremely educational."

He took my hand and pressed it warmly. "You are the best friend in the world, Amelia. We could not get on without you. You will—you will take care of yourself, won't you?"

"I always do," I said, laughing. "And so does my dear Emerson. What makes you say that, Cyrus?"

"Well, I just sort of figured you were up to something, since you always are. The quieter things look, the more I expect an explosion. You wouldn't refuse me the chance to help, would you?"

"Dear Cyrus, you are the truest of friends. At the moment, however, I am not up to anything. I only wish—"

But at that moment Emerson called my name, ostensibly to request that we come join in the singing. Emerson had quite got over his jealousy of Cyrus, but he does not appreciate having other men hold my hand quite so long or quite so warmly.

I am extremely fond of music, but it was the genial company rather than the quality of the performances that made our little impromptu concerts so enjoyable. Emerson cannot carry a tune at all, but he sings very loud and with great feeling. His rendering of "The Last Chord" was one of his best. (A good deal of the melody is on the same note, which was all to the good.) We did a few of the jollier choruses of Gilbert and Sullivan, and Nefret badgered Ramses into joining her in a song from the new Victor Herbert operetta. Cyrus always brought the latest American music out with him, and none of us had heard this one.

"It's a duet," Nefret pointed out. "I can't sing two parts simultaneously, and you're the only other one who can sight-read."

Ramses had been reading the words over her shoulder. "The lyrics are even more banal and sentimental than usual," he grumbled. "I won't be able to keep a straight face."

Nefret chuckled. "What's wrong with golden hair and eyes of blue? It's hard to find words that rhyme with 'brown.' You come in on the chorus: 'Not that you are fair, dear...'"

I must confess they sounded very well together, even though Ramses could not resist breaking into a tremulous falsetto on the last high note.

After the impromptu concert had concluded with Cyrus's rendition of his favorite "Kathleen Mavourneen"—making calf's eyes at his wife the whole time, as Emerson inelegantly expressed it—we went out to the courtyard to wait for the carriage. The night was beautifully cool and the stars blazed as bright as Mrs. Stephenson's diamonds. Katherine, all afire with her new scheme, suggested we go to Luxor next day to call on Fatima's teacher.

"Impossible," said Emerson.

"Why?" I demanded. "You can certainly spare me for a few hours. That nasty number Fifty-three—"

"We are not going to work at Fifty-three. I have a little surprise for you, Peabody. Great news! Tomorrow we start on tomb Five!"

"How exciting," I said hollowly. There could be nothing of interest in that rubble-filled tomb, and the labor involved would be monstrous.

"How'd you manage that?" Cyrus asked. There was a note of envy in his voice. He missed the Valley where he had excavated for so many years without success, but with great enjoyment.

"Tact," said my husband smugly. "I simply pointed out to Weigall that nobody else would ever bother with the confounded place, especially Davis, who is such an egotistical ignoramus—"

"You didn't say that!" I exclaimed, as a ripple of laughter ran through the group.

"What difference does it make what I said? Weigall has agreed, and he is the man in charge."

"It was very kind of him to overlook your knocking him down the other day."

"I did it for his own good," said Emerson hypocritically. "Never mind that. We are going to need more men than we have been using with the smaller tombs. I will need Nefret and David as well, for I mean to take quantities of photographs."

Emerson sent us all off to bed after we got home, since he meant to make an early start next day. After I had brushed and braided my hair I put on my dressing gown and slipped out of the room, leaving him bent over his notes.

Nefret responded at once to my soft tap on the door. She was alone except for the cat, who occupied the precise center of her bed. "Is something wrong, Aunt Amelia?" she asked.

"Nothing. I am only a little curious. Was it you who persuaded Mr. Weigall to give in to Emerson's request? I do hope, my dear, that you did not resort to underhanded means. Mr. Weigall is a married man, and—"

"Quite devoted to his Hortense," said Nefret, trying not to smile. "I never flirt with married men, Aunt Amelia. I am shocked that you should suggest such a thing."

"Ah," I said. "Mr. Davis is not a married man, is he? And Mr. Weigall does whatever Mr. Davis tells him to do. I noticed the other evening—"

Nefret burst out laughing. "So did Ramses. He accused me of flirting with Mr. Davis. Mr. Davis is quite harmless, Aunt Amelia, but like many older men he is particularly susceptible to flattery and compliments. I did it for the Professor."

"Hmmm. Do you have an idea as to why he is so set on working in that part of the Valley?"

"An idea did occur to me. It must have occurred to you as well."

"Yes." I sighed. "We must hope Mr. Ayrton does not come across any interesting tombs this season."

I refer the Reader to my plan of the Valley and invite him to note the relative areas of tomb Five and the area in which Mr. Ayrton was working. If there were unknown tombs in the Valley of the Kings, such areas were precisely where one might expect to find them. And if Ned did find such a tomb, Emerson would be there, watching every move he made and criticizing everything he did.

I expected trouble and I was (of course) right. But not even *I* could have anticipated the magnitude of the disaster that actually occurred.

BOOK TWO

THE GATES OF THE
UNDERWORLD

O great apes who sit before
the doors of heaven:
take the evil from me, obliterate my sins,
guard me, so that I may pass between
the Pylons of the West.

7

The approach to the Valley had changed a great deal since our first days in Egypt. A rough but serviceable road led through the forbidding cliffs and a wooden barrier now barred the entrance to those who lacked the requisite tickets. Our horses were among the first occupants of the donkey park, for the sun had not yet risen over the eastern hills when our caravan left the house. We had taken this longer but less arduous route, instead of the footpath that led over the hill from Deir el Bahri, because tomb Five lay near the entrance, just outside the barrier.

Ramses and David were not with us. I had, quite by accident, happened to overhear part of a conversation between them that morning. They were in Ramses's room; the door was slightly ajar and both their voices were rather loud, so inadvertent eavesdropping was unavoidable.

The first words I heard were David's. "I am going with you."

"You can't. Father has asked—excuse me, demanded—your help today."

"He will change his mind if we ask him. You promised you would not—"

Ramses cut him off. "Don't be an old granny. Do you think I can't take care of myself?"

I had never heard him speak so brusquely to David, or sound

151

so angry. Intervention was obviously in order. I tapped lightly at the door before pushing it open.

They were both on their feet, facing one another in attitudes that could only be described as potentially combative. David's fists were clenched. Ramses appeared unmoved, but there was a set to his shoulders I did not like.

"Now, boys, what is this?" I asked. "Are you quarreling?"

Ramses turned away and reached for his knapsack. "Good morning, Mother. A slight difference of opinion, that is all. I will see you this afternoon."

He slipped neatly out of the room before I could inquire further, so I turned to David, who was not as quick or as rude as my son. When I questioned him, as I felt obliged to do, he insisted that he and Ramses had not been quarreling, and that nothing had happened to give him cause for concern.

Except for Ramses's ungovernable habit of getting himself in trouble, I thought. A stentorian shout from Emerson summoned us to our duty, so I allowed David to depart and followed him into the sitting room in time to overhear another loud exchange. This time it was between Ramses and Nefret, and I must admit that she was doing all the shouting. She broke off when I entered, and I said in exasperation, "What is wrong with you three? It must be Ramses who is responsible for all the arguing, since—"

"We were not arguing, Aunt Amelia." Nefret's face had turned a charming shade of rosy brown. "I was just reminding Ramses of a certain promise he made me."

Ramses nodded. He was wearing what Nefret calls his stone pharaoh face, but his high cheekbones were a trifle darker than usual—with pure temper, I supposed. "If you are coming with me, David, let us go."

He strode out without waiting for a reply. David and Nefret exchanged one of those meaningful glances, and David hurried out. I decided not to pursue the subject. Even the best of friends have little differences of opinion from time to time, and I would have enough on my mind trying to keep Emerson from harassing poor Ned Ayrton—for I felt certain that was what he intended to do.

The young man arrived with his crew shortly after us. He had to pass us in order to reach the area where he had begun work the day before, on the west face of the cliff along the tourist path. As I had expected—and hoped—Davis was not with him. The American was not interested in the tedious labor of clearance; he only turned up when his "tame archaeologist" sent to tell him something interesting had been found.

Ned's innocent countenance brightened with surprise and pleasure when he saw Emerson, who had been lying in wait for him.

"Why, Professor—and Mrs. Emerson, good morning to you, ma'am—I thought you were working at the other end of the Valley. Tomb Five, is it?"

"As you see." Emerson moved out of the way of a man carrying a basket of rock chippings. "Weigall *kindly* gave me permission to investigate it."

"I don't envy you the job, sir. The fill is packed as hard as cement."

"As it was in the tomb of Siptah," said Emerson, "which you never finished clearing. Left the job half-done. Well, young man, let me tell you—"

"Emerson!" I exclaimed.

Ned flushed painfully, and Nefret turned from the camera she was inspecting. "Don't scold Mr. Ayrton, Professor, you know the decision was not his. How are you getting on, Mr. Ayrton? Any sign of a tomb?"

The young man gave her a grateful look. "Not yet, Miss Forth, but we have only been at it for two days. There is quite a large accumulation of limestone chips along the face of the cliff, probably from another tomb—"

"Ramses VI," said Emerson.

"Er—yes, sir. Well, I must be off."

The area in which he was working was only a few hundred feet south of us, on the same side of the path, but a shallow spur of rock cut off our view. As the sun rose higher and the first influx of tourists streamed through the barrier, their foolish laughter and babble drowned out the voices of Ned's crew, to the visible annoyance of Emerson, whose ears were practically standing out from his head. (I speak figuratively; Emerson has particularly handsome ears, somewhat large but well-shaped and lying flat against his skull.) He knew, as did I, that a new discovery might be heralded by cries of excitement from the workmen.

There was really nothing for me to do, since several tons of rock

had to be removed before the entrance could be fully exposed. Howard had told us he had done some clearing in '02, but all evidence
of his work had been filled in since by rockfalls and debris. I had
leisure therefore to indulge in my favorite occupation of watching
my husband. Booted feet wide apart, bare black head shining in the
sunlight like a raven's wing, he directed the work with cries of encouragement or advice. My attention being on him, I observed him
sidle away and called to ask where he was going.

"I thought I would ask Ayrton to join us for our mid-morning
tea," said Emerson.

"What a kind thought," I said.

There may have been just the slightest edge of sarcasm in my
voice. Emerson shot me a reproachful look and went on his way. I
decided I had better go after him. Not that I was at all curious about
what Ned was doing, but I knew Emerson would not proffer the
invitation until after he had inspected the excavation and lectured
at length on methodology.

The task the young fellow had undertaken was indeed formidable. The Valley, as I have explained, but will repeat for the benefit
of Readers unfamiliar with it, is not a single flat-floored canyon but
a complex of smaller wadis running off at all angles from the main
path. The paths wind round outcroppings of stone, some natural,
some formed by the stone removed from nearby tombs. One such
rocky mound formed the western face of the central path, and
against it lay a pile almost fifty feet high of limestone chips. It is
under such piles of man-made debris that excavators hope to find
forgotten tomb entrances.

The sun, now near the zenith, reflected off the pale rock in a
blinding dazzle, unrelieved by vegetation or shadow. The fine dust
stirred up by tourist boots resembled pale fog. As I approached the
site, the cloud rose into a towering cumulous cloud. Ned's men were
hard at work piling the loose rock into baskets and carrying them
away to a dump site nearby.

He had dug a trench straight down the rock face, obviously without result, since he was now in the process of extending it. As I had
anticipated, Emerson was giving the young man the benefit of his
advice. I put an end to that, and removed both of them. The sweating
workers were glad to stop for a while.

I make it a habit to set up a little shelter near our place of work with a rug on the ground and a small folding table, for I see nothing wrong with comfort if it does not interfere with efficiency. On this occasion I had taken advantage of a nearby tomb entrance, that of Ramses II. Choked with rubble and dismissed by Baedeker, it was not approached by tourists, so we could count on a modicum of privacy while we rested and refreshed ourselves.

Ned was visibly disappointed to find that Ramses was not with us, but he appeared to enjoy the brief interlude. Emerson behaved himself very well, but when Ned rose to leave, my spouse could not resist a final shot.

"If you find a tomb, Ayrton, do me the favor of clearing the cursed place out completely. I am tired of tidying up after you and the others."

There is a saying: "Take care what you wish, for it may be given unto you." Emerson got his wish, and he did not like it at all. In later years he was to refer to the business as "one of the greatest disasters in Egyptological history."

It began that same afternoon, when Ned's perspiring workers came upon a niche containing several large storage jars. The discovery was not in itself exciting enough to warrant a shout of triumph from the men who found it; we did not learn of it until Ned came by with his crew on their way home.

"Stopping already?" asked Emerson, advancing to meet them.

"Yes, sir." Ned removed his hat and pushed the damp hair back from his brow. "It is very warm, and I have—"

"Any luck?"

So the news was told. "They are nothing to be excited about," Ned added. "Plain storage jars—Twentieth Dynasty, I believe. Well, then, I look forward to seeing you all tomorrow."

Emerson did not even have the decency to wait until he was out of sight. I followed my irritating husband around the rock spur and found him climbing up the rubble. The opening was a good thirty feet above bedrock and when I would have followed he waved me back.

Upon returning he remarked, "Eighteenth Dynasty."

"Why are you making such a fuss about it?" I demanded. "One is always coming across isolated finds of that sort. Rough storage jars cannot contain anything of interest."

"Hmph," said Emerson. He turned and looked up the slope.

"Now, Emerson, leave them alone! They are not *your* jars. I suggest we follow Ned's example and stop work. It is very warm, and I don't want Abdullah having another attack."

Emerson swore a great deal, but he has the kindest heart in the world and I knew the appeal would have its effect. It was late in the afternoon before we reached the house. The vine-shaded verandah looked very pleasant after our long hot ride. Horus, stretched out on the settee, examined us with a critical eye and began washing himself.

It seemed an excellent idea. I had a luxurious soak in my nice tin bath and changed into comfortable garments. When I returned to the verandah Fatima had brought tea. Nefret was pacing up and down, looking out.

"They are late," she said.

"Who? Oh, Ramses and David. Not really. Ramses has no notion of time, he will go on working until it gets too dark for him to see anything. Come and have your tea."

She obeyed, but even the bulk of Horus, who promptly spread himself across her lap, did not prevent her from fidgeting. I remembered the exchanges I had heard between the three that morning, and an unpleasant suspicion began to form in my mind. Since I do not allow such things to fester, I brought it out into the open.

"Nefret, are you concealing something from me? You are uncommonly edgy this evening; were the boys planning some expedition that is likely to lead them into danger?"

Emerson banged his cup into the saucer. "Curse it!" he exclaimed, but did not elaborate since Nefret spoke first.

"So far as I know, they are working at the Seti temple just as they said they would."

"Oh." Emerson's rigid form relaxed. "I do wish, Peabody, you would stop looking for trouble. No one has bothered us since that wretched man's body was found. He was the instigator of the other attacks; now that he has been—er—removed, we have nothing to fear."

I settled back to enjoy myself, for our little detectival discussions are always stimulating. "You are of the opinion that there is no connection between those attacks and the one against me in London?"

"That was Sethos," Emerson said. "He is still in England. I made the rounds of the cafés and coffee shops, as did Ramses. We found no indication that he has returned to his old haunts."

"Sethos may not have been responsible for the original encounter, Emerson. I have other enemies."

"You needn't brag about it, Peabody." Emerson reached for his broken cup, cut his finger, swore, and went to the table. Splashing soda into a glass, he said over his shoulder, "And don't try to exonerate that bas—— that man. We know it was he. The typewriter, Peabody. Remember the typewriter."

"I don't believe for a moment in Ramses's egotistical deductions," I replied, taking the glass Emerson handed me and nodding my thanks. "It is impossible to tell one machine from another, and furthermore, the incident in Fleet Street lacked Sethos's characteristic touch. He is not so crude or so . . . My dear Nefret, what are you staring at? Close your mouth, my dear, before an insect flies in!"

"I—uh—I had just remembered something, Aunt Amelia. A—a letter I promised to write."

"I hope Sir Edward is not your correspondent, Nefret. I do not approve. He is too old for you, and you have seen entirely too much of him lately."

"Only half a dozen times since Christmas Day," Nefret protested. "And once was at the party, with a hundred people present."

Emerson got to his feet. "If you are going to gossip I will leave you to it. Call me when dinner is ready."

The eastern cliffs shone in the last rays of the setting sun. There is no color anywhere on earth like that one, nor can words describe it—pale pinky gold with a wash of lavender, glowing as if lit from within. The lovely dying light lay gently on Nefret's sun-kissed cheeks, but her eyes avoided mine and she cleared her throat nervously before she spoke.

"May I ask you something, Aunt Amelia?"

"Why, certainly, my dear. Is it about Sir Edward? I am glad you want to consult me. I have had a good deal more experience in these matters than you."

"It is not about Sir Edward. Not exactly. Speaking of experience in such matters—er—you seem to believe he—Sethos—is sufficiently—uh—attached to you that he would not . . . Oh dear. I didn't mean to offend you, Aunt Amelia."

"You have not offended me, my dear, but if I understand what you are driving at, and I believe I do, the subject is not one I care to discuss."

"It is not idle curiosity that prompts me to introduce it."

"No?"

Nefret's slender throat contracted as she swallowed.

"Enough of that," I said in a kindly manner. "Goodness, how dark it has become, and the boys not back. I wonder if they decided to spend the night on the dahabeeyah."

"They would have told me if they had," Nefret said. "Damnation! I knew I ought to have gone with them!"

From Manuscript H

The mummy wrappings fitted close around his body, muffling his mouth, blinding his eyes, binding his arms and legs. They had buried him alive, like the miserable man whose mummy his parents had discovered at Drah Abu'l Naga. Someday another archaeologist would find him, his body brown and shriveled, his mouth open in a silent scream of terror, and . . .

He came awake in a desperate spasm that tore at every muscle in his body. It was still dark and he was as incapable of movement as any mummy, but the cloth covered only his mouth. He could breathe. Concentrating on that essential activity, he forced himself to lie still while he drew air in through his nostrils and tried to remember what had happened.

They had been copying the reliefs in one of the side chambers off the hypostyle hall and were about to stop for the day when they heard the thin, high wailing. It was impossible to tell whether it came from a human or another kind of animal, but the creature was obviously young and obviously in distress. Scrambling over fallen blocks and along shadowy aisles, they followed the pitiful, intermittent cries back into the sanctuary, where shadows lay like pools of dark water . . . Then nothing. His head ached, but so did every other part of his body. How long had he been unconscious? It must be night now; if the sun were still shining he ought to see streaks of light from windows or door, even if they were shuttered.

With considerable effort he rolled over onto his side. No wonder he had dreamed of mummy wrappings; they had been extravagant with the rope. His hands were tied behind him and his arms were bound to his sides; the other end of the rope round his ankles must be fastened to some object he couldn't see, since he was unable to move his legs more than a few inches in any direction. Flattering, in a way, he supposed. His father's reputation must have rubbed off onto him. Not even the mighty Father of Curses could burst these bonds. There was nothing for it but to wait until someone came. He didn't doubt that someone would eventually. They hadn't gone to all this trouble in order to leave him to die of hunger and exhaustion.

But the idea brought him dangerously close to panicking, and he forced himself to lie still and breathe steadily. The gag rasped his lips. There was no saliva left on it or in his mouth, which felt as if it were filled with sand.

The air was close and hot and the smell . . . Every culture has its own distinctive collections of odors, varying with social class and personal idiosyncrasies, but easily distinguished by someone who has made a study of them. Cooking odors were particularly distinctive. Even with his eyes closed he could tell whether he was in an English manor house or a cottage kitchen, an Egyptian coffeehouse or a German bierstube. This room wasn't a kitchen, but it was a room, not a cave or a storage shed. It held the indefinable but unmistakable smell of Egypt, but at one time it had been occupied by someone with European taste—expensive taste, at that. He couldn't name the perfume, but he had encountered it before.

The surface on which he lay was softer than a floor, even one covered by a rug or matting. It gave slightly when he moved and made a faint rustling sound. A bed, then, or at least some kind of mattress.

He lay quiet and held his breath, listening. There were other sounds, some faint and far off and undistinguishable, some small and near at hand. A mouse, reassured by his stillness, ventured out on little clawed feet and began to gnaw on something. Insects whined and buzzed. The sound he had half-hoped, half-feared to hear, that of another pair of straining human lungs, was not audible. Had they carried David off too, or had they left him dead or wounded on the floor of the temple?

Since there was nothing else he could do, he willed himself to sleep. He hadn't supposed the meditation techniques taught him by the old fakir in Cairo would work under these conditions; but his eyelids were drooping when a new sound brought him to full wakefulness. There was a line of light in front of him, lower down, at what must be floor level. It widened into a rectangle.

She slipped quickly into the room and closed the door. The lamp she carried was dim and flickering, just a strip of rag floating in oil, but after the darkness it half blinded him. She put the lamp on a table and sat down on the bed next to him. She wore red roses in her hair this time, and silver shone at her wrists.

"I brought you water," she said softly. "But you must give me your word you will not call out if I remove the gag. You would not be heard outside these walls, but I would be punished if they knew I had come here."

She waited for his nod before she slit the cloth with a knife she took from her sash. The relief was enormous, but his throat was so dry he could not speak until after she had raised his head and dribbled water from a clay cup between his lips.

"Thank you," he gasped.

"Always the proper English manners!" Her full mouth curved in a sardonic smile. She held the cup to his lips again and then lowered his head onto the mattress.

"You can't replace the gag now that you've cut it," he said softly. "Will they blame you? I don't want—"

Her ringed hand left a smarting path across his face. He shook his head dizzily.

"Sorry. Was I talking too . . ."

"Don't do that!" She bent over him and imprisoned his face between her hands. It was not a caress; her fingertips dug into his aching temples. "Don't care about me. Why were you fool enough to let them catch you? I tried to warn you."

"You did?"

She let go of his head and raised her hand. He braced himself for another slap. Instead she ran the tip of one finger slowly across his lips. "Do you know what brought me here?" she asked.

Several possibilities occurred to him, but it would not have been politic to mention any of them. He said, choosing his words with care, "The tenderness of your heart, lady."

She let out a little sound that might have been a muffled laugh. "That reason will serve as well as another."

She reached for the knife and freed him in a series of quick slashes. With equal deftness she unlaced his boots and drew them off. Numb with long confinement—and sheer astonishment—he let her rub his hands and feet until they began to tingle with returning circulation.

"Wait in the doorway," she said. "When you hear me call out 'Beloved,' count to ten, then go straight down the stairs. There are two men; you will have to deal with one of them. I think you will have no difficulty. After you have done so, go straight out the door. Do not stop, do not turn back."

"My friend," Ramses said. "Is he here?"

She hesitated for a moment and then nodded. "Don't waste time searching for him, it would be too dangerous. Go and bring help."

"But you—"

"I will be gone when you come back. Inshallah." She added, with a faint smile, "You owe me a debt, young lord. When I call on you to make it good, will you come?"

"Yes."

Her mouth found his. He met it with an appreciation that was not entirely due to gratitude, but when his arm went round her shoulders she twisted away and stood up.

"Another time," she said. "Inshallah. Come now."

She blew out the lamp and eased the door open. Silent on stockinged feet, he followed. By the time he reached the door she had gone ahead, along a corridor lit only by a glow from below. The house was of good size; there were three other closed doors and a lower floor. He waited until she had started down the stairs before he tried the other doors. None were locked. None of the rooms were occupied. A narrow flight of stairs, hardly more than a ladder, led to an opening through which he saw the glow of starlight. No need to look there, the ladder must go to the open roof.

The signal came sooner than he had expected. Abandoning caution, he ran for the stairs. He had known what she meant to do. All part of the day's work for her, perhaps, but he couldn't let her do it—not for him.

They were in the room opposite the foot of the stairs. The second man had his ear pressed to the flimsy panel of the door—waiting his turn, as he erroneously believed. He was too absorbed to hear the rush of unshod feet until it was too late. Straightening, he reached for the knife at his belt and opened his mouth to shout a warning. Ramses closed it for him and he fell back against the door, bursting it open. Ramses elbowed the inert body out of his way and went in.

He hadn't realized how angry he was until after the other man lay sprawled on the floor at his feet. Rubbing his bruised hands, he watched Layla rearrange her clothing and sit up.

"Fool," she snapped. "Why don't you go?"

"You first. They'll know it was you who freed me."

She swore at him. He laughed aloud, giddy with the dangerous euphoria that follows a winning fight, and as she darted toward the door he swung her into his arms and kissed her.

"Fool," she whispered against his lips. "You must hurry! They are coming soon, to move you to another place. If you knew what they plan for you, you would not linger."

"Where is he?"

"I will show you, but don't think I will stay to help you. The fate meted out to traitors is one I would not face."

The man near the door was stirring. There wasn't time to tie him up. Ramses turned him over and hit him again.

Layla had gone up the stairs. She was back immediately, wearing a dark cloak and carrying a loosely tied bundle. She must have got her things together in anticipation of flight before she freed him. A woman of many talents, Ramses thought.

Gesturing him to follow, she ran toward the back of the house and unbolted a door that led into a walled courtyard.

"He is there," she said, indicating a shed against the far wall. "Ma'as salama, my lord. Do not cheat me of my payment."

Moonlight framed her for a moment and then she was gone, leaving the gate through which she had fled ajar. Ramses headed for the shed, trying to avoid the squashier debris that litters Egyptian courtyards. Pebbles pressed into the soles of his feet. The euphoria was passing and he was beginning to wonder if he had made the right decision. He had been lucky so far, but the long hours of confinement had taken their toll, and that last blow had been a mistake. He'd been too drunk with imbecile heroism to feel it at the time, but his right hand ached like a sore tooth, and he couldn't bend the fingers. If the door of the shed was locked he would have to go for help before the guards woke up and came looking for him.

The door had not been locked or barred. As soon as it opened he knew why.

They hadn't handled David as considerately as they had him. They must have tossed him in and left him to lie as he fell, because his head was bent at an awkward angle and his legs were twisted. Not even a pile of moldy straw lay between his body and the hard earthen floor, which was littered with ancient animal droppings. They hadn't stinted on the rope, though, and the dirty gag covered his nose as well as his mouth.

There was a lamp. The guard would have insisted on that.

He had been sitting on the floor with his back against the wall, and he must have been dozing, for he was slow to react. When he rose, Ramses's stomach twisted. The fellow was as tall as he and twice as broad. His belly rounded the front of his galabeeyah, but not all the weight was fat. And he had a knife.

For a moment they stared at one another in mutual stupefaction. The guard was the first to recover. It wasn't difficult for Ramses to read his mind; his round sweaty face mirrored every slow-moving idea. No need to call for help against an opponent as wretched-looking as this one. Recapturing the prisoner single-handed would win him praise and reward. He drew his knife from its scabbard and started forward.

Ramses wasn't thinking fast either, but the options were too obvious to be overlooked. One backward step would take him out the door. There was a bar. By the time the guard broke down the door or summoned help, he would be long gone. It was the only sensible course of action. Unarmed and exhausted, he wouldn't last ten seconds against a hulking brute like that one. No one would know he had run away. David was unconscious. Or dead.

He launched himself forward and down, at an acute angle that would—he hoped—take him under the blade of the knife. The move caught even him by surprise; his chest hit the floor with a force that knocked the breath out of him, but his hands were already where he wanted them to be, gripping the bare ankles under the ragged hem of the galabeeyah. He yanked, with all the strength he could muster.

It wasn't much. His right hand gave way, but the left was still functioning, and it was enough to pull the man's feet out from under him and get his attention off the knife. He sat down with a thud that must have rumbled up his spine into his skull, and his head hit the wall. The blow only stunned him but it gave Ramses time to finish the job. Then he picked up the knife and crawled through the dung and dust to David.

He was alive. As soon as his mouth and nose were uncovered he sucked in a long shuddering breath. Ramses heaved him over and began slashing at the ropes. He had freed David's hands and arms before he realized that not all the dark stains on David's shirt were dirt. He breathed out a word even his father seldom employed.

"Ramses?"

"Who else? How badly are you hurt? Can you walk?"

"I'll give it my best try as soon as you free my ankles."

"Oh. Right."

After he had done so Ramses stuck the knife in his belt and bent over David. "Put your arm over my shoulders. We're on borrowed time as it is; if you can't walk I'll carry you."

"I can stumble at least. Help me up."

At first he couldn't even stumble. Ramses had to drag him out the door and across the courtyard to the gate Layla had left open. They weighed about the same, but Ramses could have sworn David had gained ten stone in the past few hours. His lungs were bursting and his knees felt like molasses. He couldn't keep this up much longer.

Then he heard a shout from the house and discovered he could. The rush of adrenaline carried them through the gate and into a patch of shadow. Can't stop now, he thought. Not yet. They were still on borrowed time, time borrowed from Layla. He prayed she had got away. He prayed they would too. Abdullah's house was on the other side of the hill and their captors would expect them to head in that direction, and they would . . . They would . . .

Something strange was happening. The patches of moonlight on the ground shivered like water into which someone has tossed a stone. The trees were swaying as if in a strong wind, but there was no wind. He couldn't catch his breath. He fell to his knees, dragging David down with him.

"Go on. Abdullah—"

"Not there, you fool. Too far."

Hands pulled at him. Layla's? She had called him a fool. He was on his feet, moving, floating, through patches of silver and black, moonlight and shadow, until a burst of sunshine blinded him, and he passed through the light into utter darkness.

I would rather not remember those hours of waiting, but some account of them must be given if my narrative is to be complete. Nefret's distress was harder to bear than my own, for mine was mitigated by familiarity with my son's annoying habits. This would not be the first time he had gone off on some ill-considered and dangerous expedition without bothering to inform me. Delay did not necessarily imply disaster; he and David were full-grown men (physically if not emotionally) and quite adept at various forms of self-defense, including the ancient Egyptian wrestling holds I had shown them.

So I told myself, at any rate, and attempted to convince Nefret of my reasoning. She was not convinced. They were in trouble, she knew it, and it was her fault for not going with them, and something must be done about it.

"But what?" I demanded, watching her anxiously as she paced up and down. She had not changed from her working clothes, and her boots thudded heavily on the tiled floor. Horus had lost all patience with her because she refused to sit down and provide a lap for him; when she passed him he reached out and hooked his claws into her trouser leg. She detached him without comment and went on pacing.

"There is no sense searching for them," I insisted. "Where would we start?"

Emerson knocked out his pipe. "At the temple. Never mind dinner, none of us has the appetite for it. If I find no sign of them there, I will come straight back, I promise."

"Not alone," I said. "I am coming with you."

"No, you are not."

We were discussing the matter, without the coolness that verb implies, when Emerson raised his hand for silence. In that silence we all heard it—the pound of galloping hooves.

"There," said Emerson, his broad breast rising in a great sigh of relief. "There they are. I will have a few words to say to those young men for frightening you so! That is Risha, or I know nothing of horseflesh."

It was Risha, running like the wind. He came to a sudden stop and stood trembling. His saddle was empty, and a broken end of rope hung from his neck.

My dear Emerson took charge as only he can. In less than ten minutes we were mounted and ready. Nefret wanted to ride Risha, but Emerson prevented her, knowing she would outstrip us. The noble beast would not stay, however. Intelligent and loyal as a dog, he guided us back along the path he had taken in such haste. It led, as we had expected, to the temple of Seti I.

We found Asfur, Risha's mate, still tied to a tree near the spring north of the temple. In one of the chambers off the hypostyle hall a thin cat sprang hissing into the shadows when the light of our candles appeared. It had been devouring the remains of the food the boys had brought. On the floor were their knapsacks, two empty water bottles, and their coats. Their drawing materials had already been packed, so they must have been about to leave when they were intercepted. There was no sign of them elsewhere in the temple or its surroundings. Lanterns and candles were not bright enough to permit a search for footprints or bloodstains.

There was nothing we could do but return to the house. Emerson was the one who paced now; Nefret sat quite still, her hands folded and her eyes lowered. Finally Emerson said, "They did not leave the temple of their own accord. They would not have abandoned the horses."

"Obviously," I said. "I am going to Gurneh to fetch—no, not Abdullah, worry and exertion would be bad for him—Selim, and Daoud and—"

"Peabody, you are not going anywhere. And neither are you, Nefret; stay here and try to keep your Aunt Amelia under control. It is a damned difficult job, take my word for it. I will go to the dahabeeyah. It's a far-out chance, but someone may have seen something of them. I will bring Reis Hassan and another of the crewmen back with me, and then we will think what to do next."

Another grisly hour dragged by. Emerson did not return. It was Reis Hassan who came instead, with a message from my husband. Someone had claimed to have seen the boys walking toward the ferry landing. If they had gone over to Luxor he would follow the trail. Mahmud was with him, and Reis Hassan would stay with us.

Nefret did not react or even look up. For the past hour she had not moved. All at once she started to her feet; Horus, who had been on her lap, rolled off it and bounced onto the floor. Over his yowls of fury, I heard her say, "Listen. Someone is coming."

The individual was on horseback, coming at a gallop, and I assumed it was Emerson. Even at a distance, however, I knew the slighter form could not be his.

"Selim," said Nefret calmly.

There could be no doubt. Selim was an excellent horseman and he was waving his arms in a wild manner that would have unseated any rider less skilled. He was shouting too, but it was impossible to make out the words until he stopped.

"Safe!" was the first word I heard. "They are safe, Sitt, safe with me, and you must come, come at once, and bring your medicines, they are sick and bleeding and I have left Daoud and Yussuf on guard, and they are safe, and they sent me to tell you!"

"Very good," said Nefret, when the enthusiastic youth had run out of breath. "I will go with you, Selim. Ask Ali the stableman to saddle Risha."

She put her arm round my waist. "It's all right, Aunt Amelia. Here, take my handkerchief."

"I do not require it, my dear," I said with a sniff. "I believe I may have a slight touch of catarrh."

"Then you should not go out in the night air. No, Aunt Amelia, I insist you stay here and wait for the Professor. You might send someone to ask Mr. Vandergelt for the loan of his carriage, in case they are . . ."

She did not give me time to suggest alternatives, but dashed into the house and came back with her bag of medical supplies. It was, I supposed, the most sensible arrangement. I had no fear for her; Selim would be with her, and nothing less than a bullet could stop Risha when he was in full gallop.

As I had expected, Cyrus and Katherine accompanied the carriage, full of questions, and demanding to be allowed to help. I was explaining when Emerson returned.

"So you're at it again," Cyrus remarked. "I thought things had been abnormally quiet this season. Emerson, old pal, you okay?"

Emerson passed his hand over his face. "I am getting too old for this sort of thing, Vandergelt."

"Not you," said Cyrus with conviction.

"Certainly not," I exclaimed. "Katherine dear, you and Cyrus must stay here. There won't be room for all of us in the carriage."

"I will make tea," Katherine said, pressing my hand. "What else can I do for you, Amelia?"

"Have the whiskey ready," said Cyrus.

From Manuscript H

When Ramses opened his eyes he knew he wasn't dead or delirious, though the face that filled his vision was the one he would have preferred to see under either of those conditions.

"I think I'm supposed to babble about angels and heaven," he said faintly.

"I might have known you'd try to be clever," Nefret snapped. "What's wrong with 'Where am I?' "

"Trite. Anyhow, I know where I—hell and damnation! What are you . . ."

The pain was so intense he almost blacked out again. Off in the distance he heard Nefret ask, "Do you want some morphine?"

"No. Where is David?"

"Here, my brother. Safe, thanks to—"

"None of that," Nefret ordered. "You two can wallow in sentiment later. We have a lot to discuss and I haven't finished with Ramses yet."

"I don't think I can stand any more of your tender care," Ramses said. The worst of the pain had subsided, though, and the hands that wiped the perspiration from his face were sure and gentle. "What the hell did you do to me?"

"What the hell did you do to that hand? It's swelling up like a balloon, and one of your fingers was dislocated."

"Just . . . leave me alone for a minute. Please?"

His eyes moved slowly around the room, savoring the sense of safety and the reassurance of familiar faces: David, his dark eyes luminous with tears of relief; Nefret, white-faced and tight-lipped; and Selim, squatting by the bed, his teeth bared in a broad grin. If he hadn't been such a fool he would have remembered Abdullah had relatives all over Gurneh. Selim's house was one of the closest. His youngest wife made the best lamb stew in Luxor.

His eyes went back to David. "You got me here. God knows how. How bad is it?"

"To put it in technical terms, the knife bounced off his shoulder blade," Nefret said. "A bit of sticking plaster was all that was required. Now let's get back to you. I want to make sure nothing else is broken before we move you."

"I'm all right." He started to sit up and let out a yelp of pain when she planted her hand firmly against his chest and shoved him back onto the pillow.

"Ah," she said, with professional relish. "A rib? Let's just have a look."

"Your bedside manner could use some improvement," Ramses said, trying not to squirm as she unbuttoned his shirt.

There was no warning, not even a knock. The door flew open, and he forgot his present aches and pains in anticipation of what lay in store. The figure that stood in the door was not that of an enemy. It was worse. It was his mother.

I have always believed in the medicinal effects of good whiskey, but on this occasion I felt obliged to prescribe something stronger, at least for Ramses. Nefret and I discussed whether his ribs were broken or only cracked; Ramses insisted they were neither, but soon would be if we went on prodding him. So I strapped him up while Nefret dealt as efficiently with his hand, which was as nasty a specimen as I had ever beheld, even on Ramses. I then attempted to administer a dose of laudanum to each lad, for though David's injuries were superficial he was gray-faced with exhaustion and strain. Neither of them would take it.

"I want to tell you what happened," David said. "You should know—"

"I'll tell them what happened," said Ramses. We had had to hurt him quite a lot, but I suspected the unevenness of his voice was due to annoyance as much as pain.

Emerson spoke for the first time. Sitting quietly by the side of the bed, he had not taken his eyes off Ramses, and once, when he thought none of us saw him, he had given his son's arm a surreptitious and very gentle squeeze. "Let's get them home, Peabody. If they are fit for it, we might certainly profit from a council of war."

So we bundled them into the carriage and took them home, with Risha trotting alongside. We retired to the sitting room, where I tried to make Ramses lie down on the settee, but he would not. Katherine moved quietly around the room lighting the lamps and drawing the curtains. Then she came and sat next to me. Her silent sympathy and support were what I needed just then; rallying, I once more took charge.

"You had better tell us what happened, Ramses," I said.

I had had occasion in the past to complain of my son's verbose and theatrical literary style. This time he went too far in the opposite direction. His concluding sentences were typical of the narrative as a whole. "The fellow hit his head when he fell. Once David was freed we ran for it. We would not have got away if he had not taken charge and made for Selim's house. I had somehow got it into my head that we must reach Abdullah."

"Is that all?" I exclaimed.

"No, it is not!" David's expressive countenance had displayed increasing signs of agitation. "I saw what you did, Ramses. I was dizzy and sick and short of air but I was not unconscious." His eyes moved round the circle of interested faces. "The guard had a knife. Ramses did not. He looked as if he could barely stand. When he fell forward I thought he had fainted, and the guard must have thought the same, but it was that trick he showed us once—you remember, Nefret, the one he told you not to try unless you had no other choice because it requires split-second timing. You have to go in under the knife and pray it will miss you, and get hold of the other man's feet before he can jump back."

Nefret nodded. "Split-second timing and long arms and the devil's own luck. That's when he cracked that rib."

"It is not cracked," Ramses said indignantly. "Only bruised. And the damned sticking plaster itches like fury. I don't know which is worse, you or—"

"He tried to carry me," David said, his voice unsteady. "I

couldn't walk, I was too stiff. He could have left me and gone for help, but—"

"But I didn't have sense enough to think of it," said Ramses. "Do you mind shutting up, David?"

"It won't do, Ramses," Nefret said. The color rushed into her face and she jumped up. "You've left out everything of importance. Curse it, don't you understand that we cannot deal effectively with this situation until we have all the facts? Any detail, no matter how small, may be important."

Emerson, who had listened in silence, cleared his throat. "Quite right. Ramses, my boy—"

Nefret whirled round and shook her finger in his astonished face. "That applies to you too, Professor—and you, Aunt Amelia. What happened tonight might have been prevented if you had not kept certain matters from us."

"Nefret," Ramses said. "Don't."

My poor dear Emerson looked like a man who has been clawed by his pet kitten. With a little cry of self-reproach Nefret flung herself onto his lap and put her arms round his neck.

"I didn't mean it. Forgive me!"

"My dear, the reproach was not undeserved. No, don't get up; I rather like having you there."

He enclosed her in his arms and she hid her face against his broad shoulder, and we all tactfully pretended not to see the sobs that shook her slim body. I had expected she would give way before long. Her temperament is quite unlike my own. She performs as coolly and efficiently in an emergency as I could do, but once the emergency is over, her tempestuous and loving nature seeks an outlet for the emotions she has repressed. So I let her cry for a bit in Emerson's fatherly embrace, and then suggested that some of us ought to retire to our beds.

Nefret sat up. The only evidences of tears were her wet lashes and a damp patch on Emerson's shirt. "Not until we have finished. Ramses, tell it again, from the beginning, and this time don't leave anything out."

We had to wring some of it out of him. Perched on Emerson's knee, with his arm around her, Nefret exhibited such skill at interrogation I was not forced to intervene.

"I am not surprised that Layla should be involved in a criminal activity," I said. "Apparently her services are for sale to anyone who can meet her price."

"Criminal activities," said my son, "enabled her to escape from a life of misery and degradation. Can one who has never been forced to make such a choice condemn hers?"

"Good gracious, how pompous you sound," I said. "I must admit the justice of your remark, however; women have a difficult enough time in this man's world, and moral scruples are luxuries some of them cannot afford."

"In this case," said Nefret, her voice smooth as honey, "Layla's moral scruples were stronger than greed. Or was there another reason why she took the risk of freeing you?"

Ramses looked quickly at her and as quickly returned his gaze to his feet, at which he had been staring most of the time. "Several reasons, I think. Even a woman devoid of ordinary moral scruples may balk at murder. Father—and Mother too, of course—have formidable reputations; had we come to harm, they would have exacted retribution. Layla implied that her employers had something particularly unpleasant in mind for me, and possibly David as well. The pronoun 'you' can be singular or plural, and I did not ask her to elaborate, since my mind was—"

"Stop that," I said irritably.

"Yes, Mother."

"You made me forget what I was going to ask next."

"I beg your pardon, Mother."

"I know what I was going to ask next," said Nefret. "It is a simple question, and vitally important. What do these people want?"

"Us," Ramses said. "Both of us, or they would have left the one they didn't want dead in the temple."

"That's too simple," Nefret snapped. "Abduction isn't an end in itself, it is a means to an end. If you hadn't got away, we would have received a demand for—what? Money? The papyrus? Or . . . something else?"

"Wait a minute," Cyrus ejaculated, tugging at his goatee. "You're getting ahead of me here. What papyrus?"

"The children picked it up in Cairo," I explained. "From a dealer—the same fellow who turned up in the Nile a few days ago, mangled by what appeared to have been a crocodile."

"But, Amelia," Cyrus began.

"Yes, I know. There are no crocodiles in Luxor. I will explain it all to you later, Cyrus. Someone does seem to want the papyrus back. Do you think that was the motive behind the boys' little misadventure, Nefret?"

"There is another possibility."

"Well? It is getting late and—"

"I will be brief," said Nefret. There was a note in her voice I did not like at all. "Let us suppose that the attack on Aunt Amelia in London and our subsequent encounters with Yussuf Mahmud are connected. If one person is behind all of them, that person must be the Master Criminal himself. All the clues lead back to him—the typewritten message, the possibility that the papyrus came from his private collection, even the fact that someone has discovered that Ali the Rat is Ramses. That is a tenuous lead, I admit, but Sethos is one of the few people who knows you found his private laboratory, and if, as I strongly suspect, he has been in touch with you since, he is probably familiar with our habits. Your turn, Aunt Amelia. It is time you told us everything you know about that man. And I mean everything!"

Goodness, but the child had a stare almost as forbidding as that of Emerson at his best! I daresay I could have stared her down, but I could not deny the justice of her charge.

"You are correct," I said. "We have encountered Sethos since, and I . . . Oh dear. There is no doubt that he knows a good deal more about all of us, including Ramses, than he ought."

8

Our discussion ended at that point, for Ramses's face had turned an unpleasant shade of grayish-green, and Nefret bundled him off to bed. He went protesting, if feebly, so I assured him we would not continue without him.

"I need to collect my thoughts," I explained. "And arrange them in a logical sequence. I do not believe I am capable of doing so at this time."

"Small wonder," said Emerson. "It has been a trying evening for you, my dear. Off to bed with you too. We will continue tomorrow morning."

Katherine cleared her throat. "Amelia, would you think me rude if I asked whether Cyrus and I might join you? Curiosity killed the cat, you know. You would not want my death on your conscience."

At that moment I would have agreed to anything in order to be left alone—to collect my thoughts, as I have said. Brief reflection assured me that affection as well as curiosity had prompted her request, and that no one could assist us better than these dear friends. Cyrus knew more of our extraordinary history than most people, and his wife's cynical intelligence had served me well in the past. Recollecting that the following day was Friday, the Moslem holy day, when we breakfasted later and more leisurely than on workdays, I invited them to join us for that meal.

My dear Emerson tucked me into bed as tenderly as a woman

might have done, and Fatima insisted on my drinking a glass of warm milk flavored with cardamom, to help me sleep.

"You are all being kinder to me than I deserve," I said. "Come to bed, Emerson, you have been as worried as I."

"Later, my dear."

"You don't mean to sit up all night standing guard, do you?"

"Not all night. David and I will take it in turn. He would have struck me, I think, if I had not agreed." Emerson's hard face softened. "He's fit enough, Peabody. Selim's young wife stuffed him full of lamb stew, and Nefret assures me the wound is negligible."

"I meant to examine him again," I murmured. "Ramses too. She wouldn't let me . . ."

Emerson took my hand. His voice seemed to come from a great distance. "She didn't mean it, you know, Peabody."

"Yes, she did. Oh, Emerson—was I in error? I honestly believed I was acting for the best . . . for their own good . . ." A great yawn interrupted my speech, and the truth dawned at last. "Curse it, Emerson! You put laudanum in the milk. How could. . . ."

"Sleep well, my love." I felt his lips brush my cheek, and felt nothing more.

I woke before the others, rested and ready to take up the reins once more. Emerson was sleeping heavily; he did not stir even when I planted a kiss on his bristly cheek, so I dressed and tiptoed out.

The others were in the same state as Emerson, even David, whose cousin Achmet had taken over the duties of guard. I stood for a while by Ramses's bed, looking down at him. Nefret must have made him take laudanum, or one of her newfangled medicines, for he was deeply asleep. When I brushed the tangled curls away from his face he only murmured and smiled.

I was on the verandah busily making notes when Cyrus and Katherine rode up, Cyrus on his favorite mare Queenie and Katherine on a placid broad-backed pony. Her straw hat was tied under her chin with a large bow, and she looked more than ever like a pleasant pussycat.

Emerson and the children came in shortly thereafter, and we sat down to breakfast. Conversation was sporadic, and not only because we were eating. One was conscious of a certain air of constraint. I was relieved to see that Ramses's appetite was normal, though he had some little difficulty eating with his left hand. I wondered how Nefret had bullied him into wearing a sling, and whether his injuries were more extensive than I had realized, and whether I ought not insist on examining him myself . . .

"The sling is just to protect his hand, Aunt Amelia. His arm is not hurt."

They were the first words Nefret had addressed to me since she had uttered those stinging accusations the night before. Her blue eyes were anxious and her smile tentative. I smiled warmly back at her.

"Thank you, my dear, for reassuring me. I have complete confidence in your skill. And thank you for tending to me so efficiently. I slept like a baby and woke refreshed."

"Oh, Aunt Amelia, I am sorry for what I said last night! I didn't—"

"You are becoming tediously repetitive, Nefret." Ramses pushed his plate away. "And you are wasting time. I see that Mother has organized her thoughts in her usual efficient fashion and in writing; shall we ask her to begin?"

I shuffled my papers together and picked them up, wishing I had thought to do so before my son's vulturine stare fell upon them. The pages had a good many lines scratched out and scribbled over. The complexity of my thought processes does not lend itself to written organization. However, I had decided what to say and I proceeded to say it.

"I agree with Ramses; we ought not waste time in apologies and expressions of regret. If anyone of us has erred, she—er—he or she did so with the best of intentions. There is nothing so futile as—"

"Peabody," said Emerson. "Please. Abjure aphorisms, if you are able."

The glint in his handsome blue eyes was one of amusement rather than annoyance. The same affectionate amusement warmed the other faces—except, of course, for that of Ramses. His expression was no more rigid than usual, however, so I concluded we were in accord once more, all grievances forgot.

"Certainly, my dear," I said. "I begin with the assumption that

you are all familiar with the history of our original encounters with Sethos. Ramses has told David and Nefret, and Cyrus has told Katherine? Hmmm, yes, I thought so. I gleaned certain bits of additional information during my—er—private interview with him. After long and thoughtful consideration of that interview I have extracted the following facts that may be relevant.

"Sethos does have a private collection of antiquities. What he said—er . . ." I pretended to consult my notes. It was not necessary; never would I forget those words, or the look in those strange chameleon eyes when he pronounced them. "He said: 'The most beautiful objects I take, I keep for myself.' "

Emerson growled deep in his throat, and Ramses remarked, with greater tact than I would have expected, "The papyrus certainly meets his criteria. What else did he say?"

I started to shake my head—caught Nefret's fond but critical eye—and sighed. "That Emerson was one of the few individuals in the world who could constitute a danger to him. He did not explain why. He claimed he had never harmed a woman. He promised . . . No, let me be absolutely accurate. He implied that he would never again interfere with me or injure those I love."

"It appears you misunderstood that one," my son said dryly.

"What else?" Nefret demanded inflexibly.

"As to his familiarity with our personal habits and private affairs . . . Well, let me put it this way. He knows enough about Ramses to suspect that he has become interested in the art of disguise, and that he could easily pass as an Egyptian. Once the suspicion arose, a clever man might be able to deduce the identity of Ali the Rat. For one thing, Ali was seen in Cairo only when we were there. I cannot think of anything else that would help us. That is the truth, Nefret."

It was the truth—or so I honestly believed. It would not be fair or accurate to say I was mistaken, for at that time none of us had the faintest inkling . . . But excuses do not become me. I was wrong, and the price I paid for my error was one that will haunt me for the rest of my life.

A pensive and (in Nefret's case) somewhat skeptical silence followed. No one questioned my statement, however. Finally Ramses said, "It doesn't get us any further, does it? There is nothing to suggest Sethos is not behind this business and nothing to prove that he is. If the incident in London is unrelated to the others, we have

another unknown foe to contend with, and it may be that he would have exchanged David and me for the papyrus. If Sethos is the mastermind, he only took us prisoner as a means of getting to Mother. Humiliating, isn't it, David? No one wants us for our charming selves."

"Could I have a look at this famous papyrus?" Cyrus asked. "It must be something darned remarkable if a fellow is willing to go to such lengths to get it back."

"It is," Ramses said.

"As papyri go," said Emerson, who is not as impressed by papyri as are some people. "Fetch it here, Ramses."

Ramses did so. Cyrus let out a low whistle. "It's darned elegant, all right. Mr. Walter Emerson is going to go off his head about it."

"Uncle Walter!" David started to his feet. "Good heavens! He and Aunt Evelyn and Lia . . . They mustn't come! They could be in terrible danger."

"Now, David, don't be so melodramatic," I said. "There is no reason to suppose—"

"He's right, though," Emerson said. "At the moment we don't know what the devil is going on, much less why. Three more potential victims would complicate the problem even further. We had better head them off."

"It is too late," I said hollowly. "They sailed from Marseilles this morning."

It was Katherine who dispelled the Gothic atmosphere with a simple statement. "Always expect the worst and take steps to prevent it."

"Just what I was about to say," I exclaimed. "Steps! We must take steps! Er—what steps?"

There was something very comforting about that calm pink-cheeked face of hers. "First, take every possible means to protect yourselves. Secure this place and don't go abroad without an escort. Second, postpone or cancel the visit of your family. I don't doubt Evelyn and Walter can take care of themselves, but the girl cannot; she would only be an additional source of anxiety. Third, find out who is responsible for this and stop them."

"That's a pretty ambitious program, my dear," Cyrus said, shaking his head. "Where do we start?"

It warmed my heart to hear him say "we," but I had expected no less of him.

"In Gurneh, obviously," said Ramses. "And, as Mrs. Vandergelt has so sensibly suggested, all together."

I had expected the village would be abuzz with excitement, for the events of the preceding night would certainly be known by now to every inhabitant, spreading rapidly along that web of gossip that is the primary source of news in illiterate societies. However, as we rode along the winding path I saw the place was abnormally quiet. A few people greeted us; others we saw only as a flutter of skirts as the wearers thereof whisked themselves behind a wall.

"That was Ali Yussuf," I exclaimed. "What is wrong with him?"

Emerson chuckled. "An uneasy conscience, my dear Peabody. Even if he had nothing to do with last night's affair, he is afraid we will hold him responsible for what happened to the boys."

"One cannot help being suspicious, Emerson. How could the miscreants have been so bold as to bring their captives here unless some of the villagers were in league with them?"

Ramses was riding ahead, but he can hear a whisper across the Nile, as the Egyptians say. He turned his head. "This was only a temporary stopover, Mother. They would have moved us under cover of darkness."

Kadija was standing in the doorway when we rode up to Abdullah's house. She informed us that neither Abdullah nor Daoud was at home. "Curse it," said Emerson. "I told Daoud to keep the old rascal out of this. Where have they gone, Kadija?"

Daoud's wife understood English though she never spoke it. Looking as mysterious as only a black veil can make one look, she gave Emerson the answer he had expected.

"Curse it," Emerson repeated. "I suppose the whole lot of them have gone there."

"Not all," said Kadija in Arabic. "Some are asking questions, Father of Curses. Many questions of many people. Will you come in and drink tea and wait?"

We declined with thanks and were about to proceed when Kadija came out of the house, moving with ponderous and dignified deliberation. Her hand, large and calloused as a man's, rested for a moment on David's booted foot before she turned to Ramses and inspected him closely. It was not Ramses whom she addressed, however. "Will you stay for a moment, Nur Misur?"

"Yes, of course. Go on," Nefret said to the rest of us.

She was only a moment. "Well?" I asked. "What is so funny?"

Nefret got her face under control. "She told me a very amusing story."

"Kadija?" I said in surprise. "What sort of story?"

"Uh—never mind. What she really wanted was reassurance about the boys. She was too shy to ask them directly how they are feeling."

We could have found the house we sought even without David's directions. It was surrounded by a crowd of people, all gesticulating wildly and talking at the top of their lungs. The black robes of the women contrasted with the white and blue and sand-colored galabeeyahs of the men, and children darted in and out like little brown beetles. The men greeted us without self-consciousness; either their consciences were clear, or they had none.

This was not the house in which Layla had once lived. I remembered that establishment very well. This was larger and more isolated, with a few dusty tamarisk trees behind it and no other house in sight. The location was well suited to the purpose it had served; a cart loaded with, let us say, sugar cane, could drive through the gates into the walled courtyard without arousing suspicion.

When I saw who stood in the open doorway I understood why none of the men had had the temerity to attempt to enter. Daoud's large frame filled the aperture from side to side and from lintel to threshold. He rushed at us with cries of pleasure and relief, embraced David, and was about to do the same to Ramses when Nefret got between them.

Abdullah awaited us inside. His snowy-white beard bristled with indignation, and a ferocious scowl darkened his venerable brow. He addressed Emerson in tones of icy reproof.

"Why did you not tell me? This would not have happened if you had taken me into your confidence."

"Now, see here, Abdullah," Emerson began.

"I understand. I am too old. Too old and stupid. I will go sit in the sun with the other senile old men and—"

"You were in our confidence, Abdullah," I interrupted. "You knew as much as we did. We were not expecting anything like this either."

"Ah." Abdullah sat down on the stairs and scratched his ear. "Then I forgive you, Sitt. Now what shall we do?"

"It appears to me that you are already doing it," said Ramses, glancing at the open door of the room on our left. It had once been comfortably furnished, with rugs and tables, a wide divan and several armchairs of European style, and a large cupboard or wardrobe against the far wall. The shutters had been flung open and sunlight streaming through the windows illumined a scene of utter chaos— rugs rolled up and thrown aside, cushions scattered across the floor, chairs overturned.

"We are searching for clues," Abdullah explained.

"Trampling them underfoot, most likely," said Emerson. "Where is Selim? I told him to . . . Oh, good God!"

A resounding crash from above indicated Selim's presence. Ramses slipped past Abdullah and hurried up the stairs, with the rest of us following.

Selim was not alone. Two of his brothers and one of his second cousins once removed were rampaging through the rooms on the first floor, "searching for clues," one presumed. Emerson's roar stopped but did not at all disconcert them; they gathered round, all talking at once as they tried to tell him what they had done.

I left Emerson patiently explaining the principles of searching suspected premises, and joined Ramses, who stood looking into one of the rooms.

It was a woman's bedchamber. The furnishings were an odd mixture of local and imported luxury—Oriental rugs of silken beauty, a toilet table draped with muslin, carved chests, and vessels of fine china behind a screen. I deduced that Selim and his crew had not had time to demolish this room, but there was evidence of a hasty search. One of the chests stood open; its contents spilled out in a flood of rainbow-hued fabric. The bedsheet was crumpled and dusty.

"This is where you were confined?" I asked.

"Yes." Ramses crossed to the bed. He picked up a piece of white cotton, which I had not seen because it was the same color as the sheet, examined it, and dropped it onto the floor. I did not need to ask what it was.

A search of the room produced nothing except a few lengths of rope, knotted and cut—and Ramses's boots, which had been kicked under the bed. I was glad to get them back, for he had only the two pair, and boots are expensive.

Nefret and I investigated the chests. They contained women's clothing, some Egyptian, some European—including a nightdress of transparent silk permeated with a scent that made Nefret wrinkle her nose.

"She must bathe in the cursed stuff," she muttered.

"She took everything of value with her," said Emerson, who had overturned the mattress and bedsprings. "There is no jewelry, no money. And no papers."

Nefret tossed the nightdress back into the chest. "She left all her clothing, though."

"There wasn't time to pack a trunk," said Ramses. "Nor would she have dared return to get her things. She said others were coming soon."

Katherine sat down on a hassock. "If she carried away only what she could put in a smallish bundle, she will have to replenish her wardrobe. We should inquire at the markets and shops."

"I was about to make that suggestion," said a voice in pure cultivated English.

He stood watching us from the doorway, clad in well-cut tweeds and gleaming boots, his hat in his hand, his fair hair as smooth as if he had just passed his brushes over it.

"Sir Edward!" I cried. "What are you doing here?"

"I have been here for some time, Mrs. Emerson. Good morning to you all," he added with a pleasant smile.

"Daoud was not supposed to admit anyone," Ramses said.

"Daoud did not include me in that interdict," said Sir Edward amiably. "He remembered me as a friend and co-worker. As a friend I could not remain aloof. The news was all over Luxor this morning. I am relieved to find it was exaggerated"—his cool blue eyes moved over Ramses and spared a glance for David—"but not entirely inaccurate. How could I not offer my assistance?"

"Unnecessary," said Emerson. "We have the matter under control."

"Ah, but have you? No one who knows you all as I do would doubt your ability to defend yourselves against ordinary enemies. The very fact that these enemies succeeded in abducting Ramses and his servant—"

"David is not my servant," Ramses said.

"—and his friend," Sir Edward corrected smoothly, "strong young men who were, I do not doubt, on the alert, suggests that they are dangerous and unscrupulous. As I told Mrs. Emerson the other evening, I am looking for something to occupy my mind. My archaeological services are not needed, it appears, so I beg you will accept my services as a guard."

"For 'the ladies,' you mean?" Nefret inquired, lashes fluttering and lips trembling. "Oh, Sir Edward, how gallant! How noble! How can we ever thank you?"

It was such an outrageous parody I was tempted to laugh. Sir Edward was no more taken in than I. He planted his hand upon the approximate region of his heart, and gazed at Nefret with the sickening intensity of a provincial actor playing Sir Galahad. "The protection of helpless females is an Englishman's sacred duty, Miss Forth."

Emerson was not amused. "What nonsense," he grumbled. "This is no laughing matter, Sir Edward."

"I am well aware of that, sir. If I have been informed correctly, the woman who owned this house was the same one Mrs. Emerson and I encountered a few years ago. I was able to be of some small service to her then. Dare I flatter myself that I may be again?"

Emerson dismissed the offer with a frown and a peremptory gesture. "We are wasting time with these empty courtesies. We have not finished searching the place."

Sir Edward was wise enough to refrain from further argument, but he followed at a discreet distance while we examined the remaining rooms and the flat roof. We found nothing of a personal nature except an empty tin that had contained opium, and a nargileh. The kitchen, a separate building near the main house, was a shambles. It reeked of vegetables that had begun to go bad, milk that had curdled, and the thin sour beer of Egypt. The only unusual item was a broken bottle of green glass. Ramses sorted through the fragments till he found one that had part of a label.

"Moët and Chandon," he said.

"The lady has expensive tastes," Sir Edward murmured.

"She has the means to indulge them," I said. "She has buried two wealthy husbands."

The only remaining place to be searched was the shed. It had been painful enough for me to see the room where Ramses had been imprisoned; the gag and the tightly knotted ropes were mute but powerful evidence of those long hours of discomfort and uncertainty. The filthy little shed was even worse. My sympathetic imagination—a quality with which I am amply endowed—pictured David lying helpless and wounded on the hard floor, despairing of rescue, fearing the worst, in ignorance of what had befallen the friend he loved like a brother. What would have been his fate, and that of Ramses, if Layla had not come to their aid? Not a clean, quick death, for their attackers could have dispatched them at any time. A number of alternatives came to mind. A shudder ran through my frame.

There was not room in the horrid little place for all of us, so I left the search to Emerson and Ramses. All they found was an overturned beer jar and a pile of cigarette ends, a rough clay lamp and a thin layer of musty straw.

We returned to Abdullah's house, hoping that the inquiries he had set in motion had produced more information. Our people had been on the job since dawn, and I must say they had covered the village thoroughly. A crowd of witnesses awaited us, some grumbling and resentful, some curious and cheerful. Abdullah brought them in one by one while we sipped the tea Kadija served.

Everyone had known of Layla's return; it had been a subject of interest, particularly to some of the men. However, when they dropped by to renew old acquaintances they had been turned away. They were indignant but not surprised; Layla had always been unpredictable, as one of them put it, adding philosophically, "That is what comes of letting women have their own money. They do what they wish instead of what men tell them to do."

"Damned right," said Nefret, after this last witness had taken his leave. "I beg your pardon, Aunt Amelia and Mrs. Vandergelt."

"Granted," said Katherine with a smile. She had got accustomed to hearing Nefret use bad language, and I had more or less given up hope of stopping Nefret from using it. She had learned a good deal of it from Emerson.

Aside from the unhelpful information about Layla, the majority of the witnesses had nothing much to say, though some of them said it at considerable length. Strangers had been seen coming and going from Layla's house; they were unfriendly people who would not stop and fahddle or answer questions. Finally Emerson put a stop to the proceedings with a vehement comment.

"This isn't getting us anywhere. If any of the Gurnawis knew those fellows they won't admit it. Layla is our best lead. We must find her. Where can she have gone?"

Sir Edward had come with us, since no one had told him not to. He cleared his throat. "Doesn't it seem likely that she would have crossed over to Luxor? The villages on the West Bank are small and close-knit; strangers are noticed. There is a certain part of Luxor . . . Forgive me. I ought not to have referred to it while there are ladies present."

"Oh, that part of Luxor," I said. "Hmmm."

"The thought had occurred to me," Ramses said, with a hostile look at Sir Edward, who smiled amiably back.

"Well, you are not to go there," I declared. "Nor David."

I did not forbid Nefret to go, because it would never have occurred to me that she would. Autopsies and mangled bodies, yes; the abodes of hardened criminals, certainly; but a house of illicit affection . . .

I cannot imagine how I could have been so dense.

Sir Edward took leave of us at the place where we had stabled our horses with one of Abdullah's innumerable young relatives. He did not renew his offer of assistance, but the meaningful look he gave me was sufficient assurance that it held and would hold. He looked very well on horseback, and Nefret's eyes were not the only ones that followed his erect figure as he rode off toward the ferry.

We turned our horses in the direction of home and Cyrus said, "I don't want to speak out of turn, Emerson, but darned if I can understand why you didn't jump at Sir Edward's offer. He's a husky young fellow and a smart one, too."

"I won't have him hanging about making eyes at my wife," Emerson growled. "Or Nefret."

"Well, now," said Cyrus, in his quiet drawl, "I don't recollect that there's any law against a fellow paying polite attentions to a lady so long as she doesn't object. And I have a feeling that if Miss Nefret did object she'd let him know in no uncertain terms."

"Damn—er—absolutely right," said Nefret. "Don't talk like a Victorian papa, Professor darling. We need Sir Edward. Especially if Lia and Aunt Evelyn and Uncle Walter join us."

"There won't be room in the house," Emerson muttered. It was the last dying rumble of the volcano; Emerson has his little weaknesses but he is not a fool, and he recognized the inevitable.

"There will be ample room if we can prevent our loved ones from coming," I said. "Sir Edward is at the Winter Palace, is he not? We will call on him, or leave a message, accepting his offer."

For once there was no argument about what we should do next. It was imperative that we attempt to locate Layla, and the sooner the better. In my opinion Luxor was her most likely destination and it was there we stood the best chance of finding a trace of her. My suggestion that Ramses should go home and rest was met with stony silence on his part and a critical comment from Nefret.

"I wouldn't trust him to stay there, Aunt Amelia. We had better let him come along so we can keep our eyes on him."

I had not intended to take her with us, but when I came to think of it, I did not trust her either. So we rode directly to the dock and two of our men took us across the river in the small boat we kept for that purpose.

From Manuscript H

"How are we going to get away from them?" Nefret demanded.

They were waiting outside the railway ticket office while the senior Emersons interrogated the stationmaster. The platform, the station house, and the path leading to it were teeming with people waiting to catch the train to Assuan. The sun was high overhead and the air was thick with dust. Nefret had taken off her hat and was fanning herself with it.

"This is a waste of time," she went on. "How can the stationmaster possibly remember one veiled woman? They all look alike in those black robes. Anyhow, *they* knew she had betrayed them, and the railway station is one of the first places they would have looked. If she is as clever as all you men seem to think, she would go into hiding until things quiet down, and there is only one logical place where she would go."

"Nefret, will you please be reasonable?" Ramses kept his voice low. "I agree that Layla might have sought refuge among her old—er—acquaintances. The only way we can manage a visit to the place is with Father's cooperation. He means to go there himself, which would not be a good idea. David and I may be able to convince him we can be more effective than he, but there is no way on earth he would consent if he thought you were going with us."

"I wouldn't consent either," David said. He stood slightly behind Ramses, his eyes moving suspiciously over the hurrying figures that passed.

Nefret slapped her hat onto her head and tied the ribbons under her chin. "We'll see about that. Here they come. What luck, Professor?"

"Better than I had expected," was the reply. "A woman purchased a ticket to Cairo early this morning. Her ornaments and clothing were those of a peasant, but the clerk remembered her because she was traveling alone and she paid for a second-class ticket. A woman of that sort would ordinarily travel third class, if she traveled at all. I am going to telegraph Cairo and ask the police to meet the train."

It took a good deal of maneuvering and distraction, and several outright lies, to arrange the matter as Ramses wished. After the telegraph office they went to the Winter Palace. Sir Edward was not there, so they decided to have luncheon at the hotel; and it was while the ladies had retired to freshen up that Ramses had the opportunity to talk with his father. The initial reaction was what he had expected—a flat, profane refusal.

"You can't mean to go yourself, Father," Ramses said. "They wouldn't talk to you."

Emerson fixed him with an icy stare. "They would feel more at ease with you?"

"Yes, sir. I believe so."

"Everyone in Luxor is in awe of you, Professor," David added. "They might be afraid to speak freely."

"Bah," Emerson said. "No. No, it is impossible. I shudder to think what your mother would say if she found out I let you boys visit a bordello."

"What will she say if she finds out you mean to visit one, Father?" Ramses asked.

"Er—hmph," said Emerson, stroking his chin and glancing uneasily at the door of the Ladies' Parlor.

"He's got you there, Emerson," said Vandergelt, grinning. "You're not a good liar. She'd see through any excuse you gave her, and she'd insist on going along. We sure don't want her traipsing around the—er—hmmm. Let the lads handle it."

Ramses had been in an Egyptian brothel only once—in the course, it should be said, of a criminal investigation. The place had sickened him, though it had been one of the less offensive of its kind, catering as it did to Europeans and wealthy Egyptians. This one was worse. The main room opened directly onto the street and was separated from it by a kind of curtain made of strips of cloth. The shutters were closed and the only light came from a pair of hanging lamps. The room reeked of dirt and sweat and cheap perfume. It swarmed with flies, whose buzzing formed an incessant droning.

Their appearance produced another sound—a musical jingle of the ornaments adorning the breasts and ears and hair of the women who reclined on the cushioned divan that was the room's principal article of furniture. Wide dark eyes framed in kohl stared curiously at them, and one of the women rose, smoothing the thin fabric over her hips in a mechanical gesture of seduction. A curt word from another woman made her cringe back. The speaker stood up and came toward them. She was older than the others. Rolls of fat wobbled as she moved, and the coinlike disks that dangled from her headdress and necklace were of gold.

David cleared his throat. They had agreed it would be better for him to speak first, but he was hoarse with embarrassment. "We are looking for a woman."

A muted chorus of laughter followed this ingenuous remark, and the proprietress chuckled. "Of course, young masters. Why else are you here?"

"It's a good thing I came," said a cool voice behind them. "You had better let me do the talking, David."

Ramses spun round. She had thrown back the hood of her cloak and her hair glimmered in the streaks of sunlight that filtered through the curtained door. She was like a flower that had sprung up in the middle of a cesspool; his first impulse was to snatch her up and carry her out of the foul place. Knowing how she would react—kicking and screaming would be the least of it—he took hold of her arm. "What in the name of God are you doing here?"

"I followed you. Mrs. Vandergelt took Aunt Amelia to the shops, and I slipped away. You're hurting me," she added reproachfully.

"David, get her out of here."

"Don't you dare touch me, David!"

By that time they had a fascinated and augmented audience. Several other women had slipped into the room. They were dressed like the others, in flimsy, brightly colored garments. Their uncovered faces ranged in shade from blue-black to creamy brown, and their hands and feet were stained with henna.

Nefret addressed the gaping proprietress in her rapid, simple Arabic.

"We search for a friend, Sitt, a woman who did us a great service and who is in danger because of it. Her name is Layla. She lived in Gurneh, but she ran away from her house last night. We must find her before she comes to harm. Please help us. Have any of you seen her?"

Not a flower, Ramses thought—a ray of sunlight in a dark cell. No stain of sin or sorrow could touch the shining compassion that filled her, or dim the brightness of her presence.

For a few seconds not even the sound of a drawn breath broke the stillness. Then someone moved; he couldn't tell which of them it was, only the soft tinkle of her ornaments betrayed the fact that movement had occurred.

The older woman folded her plump arms. "Get out," she said harshly. "We cannot help you. What sort of men are you, to let one such as she come to this place?"

"Excellent point," said Ramses, recovering himself. He'd been reading too damned much poetry, that was his trouble. "Nefret, it's no good. Come away."

She stood her ground. "You know who we are, where we live. If any of you know anything—if you want to leave this terrible life—come to us, we will help you escape—"

The old woman burst into a flood of invective and shook her fists at them. Nefret didn't budge. She raised her voice and went on talking until Ramses and David dragged her out the door.

"That was brilliant," Ramses said, once they had retreated to a safe distance. "Nefret, may I venture to suggest once again that you hold your tongue and control your emotions until you've given some little thought to what you are doing? You might have endangered yourself, and us."

"They wouldn't dare attack us," Nefret muttered.

"Perhaps not. The women are another matter."

"But I didn't mean . . . Oh, good heavens, do you think . . ."

She looked so stricken he hadn't the heart to continue scolding her. "All I'm saying is that we didn't go there on a rescue expedition, admirable as that aim might have been. We were attempting to extract information, and trying to remove the merchandise is not the way to win a merchant's confidence."

"How can you joke about it?" Her blue eyes shone with tears of rage and compassion.

"The only alternative is to curse God. Neither does any good." His hands lingered as he adjusted the hood of her cloak over her bright head. "Let me try once more."

"You are not going in there alone, Ramses," David announced.

"You can keep watch. Wait for me here."

"If you aren't out in five minutes I'll come after you," Nefret said.

He was out in less than five minutes. "Nothing," he reported. "No one saw her, no one would admit knowing her."

"I'll try another place," David said heroically. His face was pinched with disgust.

"No. I haven't the stomach for more either," Ramses admitted. "The word will spread now—and one of the words I mentioned was 'reward.' I didn't suppose any of them would dare speak up before the others. Come, let's get out of this."

When they reached the riverbank David had found a new source of worry. "Aunt Amelia will want to know where we were. What shall we tell her?"

"That we went to the Luxor garden for a cup of tea," Nefret said. "We'll go there now, so it won't be a lie."

She was more composed now, her face pensive instead of angry. After they had found a table and ordered tea, she said, "I did make a mess of things, didn't I? "

"Not necessarily," Ramses said. "One never knows; an impulsive word from you may have had more effect than my methods."

"I won't ask what methods you used." She smiled at him and took his bandaged hand gently in hers. "I've been wanting to ask you about this—and a few other things. You must have hit someone very hard to do so much damage."

"There were two of them," Ramses said, wondering what she was getting at.

"In the house, you mean? You took on both of them at once? That was very brave of you."

"Not very."

"And what was Layla doing while you fought two men?"

Her eyes were wide and innocent and as blue as the sea, and that was where she had maneuvered him—between the devil and the deep blue sea. He tried to think of a convincing lie and failed miserably; he couldn't remember precisely how much he had told them, but he must have said enough to get that quick, intuitive mind of hers on the right track.

"Precisely what you suspect," he said with a sigh. "At least that was what she intended to do. Don't despise me, Nefret, I got there in time to prevent it. How the devil do you know these things?"

Her fingers stroked his wrist, sending tremors all the way up his arm. "I know you, my boy."

"Don't let your emotions get the better of you, Nefret. There's Mother. I might have known she'd track us down." His mother was advancing with her usual brisk stride; there was only time for him to add with a faint smile, "I hadn't much choice, dear. If you ever found out I had slunk away and left her, you'd have used my skin for a rug."

I have never succumbed to the lazy Eastern habit of sleeping in the afternoon, but I firmly believe that an active mind is in need of brief intervals of relaxation. After we had returned home after our busy, if fruitless, investigations, I lay down on my bed and picked up a book.

I was roused from the meditative state into which I had fallen by sounds that made me start up with heart pounding. Steel ringing on steel—raised voices—the sounds of mortal combat! Rushing to the door, as I believed, I found myself tugging at the window shutters, which I had closed against the heat of the afternoon sun.

This momentary confusion was soon overcome and I emerged into the courtyard, where I stood transfixed. The sight was terrible: Ramses and David, barefooted, stripped to trousers and shirt, striking fiercely at one another with the long knives used by the Tourag. Mute and motionless with horror, I saw Ramses's knife drive home against David's breast.

The paralysis broke. I shrieked.

"Good afternoon, Mother," said Ramses. "I am sorry if we woke you. Confound it, David, you were holding back. Again."

David rubbed his chest. "Honestly, I was not. Good afternoon, Aunt Amelia. I am sorry if we—"

"Oh, good Gad!" I exclaimed. He was upright and smiling, without so much as a drop of blood spotting the white fabric. On a bench against the wall Nefret and Emerson sat side by side, like spectators at a performance.

"Hallo, Peabody," Emerson said. "Here, boys, let me have a go."

He jumped up and began tugging at his shirt. A button popped off and fell to the ground. Emerson's hasty method of removing his garments makes it necessary for me to spend far too much time sewing on buttons. When I fix them firmly, the fabric tears instead, ruining the shirt.

"Please, Emerson," I said automatically. "Not another shirt. What the devil is going on here?"

I saw now that the knives had been blunted by strips of leather bound round the edge and sharp tip. Emerson said cheerfully, "Ramses wanted some practice at fighting left-handed. It is a useful skill, don't you agree, Peabody?"

"Quite," I said.

Emerson removed his shirt, losing only one more button in the process, and tossed it onto the bench. "Let me have your knife, Ramses."

"Take David's," said my son. Perspiration beaded his face and trickled down his throat. He had discarded the sling, and I observed that the bandage on his hand was a peculiar shade of green. "He can't even attack *me* as hard as he ought; sheer awe of you would paralyze him."

"But not you, eh?" Emerson grinned. "Right! Have at you, my boy!"

Taking the knife from David's limp grasp, he stood poised, his knees flexed and his arms outstretched.

I made my way to the bench and sat down next to Nefret. "Those leather strips . . . What if they came undone?"

"I fastened them on myself." Nefret's brow was slightly furrowed. "Ramses was keen on the idea, so . . . They look splendid, don't they?"

I suppose they did. Emerson's magnificent muscles slid smoothly under his bronzed skin as he shifted his weight from one foot to the other. Ramses matched him in height if not in bulk; he was breathing rather quickly, but he was as light on his feet as his father. They circled one another slowly. Ramses was the first to attack; his knife drove at Emerson's ribs. Emerson twisted aside and struck Ramses's arm away. Ramses jumped back, throwing out his other arm to maintain his balance, and his father slashed at his unguarded breast. It was not a hard blow, but Ramses dropped his knife and doubled over, clutching his side.

"Oh, curse it," Emerson said, hurrying to him. "Forgive me, my boy. Come and sit down."

Ramses pulled away from his father's affectionate grasp and straightened. The blunted tip of Emerson's knife had caught in the opening of his shirt and pulled it apart. The bruise over his rib cage was the size and color of a tarnished silver saucer. "It's quite all right, sir. Shall we try again?"

Emerson began, "I will not take advantage—"

"The point of this exercise," said Ramses, breathing hard, "is learning to deal with an opponent who is delighted to take any advantage he can. I daresay I have had more practice at this than you, Father. Don't be afraid of hurting me again. I won't let you."

"That's enough," Nefret said, jumping up. "Curse you, Ramses, you bloody idiot!"

"More than enough," said Emerson. "Ramses, my boy—"

"No harm done, sir, I assure you." Ramses picked up his knife. "If you will excuse me, I will go and clean up."

"If you will excuse *me*," said Nefret to us, "I will go and deal with Ramses. I *told* him not to take those bandages off!"

Emerson cleared his throat. "Er—Nefret, my dear, I know you mean well, but don't you think he might be more amenable if you—er—asked him nicely instead of—er—calling him names?"

"Hmph," said Nefret—but she looked a little self-conscious. "All right, sir, I will try. Come and help me, David. If gentle persuasion doesn't do the job, you will have to hold him down."

"What's wrong, Peabody?" Emerson inquired. "I am a confounded clumsy idiot, but I don't believe he is much hurt."

"I am sure he is not."

My voice was not entirely steady. Emerson put a manly arm round my shoulders and made comforting noises. He seldom gets the chance to treat me like a timid little woman, and he enjoys it very much.

Absolute nonsense, of course. I am quite accustomed to deadly weapons of all varieties. I carry several myself: pistol and knife, and of course my parasol. Nor had my conscious mind been misled by the mock combat between the two boys; I had seen them practice before, with bare hands and with knives, and I knew either of them would have rather died than harm the other. Why then had I felt a sensation as of icy hands closing over my heart? Could it be that I had beheld not the harmless present but the deadly future—the portent of an encounter yet to come?

At dinner that evening David again raised the question of what we were to do about those dear ones who were even then on their way to us. I assured him I had not forgot the matter, but had only postponed it since we had had more pressing problems to deal with.

"They sailed from Marseilles yesterday morning and will not

arrive in Alexandria until Monday next," I explained. "That gives us two more days."

"One," said Ramses. "The steamer arrives early in the morning, so if we want to head them off one of us should take the train to Cairo on Sunday."

"I believe we became a bit overexcited the other evening," I said. "The danger to them is surely minimal, and they will be disappointed not to come on."

"Especially Lia," Nefret said. "She has looked forward to this so much. She has been studying Arabic all this past winter."

"They must be warned, at least," I said. "I will take the train—"

"Not on any account, Peabody," said Emerson, glowering at me. "Do you suppose I don't know what you intend? Your mind is an open book to me. I will not have you perambulating around Cairo interrogating antiquities dealers and harassing the police and—"

"One of the boys could come with me."

"No," said Nefret, as emphatically as Emerson. "Never mind Cairo, the journey itself is too risky. Fourteen hours on the train, with several stops—good Gad, all it would take is a gun in your ribs or a knife at your back."

"Then what do you propose?" David asked with unusual heat. "One of us must go, there is no question of that, and surely I am the most logical person. They won't bother with me."

I believe the others were as taken aback as I. For a moment the only sound that broke the silence was the fluttering of insects round the lamp. A moth, drawn by the fatal lure of the flame, dropped down the glass chimney and expired in a brief burst of glory.

"Don't talk like a damned fool," Ramses said brusquely.

"I would not have put it that way, but I endorse the sentiment most emphatically," I said. "David, how can you suppose we would be indifferent to a threat directed at you? You are one of us."

"Quite," said Emerson. "None of us is going. I would take on the job myself, but I cannot trust the rest of you to behave yourselves. I am sending Selim and Daoud."

"Brains and muscle," I said, smiling. "That is the ideal solution, Emerson. They can carry a letter from me, explaining the situation and urging Walter to take the next boat back to England. Unless, of course, we can solve the case before then."

"Before Sunday morning?" Ramses inquired, raising his eyebrows.

"Don't be absurd, Peabody," Emerson grunted.

"Hmmmm," said Nefret.

"We can at least make a start," David said. "Tomorrow in Luxor—"

"What are you talking about?" Emerson stared at him. "Tomorrow is a workday."

"Oh, come, Emerson, you surely don't intend to resume work as if nothing had happened," I exclaimed.

"I do not intend," said Emerson, "to allow anyone, male, female, or fiend in human form, to stop my excavations. What the devil is wrong with you, Peabody? What the devil is wrong with all of you?" He raked our faces with his glittering blue gaze. "We've been in situations as difficult as this before, and faced enemies as unscrupulous. Riccetti and Vincey and—"

"Never mind the rest," I said. "It is a long list, Emerson, I admit. Perhaps you are right. We will not huddle in the house starting at shadows. We will not be intimidated!"

"Bravely spoken, Mother." Ramses sounded amused, though his countenance did not display that emotion or any other. "However, I trust you won't object to taking a few precautions."

"Such as?"

"The same precautions Mrs. Vandergelt suggested. Guards, several of them, here at the house by night and by day. None of us is to go anywhere alone, or with only one other person. Keep your eyes open and trust no one."

"That applies to you and David as well," said Emerson, studying him keenly. "You are coming with us tomorrow, to the Valley."

"Yes, sir."

Emerson had not expected such ready agreement. His stern face relaxed into a smile. "You'll enjoy it, my boy. We have cleared the entrance to tomb Five, and Ayrton has found a cache of storage jars!"

"Indeed. That is exciting news, sir."

"Yes. You know the terrain." Emerson pushed his plate away and took a handful of fruit from the bowl. "Here is number Five, this fig is the entrance to Ramses the Sixth. . . ."

Not even a threat of murder can distract Emerson indefinitely from the joy of excavation. I did not object when he poured a pile of sugar onto the table and demonstrated the approximate location of Ned Ayrton's find. His superb self-confidence had restored mine. I felt ashamed of myself for yielding, however briefly, to weakness. And how foolish had been that earlier fantasy of discord! We were utterly devoted to one another. Brothers could not be closer than Ramses and David.

From Manuscript H

Sitting on the window ledge he waited for a long time, watching the slits of light that showed through the shuttered window of his parents' room. They must be arguing. Nothing surprising about that. It would end as it always did, but it was taking them devilish long tonight.

The courtyard lay quiet under the moon. His father had brushed aside his mother's suggestion that it be lighted, and he was in full agreement. The best possible solution was not to deter invaders but to catch them in the act. It wasn't likely that anything of that sort would happen, though. "They" wouldn't risk entering the house when there were easier ways.

A few of the precautions he had suggested had been taken. There were bars on the outer windows now, those of his—formerly Nefret's—room and of his parents'. They could be removed, but not without making a lot of noise. The gates were barred and the glow of a cigarette in one corner betokened the presence of Mustafa, Daoud's second son.

Finally the slits of light at his parents' window disappeared. He waited a little longer before lowering his feet to the ground.

Nefret was still awake. She was not alone. The voices were soft, he couldn't make out the words. Was she talking to the damned cat? Somehow he didn't think so.

Eavesdropping was a despicable habit. But, as he had once told his mother, cursed useful. I oughtn't do this, he thought, as he put his ear against the panel.

"You should tell him, David. It isn't fair not to."

"I know." David's voice was so low he could barely make out the words. "I've tried, but—"

He was not consciously aware of pressing the latch. The door seemed to open by itself. They were sitting side by side on the bed. Nefret's arm was around David, and he had covered his face with his hands.

David lowered his hands. "Ramses!"

"Excuse me." He stepped back. "I didn't know you were here."

"We were just about to go looking for you," Nefret said, jumping up. "Come in and close the door."

"No. I apologize for intruding. I'll go."

"What's the matter?" Nefret asked. "Is your hand bothering you?"

"No, not at all. I—"

"Close the damned door."

She did it for him and pushed him into the nearest chair. "I want to dress your hand again. David, get me a basin of water, will you?"

She cut through the cloth and guided his hand into the water. A green stain spread out, and Nefret eased the bandage off. "Amazing," she murmured. "The confounded stuff does seem to be effective. The swelling has gone down."

"It looks horrible," David said in a smothered voice.

"That's because it's green," Nefret explained.

"It does rather suggest rotting flesh," Ramses agreed. "But it feels considerably better. I suppose Kadija gave you the ointment this morning?"

"She slipped it to me while Aunt Amelia wasn't looking. Daoud got it from her, did you know that? She says the women of her family have handed the recipe down for generations. One of these days I must take a sample home and have it analyzed. Now, this is going to hurt. What shall we talk about that will prove sufficiently distracting? I know! Sir Edward. Do you think he's the Master Criminal in disguise?"

It did hurt. He set his teeth. "So that occurred to you, did it?"

"Really, Ramses, you are so exasperating! You might at least look surprised when I announce a startling theory. I've been thinking about the fortuitous appearance of the gallant Sir Edward. The last time we saw him was the year we had all that trouble with Riccetti and the rival gang of antiquities thieves. It was Sir Edward who rescued Aunt Amelia from one of the latter group. He had followed her that day for reasons that have never been satisfactorily explained—"

"That was just Father being sarcastic," Ramses said impatiently. "He thinks every man Mother meets falls madly in love with her."

"But Sir Edward wasn't madly in love with her, was he? So why *did* he follow her that day? Riccetti was trying to reestablish his control over the illegal antiquities game in Egypt. So were other people. Why should not one of them have been the Master Criminal himself?"

"It's an interesting idea," David said thoughtfully. "Sir Edward does match her description, doesn't he? Just under six feet tall, well-built, athletic. And an Englishman."

"He's too young," Ramses objected.

"Too young for what?" David asked. "He appears to be in his middle to late thirties, but the man is an expert at disguise. And you don't know how old Sethos was when you first met him. A very young man can be brilliant, and be capable of a grand passion."

Ramses stiffened. Nefret paused in the act of winding the bandage round his hand. "Too tight?"

"No. Get it over with, can't you?"

"Ungrateful brute," said Nefret without rancor. "There's another suspicious point about the gentleman. When we first knew him, he called himself a poor relation, a younger son who had to work for a living. You heard what he said the other night, about an inheritance from an uncle that had made him financially independent. So what's he doing in Egypt? He did demonstrate some interest in and talent for archaeology, but if that interest had been sincere he'd have come back before this, wouldn't he? Why has he turned up now? There you are, my boy. All done."

"Thank you." He wriggled the fingers she had left protruding. "Far be it from me to cast cold water on an intriguing theory, but I can think of another reason for Sir Edward's reapparance that has nothing to do with criminal activities."

Nefret sat back on her heels and smiled at him. "Me."

"You. Yes."

"Oh, he's interested," Nefret said calmly. "He might be even more interested if I gave him any encouragement."

"You've flirted outrageously with him!"

"Of course." Nefret chuckled. "It's fun. Ramses, you are such an old Puritan! If it will relieve your mind, I am not in love with Sir

Edward. He's extremely attractive and utterly charming, but I don't care for him that way."

"Then he wasn't the man you were seeing in . . . Sorry. None of my affair."

"In London?" The soft chuckle deepened into a laugh. "No, it isn't your affair, but if you hadn't been so confounded inquisitive I'd have told you. He was one of the medical students from Saint Bart's. I thought, innocent creature that I am, that he was interested in my *mind*. He wasn't. Now can we get back to business?"

Ramses nodded. A few days earlier he would have been delighted to learn she wasn't interested in Sir Edward or the unfortunate medical student (he wished he had been on the scene when Nefret dealt with the fellow's advances). Now there was another, far more dangerous rival. Or was there? He wondered if he was losing what was left of his mind.

"I suppose he can't be Sethos," Nefret admitted. "It's a pity. Aunt Amelia needs all the protectors she can find. Sethos would die to keep her from harm!"

"My God, you're beginning to romanticize the fellow," Ramses said in disgust.

"He is romantic," Nefret said dreamily. "Suffering from a hopeless passion for a woman he can never have, watching over her from the shadows . . ."

"You've been reading too many rotten novels," Ramses said caustically. "If Sethos is still in love with Mother, he'll be after her himself. If he isn't, he won't bother defending her."

"Goodness, what a cynic you are!" Nefret exclaimed.

"A realist," Ramses corrected. "Disinterested passion is a contradiction in terms. What man outside a romantic novel would risk his life for a woman he can never possess?"

"Didn't you risk yours, for Layla?"

Ramses shifted uncomfortably. "How the devil do we get onto such subjects? What I meant to say was that a second party who has designs on Mother is a complication we don't need. When is Sir Edward joining us?"

"Tomorrow. There's plenty of room if Uncle Walter and the others don't come."

Ramses nodded. "I only hope . . ."

"What?"

"That they can be persuaded to return home." Absently he rubbed his side.

Nefret put her hand over his. "Does it hurt? Let me give you something to help you sleep."

"It doesn't hurt, it itches. I don't need anything to help me sleep. I think I will turn in, though. It's been rather a long day."

It was a longer night. He dreamed again of fighting blindly in the dark, of hands that clawed and pounded at his face, of his own hands fumbling and failing, and finding at last the only hold that might save them. Again his stomach turned at the sound of shattering bone, again the brief flare of a match illumined the dead face. But this time the face was David's.

9

When I approached the verandah next morning I heard the murmur of voices and wondered who was up so early. Emerson had been splashing and sputtering over his ablutions when I left the room, so I concluded it must be the children.

I was in error.

"Good morning, Sir Edward," I said, surprised. "And—Fatima?"

"I intended to creep onto the verandah without disturbing anyone," he explained, rising to his feet. "But this kind woman found me and brought me tea."

Fatima ducked her head. "She has been good enough to allow me to practice my Arabic," Sir Edward went on easily. "I hope I am not too early? I wanted to be in time to accompany you to the Valley, and I know the Professor's habits."

"Excellent," I said. "The others will be here soon, Fatima; you may serve breakfast. Thank you."

"She understands English?" Sir Edward laughed ruefully. "I might have spared her my appalling Arabic had I known."

"She has been studying English, and learning to read as well. Ambition and intelligence and the love of learning are not limited to the masculine gender, or to a particular race, Sir Edward. We are all brothers and sisters in the eyes of heaven, and if education were available to Egyptians—"

"Lecturing again, Peabody?" said Emerson from the open door.

"Good morning, Sir Edward. Come and have breakfast, we must be off in a quarter of an hour."

It was nearer half an hour before we left the house, primarily because Ramses and Nefret got into another argument. She wanted him to wear the sling and he said he would not.

"You will keep hitting your hand," she insisted.

"It will be my own damned fault if I do," said Ramses.

I told Ramses not to swear and Nefret said he was a damned stubborn fool, and everyone added his opinion, except Sir Edward, who would have feigned a courteous deafness had that been possible, which it was not, since all their voices were quite loud. Emerson finally put an end to the discussion by shouting louder than anyone else and demanding that we get off at once.

I was especially glad that day that we had got into the habit of hiring horses for the season instead of relying on donkeys and our own feet. One feels—and is—much more vulnerable mounted on a little animal not much taller than oneself, which does not take kindly to moving faster than a trot. The boys' splendid steeds could outrun anything on four feet, and even the horses we had hired were in excellent condition, especially after I had attended to them as I always did animals that came under my care.

Sir Edward had borrowed one of Cyrus's mounts. It and the other horses were waiting when we emerged from the house. I watched Ramses out of the corner of my eye, wondering how he would manage; he had of course lost the argument and his right arm was enveloped in what appeared to be a bedsheet, for Nefret did nothing by halves. Risha snuffled inquiringly at the fabric, and, with an uncanny appearance of understanding the difficulty, adjusted his hindquarters in the position required for the spectacular flying mount Ramses used when he wanted to show off. Success depended in part on the strength and length of the rider's lower limbs, and Ramses accomplished it without visible effort.

We left the horses at the donkey park in charge of one of the attendants. The men, headed by Abdullah, were already at work. A cloud of pale dust surrounded the entrance of number Five, from which one of our brave fellows emerged carrying a basket of broken rock. The sound of pickaxes could be heard from within. Cursing, Emerson stripped off his coat and threw it on the ground. "Late!"

he cried, in poignant, generalized accusation, and without further ado plunged into the dark opening. Ramses promptly followed.

"Doesn't the Professor trust Abdullah to direct operations?" Sir Edward asked.

"As much as he trusts anyone. He believes he should be the one to make the decisions and take the risks."

"Risks?" Sir Edward glanced betrayingly at Nefret, who was helping David with the cameras.

"There are always risks entering a new tomb," I replied, dusting off Emerson's coat and putting it over my arm. "And this one is quite nasty—filled to the ceiling with broken rock and debris."

"Why bother with it, then?"

Emerson reappeared in time to hear the question. His black hair looked as if it had been powdered. "Why bother?" he repeated. "That, sir, is a stupid question from someone who claims to have an interest in Egyptology. However—" He turned and shouted, "Ramses! Come out of there!"

When Ramses had done so, Emerson said, "I am about to explain the interesting features of this tomb to Sir Edward. You and David have not been with us, so you may as well listen too."

Ramses opened his mouth, caught his father's eye, closed his mouth, and nodded.

"Ahem," said Emerson, removing a sheet of paper from his notebook. "This tomb is described by Baedeker and other sources as a short corridor tomb without inscriptions. This is not correct. Burton actually entered the place in 1830. His plan shows an arrangement quite unlike any other sepulchre in the Valley: a great sixteen-pillared hall, with smaller rooms on all four sides, and an extension of unknown length beyond. Burton couldn't get any farther. However, in two places he found traces of the prenomen of Ramses II. Wilkinson—"

"Emerson," I said, anticipating the interruption I could see hovering on the lips of my son, "you needn't go into such detail. You are boring Sir Edward."

"Not at all," said that gentleman with a winning smile. "The Professor is playing a little game with me, I think, or perhaps testing me. This cannot be the tomb of Ramses II, for his lies just across the way. Number Seven, isn't it?"

"Yes," said Emerson. "As I was saying before my wife interrupted me, the unusual plan and certain other evidence suggest this was a multiple burial. We have begun the clearance of the first chamber. It is slow going, since the cursed place is packed hard with rubble. I won't be needing you for a while, Ramses; you might—er—just go along and say hello to Ayrton. He missed you the other day. And," he added emphatically, "we missed him this morning because of being so confounded late."

"Yes, sir," said Ramses.

He and David, who of course accompanied him, were gone quite some time. We were about to stop for our mid-morning tea when they turned up, and Emerson immediately demanded to know what was going on.

"Nothing of interest," said Ramses, accepting a glass of tea. "Ned sent off a message to Mr. Davis yesterday informing him he had found a tomb, but—"

"What?" Emerson exclaimed. "Not that niche with the storage jars? That is obviously—"

"Yes, sir," said Ramses. "Some feet below that niche was a surface that had been squared off and smoothed, suggesting that a tomb might have been begun. That was why I remained, to see what came of it, but there was no entrance. Ned has just dispatched another messenger to tell Mr. Davis it had been a false alarm."

"What's he done with the jars?" Emerson asked greedily.

"Sent them to his house, I believe. Mr. Davis," said Ramses without expression, "will want to investigate them himself."

"Curse it," said Emerson.

The day passed without further discoveries by Ayrton or ourselves; there were reliefs on the walls of the first chamber, but not until later in the day, after the dust raised by the feet of the men had settled, were we able to examine them by candlelight. Though damaged, enough remained to arouse the interest of my hypercritical son.

"The scenes are reminiscent of those in the princes' tombs S. Schiaparelli found in the Valley of the Queens," he remarked. "We ought to get at them as soon as possible, Father, the plaster is loose and the least vibration—"

"Confound it, Ramses, I am only too well aware of that," Emerson replied. "It will have to wait until we have got the place cleared out a bit more. We will need better light. Reflectors might do it, but if I can run an electric wire . . ."

He stopped speaking, his face glum. He was remembering the happy days when Howard Carter held the post of Inspector. Emerson's slightest wish had been Howard's command, and Mr. Quibell, his successor, had been almost as obliging. It remained to be seen whether Mr. Weigall would agree to Emerson's request for a wire to be run from the electric engine in the tomb of Ramses XI. I was not particularly sanguine about it.

We returned to the house and dispersed in various directions—the children to the stable with the horses, Emerson to his desk in the sitting room. Sir Edward's luggage had been brought over from the hotel, so I showed him to his room and left him to unpack. After refreshing myself and changing my dusty clothes I told Fatima to serve tea and settled down on the verandah to read the messages that had been delivered.

There was only one of particular interest. After the others had joined me, I handed it to Emerson, to whom it had been addressed. With a sour look at me, he tossed it onto the table.

"I see you have already read it, Peabody. Why don't you just tell us what it says?"

"Certainly, my dear. It is a telegram from the Cairo police. They met the train, as we requested, but found no woman answering to Layla's description."

During the course of the day I had told Sir Edward about the steps we had taken, so he understood the reference. He shook his head doubtfully.

"She could easily have eluded them. You know what utter confusion reigns at the station—masses of people shoving and shouting, all trying to get on and off the train at the same time."

I had requested Nefret to pour. She looked very dainty and ladylike in her white muslin frock, though the bulk of Horus filling her lap and overflowing onto the settee rather spoiled the picture. The cat raised his head and growled at Ramses when he approached the table to take the cup Nefret had filled for him; being accustomed to Horus's little ways, he managed to get hold of it without being clawed. Retreating to the ledge, he said, "It is possible she never took the train, or intended to do so. She could have purchased the ticket as a blind, to mislead the others."

"That possibility occurred to me, of course," I said.

"Of course," Ramses echoed. He fished something out of his cup. "Nefret, could you keep that cat from dipping his tail in the tea?"

Sir Edward laughed and removed another hair from his upper lip. "They do shed in warm weather, don't they? That is a very handsome animal, Miss Forth. Yours, I presume?"

"If you are going to blather on about cats I am going to my study," Emerson grunted.

"I assure you, Emerson, I have more serious topics in mind," I told him. "But allow me to remind you that you were the one who complained the other day about conversation unsuitable for the tea table."

"On that occasion we were discussing mutilated bodies and hideous wounds," Emerson retorted, animation warming his tanned, well-formed features. "And murder cults. You were the one who brought up that absurd idea!"

"It has not been disproved. The crocodile god—"

"Has nothing to do with anything! Yussuf Mahmud—"

"Crocodiles!" Sir Edward exclaimed. He took a sandwich from the plate Fatima offered and gave her a smiling nod. "Forgive me for interrupting, sir, but I presume you are referring to the body drawn from the river last week. Do you believe that that bizarre incident is related to your present difficulties?"

"Not at all," said Emerson. "Mrs. Emerson is always getting off the track."

I would have pointed out the injustice of the charge had my mouth not been full of tomato sandwich. Before I could swallow, Ramses said coolly, "An interesting suggestion, Sir Edward. How much do you know about our present—er—difficulties?"

"Only what has occurred since my arrival in Luxor" was the prompt reply. "Far be it from me to inquire into matters of a private nature, but I would be better able to serve you if I were made cognizant of the relevant facts."

"The difficulty," I admitted, "is in knowing what facts are relevant. However, certain earlier incidents are almost certainly part of the business, and I agree you are entitled to hear of them."

I waited for an objection, but there was none, though Emerson scowled and Ramses looked particularly blank. I therefore proceeded to narrate the adventure of the three comrades and the Book of the Dead.

"Good God!" Sir Edward exclaimed. "*You* went to el Was'a, Miss Forth?"

Nefret banged her cup into her saucer with almost as much force as Emerson would have employed when in a similar state of indignation. "You may as well get one thing straight, Sir Edward, if you are to join our company. I am an adult, independent woman, and I won't allow any man, including you, to wrap me in cotton wool."

He apologized, fulsomely and at length, and at Nefret's request Emerson went and got the papyrus. Sir Edward studied it with the fascinated attention of a true scholar.

"Astonishing," he breathed. "What are you going to do with it?"

Ramses, who was standing guard over the scroll, replied, "It will go to a museum eventually, but not until after I have copied and translated it."

"It appears to be in excellent condition." Sir Edward reached out his hand. Ramses slid the lid over the box.

"It will not remain in that condition if it is handled repeatedly."

I resumed my narrative. When I had finished, Sir Edward said, "As I once mentioned, Mrs. Emerson, your narrative style is remarkably vivacious. You believe, then, that the papyrus is the object of the attentions you have received?"

"It is one possibility," said Ramses.

"Yes, quite. What are your plans, then? For I feel sure you don't mean to sit idly by until something else happens."

"There is not a great deal we can do," said Ramses, who had obviously appointed himself spokesman. "Layla is the only person we know about—the only one who isn't dead, that is—and we have not yet succeeded in tracing her. She is not in Gurneh. Abdullah and his people conducted a house-to-house search, and I assure you, they were thorough."

"Have you questioned her former—er—associates?"

He looked apologetically at Nefret, who said, "Prostitutes, you mean."

"Er—yes."

"We have already investigated that group," said Ramses.

"We?" Sir Edward repeated, raising one eyebrow.

"We!" I exclaimed. "What have you done? Ramses, I strictly forbade you and David to . . . Where did you go—and how, if a mere mother may ask, did you *know* where to go?"

"Now, Peabody, calm yourself," Emerson began.

"Emerson, how could you allow them to do such a thing?"

"Someone had to," Emerson insisted. "Layla might have sought temporary refuge with her—er—sisters in misfortune. Don't be such a bloo—blooming hypocrite, Peabody, you know perfectly well you would have gone yourself if I had given you the chance."

"None of them admitted knowing anything," said Ramses. "But one would not expect them to, in front of the others. I mentioned a reward. We may yet receive information from one of the—er—ladies."

"Girls, you mean," Nefret muttered. "Some of them no older than—"

Ramses broke into a fit of coughing, and Nefret said hastily, "I'm sure you would like more tea, Sir Edward. Do bring me your cup."

He rose obediently, smiling a little, and approached her.

"And how," I inquired, "do you know their ages?"

"Curse it!" said Nefret.

"Damnation!" said Sir Edward, dropping his cup. Tepid tea and bright red blood dripped onto Nefret's skirt. Growling, Horus withdrew the paw that had raked Sir Edward's hand.

I administered first aid and apologies, which Sir Edward accepted with the comment that he was pleased to know Miss Forth had such a faithful guardian. Nefret made good her escape, with the excuse—which had a certain validity—that she must change and rinse the blood out before it set. Emerson declared he had work to do before dinner. Sir Edward said he believed he would take a stroll. How the boys eluded me I do not know, but when I looked round I realized I was alone.

I went after Ramses first, but could not locate him or David anywhere in the house. Nefret had barred her door. She pretended not to hear my knock, so I went round to the window and banged on the shutters until she opened them.

We had a little chat.

When I left her I looked for Emerson and found he had gone to earth in a quiet corner of the courtyard. He was smoking his pipe and talking with Ramses. Ramses got to his feet when he saw me.

He may have been exhibiting the good manners I had taught him, but his pose strongly suggested that he was about to bolt.

"Don't scold the lad, Peabody," Emerson said, making room for me on the bench. "He came to me, in a very manly fashion, and attempted to take full responsibility for Nefret's behavior. I do not hold him accountable." He sighed. "I do not hold anyone accountable for Nefret."

"I have just talked with her," I said.

"Ah," said Emerson hopefully. "Did she promise she would never do it again?"

"No. She said she would do it again as soon as she could, and as often as possible." I smiled somewhat ruefully at my son. "Sit down, Ramses, and don't look so wary. I do not blame you. Nefret is . . . In a nutshell, she is precisely the daughter I would have chosen! She is determined to help those unfortunate women, and I believe she can and will."

"She wants to help the whole bloody suffering world," Ramses said. He appeared to be watching a beetle that was heading purposefully for a bit of bread crust. "She'll break her heart, Mother."

"Broken hearts can be mended," I said. "A heart that is impervious to pain is also impervious to joy."

Emerson snorted, and Ramses looked up. "No doubt that is true, Mother. However, we must also consider the risk to Nefret's—er—body. Aside from the other dangers involved in attacking a business enterprise of that sort, there is the strong possibility that some of the women in the House of the Doves are in the pay of our unknown enemy."

"Damned right," said Emerson. "None of you is to go to that quarter again, do you hear?"

"I doubt additional visits would produce useful results," Ramses replied. "We have done what we could."

"Agreed," I said. "Now go and find David, Ramses, and tell him it is safe to come out of hiding. Dinner will be ready shortly."

After he had taken a cup of postprandial coffee with us, Sir Edward begged to be excused. "I have letters to write," he explained with a smile. "My dear mother is quite frail; I try to write at least three times a week."

"If she is that confounded frail, why doesn't he stay with her?" Emerson inquired after the young man had left the room.

"That was only a courteous excuse, Emerson. He does not wish to intrude on our privacy. Speaking of letters, we have messages of our own to write. I will write Evelyn; will you pen a line to Walter? The rest of you may include messages if you like; remember, we must convince them to return home at once, but avoid alarming them."

"Not such an easy task," Ramses murmured.

Nor was it. I labored for some time over my note, rubbing words out and changing them. When at last I was satisfied I had done the best I could, I put down my pencil. His pen poised, David was frowning over the paper on the table before him. The others, including Emerson, were reading.

"I thought you were going to write Walter, Emerson," I said.

"I have."

I picked up the paper he indicated. It read: "Catch the next boat home. Sincere regards, R.E."

"Really, Emerson," I exclaimed.

"Well, why repeat information you have probably given in excruciating detail? You've been at it for hours, Peabody."

"Hardly so long, my dear. I have given them all the necessary information, however. Nefret, do you want to add anything?"

"That depends on how detailed that information of yours is," Nefret replied. "What did you say about Ramses and David? You know how Aunt Evelyn worries."

"You may read the letter if you like."

Ramses leaned over her shoulder and read with her. "Hmmm. You have vivid powers of description, Mother. Perhaps I had better add a few lines of reassurance."

"With your left hand?" Nefret shook her head. "My dear boy, a scrawl like that would only worry Aunt Evelyn more. I know; I will append a medical report. The facts will be less alarming than the fancies a loving imagination can invent."

She was still writing when Selim and Daoud came in. They were to catch the morning train, so Emerson gave them money for expenses and warned them again to be on the alert.

"Stay until you have seen them board the boat," he instructed. "No matter how long it takes. Curse it," he added gloomily, contemplating the reduction of his work force by two of its most valuable members.

"What if Mr. Walter Emerson will not go?" Selim inquired.

"Knock him on the head and—"

"Now, Emerson, don't confuse the lad," I said, for Selim's eyes and mouth had gone wide with consternation. "You must just ... Well. What should he do?"

"It is high time someone asked that question," said Ramses. "We've been talking about them as if they were parcels to be dispatched at our convenience. I've seen Aunt Evelyn in action, and I assure you she will not take kindly to being ordered about."

"Walter won't want to go either," I agreed. "But there is the child. They cannot send her home unaccompanied, and they surely won't expose her to danger. No loving parent would."

The silence that ensued was not precisely uncomfortable. Not precisely. Ramses, who was standing behind Nefret with his hands resting on the back of her chair, stared off into space with a particularly blank expression.

"Hmph," said Emerson loudly. "Selim was quite right to raise the point. There is a possibility, I suppose, that Walter will pack Evelyn and the child onto the boat and come on here himself. Evelyn might not like it, but she would accept it. Not even she would expect him to let her come alone, or bring Lia."

"I wouldn't count on that," I said. "If one or all of them insists on coming here, Selim, he—or she!—must do as she likes. They are free agents, after all. We can only advise and warn, we cannot command them."

We gave the letters to Selim and wished him and Daoud a good journey. Daoud embraced David and wrung Ramses's and Emerson's hands. He was a very silent man, but he had followed every word with extreme interest, and he was obviously pleased and proud to have been selected for such an important mission.

We dispersed shortly thereafter. Emerson went off arm in arm with Nefret; I knew he would find some transparent excuse to search her room before he let her enter it. I followed Ramses, and caught him up at the door of his room.

"Yes, Mother?" He raised an inquiring eyebrow.

"How is your hand? Would you like me to have a look at it?"

"Nefret changed the bandage before we went to dinner."

"A little laudanum to help you sleep?"

"No, thank you." He waited for a moment, watching me. Then he said, "You didn't expose me to danger, Mother. You did your damnedest to keep me out of it."

"Don't swear, Ramses."

"I beg your pardon, Mother."

"Good night, my dear."

"Good night, Mother."

I had long since despaired of persuading my family to attend church services on Sunday. Their religious backgrounds were diverse, to say the least. David's father had been a Christian, in name at least, though, in Abdullah's picturesque words, he had "died cursing God." Nefret had been Priestess of Isis in a community where the old gods of Egypt were worshiped, and I had a nasty suspicion she had not entirely abandoned her belief in those heathen deities. Perhaps she shared the views of Abdullah, who was something of a heathen himself: "There is no harm in protecting oneself from that which is not true!" Emerson's views on the subject of organized religion ranged from the blasphemous to the merely rude, and Ramses never expressed his views, if he had any. So for us the Sabbath was a workday like any other, since we allowed our Moslem workers their day of rest on Friday. We were therefore up bright and early and ready to return to the Valley. It had been a quiet night, without incident.

Later that morning Ned Ayrton joined us for a brief period of refreshment, as he had got into the habit of doing. Let me add that this was in no way a reflection upon his work habits, which were conscientious to a fault. Many excavators do not pause for breakfast until after they have been at work for several hours. We always took a little rest and a cup of tea at around ten in the morning, and so did Ned. I do not believe I will be accused of vanity when I say that he enjoyed our company. In response to Emerson's pointed inquiry he said his men were sinking a pit below the squared-off area they had discovered the day before.

"It has been rather hard going," he explained. "The limestone chips have been soaked by water and are fused together like cement."

"Not a good sign," said Emerson, stroking his chin.

"No. One can only hope that if there is a tomb entrance below, the rain did not penetrate so far. Well, I have been too long away; it is the pleasure of your company, Mrs. Emerson, that is to blame."

After he had gone, I said, "Mr. Davis's expectations are so high they must make Ned very nervous. I cannot suppose he will find anything where he is digging now."

"Hmmm," said Emerson.

I am convinced my husband has a sixth sense for such things. It was not until later in the afternoon, just as we were about to stop for the day, that Ned came running back to tell us the news. "Eureka!" was his first word, and his last for a time; he was too out of breath to continue.

"Ah," said Emerson. "So you've found a tomb entrance, have you?"

"Yes, sir. Rock-cut steps, at any rate. I thought perhaps you might want to have a look."

It was a polite way of putting it. Wild horses could not have kept Emerson away. The rest of us followed.

The opening lay directly to the right of the open entrance to the tomb of Ramses IX. Mounds of debris still surrounded it, but the top of a stone-cut stair was clearly visible.

Ned's men were still at work shoveling rock into baskets, clearing down the steps. Emerson snatched a shovel from one of them. His eyes were glazed, his lips half parted. Those who have felt that passion for discovery, and have been deprived of it for too long, can comprehend the intensity of his emotion at that moment. I can only compare it with the feelings of a starving individual who sees a platter of rare roast beef. He does not care that it is not *his* roast beef. If he is hungry enough, he will have it, whatever the consequences.

It well-nigh broke my heart to stop him, but I knew I must. "Emerson, my dear, Mr. Ayrton's men are shoveling quite nicely. You will only get in their way."

Emerson started and came out of his trance. "Er—hmmm. Yes. It—er—certainly looks promising, Ayrton. Good clean fill just here; no water. Typical Eighteenth Dynasty type. Probably undisturbed since the Twentieth Dynasty."

Ned smiled and brushed the damp hair away from his perspiring face. "I am glad to hear you say so, sir. You see, I rather jumped the gun day before yesterday—sent Mr. Davis a message saying I'd found him a tomb, and then had to take it back. I didn't want to make the same mistake a second time."

"The place could have been robbed ten times over before the entrance was concealed under the debris," Emerson said. "Almost certainly was. Hmph. It shouldn't take more than a few hours to . . ."

Then, dear Reader, the true mettle of the man I had married was displayed. At that moment there was nothing on earth Emerson desired more than a glimpse of what lay at the bottom of those stone-cut steps. If the discovery had been his—as it ought to have been—he would have uncovered the entrance that day, with his bare hands if need be, and camped on the spot all night to protect his find. The struggle was intense, but professional honor won out over envy.

Emerson squared his mighty shoulders. "Stop," he said.

"Sir?" Ned stared in wonderment.

Like myself, Ramses knew his father had gone as far as he was capable of going. He put a friendly hand on the young man's shoulder. "You don't want to expose the entrance and leave it open overnight."

"Good Lord, no, I couldn't do that. Mr. Davis will want to be here when we open it."

"Unless you think he will want to come round this evening, you had better stop, then." Ramses ran an expert eye over the rough opening. "It's likely there are not more than a dozen steps, and the fill is loose here."

"Yes, of course." Ned smiled apologetically. "You must think me a blundering fool. I suppose I was a bit excited. It is always rather exciting, isn't it—a new tomb? Not knowing what might be there?"

"Yes," said Emerson morosely. "It is. Rather."

Ned went with us as far as the donkey park and then struck off on foot, heading for the house Davis had had built for him near the entrance to the Valley. No wonder he was pleased. Even if the tomb turned out to be unfinished or completely plundered in ancient times, it was a good sign to find one at all.

We had been invited to attend one of Cyrus's Sunday-evening soirees that night. He was a sociable individual, and took even greater pleasure in entertaining now that he had Katherine as his hostess.

I was of two minds about going. Ordinarily I take pleasure in respectable social events, and Cyrus's entertainments were always elegant and refined. Many of our friends would be present, including two of the best—Katherine and Cyrus themselves.

Yet I found myself disinclined that evening for pleasure. My thoughts were otherwise engaged, following in imagination the activities of those who were far away. Selim and Daoud were still on the train. They would not arrive in Cairo until later that evening, with the briefer journey to Alexandria still ahead. If it was not delayed, the steamer would soon arrive in the harbor, where it would drop anchor; the passengers would disembark the following morning. We could not expect news until later that same day, for explanations and decisions would take time, and it was possible Walter would decide to go on to Cairo, where we had booked rooms for them at Shepheard's. To take Lia home without a glimpse of even the pyramids and the Sphinx would be too cruel, after her high expectations; a father as fond as Walter would surely be unable to resist her pleas. If they remained in Cairo for a time, perhaps I could just run up to see them, and have a little look round . . .

Too many ifs! I would have to wait another twenty-four hours, at least, before I knew what they intended.

I came to the logical conclusion that brooding would not be good for us. There was nothing we could do that evening anyhow.

I discovered that the others had expected we would go and that even Emerson was resigned, if not enthusiastic. He gave me the usual argument about wearing formal dress, which, as usual, I won. Cyrus had sent his carriage for us. Since it would have been a bit of a squeeze for our entire party, Sir Edward announced he would ride horseback. Emerson had cast a reproachful glance at me when he found that Sir Edward and the boys were not in evening kit. I was hardly in a position to lecture Sir Edward; when I lectured Ramses, he explained disingenuously that studs and links were too difficult to attach with only one hand.

I decided to let him off this time, but there was another question I wanted to ask. I had feared he might use his damaged hand as an excuse for letting his beard grow; men seem to favor the cursed things. He had remained clean-shaven, however, and as I straightened his cravat and tucked his collar in I asked how he managed it.

"I have been using a safety razor for several years now, Mother," was the reply. "I am surprised you did not know."

"I am not in the habit of searching your personal belongings, Ramses," I said.

"Of course not, Mother. I didn't mean to imply—"

Emerson interrupted with the remark he always made on such occasions—"If we must do this, let's get it over with."

The electric current, which was notoriously erratic, appeared to be functioning that evening. The windows of the Castle shone hospitably through the darkness, and Cyrus was waiting to greet us. There was only time for his question—"Anything new?"—and my brief reply in the negative before the arrival of other guests recalled him to his duties as host.

Familiar faces and forms filled the great drawing room; familiar voices were raised in laughter and conversation. Yet as I stood a little to one side, sipping my wine, I found myself studying those faces with a new interest. Was there among them a new, unknown enemy—or an old one?

There were always a good many strangers in Luxor during the season. Some of them I knew slightly. Emerson was engaged in conversation with one, a certain Lord . . . for the moment the name escaped me, but I remembered that he had recently come to Egypt for his health and had become interested in excavating. He was tall enough, but since he was a married man I assumed his wife would notice a substitution. Unless she was also . . .

Nonsense, I told myself. Sethos could not be among those present. I had known him in London; I would know him in Luxor, in any disguise he could assume.

As for unknown enemies—well, that offered infinite possibilities. Most of the dealers in illegal antiquities were Egyptians or Turks, but as painful experience had taught me, Europeans also engaged in that ugly trade, and they were likely to be more dangerous and unscrupulous than their native counterparts. Since Sethos's retirement a number of people had attempted to take over all or part of his organization. The stout German baron, the elegant young French-man who was gazing soulfully at Nefret, the red-faced English squire—any one of them could be a criminal.

A touch on my arm roused me from my thoughts, and I turned to see Katherine beside me. She was wearing a gown she had had made up in London, incorporating panels of Turkish embroidery and green silk, and the parure of emeralds that had been Cyrus's wedding gift.

"No corsets," she whispered with a conspiratorial smile. "Come and sit down for a moment, I have been on my feet for hours."

We withdrew into a retired corner, and Katherine said, "I want to talk with you about my new project, Amelia. I spoke with Miss Buchanan at the American School for Girls a few days ago. It made me feel quite ashamed of my nationality. The Americans have done so much more than we English to improve the lot of Egyptian women—schools and hospitals all over the country—"

"As well as churches," I said. "I would be the last to deny the great good these dedicated persons have done, but they are mis-sionaries and their primary aim is to convert the heathen."

"Wasn't it Henry the Fourth who remarked that 'Paris is worth a mass' when his claim to the throne of France was made dependent on his conversion to Catholicism? Perhaps education is worth a prayer." I smiled wryly in acknowledgment, and Katherine went on, "However, there is certainly room here for a school that makes no such demands, and that opens education even to those who cannot afford the fees of the Mission School. Miss Buchanan amiably agreed, and offered to assist me in any way she could."

"Splendid," I said heartily. "I am delighted that you are going ahead with your project, Katherine, and I promise I will do my part. I meant some days ago to make the acquaintance of Fatima's teacher, but I have not had the time to do so."

"I have. Fatima gave me her name, and I called on her yesterday. She is an interesting woman, Amelia—handsome and well-educated and obviously of a superior class. Admirable as are the methods of the Americans, we can learn something from teachers like Sayyida Amin."

"Ah, so she prefers the title Sayyida to that of Madame? That suggests she is not in sympathy with Western ideas of emancipa-tion."

"A good many educated Egyptians, male and female, resent our presence and our ideas," Katherine said soberly. "It is not surprising that they should."

"Quite. Kindly condescension can be as infuriating as outright insult. Not that either of us would fall into those errors! I am sorry I was unable to go with you, Katherine. I have been just a little preoccupied recently."

"You certainly have!"

I told her of the present progress of the investigation—or, to be more accurate, the lack of progress. I would not have ventured to tell any other woman of my acquaintance about Nefret's visit to the house of ill fame, but I felt certain Katherine's unorthodox background would make her more tolerant of those who have, often through no fault of their own, strayed beyond the bounds of conventional society. As usual, my judgment was correct.

"She is a remarkable girl, Amelia. One can only admire her courage and compassion—and fear for her well-being. You are going to have your hands full."

"They are already full. Ramses is enough to drive any parent over the brink of sanity, and I daresay even David will have his problems."

I had observed him talking with a girl who was a stranger to me—one of the recent crop of tourists, I assumed. She was fair-haired and elaborately dressed in a frock of azure blue embroidered with rosebuds that bared plump white shoulders. It was unusual to see David without Ramses or Nefret or both; he was rather shy with strangers, but he appeared to be responding to this young woman, who was flirting with him over her fan.

At that moment a stocky older lady, whom I took to be the girl's mama, bustled up to them. Taking the girl firmly by the arm, she drew her away, without so much as a nod at David.

"I daresay he already has a good many," Katherine said thoughtfully. "He is a handsome young fellow, and those exotic looks of his cannot but be intriguing to the girls; but what responsible mama would allow her daughter to become seriously involved with him?"

"She needn't have been so rude about it. Goodness, Katherine, we sound like a pair of empty-headed gossips."

At that point Katherine was called away by guests who were about to take their leave. I remained where I was, observing that

Ramses had joined David, and that Emerson had collared Howard Carter and was lecturing him about something, and that Nefret was . . . Where was she?

My agitated gaze soon found her, the center of a group of young gentlemen, but that pang of alarm, brief though it had been, made me decide we had better return home. I do not often suffer from nerves, but I did that night.

I collected my family and Sir Edward and we made our excuses. As we stood waiting for the carriage, Cyrus's gatekeeper, an elderly Egyptian who had been with him for many years, came up to me.

"A person gave me this, Sitt Hakim. She said it was for Nur Misur, but—"

"Then you should give it to me, Sayid," Nefret exclaimed. She reached for the grubby little packet, barely an inch square, that rested on the gatekeeper's palm.

Ramses's hand got there before hers. "Hold on, Nefret. Who was it who gave you this, Sayid?"

The old man shrugged. "A woman. She said—"

We extracted a description, such as it was. Veiled and robed, the anonymous figure had not lingered or spoken more than a few words. She had not given him money, but he assumed . . .

"Yes, yes," said Emerson, handing over a few coins. "Let me have that, Ramses."

Nefret let out an indignant exclamation.

"I suggest," said Ramses, closing his fingers tightly over the packet, "that we wait until we get home. It is too dark to see clearly, and too public."

The sense of this could not be gainsaid, but we were all on fire with curiosity by the time we reached the house, and without a moment's delay we hurried into the sitting room. Fatima had lit the lamps and was waiting to see if we wanted anything.

Ramses put the packet down on the table in the glow of a nearby lamp. The cheap coarse paper had been folded tightly into multiple layers. It was very dirty, but I thought I saw traces of writing.

"I recommend it be handled with care," Ramses said. "Father?"

I felt certain he would not have left it to Emerson if he had had the use of both hands. For once I did not volunteer. The folded paper filled me with a strange revulsion. I did not believe it contained anything dangerous, but I did not want to touch it.

With the same delicacy of touch he displayed when handling fragile antiquities, Emerson unfolded the paper, placed it on the table and smoothed it out. There was writing on it—only a few words, in crudely formed Arabic letters.

" 'Sunrise,' " Emerson read. " 'The Mosque of Sheikh el . . . Graib,' is it?"

"Guibri, I think," Ramses said, bending over the paper. "There are two more words. 'Help me.' "

For a moment no one spoke. The lamplight shone on the strong hands of Emerson, flat on the table, the crumpled paper between them, and on the intent faces bent over the message. Nefret let out a long breath.

"Thank heaven. I hoped she would trust me! Now I can—"

"There were a dozen women there," Ramses said flatly. "Which one are you talking about?"

"She was wearing . . . Oh, never mind, you wouldn't have noticed. It was the way she looked at me."

"Hmph," said Ramses.

"Er—yes," said Emerson. "Does it matter which one it is? One of them, it seems, is asking for our help—and, it may be, offering hers. I will go, of course."

"*My* help," Nefret said. "It was I to whom she directed the message."

"Damn it," said Ramses. "Excuse me, Mother. Stop and think, all of you. This message cannot have come from one of those women. None of them knows how to write!"

"You don't know that," Nefret said.

"It is a reasonable assumption, however," Emerson agreed. He stroked his chin. "A public letter writer?"

"She wouldn't risk it," Ramses insisted. "Anyhow, it's too crudely written."

"It reminds me," David began.

He was not given the opportunity to finish. Emerson declared that someone must keep the assignation. Nefret insisted it must be she. The table shuddered; Horus, returning from one of his nightly strolls, had leaped onto it and was trying to get Nefret's attention. Failing in this, he sniffed curiously at the note.

"Get it away from him, Nefret," I ordered.

It was too late. Horus hissed and spat and shredded the paper with his claws.

"I hope," said Emerson, "that you won't take this as one of your confounded omens, Peabody."

It would have been difficult to interpret Horus's actions as symptomatic of anything in particular. I needed no such portent to make me regard the forthcoming expedition with extreme trepidation. We had agreed it must take place; if the appeal was genuine it could not be ignored. Ramses insisted it must be a trick, but even he admitted the place and time of the assignation were those such a woman might have chosen. The mosque in question was not far from the house they had visited, and early morning, while the others were resting, offered the best opportunity for her to slip away.

What with one thing and another I did not enjoy a quiet night's repose. I do not believe Emerson slept at all. When he shook me awake it was still dark outside, and sunrise was several hours away when we assembled in the sitting room for a hasty breakfast. Since we had not been able to agree on which of us should go, we were all going, including Sir Edward.

He had said very little the night before, and he applied himself to his food in thoughtful silence.

"You have said very little, Sir Edward," I remarked. "I have the impression you do not approve of this."

He looked up, his brow furrowed. "I have a number of reservations, Mrs. Emerson. I cannot believe one of those women would venture to communicate with you, or be able to do so in writing. What Miss Forth said to them must be known by now to most of the residents of Luxor. A resourceful enemy could make use of it to lure you into a trap."

"We went over all that last night," I reminded him. "And agreed that the chance must be taken."

"Then there is no use in my trying to dissuade you."

"None at all," said Nefret.

He bowed his head in silent acquiescence, but as we proceeded to mount the horses I saw he was fingering something in his pocket.

A pistol? I rather hoped it was. I myself was armed "to the teeth," as Emerson caustically remarked: my little pistol in one pocket, my knife in the other, my parasol in my hand. My belt I had left behind, but most of its useful accoutrements had been distributed among my other pockets. One never knows when a sip of brandy will be needed, or the means of striking a light.

The first faint blush of dawn outlined the eastern mountains when we disembarked on the quay in Luxor. We were not the only early risers; lighted windows in the hotels indicated that the tourists were up and dressing, and shadowy forms in long galabeeyahs moved along the street on their way to work or to prayers. We were in good time, for our destination was not far distant.

"Wait," Ramses said suddenly.

"Why? What?" I cried, raising my parasol and darting suspicious looks all round.

"Wait until it is light enough to see where we are going," Ramses elaborated. "Confound it, this is dangerous enough by daylight."

In another ten minutes Emerson decreed it was safe to go on. Though it had fewer than twelve thousand inhabitants, Luxor boasted eight or nine mosques, none particularly distinguished for antiquity or architectural distinction. That of Sheikh el Guibri was less than half a mile from the riverbank. The street on which it was located was no more than a country road, unpaved and dusty. We had not quite reached it when the first call to prayer rose into the clear morning air. The muezzins are individualists, defining the exact moment of sunrise according to their own notions. This earliest call came from one of the mosques farther south, but Nefret quickened her pace and was only restrained from drawing ahead of the boys by Emerson, who held her hand tightly in his. We had her safely surrounded, since Sir Edward and I brought up the rear, but I doubted she would accept this state of things for long.

The mosque stood back a little from the road. Through the open arch of the entrance we could see into the courtyard with its fountain and surrounding libans. An adjoining structure with a domed roof presumably housed the tomb of the holy man after whom the mosque was named. From the minaret, the muezzin added his voice—baritone, cracked with age—to the chorus.

There were a number of people abroad, walking or riding donkeys, or driving carts loaded with produce. A woman balancing a load of reeds on her head gave us a curious look as she passed. We were certainly conspicuous; few tourists came this way.

"I am going into the courtyard," Nefret said in a low voice. "She wouldn't approach me here on the road."

"Not a good idea," said Ramses. "She would be even more conspicuous inside. Women are not encouraged to pray in public. The rest of you go on, toward the tomb. We will wait here."

"We? Curse it, Ramses, you agreed—"

"I lied," Ramses said coolly. "We can't take the chance, there are too many people about. She's seen me and David with you, and if her intentions are honorable she wouldn't expect you to be alone."

We waited for another quarter hour, until the last dilatory notes of the call to prayer had died away and the red globe of the sun had lifted over the eastern mountains. Emerson was getting restless. We joined the children, who were—not surprisingly—arguing.

"Are you sure this is the right place?" Nefret demanded.

"No." Ramses kept glancing uneasily around. "The writing was atrocious, and there are two mosques with similar names. I'd have had another look if the damned cat hadn't ripped the paper to shreds."

"She's not coming," Emerson said. "Or she never meant to come. Or—"

"Or Sir Edward was correct," I said, glancing at that gentleman, who did not reply. Like Ramses, he was watching the passersby. "This was a trap that failed. They did not dare attack all of us."

At Nefret's urging we stopped by the other mosque—that of Sheikh el Graib—on our way back to the quay. It was in a more populous section, closer to the Luxor Temple. The street was teeming with the usual morning traffic by that time, but the mosque itself was quiet, morning prayers being over. Nefret had not given up hope of a message, at least; she walked slowly along the facade of the building, looking from side to side; but it was Ramses, close on her heels, who spotted the small object lying in the dust.

It was a thin gold disk, pierced by a small hole—the sort of ornament that hangs from the earrings and headcloths of Egyptian women.

10

What was the import of that little golden disk? Most probably nothing. Such ornaments were common, and even if it had belonged to the woman who had written us, it might have fallen unnoticed from a piece of jewelry. Nefret insisted it had been left deliberately, as a sign that the girl had kept the appointment but had been unable to remain. I considered this unlikely. The woman must have known such a token would not have been left lying in the dust for long. To an indigent peasant the bit of gold represented food for days.

In my case at least relief won out over disappointment, and I fancy most of the others felt the same. If what we hoped had not occurred, at least that which we feared had not happened either. Studying Nefret's crestfallen face, observing the determined set of her jaw, I decided I had better have another little chat with her. No one admired her courage and compassion more than I, but it would be madness for her to venture again into the house of ill fame.

On our way back to the riverbank we passed near the telegraph office, but I did not suggest we stop. We could not expect a message from Walter so soon, and Emerson would have objected to any further delay. He had already lost several hours on what he was pleased to call a wild goose chase, and he grudged every minute away from his work.

It had proved to be more onerous than even he had expected. The debris that filled the first chamber contained hundreds of bits and pieces: fragments of pottery and alabaster jars, beads of all varieties, scraps of wood and scraps of people—mummified people, that is. By Emerson's meticulous standards every scrap had to be preserved and recorded. Dedicated scholar that he is, he became quite interested in the proceedings and (to my relief) did not even send anyone down the path to spy on poor Ned Ayrton.

Early in the afternoon I suggested to Emerson that we return to the house. "We ought to have had a message from Walter by now. I asked him to telegraph at the earliest possible moment."

Emerson looked blank. So obsessed was he by archaeological matters that it took him a moment to understand my reference. "I don't know why you are making such a fuss, Peabody. Either Walter has sent a telegram or he has not. What you expect me to do about it?"

"Send one of the men to the telegraph office. You know how dilatory the clerks are, messages sometimes lie on the desk for days."

"Oh, bah," said Emerson. "I cannot spare another man, Peabody. I am short-handed as it is with Selim and Daoud gone."

So I sent Abdullah. It was a very warm day, and I wanted to get him out of the infernal heat and dust of the tomb. After I had given him my instructions and told him to meet us back at the house, Nefret beckoned to me from the rubbish heap in a conspiratorial manner.

"Mr. Davis just went past," she whispered.

"Which way? In or out?"

"Out. He must have got past us earlier without being seen. He was looking very pleased with himself, Aunt Amelia."

"Oh? Well. Perhaps those steps of Ned's led to something after all. How nice for Mr. Davis."

Nefret's conspiratorial smile broadened into a grin. "Yes, isn't it? Do you mind if I go over there and see?"

"Do as you like, my dear."

"Don't you want to come with me?"

"Now that you mention it . . ." I said.

Somehow I was not at all surprised to find Ramses already there. The last time I had set eyes on him he had been in a far corner of the tomb chamber squinting at a cartouche, but he was an expert at eluding people—especially his mother. He and Ned stood partway down the steps, gazing at what lay below.

The full length of the stairs was now exposed, though they had not been completely cleared. At the bottom was a wall of rough stones, unmortared and unevenly cut. It filled the neatly cut rectangular space that was undoubtedly the entrance to a tomb.

"Has the wall been breached?" I demanded.

"One can always count on you, Mother, to go straight to the heart of the matter," said Ramses, reaching up a hand to help me as I scrambled down. The steps were a bit treacherous, littered with smaller pebbles and quite steep. "It appears it has not been. It's a rather makeshift construction, though; Ned and I have just been discussing the possibility that it may not be the original blockage. We . . . Nefret, don't come down, there's not room for another person."

"Then you come up. I want to see."

After she had had her turn, I said, "How splendid, Ned. I suppose Mr. Davis is anxious to have that wall down. Are you going to take photographs this afternoon, or will there be time tomorrow morning?"

"He directed me to have everything prepared for him in the morning."

It was a somewhat evasive answer. Ramses caught my eye—Ned was carefully not looking at either of us—and said casually, "I was about to tell Ned we would be happy to take a few photographs for him. We have our equipment here, and it wouldn't take long."

"That would be good of you," Ned said, looking relieved. "I haven't a camera with me, and the light will be fading soon, and—er—"

"Quite," I said briskly. "Nefret?"

She hurried away. Turning back to Ned, I said, "Have you notified Mr. Weigall? Since this is a new tomb, it becomes the responsibility of the Inspector."

"He and Mrs. Weigall are having tea with Mr. Davis. I believe he plans to inform him then."

When Nefret returned, Emerson was with her. I had been afraid he would, but there was nothing I could do about it.

I asked Ned to come back to the house with us and have tea, but he declined, saying he had a great deal of work to do. The truth was, an hour of Emerson's company was about all he could stand. Emerson was not rude—not by his standards, that is—but his enormous energy and emphatic lectures are hard on the young and timid.

Abdullah had returned with the longed-for telegram, which the clerk assured him had just that minute arrived. "Your messages received," it read. "Discussions underway. Will wire tonight or tomorrow. Take care."

"Sent from Cairo," I said.

"I hope they will make up their minds soon," Emerson grumbled. "I cannot spare Daoud and Selim."

We were at the dig at our usual hour next morning, shortly after sunrise. It was not until after 10 A.M. that Mr. Davis and his entourage appeared.

There were dozens of them! The Weigalls, Mrs. Andrews and her nieces, the Smiths, servants carrying cushions, sunshades, and baskets of food and drink, and several elegantly costumed individuals I did not know—distinguished visitors who had been invited to watch Mr. Davis find a tomb. It looked for all the world like a group of Cook's tourists on a sight-seeing jaunt.

Mr. Davis was attired in his favorite "professional" garb: riding breeches and buttoned gaiters, tweed jacket and waistcoat, and a broad-brimmed felt hat. He nodded at me, but I doubt he would have stopped had not Emerson hailed him.

The contrast between them was ludicrous: Mr. Davis, dapper and neat, if somewhat ridiculous, in those old-fashioned garments; Emerson, trousers and boots white with dust, shirt open to the waist and sleeves rolled to the elbows. I could see he had determined to be cordial if it killed him. Baring his teeth in a friendly grin, he strode forward and offered his hand. Dripping with a pale paste composed of dust and perspiration, covered with bleeding scratches, it was not the sort of object one would wish to grasp, but Mr. Davis could not avoid doing so because Emerson seized his hand before he could back away, and wrung it vigorously. He then congratulated Mr. Davis on "another interesting discovery," and Weigall, who had watched the performance in mild alarm—for the sight of Emerson being affable understandably aroused his suspicions—said they must be getting on.

"May I come and watch?"

No one would have had the audacity to make a request like that except Nefret. She had not shirked her duties that morning; but she was one of those fortunate young women who looks even prettier when her face glows with exertion and her loosened hair coils in shining tendrils around temples and cheeks. As she spoke she turned the full battery of eyes, smile, curls, and slim brown hands on Mr. Davis. As Ramses remarked later, the poor old chap didn't stand a chance.

They went off arm in arm. "Emerson," I said, taking pity on my afflicted spouse, "why don't you go with them?"

"I was not asked," said Emerson. "It was a conspicuous omission. I do not thrust myself in where I am not wanted."

"Nefret will let us know what is happening," I said.

Indeed, it was not long before Nefret came running back. "Bring the plates, David," she gasped, picking up the camera.

"What is going on?" I demanded.

"They have taken down the wall. There is another behind it, plastered and bearing the official necropolis seals. I—"

"What?" The word burst from Emerson like an explosion.

"I persuaded Mr. Davis to wait until I could take a few photographs," Nefret explained breathlessly.

Sir Edward cleared his throat. "I would be more than happy to assist, Miss Forth."

She spared him a quick warm smile. "I don't doubt you could do the job better, Sir Edward, but Mr. Davis doesn't like people interfering. He only gave in to me because I begged and wheedled."

Emerson's subsequent remarks cannot in decency be reproduced. I caught hold of him and dug in my heels. "No, Emerson, you cannot go there, not while you are in this state of mind. You know we agreed that tact is our best . . . Ramses, don't let him get away!"

"I daren't wait, Mr. Davis was hopping with excitement." Nefret hurried off, followed by David.

"Bah!" Emerson exclaimed. "All right, Ramses, unhand me. I am perfectly composed."

Of course he was not. I do not know whether I can convey to the Reader the import of Nefret's statement. The outer blockage of rough stones was obviously secondary; the inner wall, stamped with the seals of the necropolis priests, must be the original. That meant that the tomb had been entered at least once in antiquity, presumably by thieves, but it would not have been blocked a second time unless something of value was still there.

"Take heart, Emerson," I said. "Now that a new tomb has been located, the Department of Antiquities will take charge. Mr. Weigall won't allow Mr. Davis to do anything foolish."

"Ha," said Emerson. "If it were Carter . . . Oh, the devil with it. I am going back to work."

After he had disappeared into his tomb I said casually to Ramses, "It is almost time for luncheon. I will just go and tell Nefret."

"How thoughtful you are, Mother," Ramses said. "I will just come with you."

Most of the members of Davis's party had scattered and were sitting in the shade mopping their perspiring faces and looking bored. Some of the men hovered near the steps. Mr. Smith gave me a cheery wave, so I went to him.

"Will you be painting in the tomb, then?" I inquired, edging closer to the opening.

Davis and Weigall were down below, getting in the way of the men who were removing the stones from the demolished wall and carrying them up to a dump nearby. The sections of plaster bearing the necropolis seals had been hacked off and tossed into a basket. I could see no more from where I stood.

"That depends on Mr. Davis," Smith replied amiably, mopping his wet forehead with his sleeve. "And on whether there is anything worth painting. They've just got the wall down, and I don't know what lies beyond. Exciting, isn't it?"

Nefret, who had been chatting with Mrs. Andrews, joined us in time to hear his last question. "It certainly is!" she exclaimed. Raising her voice to a piercing soprano scream, she called out, "Mr. Davis, may I see? I am so excited!"

"Later, child, later." Davis came creaking up the stairs, looking very tired and hot but very pleased. He was not a young man; one had to give him credit for enthusiasm, at least. He patted Nefret on the head. "We are stopping for lunch now. Come back in a few hours if you like. And," he added with a smug smile, "do bring Professor Emerson with you."

Mr. Davis's luncheons, which were served in a nearby tomb, were notoriously long and luxurious. We finished our own modest repast in short order, so we were back on the spot well ahead of him. Bareheaded in the boiling sun, Emerson seated himself on a boulder and lit his pipe. Ramses and David went off to talk with Davis's reis, who was sitting in the shade with the other men, awaiting, with the stolid resignation of their class, the return of their employer. I couldn't make out what they were saying, but there was quite a lot of laughter, and David kept blushing.

When Mr. Davis returned, accompanied by the entourage, he greeted us with unusual warmth. "I thought you'd want to have a look," he remarked. "I've done it again, you see. Found myself another tomb."

Emerson bit down hard on the stem of his pipe. "Hmph," he said. "Yes. Anything I can do, of course."

"Not necessary," Davis assured him. "We have everything under control."

I heard something crack and hoped it was only the stem of Emerson's pipe, and not one of his teeth.

In fact, it was not long before work ended for the day. The ladies of Davis's party were complaining of the heat, and Weigall was looking rather grave. I overheard him say something about the police. Unable to repress my curiosity any longer, I joined the group, which consisted of Weigall, Davis, Ayrton and Nefret.

"What is going on?" I inquired.

"Have a look if you like," Davis said amiably. His mustache was limp with sweat and his eyes shone.

Ned politely gave me a hand down the stairs. The entrance gaped open except for a few courses of stone remaining at the base. The descending passage typical of Eighteenth Dynasty tombs sloped down into darkness. It was filled to within three feet of the rock-cut ceiling with loose rubble, and on top of the rubble was the strangest object I had ever seen in an Egyptian tomb. It filled the passage from wall to wall, and the entire surface shone with gold. I leaned forward, not daring to move, hardly daring to breathe, for even as I looked a golden flake the size of my thumbnail shivered and dropped from the side of the object onto the stones under it.

"What is it?" I whispered.

"A panel covered with gold leaf, possibly from a shrine." Ned's voice was as soft as mine. "There is another gilded object lying on top of it—perhaps a door from the same shrine."

"And beyond—at the end of the passage?"

"Who knows? More stairs, another chamber—perhaps the burial chamber itself. We will find out tomorrow. Weigall is going to run a wire down, so we will have electric lights."

Now that he had given me a clue I was able to make out a few more details. There appeared to be reliefs and inscriptions on the panel.

"The gold leaf must have been applied over a layer of gesso, which is already loose. You aren't going to let that doddering old idiot climb in over it, are you?"

In my indignation I spoke almost as bluntly as Emerson would have done (he would have added several other adjectives).

"There is no question of that," Ned said. "I'm not entirely certain how we are going to proceed. Perhaps, Mrs. Emerson, you will give us the benefit of your advice."

Naturally I was happy to give it. Mr. Weigall had been quite right in suggesting that the police be notified and guards set over the tomb. The mere mention of the word "gold" was enough to arouse the interest of every thief in Luxor, and before nightfall every thief in Luxor would know of it. I was not surprised to discover that Mr. Davis was determined to get into the tomb next day, by one means or another. Weigall's attempts to persuade him to wait until the panel could be stabilized, or at least copied, were halfhearted and soon overcome.

"Ayrton, get the thing out of there before tomorrow morning," Davis ordered. "Carefully, of course. Don't want it to be damaged. Come back to dinner, Weigall?"

"Er—no, thank you, sir, I believe I will camp in the Valley tonight. I would be shirking my responsibility if I left the tomb unguarded."

"Quite right," Davis agreed. "Tomorrow, then. Have everything ready. I want to see what's down there."

He walked away without waiting for an answer, since in his estimation only one was possible. I was reminded of one of my favorite Gilbert and Sullivan operas: "If your Majesty says do a thing, that thing is as good as done. And if it is done, why not say so?"

(I paraphrase, but that is the general idea.)

Ayrton and Weigall exchanged glances. They did not get on well, but for the time being, mutual consternation made them allies. Weigall muttered, "It can't be done. Not without ruining it."

Ned squared his shoulders. "I will tell him. Unless you prefer to do so."

"My position with regard to Mr. Davis is a delicate one," Weigall replied stiffly.

In my opinon Ned's position was even more delicate. This was not the time for argument or recrimination, however. The situation was critical. If Emerson had been in charge, not a stone would have been touched and not a person would have entered until the panel had been examined, photographed (if possible), and copied (by David), and every possible effort made to stabilize the fragile gold. This was obviously not going to be done. My duty, as I saw it, was to suggest ways of minimizing the damage.

"Perhaps it would be possible to arrange a kind of bridge over the panel," I suggested. "Our reis, Abdullah, has had considerable experience with that sort of thing."

Weigall's face brightened. "I was just about to propose that," he said. "I think I know where I can lay my hands on a plank of the right length."

"I will tell Abdullah," I said. Weigall did not object, though he must have known I would also tell Emerson.

Emerson behaved better than I had expected—though I ought to have known that he could be depended upon to act sensibly in a crisis. This was a crisis, in archaeological terms; only one of many, alas, and possibly less disastrous than other horrendous errors in methodology the Valley of the Kings had seen. But on this occasion we were there, on the spot. It would have been impossible to remain aloof.

"Face it, Father," said Ramses, after Emerson had run out of expletives. "You cannot keep Mr. Davis out of the place. Mr. Weigall is the only one who has the authority to prevent him, and it seems he won't exercise it."

Even Sir Edward, ordinarily so cool, had been infected by the general consternation. "Have they arranged for a photographer? I will offer my services, if you think they would be accepted."

"Mr. Davis is sending to Cairo for someone," Nefret replied. "A

Mr. Paul, I believe he said. He can't be here for another day or two, though."

By the time we left the Valley the job had been done, thanks primarily to Abdullah. The plank was only ten inches wide, but it was long enough to extend from the tomb entrance to the far wall of the corridor, and Abdullah managed to wedge it in such a way that it did not touch the panel. Mr. Weigall had strung his wire so we had electric light, and the glimmer of it on the incised gold was enough to stir the feeblest imagination. Imagination was all we were allowed, however; Weigall refused to allow anyone to test the bridge. Emerson did not argue with him. His self-control was terrifying, his face set. He was unnaturally silent during the ride back, and went unresisting when I suggested a bath and a change of clothing.

Though I was sadly in need of freshening myself, I went first to the sitting room to look through the messages that had been delivered that day.

"Curse it," I said to David, the only member of the group who had come with me. "There is nothing from Cairo. We ought to have heard again from Walter by now."

"I'll go over to the telegraph office," David said. "You know how slow they are."

He looked so serious that I gave him an affectionate pat on the arm. "Now don't worry, David, I am sure everything is all right. You mustn't go off alone. I will send one of our fellows."

By the time I had located Mustafa and given him his instructions it was getting late, so I contented myself with a hasty splash in the washbasin and a rapid change of clothing. Fatima brought the tea tray to the verandah, where Horus was sprawled insolently across the entire length of the settee. I gave him a gentle but emphatic shove, since I had selected that seat for myself, and he jumped onto the floor, swearing and switching his tail. Ramses, who had just emerged from the house, let out an exclamation of surprise.

"How did you do that?"

"Avoid being scratched, you mean? It is a question of mental and moral superiority."

"Ah," said Ramses. He took the cup I handed him and settled down on the ledge, lounging comfortably against the square pillar.

A restful silence followed. For once Ramses did not seem inclined toward conversation, and I was happy to sip my tea and enjoy the peace and quiet. How nicely my vines had grown! They hung like draperies of living green, half-veiling the apertures, rustling softly in the evening breeze.

The others soon joined us, and we were deep in an animated discussion of the day's discoveries when Ramses sat up, parted the curtain of vines next him, and looked out. His soft exclamation drew me to the doorway.

A carriage was approaching—one of the rather rattletrap conveyances for hire at the boat landing. It drew up before the house and stopped. The vehicle swayed and creaked as a large man descended. Though his long robe was crumpled and stained, it was of fine linen fabric, and a pair of dusty but elegant leather sandals encased his feet. He looked strangely familiar. He resembled . . . He was . . .

Daoud! There was barely time for me to assimilate that amazing sight when another equally astonishing vision materialized—a woman, robed in black, whom Daoud tenderly assisted from the carriage. Holding her hand, he led her to me. His broad, honest face shone with pride.

"I have brought her, Sitt," he announced. "Safe and unharmed, as you told me to do."

Curling fair hair had escaped the scarf that covered her head, and her face was unveiled.

"Evelyn?" I gasped.

It was not she. It was my niece, my namesake, my little Amelia—white-faced and hollow-eyed, and most astonishing of all—here! I looked again at the carriage. No one else was in it.

"Where are your mother and father?" I demanded. "Good Gad! You didn't come alone, did you? Lia—Daoud—"

Instead of answering me, the girl held out a trembling hand. Still dazed with disbelief, I took it in mine. She raised sunken blue eyes, and a faint smile touched her white lips. They parted. But before she could speak, Nefret pushed past me and put her strong young arms round the other girl.

"She is exhausted," Nefret said. "Leave her to me, Aunt Amelia, I'll take care of her. David, will you help me?"

The others had hastened to the doorway. For once even Ramses appeared to be struck dumb. Nefret's appeal roused David from his paralysis of astonishment; stepping forward, he lifted the swaying little figure. She nestled in his arms like a kitten and hid her face against his breast. Following Nefret, he carried her into the house.

"If ever there was a time for whiskey and soda," said a deep voice behind me, "this is that time. Sit down, Peabody, before you fall over."

Daoud had begun to suspect something was amiss. A look of apprehension rippled slowly across his face, taking several seconds to complete the process because of the size of that countenance. "Did I do wrong, Sitt Hakim? You said to me, if one wishes to come—"

"You did not do wrong," Ramses said, glancing at me. "Mother, get him a cup of tea. Now, Daoud, my friend, sit there and tell us all about it, from the beginning to the end."

I had been told Daoud was the best storyteller in the family, but I had found it hard to believe; he was usually a silent man. Now, with an audience as rapt as any raconteur could wish, he came into his own. His voice was deep and musical, his metaphors were poetic, the movements of his hands hypnotic. In fact, his metaphors were so poetic I believe I had better summarize the story, and add a few interpretations that had completely eluded the innocent man.

I would never have supposed that inexperienced girl was capable of such cold-blooded, calculating manipulation! While her parents debated and argued, she had instantly determined on a course of action. There was one sure way to get them to go on to Luxor: to go herself. She had had sense enough—thank God!—to know she ought not attempt the journey alone, and it had not taken her long to realize she could never convince Selim to take her. Daoud—poor Daoud, the gentlest and kindest and not the most intelligent of men—was easy prey. And then there was my own careless statement—I could have kicked myself when I remembered! "If any of them decides to come on, he or she..." Ah, yes, I had said it, or something like it, and Daoud had taken it literally. Why not? He had seen me and Nefret, and even Evelyn, make our own decisions and act independently of men. It was not the way of the women of Egypt, but we were a different breed. And how could there be any danger if he was with her?

The whiskey and soda helped a great deal. I settled down to listen with interest to Daoud's animated account of the journey. He had had the return tickets—first class, for we do not allow our men to suffer unnecessary discomfort—and plenty of money. Lia had met him outside the hotel, after pretending to retire. Exchanging her muffling cloak for the robe and veil she had asked him to purchase, she had accompanied him to the station and onto the train. It had been a long, tiring trip, but he had done all he could to make her comfortable, purchasing fresh fruit and food at various stops and bringing her water to bathe her hands and face. She had slept a good deal of the time, in the respectful shelter of his arm.

"And so we came," Daoud concluded, "like a dove fluttering home to its nest she came, and I watched over her, Sitt Hakim, I let no bird of prey come near her."

Darkness had fallen by the time he finished. Fatima had brought out the lamps, and had lingered to listen.

Emerson drew a deep breath. "Well told, Daoud. And—er—well done. I understand how it came about, and you are not to—that is, you acted for the best. You too must be weary. Go home and rest now."

Nefret came out in time to add her thanks, in the form of a hearty hug, and Daoud went off looking as if he had received a medal. "She is asleep," Nefret said, before I could ask. "David is with her; I thought it would be good for her to see a familiar face if she woke and could not remember where she was. Should we not go in? I think dinner is ready; Mahmud is banging his pans around, the way he does when we are late."

Fatima let out a hiss of dismay and darted into the house. I could not blame her for forgetting her duties; we had all forgot everything except the interest of Daoud's narrative.

"Well!" I said, after we had taken our places round the table. "I had believed myself an excellent judge of character, but I confess Lia has shaken that opinion. To think she is capable of such slyness!"

"And such courage," Ramses said quietly.

"Yes," I admitted. "When I think of that dainty little creature braving the shouting, shoving mob at the train station, and that long, uncomfortable trip—all of it new and strange and frightening. What did she have to say, Nefret?"

"Not a great deal." Nefret planted her elbows on the table, a rude habit she had got from Emerson and of which I had been unable to break her. "She was so tired she kept falling asleep while I bathed her and got her into bed. She kept insisting we were not to blame Daoud, that it was all her doing. She left a note for her parents—"

"Good Gad!" I cried. "How could I have forgot about them! Poor souls, they must be beside themselves."

"I expect they are already on their way here," said Ramses.

This proved to be the case. We located the messages Mustafa had brought over from the telegraph office; finding us engaged when he returned, he had left them on the table in the parlor. The first had been sent early that morning, after Walter and Evelyn discovered Lia was missing. The second announced that they and Selim were taking the next express. It would arrive in Luxor around midnight. The next question was who would meet them. Emerson settled that at once.

"Ramses and David and I. No, Peabody, contrary to your opinions on the subject, we do not need you to protect us. Need I caution you to remain in the house? Should you receive a message written in blood asking you to rush to my rescue, you may assume it did not come from me."

Then followed a period of rushing about, as on the eve of Waterloo. Lia had certainly disrupted our plans to an amazing degree; but when I saw the tumbled curls and pale little face I could not find it in my heart to be angry with her. She was curled up in Nefret's bed, sound asleep. David had pulled a chair close to the bed. When I saw how drawn and anxious his face was, I put a reassuring hand on his shoulder.

"Go and have something to eat, David. There is nothing to worry about now, she is safe, and Evelyn and Walter are on their way. Selim is with them. Emerson wants you to go with him to meet the train."

"Yes, certainly. You won't—you won't scold her, will you, Aunt Amelia?"

"Perhaps just a little," I said with a smile. "Your brotherly affection does you credit, David, but don't be concerned; I am too relieved to be angry. One must admire her courage, if not her good sense."

After observing her color and listening to her quiet breathing, I concluded there was nothing wrong with the child that rest would not put right. My medical experience informed me that she would sleep through until morning unless she was disturbed, so, leaving the lamp alight and the door ajar, I went in search of the others. The sitting room was deserted except for Fatima—and Sir Edward, who listened with an expression of intense interest as she spoke.

She broke off when she saw me and bustled out, muttering about bed linen and towels and water in the basins.

"She has been telling me about your niece," said Sir Edward. "I look forward to meeting Miss Emerson; she appears to be as adventurous and independent as the other ladies in the family."

"A little too independent for a girl of seventeen," I replied. "However, all's well that ends well. If you will excuse me, I must go and see that the guest room is got in order."

"And I will clear my belongings out of my room."

"There is no hurry about that. Lia will share Nefret's room to-night, and it may be that Walter and Evelyn will turn right round and take her back to Cairo tomorrow."

"It might be advisable for them to do so. Mrs. Emerson—"

But he was interrupted by Emerson bellowing my name, and I exclaimed, "Good Gad! He will wake the child. Excuse me, Sir Edward."

Another had had the same thought; when I went to Nefret's room I met David coming out. "She is still sleeping," he reported.

"Good. Now go along, Emerson is waxing impatient. And don't forget to tell Selim he must not be hard on Daoud."

Emerson had wanted my assistance in locating his coat, which was hanging on a hook in plain sight. I helped him into it and smoothed the lapels and bade him take care; and indeed, the sober faces of Emerson and the lads more resembled those of a rescue expedition than a group of gentlemen going to meet friends. I suggested Sir Edward might accompany them, but Emerson shook his head.

"He had better stay here with you. Now, Peabody, remember what I told you . . ."

I cut the lecture short and sent them off with a cheery smile. The train might be late, it often was; but they wanted to be on the platform when it came in. My dear Evelyn would be in a fever of anxiety for her child. She must learn at the earliest possible moment that Lia had arrived safe and sound.

There would be no sleep for any of us that night. Nefret had gone back to Lia, but I was too restless to settle down. I asked Fatima to make coffee and followed her into the kitchen.

"I see you and Sir Edward have become friendly," I said casually.

"He is very kind," Fatima said. She reached for a tray. "Should I not talk with him, Sitt Hakim?"

"Of course you may. What do you talk about?"

"Many things." Her busy hands arranged cups and saucers, sugar bowl and spoons. "What I do, and what my life was like before, and what it is now; about . . . Oh, all little things, Sitt Hakim; I cannot speak of great matters, but he smiles and listens. He is very kind."

"Yes," I said thoughtfully. "Thank you, Fatima. Why don't you go to bed? It is late."

"Oh, no, Sitt, I could not do that." She turned to me, her eyes wide. "They will want food when they come, and they will be tired, but so happy to see their child. It will make me glad to see their happiness. Will they be very angry with Daoud, Sitt Hakim? He meant no harm. He is a good man."

"I know." I patted her shoulder. "I believe I can make them understand, Fatima. They are both very fond of Daoud."

My questions about Sir Edward had not been prompted by suspicion, for even my fertile imagination could not think of any sinister motive for his interest in Fatima. It was unthinkable that her loyalty could be shaken by bribe or threat, and anyhow, she knew nothing that could be used against us. His kindly interest displayed a new side of his character. Perhaps, I mused, it had been his association with us that had broadened and softened that character.

I carried the tray to Nefret's room, where I found her sitting by the bed reading. She said she did not want coffee, and would stay with Lia. I had the distinct feeling that I had been dismissed, though I could not have said why; so I let my restless feet take me to the courtyard, where moonlight spilled through the leaves of the trees and the night breeze cooled my face. I made out the motionless form of the guard, a pale shape in the shadows, and wondered if he had dropped off to sleep. When something stirred along the wall to my right, I started. A soft voice was quick to reassure me.

"Don't be alarmed, Mrs. Emerson, it is only I."

I made my way to the bench where he was sitting. "I thought you had retired, Sir Edward."

He rose and took the tray from my hands. "One of your valiant guards is already dozing," he said lightly. "I could not sleep anyhow. But coffee would be welcome. May I give you a cup?"

I accepted, and watched his well-groomed hands move deftly among the implements on the tray. "Is there some particular reason why you are wakeful tonight?"

He was silent for a moment. Then he said, "I was trying to decide whether to tell you. Far be it from me to add to your concern, but—"

"I prefer facts, however unpalatable, to ignorance," I replied, taking the cup he offered me.

"I suspected as much. Well, then, I did not tell you the whole truth about my plans for this evening. I did dine at the Winter Palace, but afterward I paid a visit to a certain establishment of which you have heard. Purely for purposes of inquiry, of course."

I didn't doubt his assurance. A man of such fastidious tastes would not be tempted by what "the establishment" in question had to offer.

"I will spare you a detailed description," he went on. "Except to say that I was somewhat conspicuous in that ambience, and that my motives were immediately suspect. I came away with my inquiries unanswered; and yet, Mrs. Emerson, I sensed that the denials given me were due to fear, not ignorance."

"What about the girl Nefret mentioned?"

His lips set in a thin line of distaste. "Several were very young, but her description was too vague to enable me to identify which one she meant. All in all, it was a singularly unpleasant and absolutely unproductive visit. I would not have mentioned it to you if I hadn't felt it necessary to warn you. You see, Mrs. Emerson, I know you well, and I know Miss Forth; she must not go there again. Must not!"

Such vehemence, from a man of his temperament, was strangely disturbing. "I agree she must not," I said slowly. "But aside from the general impropriety of such an act, you seem to feel there is a particular reason—a particular danger. I beg you will be more specific."

"Don't you see?" He put his cup down and turned to face me.

"Her first visit there caught them unawares. They had not expected she would come; who would?"

"Presumably they had not expected Ramses and David either."

"No; but it was her behavior, her open-hearted, generous appeal to those miserable women, that may have suggested to someone a means of luring her into a trap. I never believed that message was genuine. If you had not intercepted it—might she not have gone alone to the rendezvous? Might she not respond to another such appeal, or brave the horrors of that place if she believed the writer of the note was threatened? You must convince her such an act would be madness!"

His voice was tremulous with emotion. Did he care for her that much? Perhaps I had misjudged him.

"Do you care for her that much, Sir Edward?"

After a few sounds suggestive of strangulation, Sir Edward remarked, "I ought to be accustomed to your forthright manners, Mrs. Emerson. You warned me once I would never succeed in winning her regard."

"Was I correct?"

"Yes." His voice was as soft as a sigh. "I didn't believe you then, but after observing her this season I know she will never be mine."

He had not answered my question. There was no need for me to repeat it. I knew the answer.

The train was late. It was after three in the morning before the long-awaited sounds brought me running to the verandah. Emerson had hired a carriage for the travelers and their luggage (I kept telling him we ought to have one of our own, but he would not listen), and before long I was able to hold Evelyn and Walter in a loving embrace. They were both haggard with fatigue, but neither would rest until they had seen their child with their own eyes.

Nefret had dozed off on the mattress we had placed beside the bed, and the two girls made a pretty sight, with the lamplight playing on their loosened hair and their faces flushed with sleep. Nefret woke at once; her first gesture was to place a finger to her lips, so we crept quietly out again, followed by Nefret.

Weary though they were, Evelyn and Walter were too keyed up to sleep. We retired to the sitting room and the heaped-up platters of food Fatima brought. Emotions were too profound and too joyful to be restrained; tears and fond embraces and broken protestations followed.

The first coherent comment I can recall came from Walter. "I cannot decide whether to beat Daoud senseless or thank him from the bottom of my heart."

"The latter," said Emerson. "He is twice your size."

"He would stand still and let you do it, though," Ramses said. "It wasn't his fault, Uncle Walter."

"So everyone keeps telling me." Walter passed his hand over his eyes. "Well, at least we are here, and it is wonderful to see you all again. You are looking well, Amelia—remarkably well, under the circumstances."

"She thrives on this sort of thing," Emerson muttered.

Evelyn had made the boys sit with her, one on either side, and was inspecting them with the tender anxiety of her motherly heart. "And you both look better than I had dared expect. Your hand, Ramses—"

"It's greatly improved," Ramses assured her. "Mother and Nefret made a great fuss about nothing."

She smiled at him and turning to David, raised her hand caressingly to his brown cheek. "We worried about you too, dear. If it had not been for Lia we would not have hesitated about coming."

Too moved to speak, David bowed his head and carried her hand to his lips.

Emerson had begun to fidget. He does not enjoy excessive displays of sentimentality—public displays, that is. "You two look like ghosts. Go to bed. We will talk again tomorrow, when you are rested. Say good night, boys, and let's be going."

"Going?" I exclaimed. "Where, at this hour?"

"To the Valley, of course. Davis will be wrecking the tomb first thing in the morning, and I mean to get there before him."

"Emerson, you can't do that!"

"Can't give him the benefit of my advice, and attempt in my most tactful fashion to persuade him to adhere to the basic principles of scientific excavation? What is wrong with that?"

"It is Mr. Davis's tomb, my dear, not yours. You should—"

"The tomb," said Emerson in the sonorous tones he employed when he was making a speech, "does not belong to Davis, Amelia. It belongs to the Egyptian people, and to the world."

He looked so self-righteous I would have laughed if I had not been so filled with horrified apprehension. Walter did laugh. He laughed so hard he had to wipe his eyes, and if there was a slight touch of hysteria in his mirth I could hardly blame him. "Never mind, Amelia dear," he gasped. "Radcliffe told us all about it on the way here. You cannot prevent him; I cannot prevent him; the entire heavenly host could not prevent him. Radcliffe, dear old chap, it *is* good to be back!"

Emerson flatly refused to take me with him; I was needed at the house, he explained, to make certain everything was safe and in order. I would not have minded so much if he had not yielded to Nefret's demands.

"Hmm, yes, you may be useful. You can get round Davis better than most people. Don't forget the camera."

Filled with the direst of apprehensions, I took Ramses aside. "Don't let him strike anyone, Ramses. Especially Mr. Weigall. Or Mr. Davis. Or—"

"I will do my best, Mother."

"And take care of Nefret. Don't let her—"

"Wander off on her own? No fear of that." A glint of what might have been amusement shone in his dark eyes. "She'll be too busy flirting with Mr. Davis."

"Oh dear," I murmured.

"It will be all right, Mother. How can an adversary lie in wait for us when even *we* don't know what the devil Father is going to do next?"

I saw them off and returned to my duties. Fatima had supplied the guest chamber with everything a visitor might need, including rose petals in the wash water; but when I went to Nefret's room to see how Lia was doing, I found her mother lying on the pallet by the bed. Both were asleep. Wiping a tear from my eye, I went to listen at Walter's door and deduced, from the sound of snoring, that he too had succumbed. Sir Edward's door was ajar and lamplight showed within; he had not joined in the joyous reunion, but he was obviously awake and alert.

I sent Fatima to bed and lay down, thinking to snatch a few hours' repose. Repose I did, but sleep was impossible with so many impressions and questions crowding into my head. Sir Edward's solemn warning—to be honest, it was a theory that had not occurred to me, but knowing Nefret as I did I feared he might be right. Then there was Lia's outrageous behavior to be considered. Her dear parents' haggard looks had made me angry with her all over again. How thoughtless and self-centered the young can be! I did not doubt her affection for us, but she owed her parents a greater affection, and I knew she had been moved in part by a selfish desire to get her own way.

Foremost in my thoughts, as always, was Emerson. Was I concerned for his safety? Well, not really. With all four of them together, on the alert and on horseback, it would have required an attack in force to overcome them—especially since, as Ramses had pointed out, no one could possibly have expected them to be abroad at that hour. I was more concerned about Emerson's formidable temper. He was already at odds with the entire Department of Antiquities, not to mention Mr. Davis. What was he doing to Mr. Davis's tomb? What was going on in the Valley in the dark of night? And what the devil was in the tomb? I am not entirely immune to archaeological fever myself.

From Manuscript H

Ramses had seen the fever mounting, and had known nothing short of physical violence would keep his father away from Davis's tomb. He had sometimes wondered whether Emerson would interrupt an interesting excavation long enough to interfere if he saw his son being strangled or battered—and then reproached himself for his doubts. Emerson would remove the attacker, knock him unconscious, inquire, "All right, are you, my boy?" and go back to work.

It was different with Nefret, of course. His father had once stated his intention of killing a man just for laying his hands on her, and

Ramses didn't doubt he had meant it. He felt precisely the same way.

It lacked at least an hour till daylight when they reached the entrance to the Valley. The donkey park was deserted except for one of the gaffirs, who had found a quiet corner and a bundle of rags on which to sleep. They answered his sleepy questions with a few coins and left the horses with him.

The moon had set. Starlight glimmered in Nefret's hair.

The men who had been left to guard the new tomb were asleep. One of them woke at the crunch of rock under their booted feet and sat up, rubbing his eyes. He responsed to Emerson's soft greeting with a mumbled "It is the Father of Curses. And the Brother of Demons. And—"

"And others," said Emerson. "Go back to sleep, Hussein. Sorry I woke you."

"What are you going to do, Father of Curses?"

"Sit here on this rock" was the calm response.

The man lay down and rolled over. Egyptians had long since concluded that the activities of the Father of Curses were incomprehensible. It was an opinion shared by many non-Egyptians.

Emerson took out his pipe and the others settled down beside him. "Aren't you going to look at the tomb?" Nefret whispered.

"In the dark? Couldn't see a thing, my dear."

"Then what are you going to do?"

"Wait."

Sunrise was slow to reach the depths of the Valley, but the light gradually strengthened and the guards woke and built a fire to make coffee. Nefret produced the basket of food Fatima had forced on her, and they passed around bread and eggs and oranges, sharing them with the guards, as those courteous individuals shared their coffee. While they were eating, Abdullah and the other men turned up and joined the party. They were all having a jolly time when they heard someone approaching.

The newcomer was Ned Ayrton, followed by several of his workmen. When he saw them he stopped and stared.

"We dropped in to see if we could lend a hand," said Emerson jovially. "Would you care for a boiled egg?"

"Uh—no, sir, thank you. I haven't time. Mr. Davis will be here in a few hours and he will wish—"

"Yes, I know. Well, my boy, we are at your disposal. Tell us what you want us to do."

What Ayrton wanted, above all else, was to have them go away. Since he was too courteous to say so, he stuttered, "I thought—I thought I might finish clearing the stairs. Get them—er—nice and tidy. Wouldn't want anyone to trip over a rock and—er."

"Quite, quite," Emerson said. With what might have been a smile—except that it showed altogether too many teeth—he got up and started for the stairs.

"What's he going to do?" Ayrton whispered, giving Ramses an agonized look.

"God knows. How soon do you expect Mr. Davis?"

"Not before nine. He said early, but that is early for him. Ramses, I must have everything ready when he arrives. He will wish—"

"I know."

"Ramses, what is the Professor going to DO?"

"Would you object to our taking photographs?"

"You can't get anything. The angle is all wrong and the doorway is in shadow, and . . . Oh, I suppose it's all right, so long as you don't let him see you doing it."

He hurried off. Ramses turned to Nefret, who had been listening with a sardonic smile. She shook her head.

"Poor Ned. He hasn't much backbone, has he? He's supposed to be in charge."

"No, Weigall is the one in charge," Ramses said. "Ned is a hired employee and Davis is the one who pays his salary. Two hundred and fifty pounds per annum may not sound much to you, but it's all Ned has."

He had spoken rather sharply but instead of snapping back at him she smiled bewitchingly. "Touché, my boy. Who's that coming?"

"Weigall. He and some of the others camped in the Valley last night."

No one could resist Nefret. Ramses knew he was infatuated to the point of irrationality, but even Weigall, who had good reason to mistrust the whole Emerson family, thawed under her smiles and dimples.

"We are breakfasting with Mr. Davis on his dahabeeyah," Weigall announced. "And returning with him. Uh—what are you doing, Professor?"

Emerson tossed the rock he held aside and began to explain. Watching with considerable amusement, Ramses realized that he had underestimated his father. The most severe critic could not have objected to what he was doing. Davis had wanted to enter the tomb; Emerson was making it possible for him to do so.

"We'll have the place all tidied up when you get back," he announced, grinning wolfishly. "Wouldn't want Davis to twist his rickety old ankle scrambling down those littered steps. Ayrton will keep an eye on us, won't you, Ayrton? Yes. Run along and enjoy your breakfast, Weigall."

He assisted the Inspector on his way with a hearty slap on the back. As soon as he was out of sight Emerson turned like a tiger on David. "Get in there and start copying the inscriptions on that panel."

David had half-expected it, but he didn't like it. "Sir," he began.

"Do as I say. Ramses, go on down the path and keep watch. Give us a hail if you see anyone I would rather not see."

Nefret started to laugh. "Don't worry, Mr. Ayrton," she sputtered. "No one will blame you; they are only too familiar with the Professor's little ways. Anyhow, no one will know unless you tell them."

Ayrton surveyed the interested audience, which consisted of his crew and most of the Emersons' men. After a moment his outraged expression relaxed into a reluctant grin. "What did you do, bribe them?"

"Bribes and intimidation," said Nefret cheerfully. "They think Ramses is closely related to all the afreets in Egypt. Have an orange."

Obeying his father's gesture, Ramses stationed himself where he could see along the path that led to the donkey park. What his father was doing violated every written and unwritten principle of archaeological ethics, not to mention his firman. Ramses—who never let principle get in his way either—was in complete sympathy. Every movement across the plank, every breath would dislodge a few more flakes of the gold leaf. Lord only knew how much of the relief would remain after a few more days of such activity. His father had offered Davis the services of Sir Edward as photographer and David as artist. Davis had flatly refused. He wanted to be in complete control of "his" dig.

Ramses flexed his stiff fingers and cursed himself for the stupidity that had made it impossible for him to join in the fun. If he hadn't been so carried away by the image of himself as a romantic rescuer he would have employed some of the dirtier and equally effective blows he had learned in various dark corners of London and Cairo, instead of punching the villain on the jaw in approved public-school style. He could do some things left-handed, but he had never acquired the delicate precision necessary for copying hieroglyphs. Layla had been right when she called him a fool. Well, she had got away, anyhow. At least he prayed she had.

The sound of someone approaching made him start. It was only Abdullah. He was looking unusually grave.

"There is something you must know, my son."

"If it's about Daoud, my father, don't be concerned. No one is angry with him. Not very angry."

"No, it is not that. You must keep it from Nur Misur if you can. There was another body found this morning in the Nile. It was like the other—torn and mangled. This body was a woman's."

11

I had not supposed that Emerson would be deterred from his work by such minor details as the arrival of his family, or the danger that hovered over us all, or the urgent necessity of planning what we were to do about both. I determined I would join him in the Valley as soon as was possible. Admittedly I was just a little curious about what was going on there, but my primary motive was the hope that I could persuade Emerson to return home early.

It would have been rude as well as risky to abandon our guests without a word, however, so I was forced to wait until the weary travelers had had their sleep out. Lia was the first to wake; her cry of surprise roused her mother, and when I went in I found them locked in a fond embrace.

When we met for a late breakfast, I was not surprised to find that the alleviation of Walter's concern had been succeeded by extreme annoyance. This is the normal parental reaction. Lia's response was normal too, for a person of her age. One night's sleep had fully restored her, and although she expressed her regret for having worried them I did not suppose she meant a word of it. Her face glowed with happiness and excitement, whereas her parents looked ten years older.

The appearance of Sir Edward made Walter put an end to his lecture. He and Evelyn were well acquainted with the young man, and expressed their pleasure at seeing him again. He was easily persuaded to join us for coffee. "I wondered whether you had decided on your plans for the day, Mrs. Emerson," he explained. "What would you like me to do?"

This reminder, tactful though it was, had a sobering effect. I explained that we had decided to wait until the others returned before discussing our plans, not only for that day, but for the immediate future. "So I may as well go on over to the Valley," I said casually. "The rest of you stay here."

The objections to this reasonable suggestion ranged from Lia's outthrust lip and mutinous look to Walter's indignant protest: "You certainly are not going off alone, Amelia."

Sir Edward and Evelyn added their remonstrances, so it was decided that the best thing would be for all of us to go. Fatima packed an enormous lunch, and we were in good spirits when we set out. The secret of happiness is to enjoy the moment, without allowing unhappy memories or fear of the future to shadow the shining present. It was a shining day, with bright sunlight and clear air; we were on our way to one of the most romantic spots on earth, with loved ones to welcome us and wonderful sights to see. Lia's excitement was so great she kept urging her little donkey to a quicker pace, and Walter forgot care in his interest in the new tomb. He was a scholar as well as a fond father, and he had excavated in Egypt for many years.

Sir Edward was on horseback, but since there were not enough horses for all of us I rode a donkey so that I could chat comfortably with Evelyn—as comfortably, that is, as the pace of a donkey permits. She had a professional reputation of her own, as an excellent painter of Egyptian scenes; but that day her interest in archaeology was overcome by her affectionate care, not only for her child, but for the rest of us.

"I really do not know what I am to do with you, Amelia! Why can't you and Emerson have a single season of excavation without becoming involved with desperate criminals?"

"Now that is certainly an exaggeration, Evelyn. The 1901–02 season . . . No, that was the Cairo Museum swindle. Or was it that season that Ramses . . . Well, never mind."

"It's getting worse, Amelia."

"Not really, my dear; it is pretty much the same sort of thing.

The only difference is that the children are taking a more active role."

I had never been certain how much Evelyn knew, or suspected, about my encounters with Sethos. There seemed no sense in keeping from her matters the children already knew, so I poured forth the entire story. Over the years I had developed a great respect for Evelyn's acumen. She was surprised—I thought she would fall off her donkey when I described the seductive garments Sethos had once demanded I assume—but when I had finished, her first comment was practical and to the point.

"It seems to me, Amelia, that you are jumping to conclusions when you assume it is this person who is responsible for your present difficulties. You have no real evidence."

"In fact I don't believe he is," I said. "It is Emerson who sees Sethos lurking everywhere. I think . . . But we are almost there. We will talk about it later."

The Cook's Tour people were leaving the Valley, and the donkey park was a maelstrom of braying and bustling. We left our steeds in the care of the attendant and walked the short distance to our tomb.

Selim was the first to greet us; he explained that Emerson and the children were with Davis Effendi. I had been afraid they would be. Walter was keen on seeing the new tomb, and I was keen on finding out what mischief Emerson had been up to, so we lingered only long enough to say good morning to Abdullah and the others. At first Daoud was nowhere to be seen. Apparently someone—most probably Selim—had explained to him that Lia's parents might be a trifle put out with him. He finally emerged from the tomb looking like a very large, very anxious child. Walter shook his hand and Evelyn thanked him, and Lia gave him an affectionate hug, and he immediately cheered up. Once that was settled, I told Selim to take the baskets to our lunch tomb and we went on down the path.

Our family was there, and to judge by the look of it, so was half the town of Luxor. Davis had brought his usual party. I waved to Mrs. Andrews, who was sitting on a rug fanning herself with such vigor that the feathers on her hat fluttered, and went directly to Emerson. I did not at all like the look of him.

"Hallo, Peabody," he said gloomily.

"What is going on?" I asked.

"Disaster, doom and destruction. There would have been a death too," he added, "if Nefret hadn't kept me away from Weigall. You won't believe this, Peabody—"

"You ought not remain here if it annoys you so much, Emerson. What good can you do?"

"Some, I think," was the response. "They all know my views on the ethics of excavation, and Weigall pretends to share them. My very presence may have a sobering effect."

At that point Mr. Davis poppped up out of the stairwell, followed by several other men. He did not look as if he were sobered by Emerson's presence. Exultation and excitement had turned his face a frightening shade of red. "It's her!" he shouted. "Aha—there you are, Mrs. Emerson. Has your husband told you? It's Queen Tiyi! What a discovery!"

"Not *the* Queen Tiyi!" I exclaimed.

"Yes, yes! The wife of Amenhotep the Third, the mother of Khuenaten, the daughter of Yuya and Thuya, whose tomb I found last year, the—"

"Yes, Mr. Davis, I know who she was. Are you certain?"

"No question about it. Her name is on the shrine. It was made for her by her son, Khuenaten. She's there, in her coffin, in the burial chamber!"

"You've been into the burial chamber?" I inquired, with an involuntary glance at Emerson. "*You* crawled along that ten-inch-wide plank?"

"Of course." Davis beamed. "Couldn't keep me out. There's life in the old man yet, Mrs. Emerson."

I had a feeling there wouldn't be life in him much longer if he went on at this rate. If Emerson didn't massacre him, he would have a stroke; he was hopping with excitement and panting like a grampus. I urged him to sit down and rest. Visibly touched at my concern, he assured me he was about to go to lunch.

"You'll want to have a look," he said generously. "And the Professor. Later, eh?"

Emerson had not moved or spoken. He was beyond outrage, I believe, and had passed into a kind of coma of disgust. I poked him gently with my parasol.

"Come to luncheon, Emerson. Walter and Evelyn and Lia are here."

"Who?"

Realizing I was not going to get any sense out of him for a while, I called to the children, and we led Emerson back to our rest tomb, where the others were waiting. Evelyn and Walter were mightily intrigued by the news that the tomb had belonged to Queen Tiyi, the mother of Akhenaton; they had first met at Amarna, the city of the heretic pharaoh (whom Davis referred to by the old reading of Khuenaten).

"I say," Walter exclaimed. "I would like to have a look. Do you suppose Mr. Davis would allow me to go into the burial chamber?"

This had the effect of arousing Emerson. "Why not? He's let a dozen people in already, most of them driven only by idle curiosity. I dare not think of the damage they have done."

"Haven't you seen the place?" I asked, shooing a fly away from my cucumber sandwich.

"No. I had some foolish notion that abstaining might shame others into emulating me. I sent Ramses instead."

It occurred to me then that Ramses had been unusually silent. His back against the wall and his knees drawn up—for his legs were so long people tended to trip over them if he extended them at full length—he was staring at his untouched sandwich. I poked him.

"Well?" I said. "Tell us about it, Ramses."

"What? Oh, I beg your pardon, Mother. What do you want to know?"

"A complete description, please," said Nefret. "I have not yet been allowed in. The ladies"—I cannot describe the contempt with which this word was pronounced—"must wait until after the gentlemen have had their turns."

"There is only one room," Ramses said obediently. "Another was begun, but never finished; it exists as a large niche, in which are four canopic jars with beautiful portrait heads. The walls of the chamber were plastered but not decorated. Leaning against the walls and lying on the floor are other parts of the shrine. The floor is several inches deep in debris of all kinds—part of the fill which slid down from the passageway, plaster fallen from the walls, and the remains of the funerary equipment—broken boxes, spilled beads, fragments of jars and so on. Against the wall is an anthropoid coffin of a type I have never before seen. The feather pattern that covers most of the lid is formed of glass and stone inlays set in gold. There had been a gold mask; only the upper portion, with inlaid eyes and brows, now remains. There is a uraeus on the forehead and a beard attached to the chin. The arms are crossed over the breast. One may assume that the hands once held the royal sceptres, since three thongs of the whip are still there, though the handle and the other sceptre are not—"

"Uraeus, beard and sceptres," Emerson repeated slowly.

"Yes, sir."

"Hmph," said Emerson.

"Yes, sir," said Ramses. After a long moment he added, "The coffin lid has unquestionably undergone modifications from its original state."

"Ah," said Emerson.

Wearying of these enigmatic exchanges I demanded, "Is there a mummy in the coffin, or could you tell?"

"There is," said Ramses. "The coffin has been damaged, by damp and rock fragments that fell from the ceiling, and by the collapse of the funerary bed on which it lay. The lid shifted and split lengthwise, but it still covers most of the mummy except for the head, which had become separated from the body and is lying on the floor."

Lia shivered with delighted horror. "Is it very disgusting?" she asked hopefully.

"Never mind that," said her father. "No wall decorations, you say? A pity. But if the place is in the state you describe, it will keep Davis happily occupied for weeks."

Ramses did not reply. He had gone back to scowling at his sandwich. Emerson pronounced several bad words, and Nefret said consolingly, "At least they have agreed not to do anything more until the photographer they sent for arrives."

"Didn't you offer them your services, or those of Sir Edward?" Walter asked. "He did a first-rate job with Tetisheri, under equally difficult conditions."

Sir Edward smiled reminiscently. "I will never forget crawling up that ramp to the top of the sarcophagus every day, with camera, tripod, and plates strapped to my back. The Professor threatened to murder me if I fell off into his debris."

"And I would have done, too," said Emerson.

"I was well aware of that, sir. It made me a good deal unsteadier than I would otherwise have been."

Emerson grimaced amiably at him. "You did do an excellent job," he conceded. "Davis declined his offer, Walter. Cursed if I know why. He dislikes giving anyone else credit for anything." He jumped to his feet. "He can't prevent us from having a look, though. I may as well add my disturbance to the rest. Who will join me?"

Evelyn decided she would not add her disturbance, and suggested she take Lia on a tour of the major tombs. I knew what she was thinking. If they decided to return home, at least the child would have seen the most famous sites in the Valley. David offered to escort them, and I sent Daoud along too.

The rest of us had our turns in the burial chamber of the new tomb, but not until after all the men in Mr. Davis's party, and three or four of the women, had been down and back. It was an astonishing and depressing sight—the broken, violated coffin, tumbled objects everywhere, and a great golden panel propped against the wall. Chunks of plaster had fallen from the walls or hung ready to fall. There had been damage in the past, from seepage and other causes; but every breath of air, every vibration disturbed the delicate objects again. As I crouched on hands and knees in the doorway, a section of gold-covered gesso fell from the panel and added itself to the pile of flakes already on the floor.

My conscience would not allow me to penetrate farther into the room. I crawled back along the narrow plank, pausing only long enough for another look at the gilded panel so dangerously close below. The queen was there, offering flowers to the Aton who was her son's sole god; another figure, standing in front of her, had been cut away. It had almost certainly been that of Akhenaton. The heretic's enemies, determined to destroy his memory and his soul, had penetrated into even this forgotten sepulchre.

When we started for home, I was still dazed by what I had seen. I do not mind confessing, in the pages of this private journal, that I was filled with the direst of forebodings. The contents of the tomb were so precious and so fragile! They came from one of the most intriguing periods in all Egyptian history; one could only guess what light they might throw on the many unanswered questions about the reign of the heretic pharaoh. They would have to be handled with extreme care, and the proceedings thus far had not given me hope that this would be the case.

Ramses had kept to himself most of the afternoon, joining us only when we were starting on the homeward path. He brought up the rear of our little procession. I stopped and waited for him to catch me up.

"A fascinating day, was it not?" I inquired, taking his arm.

"Quite," said Ramses.

"Very well, Ramses, out with it. What is worrying you? Not the tomb, surely."

We had reached the donkey park. The others had gathered round the boys' beautiful Arabians, and Lia was demanding that she be allowed to ride Risha. Everyone appeared to be in a merry frame of mind; even Emerson looked on, smiling, as Walter attempted to dissuade his daughter and Nefret laughed at both of them, and David lifted Evelyn onto his mare. The only gloomy face was that of my son. I was about to repeat my question when he sighed and said, "There is no keeping anything from you, is there? I don't know why they call *me* the Brother of Demons."

"Now that I think about it, that name casts rather rude aspersions on me," I said. "Well?"

"I must go over to Luxor this evening. Can you keep Nefret occupied so she won't insist on coming along?"

"Why?"

He told me. "Abdullah said I must not let Nefret know. That's impossible, of course, but I don't want her examining this body. The other was bad enough. This would be unbearable."

"Not pleasant for you either," I said, concealing my own shock and distress with my customary fortitude. "Good Gad. No wonder you have been looking so strange all day. You think it may be—that woman? Layla?"

"It is a possibility. Someone must find out."

"I will go with you."

"To hold my hand?" Then the bunched muscles at the corners of his mouth relaxed, and he said quietly, "I apologize, Mother. It is good of you to offer, but I can deal with this unassisted. You must keep Nefret and the others in the dark, at least until we know for certain."

"Very well. I'll think of something."

"I'm sure you will. Thank you."

By the time we reached the house I had, of course, come up with a plan. I had no intention of allowing Ramses to go over to Luxor by himself, or even with David. Safety lay in numbers. I proposed my scheme; and everyone agreed that it would be a pleasant diversion to dine at the Winter Palace Hotel. Sir Edward said he would cross over with us, but that he had another engagement. It might have been only a courteous excuse to leave us to ourselves, but I was beginning to wonder whether Sir Edward had found himself a friend—of the female persuasion, that is. Perhaps he really had abandoned his hope of winning Nefret. She had not given him any encouragement that I had seen—and it is not difficult for a trained eye like mine to observe the little signs that indicate interest of a romantic nature. Sir Edward was not the man to waste time on a hopeless cause, especially when there were other ladies who found his charming manners and handsome looks irresistible. If such was the case I could only be grateful to him for his disinterested help.

The others went off to bathe and change. I lingered for a moment on the verandah, admiring my pretty flowers and thinking about the unknown woman who had met such a ghastly fate. What a strange world it is! Beauty and happiness, tragedy and terror inextricably entwined, making up the fabric of life. My offer to Ramses had been sincere, but I was not sorry to be let off that ugly task. I only wished it were possible to spare him. Someone had to do the job, though, and he was the most logical person to do it.

No one objected when I announced that Daoud and his cousin Mahmud would accompany us, but Walter gave me a sharp look. What he and Evelyn would say when they learned of the latest death—well, I did not doubt what their reaction would be. It could not be kept from them, but, I reasoned, why not put it off as long as possible so that we could enjoy the evening?

I managed to keep them off the subject during dinner, assisted in no small measure by Lia. She could talk of nothing but her pleasure in being with us, her enjoyment of the visit to the Valley, her admiration of Moonlight. She babbled and laughed and sparkled. Nefret joined in with her customary vivacity, but the others were not much help. The faces of Lia's parents became longer and longer; her delight would make the curtailment of that delight harder to insist upon. Ramses ate almost nothing, and David, who was to accompany him, ate even less.

They slipped away after dinner, taking (at my insistence) Daoud and Mahmud with them. I managed to distract the others for a while by showing them the amenities of the hotel, but when we returned to the salon for coffee, the questions began. My feeble excuse, that they might be visiting some of the antika dealers, was met with the skepticism it deserved.

"What the devil!" Emerson ejaculated. "If they have gone off by themselves—and you knew of it, Peabody—and did not tell me—"

Indignation stifled his speech. I winced under the power of a pair of furious blue eyes.

There was no comfort to be found in the other eyes. Nefret's blazed, Lia's were wide with distress, and even Evelyn's reproached me.

"They are in no danger," I said quickly. "Daoud and Mahmud are with them, and they have not gone far, or for long. They will soon return, and then we will discuss—"

"Never mind, Amelia." It was Walter who spoke, and the quiet authority in his voice silenced even his irate brother. "Evelyn and I have already had our discussion, and I doubt anything will change our minds. I was able, before we left Cairo, to inquire about bookings. There is space on a steamer leaving Port Said on Tuesday next. I will go back to Cairo with Lia and Evelyn, put them onto the boat, and return."

If Walter believed this would settle the matter, he did not know his family. Everyone had a different opinion, and did not hesitate to express it. Lia's voice rose to a pitch that forced me to take her by the shoulders and give her a little shake.

"For pity's sake, child, don't make a scene," I said severely. "Not in public, at any rate."

"No," said Nefret. "We Emersons do not give way to our feelings in public, do we? Aunt Amelia, how could you?"

"I had hoped to postpone this until later," Walter said, sounding a trifle rattled. "But . . . Lia, child, don't cry!"

"Not in public," said Nefret between her teeth.

She looked as if she wanted to take *me* by the shoulders and shake me. So did Emerson. The only thing that saved me from further recriminations was the return of Ramses.

So animated had the discussion become that no one saw him come into the room—except Nefret. She jumped up and would have gone to meet him if I had not caught her arm.

"Not in public," I said, and was rewarded with a really hateful look. She sat down, however, and folded her hands tightly in her lap.

Eyebrows raised, Ramses came to stand by Nefret. "I could hear you clear out in the street," he remarked. "What seems to be the trouble?"

His pretense of nonchalance might have deceived the others, but the affection of a mother could not miss the signs of perturbation. Meeting my anxious gaze, he shook his head.

I was unable to repress a cry of relief. "Thank God!"

"You creeping, crawling, despicable traitor," Nefret said. "Where is the other one?"

"Coming." Ramses gestured. I saw David standing near the door. David lacked Ramses's talent for dissimulation; he was probably still trying to get his ingenuous countenance under control. Even if the dead woman was not Layla, the sight must have been dreadful, especially for a sensitive lad like David. I took a closer look at Ramses, and rang the bell for the waiter.

"Be still, Nefret," I said sharply. "He wanted to spare you a horrible task, and you may be grateful that he did. Whiskey, Ramses?"

"Yes, please." He dropped heavily into a chair.

"I have a feeling I had better join you," said Emerson grimly.

By the time the tale was told Walter had also joined us, and I had prescribed a glass for David. He never drank spirits, but I insisted that he do so on this occasion—for medicinal purposes.

Ramses nodded approval. "He was sick." With a glance at Nefret, he added, "So was I."

With one of her graceful, impulsive gestures she took his hand in hers. "All right, my boy, I forgive you this time. I suppose you didn't really break our rule, since you told Aunt Amelia. So it wasn't Layla?"

"No."

I wondered how he could be so sure. He had not gone into detail, but remembering the horrible mutilations inflicted on Yussuf Mahmud, I assumed the face had been unrecognizable. I decided perhaps I had better not ask—at least not in front of Lia.

I might have known Nefret would ask. When she did, I saw Ramses's self-control slip for a moment.

"She was . . . younger. Much younger."

It was decided—somewhat belatedly, in my opinion—that we had better go home at once. Even those who had been spared a detailed description of the first mutilated body were horror-struck, and Walter heaped reproaches on Ramses for discussing such a disgusting subject in front of Lia. It seemed to me it had been Walter's responsibility to remove the girl—who was, in fact, less painfully affected than her elders. She had never encountered violent death, thank heaven, and her very innocence rendered her less vulnerable.

Daoud and Mahmud were waiting, and we went to the quay. It was interesting to observe how people paired off: Walter and Evelyn, talking in low voices, David and Lia behind them, then Emerson and I, with Ramses and Nefret bringing up the rear. Emerson said very little (I suspected he was saving himself for later), so I was able to overhear some of the conversation between Nefret and Ramses.

"When did you find out?" Nefret asked.

"This morning. Abdullah told me."

"So all day, since this morning, you have been afraid it was Layla. Oh, Ramses!"

There was no reply from Ramses. After a moment Nefret said, "I'm glad for your sake it wasn't she."

"My sake? I assure you, Nefret, that Layla's death would mean no more to me than—"

"Yes, it would. Don't pretend." Her voice broke. "If she had been killed, it would have been because she helped you. You would feel guilty. Just as I feel."

"Nefret—"

"This woman—this girl—was a prostitute, wasn't she? Someone must have identified her by now, or at least determined that no . . . no respectable girl that age is missing. She knew something—she asked for our help—and they killed her. I brought that child to her death.''

Emerson had heard too. He heard the little sob, and a wordless murmur from Ramses. He did not stop or turn, but his hand closed over mine with a force that bruised my fingers.

Nefret had composed herself, outwardly at least, by the time we reached the house. We had rather taken to avoiding the verandah, especially after dark, so we went to the parlor instead. Evelyn took Lia off to bed, over the latter's strenuous protests, but not even Nefret defended her right to remain. It was clear that there was still a good deal to be said, and since everybody knew what Lia's views were likely to be, there was no sense in allowing another excitable person to join in the conversation.

Emerson made the rounds checking doors, gates and windows. When he returned he reported that Daoud had insisted on remaining on guard.

"He wasn't quite so assiduous before," he remarked. "Apparently he has taken Lia under his wing."

"And a very large wing it is," I said with a smile. "She could not be safer than with Daoud."

My little attempt at humor did not lighten the atmosphere appreciably, nor did the platters of food Fatima insisted on serving. Sir Edward had returned from wherever he had been, and had joined our council of war.

He had heard the news about the dead girl and was visibly disturbed by it. Shaking his head, he said, "Even Daoud is mortal. I hope you will believe I speak as a friend when I urge Mr. and Mrs. Emerson to take their daughter home as soon as possible."

It would have been amusing if it had not been so pathetic to see the indecision on Walter's face. He was at heart a dedicated Egyptologist, and he had been long away from the scene of his work. The day in the Valley had whetted his interest afresh. And, like any true Briton, he was unwilling to abandon loved ones in peril.

"Are we starting at shadows, though?" he asked. "It sounds to me as if you have got yourself mixed up with some gang of Egyptian thieves, a little better organized and less scrupulous than most, but not as dangerous as some of the villains you have encountered in the past. The people who have been killed were both Egyptians—"

"Does that make their deaths less important?" Emerson inquired softly.

Walter frowned at him. "Don't try to put me in the wrong, Radcliffe. I didn't mean that, and you know it. The shameful fact is that it is a good deal safer to murder an Egyptian than a European or Englishman. The authorities don't trouble themselves to pursue such cases. The vicious method of murder they used is significant too."

"You are absolutely right, Walter," I exclaimed. "I pointed this out earlier, but no one believed me. A cult! A murder cult, like that of Kali—"

Emerson interrupted me with a loud snort.

"Why not?" Walter asked. "The Thuggees claim to be sacrificing to their goddess, but they aren't above robbing the victims. A secret organization, with all the appurtenances of a cult—ritual murder, oaths sworn in blood, and the rest—is easier to control than an ordinary gang of thieves."

"It is a point worth considering, Uncle Walter," Ramses said politely. "Religious fanaticism has been responsible for a number of hideous crimes."

Walter looked pleased. It wasn't often that his ideas were received with such approval. Thus encouraged, he proceeded with even greater enthusiasm. "The leaders of the group need not be—often are not—believers themselves. Sordid, cynical gain is their motive, and they employ superstitious terror as a weapon to control their underlings. Don't forget, this business began when you young people walked off with the papyrus. Is it valuable enough to inspire such a reaction?"

"That's right, you haven't seen it." Ramses got to his feet, and then looked at his father. "May I get it, Father?"

"Certainly, certainly," said Emerson, chewing the stem of his pipe and scowling.

Walter was full of admiration, not only for the papyrus, but for the container David had designed. The lad flushed under his praise. "We are being very careful, sir," he explained. "But we felt we ought to make a copy, just in case."

"Yes, quite," said Walter. Adjusting his eyeglasses, he bent over the papyrus. I went to have a closer look myself, since the vignette was one I had not seen. Four little blue apes squatted around a pool of water, their paws folded over their rounded bellies.

"The spirits of the dawn," Walter murmured, his eyes moving down the column of hieroglyphs under the painting. "Who content the gods with the flames of their mouths."

"Enough," Emerson broke in. "You can have the photographs, Walter, if you want to translate the cursed thing."

"I'll leave it to Ramses, I think," Walter said. "I doubt the text offers any new material. Well. It is a splendid example of its type, but it is certainly not unique. Could it have some particular religious significance for our postulated cult?"

Evelyn came in and joined the group around the table. "Is this the famous papyrus? What charming little baboons."

"You look very tired, my dear," I said. "Sit down and have a cup of tea."

She shook her head. "It is not so much physical as mental exhaustion. I have had quite a time with Lia. Never have I seen her so unreasonable! And you know, Amelia, that although one becomes extremely exasperated, it is difficult for a mother to refuse a child something she wants so badly."

Emerson stopped mangling the stem of his pipe and came to life. "I have a compromise to propose."

The word "compromise," coming from Emerson, was so astonishing we all stared. Taking this for intense interest, he smiled broadly and elaborated. "You cannot leave for a few more days, in any case. Suppose we give the child a whirlwind tour—Medinet Habu, Deir el Bahri, and all the rest. We will wine her and dine her and wear her out, and send her home, if not rejoicing, at least resigned."

I had a feeling it would not be so easy as that. The word compromise is almost as unknown to the young as it is to Emerson. However, if it were put to the girl in that way she would have less to complain of.

"You mean you would give up two days' work?" Walter asked. "You? What a sacrifice!"

"I beg you will not be sarcastic, Walter," said Emerson with offended dignity. "I certainly don't intend to let you wander around without me. We will travel in a body, like a confounded bunch of Cook's tourists and surrounded by—"

"By Daoud," I said, laughing. "Emerson, it is a splendid compromise. We will dine with the Vandergelts—they would be sorely disappointed not to see you, Walter and Evelyn—and show Lia the Castle, and the *Amelia* and—"

"And Abdullah's house," Ramses said. "He would be offended if we did not come for a meal. Daoud has already spoken to me about it. Kadija began cooking yesterday."

From Manuscript H

". . . I brought that child to her death!" Nefret's voice broke in a sob. Ramses put his arm round her and she turned her face into his shoulder; but there was no way he could console her, not even by taking his fair share of the blame. God knew it had haunted him ever since he had seen the slight broken body and known whose it must be.

"You cannot be certain it was your appeal that was responsible, Nefret. It might have been the reward, or even some private revenge."

"Not the last. It's too coincidental and too . . . too horrible. What sort of people are they?"

She wiped her eyes with her fingers. Ramses fumbled in his pockets, and that finally won a tremulous laugh from her.

"Never mind, my boy, you never have a handkerchief. Where's my bag?"

It was an absurd little thing, made of some shiny cloth and hanging from her wrist by a golden cord. She moved away from him and he lowered his arm. He had that to remember, at least, and the gentleness of her voice when she said, "You don't fool me, Ramses dear; you aren't as hardened as you pretend. Come and talk about it before you go to bed."

When they reached the house Sir Edward was there, bland and smiling as usual. The discussion that followed was typical of their family talks—full of sound and fury (most of it from his father) but surprisingly productive in the end. Two days of uninterrupted sight-seeing and entertainment would have to suffice, and if Lia didn't like it (he was fairly sure she wouldn't) she would have to lump it.

Ramses knew why his father was willing to take the time. He would sacrifice two days in order to have them out of the way when he went after the murderers. The girl's death had been the last straw for Emerson. Ramses had seen that look on his father's face before, and he knew what it portended.

Once they had agreed, his mother ordered them all off to bed. Ramses, putting the papyrus into its container, was the last to leave the room, or so he believed until he saw his father standing in the doorway.

"Yes, sir?" he inquired, wondering if he would ever be old enough to abandon that form of address.

"I thought you might need a bit of help with that," his father said. "How is your hand?"

"It's all right, sir. I could leave off the cursed bandage anytime if Nefret would allow me."

"She takes good care of you boys. And you of her."

"We try. It is damned difficult. You know how she is."

"I have had years of experience dealing with determined females," his father said with a faint smile. "But we wouldn't—er—care so much for them if they were not like that, would we?"

"Love" was the word he meant. Why couldn't he say it? Ramses wondered. Presumably he said it to his wife.

"No," he agreed.

"Er—you managed to spare her a most distressing scene tonight. It was—er—distressing for you too. And for David. Well done, both of you."

"Thank you, sir."

"Good night, my boy."

"Good night, sir."

David had refused to wait outside the dirty little room where the girl's body lay. He had stood at Ramses's side when the worn sheet was pulled back and he had waited, swallowing down the bile that kept rising in his throat, until Ramses was ready to go.

But when Ramses went later to Nefret's door, he heard David's voice, low-pitched and intense, and he left without knocking. That night he killed David again, digging his fingers deep into his friend's throat and smashing his head against the stone floor. He woke with a strangled cry and lay sleepless until dawn, with his murderer's hands covering his face.

Breakfast was not a pleasant occasion, despite my efforts to be cheery. Walter kept shooting apologetic glances at his daughter, Ramses looked like a ghost and David like a man with some guilty secret on his conscience—though I could not imagine what it might be, since the poor boy was one of the most harmless individuals I had ever known. From time to time a spasm of rage distorted Emerson's handsome face, and I knew he was picturing endless processions of Mr. Davis's clumsy-footed friends bumbling into the burial chamber of the new tomb. At least our plan would keep Emerson away from the Valley, which was all to the good.

Lia had been informed of that plan by her parents in the privacy of their room. According to Evelyn—who was looking worn and unhappy—she had taken it more quietly than they had expected. I had my forebodings, however. Lia did not in the least resemble her uncle, but that morning there was something strangely familiar about the set of her chin.

Sir Edward put himself out to be charming, however, and between his efforts and mine the atmosphere gradually improved. We were to spend the whole day away, starting at the temples of the Ramesseum and Medinet Habu and working our way back to Gurneh, where we had been invited to lunch with Abdullah and his family.

I will not bore the Reader with descriptions of the sights of Luxor. They can be found, not only in my earlier volumes, but in Baedeker. To say we had become blasé about them would not be entirely accurate, for I will never tire of any monument in Egypt; but I believe our pleasure derived primarily from that of Lia. The joy of the present overcame her dread of the future; face flushed, curls bouncing, she took everything in with the appreciation of a dedicated student. I had not realized how intensively she had applied herself to her studies during the past year. Evelyn had told me David had kindly agreed to tutor the child over the past summer. He had been an excellent teacher. She knew the names and the complicated history of the sites; and the glow on her face when she traced the cartouche of Ramses II with a reverent finger, and read off the hieroglyphs, made me regret even more the peculiar circumstances that must curtail her visit. How well I remembered the thrill that had pervaded my entire being when I first beheld the reality of the pyramids and penetrated the dim interiors of those admirable monuments! Well, we would make it up to her another year.

Our visit with Abdullah was an unqualified success all round. The house was decorated as if for a wedding, with flowers and palm branches, and Kadija had prepared enough food for twenty people. Lia ate of every dish and tried to sit cross-legged like Nefret. Her attempts to talk Arabic brought a smile even to Abdullah's dignified face. She treated the dear old fellow with an anxious deference that was very engaging. She was not at all self-conscious about mispronunciations and bad grammar, and managed to make her meaning understood.

As she had done with Daoud, I thought, glancing at that individual's beaming face. He had a heart as large as his body, and now he had found someone else to love.

After we had finished, the men went outside to fahddle, so that we could spend a little time with Kadija. She said very little—apparently Nefret was the only one to whom she told her jokes!—but it was evident that she too had enjoyed the visit.

We stopped on the way home to see a few of the nobles' tombs. Lia would have gone on indefinitely, but I thought Evelyn looked tired, so I reminded the others that we were to dine with Cyrus and Katherine that evening.

"Quite a full day," said Emerson, drawing me apart.

"In every sense of the word." I patted my stomach. "I doubt I will be able to eat a thing tonight. But the child is enjoying herself. What a pity she must leave so soon. Is it really necessary, Emerson?"

"Better safe than sorry, Peabody." He smiled at me. "I can quote aphorisms too, you see."

"What did Abdullah tell you?"

"Curse it, Peabody, I hate it when you read my mind that way."

"It is your face I read, my dear. I know every lineament of it. And yours is not a countenance that lends itself to deception."

"Hmph," said Emerson. "Well, I intended to tell you anyhow. The body has been officially identified, thanks to Ramses's insistence that the police question the—er—proprietress of the house. They would not have bothered if he had not demanded it, and she would not have come forward of her own accord."

"It was the girl Nefret meant?"

"Impossible to determine, Peabody. There were several of a—a young age."

His steed snorted and I saw that his hands were clenched on the reins. "Sorry," said Emerson—to the horse. To me he said, "The only way of being certain would be for Nefret to inspect the girls."

"Out of the question, Emerson!"

"I quite agree, my dear. There is at least a strong suspicion that it was the same girl. Was she murdered because she was trying to escape that hellish den, or because she knew something about Layla, or—for some other reason?"

"We will find out, Emerson."

"Yes, my dear Peabody, we will."

It was a vow, and I knew he would keep it. I also knew I would have to watch him closely once the younger Emersons had departed. My dear Emerson is inclined to be reckless when his emotions are aroused.

The Vandergelts had hoped to give a large reception in honor of our visitors, but in view of the brevity of their stay the party that evening was small—only Sir Edward and Howard Carter in addition to ourselves. The others had heard of the latest murder, for news, especially grisly news, spreads quickly, but the topic was avoided out of consideration for the youthful innocence of Lia. (At one time Howard would have extended the same consideration to Nefret, but he had learned better.)

So we talked of Mr. Davis's tomb instead. It is a rare pleasure to be in the company of individuals who are as well informed about and interested in a subject as oneself. Lia was not as well informed as the rest of us, but her eager questions inspired the gentlemen to elaborate and explain, which gentlemen always enjoy doing.

Howard, who had not yet been inside the tomb, was mightily intrigued by our description of the coffin. "Who else can it be but

Elizabeth Peters

Akhenaton himself? Oh, yes, I know he had a tomb at Amarna, but his mummy wasn't there; after the city was abandoned, the royal dead may have been moved to Thebes for safekeeping."

"Possibly," Emerson agreed. "But there are a number of pharaohs of that period missing. How is that you haven't been asked to participate in the so-called clearance, Carter? You've worked for Davis before; I would have thought he'd ask you to make drawings or paintings of some of the objects in situ."

"I'd give a great deal to be allowed to do that," Howard declared. "But—well—Mr. Smith is an artist and a close friend of Mr. Davis; I suppose he'll be asked."

"He hasn't your touch," Nefret said.

"So long as someone does it," Emerson muttered. "Thus far Davis hasn't done a cursed thing about copying or preserving the objects. Supervision is criminally inadequate too. Keep your eye on the antiquities dealers, Carter, I wouldn't be at all surprised if objects from the tomb start turning up in Luxor."

"Nor would I," Howard said. "I was talking with Mohassib the other day . . ." He broke off long enough to explain, "He is the most respected of the antiquities dealers in Luxor, Miss Lia, been in business for over thirty years. He asked to be remembered to you, Mrs. Emerson. He's been ill, you know, and I think he'd appreciate a visit."

Though he had concealed his chagrin with gentlemanly courtesy, I thought Howard had been hurt by Mr. Davis's employing another artist, one without his experience or his need. I found an opportunity later that evening to speak an encouraging word.

"Do not be discouraged, Howard. Contemplate the future with courage and optimism."

"Yes, ma'am." Howard sighed. "I'm trying. I do get discouraged at times, but I cannot complain when I have friends such as you and the Professor. You know how much I admire him."

"Er—quite," I said. Emerson is the most remarkable of men, but certain of his characteristics are better avoided. Howard's stubbornness during the affair of the drunken Frenchmen had been only too reminiscent of the way Emerson would have behaved under those circumstances.

I patted Howard's hand. "This is not the end of your career,

Howard, it is only a temporary hiatus. Take my word for it. Something is going to turn up!"

With the tact I had come to expect of him, Sir Edward excused himself as soon as we got home. Yawning in an unconvincing manner, he declared he was excessively fatigued and would retire at once. In my opinion, several of the others looked as though they could do with a rest. Lia was not one of them. She announced she did not intend to waste her few precious hours sleeping.

"You must have some rest," I said sympathetically but firmly. "Tomorrow will be another tiring day."

"I don't want to go to bed," declared Lia, sounding like a spoiled child and looking, in the chin area, alarmingly like Emerson.

"Come and talk for a while," Nefret said, slipping her arm through that of the other girl. "I haven't shown you the new robe I bought in Cairo."

With the hour of leave-taking so close upon us I was reluctant to part from my dear Evelyn, and I believe Emerson felt the same about his brother. They were deeply attached to one another, though their British reticence prevented them from saying so. At Walter's request Emerson got out the papyrus again, and they began an animated and amiable argument about the reading of certain words. After a time I noticed that Ramses was not taking part. This was enough to arouse my maternal concern, so I went to him, observing that David had already slipped out.

"You don't look at all well, Ramses," I said. "Is your hand bothering you?"

"No, Mother." He held out the member in question for my inspection. He had removed the bandage. There was still some swelling and discoloration, but when I bent each finger in turn, he endured it without visible signs of discomfort.

"Something to help you sleep?" I inquired. "You had a particularly unpleasant experience yesterday."

"Unpleasant," Ramses repeated. "You have a talent for understatement, Mother. Thank you for your consideration, but I don't need any of your laudanum. I believe I will go to bed, though. Say good night to the others for me, I don't want to disturb them."

Evelyn's golden head now rested upon a cushion, and her eyes were closed. I covered her with an afghan and tiptoed out. Though why I bothered to tiptoe I do not know, since Emerson and Walter were talking in loud voices.

Fatima was in the kitchen, her chin propped on her hands and her eyes fixed on some object on the table in front of her. So intense was her concentration that she started and squeaked when she realized I had come in. I saw that the object was a book—the copy of the Koran Nefret had given her.

"You shouldn't read by candlelight, Fatima, it is hard on your eyes," I said, putting my hand on her shoulder. "I am ashamed I have not been of more help to you with your studies."

"All help me, Sitt Hakim. So kind. Shall I read to you?"

I could not refuse. She faltered once or twice, and I supplied the words; then I praised her again and told her to get some sleep.

Peeping into the parlor I saw the men were still at it and that Evelyn was sleeping sweetly. I decided I would check on my other charges. I went down the passageway and into the courtyard. My soft evening slippers made no sound on the dusty ground. I put my ear to Ramses's door, thinking as I listened how quiet and beautiful the place looked in the pale moonlight. My little garden was flourishing, thanks to Fatima's care. The hibiscus plant in the far corner was a good-sized tree now, almost as tall as I and luxuriant with foliage.

Then I realized I was not the only one to enjoy the moonlight. A gust of wind stirred the leaves of the hibiscus and I caught a glimpse of someone standing beside it. No—not one person—two persons, so close to one another that they appeared to be a single form. All I could see of her were the slender arms twined round his neck and the flowing lines of a full white skirt. His back was to me, but as the breeze moved the leaves and the pale light shifted across his form I saw the dark head bent over the girl's, and the long length of him, and the way his shirt strained across his back. Nefret had worn emerald-green satin that night. The girl was Lia—in the ardent embrace of my son!

I don't suppose they would have heard me if I had screamed aloud. I could not have done so, in fact; astonishment—for I had not had the least notion that any such thing was going on—kept me mute. I must have made some sound, however, or leaned against the door; for it opened suddenly and I would have toppled over backward if hands had not caught and steadied me.

The hands were those of Ramses. There could be no doubt of that, for the rest of him was there too, standing just behind me—not in the courtyard with Lia in his arms.

He saw them too. I heard his breath catch and felt his hands tighten painfully on my ribs, and then at last I was able to speak.

"Good Gad!" I cried.

The guilty parties broke apart. He would have moved away from her, but she caught hold of his arm with both hands and held him fast. My outcry had not been loud; Nefret must have been awake and listening. Her door opened. She looked from me to the miscreants, and then back at me.

"Damn!" she said.

"What is the meaning of this?" I demanded.

"Now, Aunt Amelia, please remain calm," Nefret said. "I can explain."

"You knew of this? For how long, pray tell?"

"Don't be angry with her." David put the girl's hands gently away and came toward me. "It is my fault."

"No, it's mine!" Lia exclaimed. She caught David up and tried to put her arms round him. "I—I seduced him!"

"Oh, God," said Ramses. There was such a strange note in his voice that I swung round to look at him. His face was alive with an emotion as strong as any I had beheld on that enigmatic countenance.

"Did you know?" I demanded.

"No."

I turned back to David. "I presume Lia's parents do not suspect this—this—"

"I am going to tell them now," David said quietly. "No, Lia, don't try to stop me; I ought to have done the decent thing long ago."

"I'm going with you," Ramses said. He picked me up, as if I had been a life-sized doll, and set me down out of his way.

"No, my brother. Let me have the courage for once to act without your help."

Elizabeth Peters

He passed into the house. Lia started after him, and Nefret said with a gusty sigh, "Well, that's done it. We may as well join in, Ramses, family arguments are the favorite form of amusement here and this looks like being a loud one."

274

12

Loud it most certainly was. I was ashamed of Walter. He behaved like an outraged papa in a stage melodrama, and I half-expected him to point a quivering finger at David and thunder, "Never darken my door again!"

David had been too nervous to break the news gently—but then I suppose it would not have mattered how he broke it. "Lia and I love one another. I know I have no right to love her. I ought to have told you at once. I ought to have gone away. I ought—"

He was not allowed to say more. Walter caught hold of his daughter, who was clinging to David's arm, and dragged her out of the room. I do not suppose he had ever laid an angry hand on her, or any of his other children; so taken aback was she that she went unprotesting. We all stood like pillars of salt, avoiding one another's eyes, until he returned to announce that he had locked her in her room.

"I must go to her," said Evelyn.

It was the first time she had spoken since David had made his announcement. Her pale, silent look of reproach hurt David even more than Walter's angry words. He bowed his head, and Ramses, who had been watching with the strangest expression, went to him and put his hand on David's shoulder.

Walter turned on his wife. "You are not to go near her. Pack your things. We will take the morning train. As for you, David—"

"That will be enough, Walter," Emerson said. His pipe had fallen from his mouth when David spoke. He picked it up from the floor, examined it, and shook his head. "Cracked. A perfectly good pipe ruined. That is what comes of these melodramatic scenes. Young people tend to be overly excitable, but I am surprised, Walter, to see a grown man like you lose your temper."

"It runs in the family," said Nefret. She went to David and took his other arm. "Professor darling, you won't let Uncle Walter—"

"I will not allow any member of this family to behave in a manner unbecoming his or her dignity."

Considering its source, this was an outrageous statement, but of course Emerson was sublimely unaware of that. He went on, "David, my boy, go to your room. Sit quietly and don't do anything foolish. If I discovered that you had polished off your Aunt Amelia's laudanum or hanged yourself with a bedsheet I would be seriously put out with you. Perhaps you had better go with him, Ramses."

"No, sir," Ramses said quietly. "He wouldn't do anything like that."

"I'm not leaving either," Nefret announced.

"Do you believe he needs advocates here, to ensure fair play?" Emerson inquired.

"Yes!" Nefret exclaimed passionately.

"Yes," said Ramses.

Nefret's slim shoulders were thrown back and her eyes blazed. Ramses's eyes were half-veiled by his lashes, and his face was no more expressive than usual, but his pose was as defiant as Nefret's. They looked very handsome and very touching and very young. I wanted to shake both of them.

"Thank you, my friends," David said softly. With a firm stride, not looking back, he left the room.

"Well now," Emerson began.

He got no farther. Nefret turned on me. I had gone to Evelyn and was sitting beside her, patting her hand.

"What have you got to say, Aunt Amelia? Aren't you going to speak up for them?"

"My dear, it is out of the question. I am sorry."

"Why?"

"She is only seventeen, Nefret."

"He would wait."

"He would wait?" Walter burst out. "The slyness of it! I welcomed that boy into my home, treated him like a son, and he took advantage of a child who—"

"False!" Nefret's voice pealed like a bugle. She looked like a young Valkyrie as she spun round to face Walter, cheeks flushed, hair as bright as a bronze helmet. "Lia made the first advance; do you think David would have dared, shy and modest as he is? He wanted to confess but she wouldn't let him. Why are you all behaving as if he has done something shameful? He loves her with all his heart and he wants to marry her—not now, when she comes of age and he has established himself."

"They cannot marry," Walter said. "Not now or ever." He passed his hand over his eyes. "I spoke in the heat of anger, and I regret it. I will tell the boy so, for I don't believe he did anything dishonorable. But marriage..."

Ramses had followed David to the door and closed it after him. Lounging against the wall, his hands in his pockets, he said, "He's Egyptian. A native. That's it, isn't it?"

Walter did not answer. Ramses was not looking at him; he was looking at me.

"Certainly not," I said. "You know my feelings on that subject, Ramses, and I am offended you should think me capable of such prejudice."

"Then what is your objection?" my son inquired.

"Well—his family. His father was a drunkard and his mother—"

"Was Abdullah's daughter. Is it Abdullah to whom you object? Daoud? Selim?"

"Stop it, Ramses," Emerson ordered. "I will not have you addressing your mother in that accusatory tone."

"I beg your pardon, Mother," said Ramses, not meaning a word of it.

"This business is too serious to be settled in a single evening of recriminations and accusations," Emerson went on. "You may remove your family tomorrow evening, Walter, if you insist, but I will be cursed if I am going to lose another night's sleep getting you to Luxor in time to catch the morning train. No, Nefret, I don't want to hear any more from you either. Not tonight."

"I was only going to ask," said Nefret meekly, "what *you* think, Professor?"

"I?" Emerson tapped the ashes out of his pipe and rose. "Good Gad, is someone asking my opinion? Well, then, I do not see what all the fuss is about. David is a talented, intelligent, ambitious young man. Lia is a pretty, spoiled, engaging little creature. They must wait, of course, but if they are of the same mind three or four years from now she could do worse. Now off to bed with you all."

Nefret ran to him and threw her arms around him.

"Hmph," said Emerson, smiling fondly. "Bed, young lady."

We dispersed in silence. Walter looked rather shamefaced. He was a kind, gentle man, and I could see he regretted his behavior, but I did not suppose he would change his mind. It was an unfortunate development. Walter had thought of David not only as a gifted pupil but as an adopted son; this disclosure must change that relationship forever. It was even more difficult for Evelyn, who had taken David to her bosom.

She kissed me good night, looking sad enough to break my heart, and went to Walter. He put a comforting arm round her and led her out. Nefret caught Ramses by the hand. "Come to David," she said, and led him out. Neither of them looked at me.

"So, Peabody," said my husband. "Another pair of cursed young lovers, eh?"

I believe in the efficacy of humor to relieve awkward situations, but I could not smile at this old joke. "They will get over it, Emerson. 'Hearts do not break; they sting and ache for . . . ' I forget the rest."

"Thank God for that," said my husband piously. His eyes followed me as I went round the room extinguishing the lamps. "It's going to be up to you, you know."

"What do you mean?"

"Evelyn relies on your judgment, and you have Walter firmly under your thumb, along with the rest of us. If you supported the young people . . ."

"Impossible, Emerson."

"Is it? I wonder, Amelia, if you yourself know why you are so intransigent."

I had put out all the lamps but one. Shadows crept into the room. I went to Emerson. He drew me into his arms and I laid my aching head on his breast. It had been an unpleasant scene.

"You'll have to come to grips with it sooner or later, my dear," Emerson said gently. "I cannot help you this time. Confound it, I could have done without this! Life is complicated enough, with a maniacal killer on the loose and Davis wrecking that damned tomb!''

From Manuscript H

Holding him firmly by the hand, Nefret led the way to David's room. Ramses was still dazed. If he hadn't been so preoccupied with his own selfish feelings, he might have noticed certain things: the way Lia had clung to David the day she arrived, the look on David's face as he held her; Nefret's efforts to give them some time alone; even the girl's deference toward Abdullah, like that of an expectant bride trying to ingratiate herself with her future father-in-law. No wonder she had trusted so unhesitatingly in Daoud! He had underestimated the child. There wasn't a scrap of false pride in her, and he honored her for it.

His mother hadn't noticed anything either. He found that amusing. She prided herself on her perception in romantic matters. Well, this wasn't the only one she had missed.

David's gloomy face brightened when he saw who it was. "What happened?" he asked.

"Just about what you might have expected," Nefret said. "Damn, I should have brought the whiskey."

"I don't need it, dear," David said with an affectionate smile.

"I do." Nefret dropped onto the bed and kicked off her shoes. "Give me a cigarette, Ramses, I need something to quiet my nerves. I'm still furious. Why are they acting this way?"

"You don't understand," David said bitterly. "It's one thing to take a stray dog off the street and train him to sit and fetch and carry, and boast of his accomplishments; but he's still a dog, isn't he?" He hid his face in his hands. "I'm sorry. I shouldn't have said that."

"*You* don't understand," Ramses said. He couldn't have explained why he was moved to defend his mother; he had criticized her himself, to her face. His mother was wrong and Nefret was right, but . . . He went on, "I expect Mother is feeling rather wretched just now. She's come smack up against prejudices she never knew existed because they were buried so deep. The same is true of Uncle Walter and Aunt Evelyn. That sense of superiority isn't so much taught as taken for granted; it would require an earthquake to shake feelings that are the very foundation of their class and nationality. It isn't easy for them."

"Harder for David," Nefret snapped.

"At least he has the satisfaction of knowing that he's in the right and they are not," Ramses said. "Don't be so self-righteous, Nefret. Have you forgot that the people of your Nubian oasis treated their servant class like animals—referring to them as 'rats,' depriving them of the most basic necessities? Prejudice of one sort or another seems to be a universal human weakness. Few individuals are completely free of it, including the ones who pride themselves on being open-minded."

"The Professor isn't like that."

"Father despises people quite impartially and without prejudice," Ramses said.

Even David smiled at that, but he shook his head. "He is different, Ramses. And so are you."

"I hope so. How did I fail you, David, that you were unable to tell me?"

"You have never failed me, my brother," David muttered. "I tried—I wanted to—but . . ."

"But you feared I would think you unworthy of my cousin? For the love of God, David, you ought to know me better than that!"

"I didn't! I do! I . . . Damn it, Ramses, don't make me feel more of a worm than I already feel. It was what you said one night, about taking advantage of a girl—expecting her to keep her promise even if she stopped caring for you—"

"Have a cigarette," Ramses said.

"Oh. Uh . . . Thank you."

"You two certainly have interesting conversations when I'm not around," Nefret remarked. "Which one of your numerous conquests were you talking about, Ramses?"

"None of your business."

She laughed, as he had expected, and he turned away to light David's cigarette, fearing his face would betray him. He had no right to feel so happy when his friend was miserable, but he couldn't help it.

"Don't feel put upon because David didn't tell you," Nefret said. "He didn't confide in me either. It was Lia who told me. Poor little thing, she wanted a confidante so desperately. It's hard to be madly in love and not be able to talk about it."

"Is it?" Ramses said.

"So I've been told." Nefret sat up, crossed her legs, and smoothed her skirt. "Now you understand why she was so determined to come on to Luxor. It wasn't selfishness; she was worried sick about him."

"And I'm worried about her," David said soberly. "It's just as well they are leaving tomorrow. If I never see her again—"

"Don't lose heart, David, we'll talk them round," Nefret promised. She yawned like a sleepy kitten. "Goodness, what a day! I'm going to bed. Come along, Ramses, you've got circles under your eyes the size of teacups."

"In a minute."

"You aren't angry with me, are you?" David asked, after she had gone, leaving the door pointedly open.

"No. But when I think of how often I whined at you—"

"Now we can take it in turn," David said, with almost his old smile. "Do you remember one night—how long ago it seems!—the night you first told me how you felt about Nefret, and I said . . ."

" 'You make such a fuss about such a simple thing.' "

"Something like that. I wonder you didn't knock me down. If it's any consolation, I've paid dearly for that smug remark."

Ramses extinguished his cigarette and got up. He put his hand on David's shoulder and looked searchingly at him. "You are all right, aren't you?"

"No." David smiled faintly. "But I'm not going to behave like some ass of a Byronic hero. I have too much to be thankful for. And I won't give up hope. I know I'm not worthy of her, but no one would cherish her more than I. If I can win Uncle Walter and Aunt Evelyn over—"

"Don't worry about them. The only one who really counts is Mother."

The ancient Egyptians had no word for "conscience," but the heart, which was also the seat of the intelligence, was the witness for or against a man when he stood in the Hall of the Judgment. That night I searched my heart in the sonorous phrases of the verses of the Declaration of Innocence, which I had recently translated. I had not driven away the sacred cattle, or stolen milk from the mouth of babes. I had not taken the lives of men (except when they tried to take mine) or been a teller of lies (except when it was absolutely necessary). "O thou who makest mortals to flourish," I whispered, "I do not curse a god. O thou of the beautiful shoulders, I am not swollen with pride..."

Was I, though? Was it false pride and bigotry that made me refuse to consider a marriage between those two? When I believed it was Ramses who held the girl in his arms—had my indignation been as strong as when I realized the man was David?

Yes. No. But that was different.

I turned onto my side and drew closer to Emerson. He did not wake, or put his arm around me. He was sound asleep. There was nothing on his conscience. Nor on mine, I told myself. But it was a long time before I emulated Emerson.

He was up before me in the morning, which was not the usual thing. I dressed in haste and went to the verandah, where I found Emerson conversing with Sir Edward, and Fatima hovering over them with coffee and tea and sugary cakes, to keep them from starving until breakfast.

I didn't doubt she knew of the most recent development. Servants always do know such things, and none of the participants in the argument had bothered to lower their voices. She was properly veiled, in the presence of the men, but her dark eyes were troubled.

"You look as if you could do with a stimulant, Peabody," remarked my husband, making room for me on the settee. "Have a seat and a cup of coffee, and leave the children alone. I have already spoken with all of them, and they have promised ... Where are you going, Sir Edward? Sit down."

"I thought you would prefer to discuss private family matters—"

"There is no such thing around this house," Emerson said acerbically. "You have become involved in our affairs, so you may as well leave off being tactful. I do not invite your opinion on the matter, however."

The lines of laughter framing Sir Edward's mouth deepened. "I would never venture to offer it, sir."

He was impeccably groomed as always, attired in well-cut tweeds and polished boots, his white shirt spotless. He returned to his chair and picked up his cup, which Fatima had refilled.

"As for other matters," he began.

"We will discuss those later," Emerson said. "After we have got my brother and his family away from here. Curse these distractions! As I was saying, Peabody, the children have agreed not to raise the subject again, so kindly refrain from doing so yourself. We will have a pleasant day seeing the sights as we planned, and put them on the train tonight."

"Pleasant?" I repeated ironically. "It can hardly be that, with everyone moping or angry or self-conscious. I trust you did not raise false hopes, Emerson. That would be too cruel."

"Let them hope, Peabody. One never knows; something may happen to change the situation."

Something did happen.

I found nothing to complain of in the manners of my companions. Everyone was excessively polite, and the topic that was foremost in all our minds was never mentioned, but the emotional atmosphere was so thick that it destroyed all comfort. There were awkward silences and sideways glances and downcast eyes and mournful faces. I wished we had put the younger Emersons on the train that morning and got it over with.

Lia behaved better than I had dared expect. Not by word or look did she reproach her parents, but she was not very forthcoming with them either. She did not speak to David, or he to her. There was no need. Their eyes were eloquent.

The attractions of the temple of Karnak, well known to me, were not sufficient to turn my thoughts into happier channels. I therefore sought mental distraction by considering the course of action I meant to take in order to solve our other problem.

We were in the Hypostyle Hall at the time. The usual clumps of tourists were there, gathered round their guides, and Ramses was lecturing our group. As I stood at a little distance from them, deep in thought, a voice hailed me, and I turned to see a lady approaching. She was rather stout and florid of face and looked familiar, but I could not recall where I had met her until she reminded me.

"Mrs. Emerson, is it not? We met at Mr. Vandergelt's soiree the other evening."

It was the bad-mannered mama who had removed her daughter so precipitately from David. She was quite smartly dressed in a costume of dark green linen and a bonnetlike hat which shaded features that I had not taken particular notice of at the time. Assuming, as people will, that I remembered her name—which I did not—she launched into a gushing monologue about the beauties of Egypt and her enjoyment of the country, ending with an invitation to dine with her that evening at the Winter Palace.

Unfortunately, Emerson and I have acquired a certain notoriety, and there are those, I am sorry to say, who seek out well-known persons in order to brag about knowing them. I could only assume that this lady—whose name I still could not recall—was moved by that unattractive and, to me, inexplicable, desire.

I expressed polite regrets, therefore, explaining that we were otherwise engaged. She did not take the hint, saying she would not be leaving Luxor for several more days, and that any evening would suit her. Such rude persistence, in my opinion, justifies a firm response. I was about to utter it when she caught hold of my arm.

"There is the native who has been following me demanding money," she said indignantly. "Come over here, Mrs. Emerson, where he won't see us."

The place toward which she was rapidly pulling me, with a grip that numbed my arm, was a doorway, now blocked, that had once admitted visitors to the Southern Precinct.

A thrill of anticipation ran through me. Was this another attempt at abduction? It hardly seemed likely, in such a crowded place, but the doorway was in a far corner and hidden by scaffolding.

Emerson stepped into view from behind an adjoining pillar. "Where the devil do you think you are going, Peabody?"

"Ah," said my new acquaintance, releasing my arm. "It is your husband. A pleasure to see you again, Professor. I was just asking Mrs. Emerson if you would do me the pleasure of dining with me one evening."

"Most unlikely," said Emerson, looking her up and down. "But if you will give me your card I will let you know."

She produced it, after fumbling in her capacious handbag and then—her purpose achieved, as she believed—returned to her group.

"Hmmm," said Emerson, fingering the little piece of pasteboard.

"Where are the others?" I asked, hoping, though not really expecting, to avoid a lecture.

"There." Emerson gestured. "Curse you, Peabody, if you are going to go on doing this sort of thing I will lock you up."

"What could possibly happen here, with a hundred tourists around? She is only a harmless bore."

"No doubt." Emerson glanced at the card. "Mrs. Louisa Ferncliffe. Heatherby Hall, Bastington on Stoke."

"Nouveau riche," I said with a little sniff. "Her accent was quite common. We met her at Cyrus's the other evening."

"I didn't."

I took his arm and we started toward the others. "Things have been tediously quiet of late, Emerson."

"Nothing is likely to happen if we all stay together, as we have done the past few days."

Accompanied as it was by a steely blue glare, this sounded like a threat. It was also, I feared, a depressing statement of fact. How were we to find our deadly enemy unless we gave him a chance to get at us?

We lunched at the Karnak Hotel. The beautiful view across the river, the excellent food, and the valiant attempts of some of us to carry on a cheerful conversation did not have much effect on the general gloom. The hours were passing; too few of them remained. Our dear visitors would not return to the West Bank but would go directly to the train station in time to catch the evening express; their luggage had been packed and would be brought to them there. From time to time Lia's eyes filled with tears and she turned her head, pretending to admire the view so that she could wipe them away. She had wanted to go to Gurneh to say good-bye to Abdullah and Daoud, but I had not thought that advisable.

By the time we finished luncheon the afternoon was well advanced. Sir Edward had been especially kind, devoting himself to Evelyn and trying to amuse her with reminiscences of the wonderful days in Tetisheri's tomb. The reminders were not as consoling as he hoped. It was during that season that David had come into our lives;

I knew Evelyn was remembering the abused, love-starved child who had won her heart—and whose heart she was now helping to break.

I believe we were all relieved when the time for departure finally arrived. We had wandered through the shops; Walter had showered gifts on his daughter: an embroidered robe, a necklace of gold and lapis beads, trinkets and souvenirs of all kinds. She received them graciously but without enthusiasm. She had behaved admirably. Not until we reached the station and saw who awaited us there did she give way.

Abdullah looked magnificent. He wore his finest robes, of white silk trimmed with gold, and his snowiest turban. His face, framed by the white of beard and turban, had the dignity of a pharaoh's. Daoud was also wearing his best, his long kaftan of striped silk and cotton, his girdle a colored Kashmir scarf. His face was not at all dignified.

Abdullah held out his hand and addressed Walter. "May God keep thee and thine in the shelter of his care, Effendi. May it be good until our next meeting."

Walter took the old man's hand and wrung it vigorously. He did not speak. I don't believe he could.

Abdullah addressed Evelyn and Lia in the formal words of farewell. Then it was Daoud's turn. Instead of taking the hand Lia offered, he placed an object on her palm—a flat gold case two inches square, covered with ornate Kufic script. It was a charm, containing verses from the Koran—very old and very precious.

"It is a strong hegab, little Sitt. It will keep you safe until you come again."

I could not blame her for breaking down. There were tears in my own eyes. They streamed down the girl's face as she threw herself into Daoud's arms.

"We must find our places, darling," Walter said, gently detaching her.

I do not like to remember that parting. The worst moment came at the end, when, having embraced the rest of us, Lia turned to David and held out a small, trembling hand. She had given her promise and meant to keep it if it killed her, and I am certain at that moment she felt as if it would.

"For God's sake, kiss him," Ramses said suddenly. "They can't deny you that much."

We stood on the platform waving until the train drew away and the cloud of smoke from the funnel dissipated in the evening breeze. Daoud and Abdullah had withdrawn to a discreet distance, but I supposed they would return to the West Bank with us; it would have been churlish not to offer them places in our boat. I found I was reluctant to face Abdullah, though there was no reason (I assured myself) why I should have been. His immense dignity and intrinsic good manners would prevent him from reproaching me, by so much as a look.

I wasn't keen on facing my children either. Nefret had been shooting me hostile glances all day, and Ramses . . . Who would have expected Ramses, of all people, to make such a romantic gesture? He had practically pushed them into one another's arms, and no one, not even Walter, had had the heart to forbid it.

We retraced our steps and, as I had expected, Emerson invited Daoud and Abdullah to return with us. Sir Edward, who had offered me his arm, announced he would remain in Luxor, since he had a dinner engagement. "With Abdullah and Daoud along, you don't need me," he added.

"You have been very conscientious and very kind, Sir Edward," I replied. "I can only assume it is your sense of British noblesse oblige that moves you, since we owe you nothing."

"The pleasure of your acquaintance and the honor of your esteem is more than sufficient reward for whatever poor services I have been able to offer."

It sounded as artificial as a paragraph out of a novel—or one of Ramses's more pompous speeches. Sir Edward was aware of this; with a sidelong smile and in a more natural tone he added, "I haven't been of much use thus far, Mrs. Emerson. It is a baffling case, and frustrating as well. Has the Professor any ideas about what to do tomorrow?"

"If I know the Professor, he will be back in the Valley tomorrow. He has lost two days' work and he will be wild to find out what Mr. Davis is doing."

Sir Edward laughed. "Of course. I will obtain a report this evening, Mrs. Emerson. The individual with whom I am dining is Mr. Paul, the photographer from Cairo. He has been working in the tomb all day, I believe."

"Indeed? Yes, I believe someone did mention he was to be here today. Have you met him?"

"We have mutual acquaintances—and, of course, a shared interest in archaeological photography."

When we reached the quay Sir Edward bade us good night and went on down the road toward the Winter Palace, whose lighted windows glowed through the dusk like those of the royal residence after which it had been called. He began to whistle and the length of his stride implied that he was looking forward to the evening. Fellow enthusiasts always have a great deal to talk about.

I felt rather as if I had lost my only partisan—or at least the only neutral party. I had to assure myself that I had acted for the best, as I always do, and that I had nothing with which to reproach myself. I had thought of suggesting that we dine in Luxor, but the scene at the railway station had convinced me that none of the others would feel there was anything to celebrate.

It is only with good friends that one can be comfortably silent. I had never been uncomfortable with Abdullah, but that evening I found myself trying to think of topics of conversation. Abdullah too seemed preoccupied. The moon had risen, sending silvery ripples across the water, and we were nearing the west bank before he spoke.

"I am looking for a wife for David."

"What?" I exclaimed. "He is still very young, Abdullah."

"When I was his age I had two wives and four children. Mustafa Karim has a daughter, young, healthy, suitable in all ways." In a tone of deep gloom Abdullah added, "She has learned to read and write."

I dared not laugh. In fact, I was quite touched. Abdullah considered education for women the most pernicious of all modern developments. He was making a great concession to demand literacy for his grandson's bride.

"Have you mentioned this to David?" I asked.

"Mention? No, Sitt. In the old days I would not 'mention,' I would tell him what I had arranged. Now, I suppose, he will want to meet her first."

Abdullah sighed. I patted his hand sympathetically. Poor Abdullah! He expected an argument from David, but I feared he underestimated the difficulty.

I didn't doubt Abdullah knew about David and Lia. Strange; it had not occurred to me that he would be opposed to that relationship. I was conscious of a ridiculous feeling of annoyance.

Selim was waiting for us with the horses, and after this changing of the guard—for that was what it was—Abdullah and Daoud set off on foot for Gurneh. Selim would not sit down to table with us, claiming he had already eaten. He went off to the kitchen to talk with Fatima.

"He means to stay here tonight," Ramses said. "I assured him it was not necessary, but he insisted."

"They are good friends and honorable men," said Nefret, glancing at David, who did not respond. He was wrapped in misery so profound one could almost see it around him like a damp black cloud. He had eaten nothing.

"Yes," said Emerson. "Very good of Selim. Especially since he has two young, pretty . . . Er, hmph."

Emerson's innocent blunder broke the wall of ice my son and daughter had raised between us. Nefret's face dissolved into laughter. "It must keep Selim very busy."

"I haven't heard him complain," said Ramses.

Nefret laughed again. Most improper, no doubt, but it was so good to see her smiling again that I decided to overlook these mild indelicacies.

"I cannot understand polygamy, though," she said, shaking her head. "I wouldn't want to share the man I loved. I would be madly jealous of every woman he so much as looked at!"

"Jealousy," I declared, "is crueler than the grave. It is— What did you say, Ramses?"

"Nothing." He pushed his plate away. "If you will excuse me, I am going to fahddle with Selim."

Nefret and David went with him. I spent the evening looking over the photographs they had taken of the funerary papyrus, for I had decided I would try my hand at a translation. I had fallen sadly behind with my literary activities. It was good to have the children out of the way for once.

289

When we arrived at the Valley next morning I saw Emerson had managed to get an electric wire run from the generator to our tomb. Selim went at once to arrange it and the lights. Abdullah watched him with a curling lip. He did not approve of modern inventions and refused to learn anything about them. Selim had once believed that Emerson and I were great magicians, with the power to read men's minds and control evil spirits. Observing the tactful manner with which he ignored Emerson's helpful suggestions, I rather suspected he no longer cherished those youthful delusions. Selim was of the new generation, young enough to be Abdullah's grandson instead of his son. I dreaded the inevitable day when he would replace his father as our reis, but I did not doubt he would be as able and as devoted.

Once the lights were arranged, Ramses and David got to work copying the reliefs. Only fragments of them remained, but they were of a high order, delicately carved and retaining some traces of color. Emerson watched for a while, and then withdrew. He could do nothing more inside for the time being, since every movement stirred up dust that would impede the artists.

Sir Edward had not returned the previous night until after we had retired, and he had been late coming in to breakfast. He had seemed tired and preoccupied, and I confess I had wondered whether it was the photographer from Cairo, or someone more entertaining, who had kept him up so late. When Emerson and I came out of number Five, we found him conversing with Nefret.

"If you don't want me for anything just now, Professor, I am going along to see what Mr. Ayrton is doing," she said.

Emerson tried to look as if the idea had not occurred to him until that moment. He did not succeed. "Hmmm, yes, why not? We may be able to help him."

"I was just about to ask you about that, sir," said Sir Edward. "You know I had dinner last night with Mr. Paul—"

"No, I did not know," said Emerson.

"Oh? I thought perhaps Mrs. Emerson had mentioned it."

"No, she did not," said Emerson.

"Oh. Well, sir, he suggested I might give him a hand today. The photographs he took yesterday did not turn out as well as he had hoped—"

"You helped him develop them?" I inquired, regretting my suspicions of the young man. Developing plates takes a long time and requires careful attention.

"Not to say help, no. He is a skilled photographer. However, as he pointed out, working in a confined space filled with fragile objects is easier with an assistant—to hold the equipment, you know, and manipulate the lights."

"Two assistants would be even better," said Nefret eagerly.

"That might be pushing Mr. Ayrton too far," Sir Edward said, smiling at her.

"Yes, the fewer people stamping around in the burial chamber the better," Emerson agreed.

"Then you don't object, Professor?" Sir Edward asked.

"You don't require my permission, you are not on my staff," said Emerson. "Go ahead, by all means. I will just go with you and make certain it's all right with Ayrton."

"What sort of person is this Mr. Paul?" I asked, as we started along the path.

Sir Edward laughed. "He's an odd little old chap. Absolutely dedicated to his work. I couldn't get him to talk of anything but photography."

Ned was alone—that is to say, Davis and his entourage were not there. He greeted us with obvious pleasure. "I thought you had lost interest, Professor, since you haven't been here for several days. Is Ramses not with you?"

Emerson explained that we had been entertaining guests, and that Ramses and David were now at work in number Five. When Sir Edward mentioned his intention of assisting Mr. Paul, Ned nodded. "Yes, he told me you would be joining him. It's up to him, of course; I don't know much about photography. Go ahead, Sir Edward. I needn't caution you to take care."

"He's already here, then?" I asked.

"Yes, he arrived at the crack of dawn. Very dedicated man."

Sir Edward descended the steps and disappeared into the tomb. "Mr. Davis decided not to come today," Ned explained. "There's not much we can do until Mr. Paul finishes the photography."

"Quite right," said Emerson. "We may as well get back to work. Care to come and have a look, Ayrton?"

Ned said he would like that. We had quite a nice, restful morning—all of us, that is, except for Ramses and David. When I called them out for mid-morning tea they were rather sticky and Ramses remarked that it was time they stopped anyhow, since it was hard to keep perspiration from dripping onto the paper. He and Ned got into an animated discussion of his photographic copying method.

"David agrees with Mr. Carter, though," Ramses explained. "That freehand copying is the best method of capturing the spirit of the original."

"That depends on the spirit of the copyist," Ned said somewhat cynically. "David's work is first-rate. I tried to persuade . . . Well, never mind."

When Emerson called a halt to the day's work, I went down the path to see whether Sir Edward intended returning with us. I realized that Ned must have left for the day, since the only persons present were a few of the guards. There were lights inside the tomb, however. I was tempted to go in, but my professional conscience intervened; obviously the dedicated photographers were still at work, and it would have been wrong to disturb them. Sir Edward would return when he was ready, as was his right.

Our pleasant teatime on the verandah lacked its usual air of affability that evening. Emerson was brooding over the iniquities of Davis and Weigall, and David was brooding over his broken heart. He even looked thinner than he had the previous day, which was impossible. I wondered if Abdullah had raised the subject of Mustafa Karim's suitable daughter, and decided not to ask.

"Mother, who was that woman with whom you were talking at Karnak yesterday morning?"

It was Ramses who spoke. The question was unexpected but welcome. At that point in time the topic of murder was less difficult than certain others.

"She claimed to be an innocent tourist," I said. "But her behavior was highly suspicious. If your father had not interfered—"

"She would have lured you behind a pillar, chloroformed you, and had you carried off by her waiting henchmen?" said Emerson. "Peabody, there are times when I despair of you."

"You had not met her before?" Ramses asked.

"I saw her at Cyrus's reception, but did not speak to her then. You did, David."

"What?" David started. "I beg your pardon?"

I repeated what I had said. "You were talking with her daughter, or so I suppose the young woman to have been. Fair-haired, rather plump? Mrs. Ferncliffe came and drew her away."

"Oh, yes." David was not at all interested, but he made an effort to be courteous. "I didn't realize the older lady was her mother. She didn't speak to me."

Perched on the ledge with his hands clasping his raised knees, Ramses said, "I've been thinking about something you said, Mother—you and Uncle Walter. Perhaps your idea of a murder cult is not so far-fetched as it sounded. Not that it is likely such a thing actually exists, but the suggestion of it, and those horribly mutilated bodies, have cast a spell of superstitious terror over the local people. They are obviously afraid to talk to us. Is it possible that our adversaries are using fear to compensate for a weakness in physical strength? How many of them are there?"

"Good thinking," Nefret exclaimed.

"Not really," said Ramses. "We have encountered only a few members of what may be a large organization. However, we've never seen more than three or four of them at a time, have we? There were only three men at Layla's house. She said more were expected, but that doesn't necessarily imply a large number."

"There were at least four in Cairo," Nefret said thoughtfully. "Two who came in through the window, two in the house across the street."

"There were three of them in the house," David said. His hand went unconsciously to his throat. "And the woman."

Three simple words, pronounced without emphasis or hidden meaning—yet their effect on Nefret was remarkable. Her breath caught in a sharp gasp.

"The woman," she repeated. "Amazing, isn't it, how we have overlooked the female participants? Yet there have been several of them, and the roles they played were not negligible. A woman who called herself Mrs. Markham infiltrated the WSPU and assisted Sethos in the robbery of Mr. Romer's antiquities. A woman tried to cut David's throat that night in Cairo. Another woman, Layla, was obviously an important member of the group. Some or all of the women in that abominable house in Luxor are also involved."

"Nefret," I exclaimed. "What are you saying?"

She cut me off with a peremptory gesture. Her eyes were shining with excitement. "I had an inkling of the truth a few days ago, when I tried to question you about Sethos, and *you* refused to discuss the matter. You said that the attempted abduction in London lacked Sethos's characteristic touch. You were right. He would not have planned such a crude, brutal attack or allowed his subordinates to handle you so roughly.

"Yet the clues that led us to suspect Sethos cannot be dismissed, expecially the clue of the typewriter. If it was not Sethos who sent that message, it was someone close to him—someone who had access to his private collection of treasures, who is familiar with the illegal antiquities business and the criminal underworld, who hates Aunt Amelia and wants to harm her. I believe that someone is a woman—and that you know who she is!"

Emerson's eyes widened. "Hell and damnation! Can it be—but it must be! Bertha!"

13

I had to clear my throat before I could speak intelligibly. "No. Impossible."

"It can't be coincidental," Emerson muttered. "She fits Nefret's criteria in every particular."

"Not every particular, Emerson. She was not . . . Oh, good Gad! Do you believe she *was*?"

Nefret's blue eyes glittered like the best Kashmir sapphires. "I hope you won't think me ill-mannered, Aunt Amelia, if I suggest you tell us what the devil you are talking about—for a change. Bertha was the woman who was involved in the Vincey affair the year you and the Professor were in Egypt without us. What has she to do with Sethos?"

"Sethos was also involved in that business," Emerson admitted. "We were unaware of it until the very end, and once again he managed to elude us."

"And so did Bertha," I said numbly. "We encountered her again the following year, at which time she was actively engaged in the illicit antiquities game."

"So it was she who abducted Nefret," Ramses said. "Then who is Matilda?"

"Bertha's bodyguard and lieutenant. It was she who helped carry Nefret off and . . . How the devil do you know that name?"

For once Ramses had no ready reply. His dark-fringed eyes,

avoiding mine, locked with those of Nefret, who squared her shoulders and spoke in a firm voice.

"We found your list, Aunt Amelia. What else can we do but eavesdrop and pry when you treat us like infants? Ramses, I forbid you to apologize."

"I hadn't intended to," said Ramses.

"No, you were trying to invent a plausible lie. No more of that! We want the truth, the whole truth, and nothing but the truth. Well, Aunt Amelia?"

"You are in the right," I said numbly, for my brain was still struggling to assimilate this unexpected revelation. "In some ways Bertha would be a more dangerous adversary than Sethos himself. She is and was a totally unscrupulous, brilliantly clever woman, and she boasted of having formed a criminal organization of women. Layla must have been one of her henchmen—er—women. Another fact that may well be relevant is that she—er—she appears to harbor a personal grudge against me."

"Why?" Nefret asked. "Did she explain?"

"Perhaps 'grudge' is not the precise word. The precise word she used was 'hate.' She said she had lain awake nights planning how she would kill me. Some of the methods she had invented were—again I quote—very ingenious."

I had not realized the recollection of that conversation would be so disturbing. I do not believe voice or countenance betrayed me, but Nefret's stony face softened, and Emerson put a supportive hand on my shoulder.

"'Grudge' does seem inadequate," said my son coolly. "What had you done to annoy her, Mother?"

"I had treated her much more gently than she deserved," I replied. "Her antipathy toward me arises from . . . Emerson, my dear, I am sorry to embarrass you, but—"

Emerson's brows drew together in a scowl. "Peabody, are you still harboring that flattering fantasy about Bertha's attachment to me? Her interest in me was transitory and—er—specific. And, I hope I need not say, unreciprocated! After the death of her paramour she went looking for another protector, for, as you once said, my dear, discrimination against women makes it difficult for them to succeed in criminal endeavors without a male partner. We now have reason to believe she found that partner."

"Of course," Nefret cried. "It is all coming together. Bertha joined Sethos and fell in love with him. She believed she had captured his heart until the mere sight of you at the demonstration caused him to betray the unaltered intensity of his devotion! Frenzied with jealousy, Bertha sent the message that would have delivered you into her vengeful hands had not your gallant defenders arrived in the nick of time. When Sethos learned of it he flew into a rage, accused her, told her he never wanted to set eyes on her again. If she hated you before, how much greater cause has she now! Cast off by the man she loves—"

"Oh, good Gad," Emerson exclaimed. "Nefret, I don't know which offends me most, your sentimental ideas or the language in which you express them. Bertha was incapable of the emotion you mention. Her original profession was—er—the same as Layla's, which would explain why she turned to women in the same business when she sought allies. However, the rest of your melodramatic plot makes a certain amount of sense. It would explain how the papyrus got to Cairo. She robbed Sethos before she left him."

"There's another thing," Ramses said slowly. "Something Layla said. 'Your lady mother knows. Ask her whether women cannot be as dangerous as men.'"

"You might have mentioned that little detail earlier," I said, not entirely displeased to find someone beside myself guilty of negligence. "It is highly significant!"

"Only in context," said Nefret, giving me a critical look.

"She claimed later that she had tried to warn me," Ramses said. He turned to me with as affable an expression as I had ever seen on his face. If his lips had been curved a fraction of an inch more, I would have said he was smiling. "A confounded oblique warning, if that is how it was meant. Never mind, Mother; it's all right, you know. Would you like a whiskey and soda?"

"Thank you," I said meekly.

The atmosphere had lightened appreciably. After Ramses had supplied me with the beverage he had offered, he went on. "This theory makes better sense than our original assumption that Sethos was once again our secret adversary. If it is true, the terms of the equation have changed—and not to our advantage. Sethos seems to be bound by a certain code of honor. Obviously no such scruples affect Bertha. She may have decided that the sweetest form of revenge would be to harm, not Mother, but those who are close to her. Viewed in that light, the attacks on us take on quite a different character. Yussuf was not sent to retrieve the papyrus; he was supposed to injure or abduct Nefret."

"He did try to get the papyrus," Nefret insisted. "That was what woke me, when he—"

"Stumbled over the box containing the papyrus," said Ramses. "That explains one of the points that troubled me—how he or any outsider would have known it was in your room. He didn't know, until he saw it or stubbed his toe on it."

"Damn it, Ramses, are you implying I was careless about hiding it?"

"Or," said Ramses hastily, "he was searching for something, anything, worth stealing. Yussuf Mahmud was a thief and a physical coward. Greed overcame him, and when you fought back he fled. The men who attacked David and me could easily have dispatched us. Uncertainty as to our fate would presumably have caused extreme mental anguish to Mother. What could be more painful than to fear for those you love, to know that they are enduring captivity, torture and a prolonged, unpleasant death?"

The hand Emerson had placed on my shoulder tightened. "Did Layla tell you that was what they had in mind for you and David?"

"Not in so many words" was the response. "But it would have been a reasonable conjecture even if she had not hinted at some such thing."

"Hell and damnation!" Nefret exclaimed. "We've got to find the cursed woman! Where can she be hiding? The House of the Doves? How I despise that name!"

"No," Ramses said firmly. "A woman who favors expensive French champagne would prefer more elegant accommodations."

"Of course," I exclaimed. "The champagne! That is another piece of confirmatory evidence. Good Gad, she was actually staying at Layla's house!"

"Part of the time," Ramses said. "She must have gone off that night to make the arrangements for our—er—removal. Another indication, perhaps, that her manpower (if you will excuse the term) is limited."

"Not limited enough," Emerson said grimly. "This isn't getting us anywhere. Damned if I can think what to do next."

"One never knows," I said. "Something may yet turn up!"

"Such as a cobra in my bed," said Nefret. But she said it lightly, and her smile at me was almost friendly.

A thump and a wild flutter of vines heralded the arrival of Horus. He sat down on the ledge and stared at Ramses, who edged away from him.

"Well, there is your guard against snakes," I said. "The sacred cat of Re, who cuts off the head of the Serpent of Darkness."

"If Re depended on that one to protect him, the sun would never rise again," said Ramses.

Nefret picked up the cat and cuddled him, crooning in a manner most inappropriate for a beast that size. "He was Nefret's hero, wasn't him?"

"Disgusting," said Ramses.

I could not but agree.

Since I had been unable to keep the appointment with Miss Buchanan at the Mission School, I had invited her and one of her teachers to dine, along with Katherine and Cyrus, of course. I had intended to ask Mr. Paul, the photographer, as well. My motives were entirely charitable; he was a stranger in Luxor, and knew few people. However, Sir Edward informed me he did not accept social invitations. "He's an odd little chap. Not comfortable in society."

Sir Edward was not with us either. His absences were becoming highly suspicious. I doubted that the odd little Mr. Paul was the attraction; Sir Edward must have struck up an acquaintance with one of the lady tourists. Not that it was my affair.

I was acquainted with Miss Buchanan, but had not met her companion, a Miss Whiteside from Boston. Like Miss Buchanan, she had trained as a nurse. Neither lady was a model of fashion; they wore rather severe dark gowns, with nice neat white collars and cuffs. They were amiable and interesting women, though rather given to introducing God into the conversation more often than was strictly necessary. This did not sit well with Emerson, but he behaved like the gentleman he is, confining his objections to an occasional grimace. The subject of education for women was of course the primary topic. My interest in the subject was considerable, but I found my thoughts wandering—not altogether surprising, after the revelation that had come to me earlier.

Was it indeed Bertha who had returned to torment me? It had been years since I had seen or heard from her, and I had honestly believed she had given up her evil ways.

I had one advantage with her that I had never had with Sethos. I was familiar with her true appearance, for I had been in close contact with her day after day for several weeks. No—two advantages. She might have learned something of the art of disguise from Sethos, but she had not his natural talents.

And yet . . . No one who has seen a society beauty in the full bloom of her evening toilette and seen that same woman when she wakes in the morning with puffy eyes and sallow cheeks could doubt a female's ability to alter her appearance. Bertha had been young and handsome. Would I recognize her if she had made herself look older and plainer?

My eyes moved from Miss Buchanan to her assistant. The latter was considerably younger than her superior, but neither could be called handsome. Both had scorned the use of cosmetics. No, I thought. Impossible. Bertha would be a fool to show herself to me or Emerson, who knew her as well as I did (but no better). A crafty villainess would lurk in the shadows, carrying out her evil schemes through intermediaries. If she had to appear in public, what better disguise than one of the ubiquitous black robes worn by middle-class Egyptian women? With her fair complexion darkened and only her eyes visible over the face veil, she could pass within a few feet of me unnoticed.

I came back to myself with a start, realizing that Miss Buchanan had asked me a question. I had to ask her to repeat it. After that I forced myself to behave like a proper hostess, but after dinner I took pity on Emerson and allowed the subject to turn to Egyptology.

No one who lives in Luxor can remain completely indifferent to the subject. Miss Buchanan was acquainted with Mrs. Andrews, and she had heard of the new tomb. She asked if we had been inside and requested a description. "It is true that the queen is wearing a golden crown?" she inquired.

Ramses immediately launched into an interminable monologue. Happily, this prevented Emerson from launching into an interminable tirade against all the persons involved with the tomb; but as Ramses went on and on and on, listing every item in the burial chamber, even Emerson stopped scowling and listened open-mouthed.

"The so-called crown is in fact a collar or pectoral," Ramses concluded. "Why it was placed on the head of the mummy is open to conjecture. It was of thin gold in the shape of a vulture—the vulture goddess Nekhbet, to be precise—so it could be bent to fit the contours of the skull. Oh—I neglected to mention a heap of approximately forty beads which had apparently fallen from a necklace or bracelet."

Cyrus eyed him askance. "Now see here, young fellow, you can't possibly remember all that. How many times were you in the burial chamber?"

Ramses's reply—"Once, sir, for approximately twenty minutes"—made Cyrus look even more skeptical. However, I recalled the time Ramses had rattled off the entire inventory of an antiquities storeroom after having been in the place for less time than that. I had forgot about this attribute—natural talent or acquired skill, as the case may be—and apparently Emerson had too. He gazed at his son in dawning speculation.

"A word with you later, Ramses," he said.

"Yes, sir."

The ladies from the Mission left early, in order to be safely removed from worldly temptation before midnight, when the Sabbath began. Miss Buchanan repeated her invitation to visit the school, which I promised I would do.

The Vandergelts were driving the ladies back to the boat landing in their carriage, but I managed to draw Katherine aside for a few words in private.

"We must make a formal appointment, it seems," I declared. "I have seen too little of you, and I have much to tell you."

"I feel the same," Katherine replied. "I believe Cyrus means to go to the Valley tomorrow. I will come with him, and perhaps we can find the opportunity for a chat."

I stood on the verandah waving farewell until the carriage disappeared into the darkness. I hoped the others would have gone to their rooms by the time I returned to the parlor, but they were still there, and I braced myself for additional questions and reproaches.

"We were wondering, Mother, whether you had heard from Uncle Walter."

Ramses was the speaker, but I knew who had prompted him to ask. My reply was directed impartially at them all.

"I am sorry I neglected to mention it. Yes, Walter telegraphed from Cairo this afternoon, and for a wonder the message was promptly delivered. They had a safe journey and they have booked passage on the steamer from Port Said on Tuesday next."

"All of them?" Nefret exclaimed. "I thought Uncle Walter intended to return to Luxor."

"I persuaded him not to do so," said Emerson, looking particularly smug.

None of us asked how he had accomplished that. I really did not care how. I did not doubt Walter's courage or his devotion to us, but it would have been deuced awkward to have him underfoot. He was a scholar, not a man of action, and every mention of Lia's name would have been—well—awkward.

"Well done, Emerson," I said.

Emerson looked pleased. David murmured a few words that might have been "Good night," and left the room.

Emerson does not brood. He has a happy facility for concentrating on the business of the moment and ignoring the things he can do nothing about. He was up next morning full of energy and ready to go back to work.

By the time Katherine and Cyrus joined us in the Valley we had put in two good hours' work. Cyrus inspected number Five without great enthusiasm. "It'll take years to get through that debris, and then the ceiling will probably fall in on you," he declared.

"It is not like you to be so pessimistic," I said.

"Well, consarn it, Amelia, I'm getting discouraged. All those years here in the Valley without any luck, and I'm having the same kind of thing over at Dra Abu'l Naga, right near where you-all found Tetisheri. Seems as if I should be due for something."

"I told you you should have hired Carter," Emerson said unsympathetically.

"Couldn't let Amherst go, could I? He's doing the best he can. How about having a look at Davis's tomb?" Cyrus added emphatically, "Darn the fellow!"

So we all went to have a look. No one was there but Ned, standing guard, or so I assumed, since nothing was going on. He explained that Mr. Paul was still photographing, so no visitors were allowed.

"Is Sir Edward with him?" I asked. I had not seen the young man that morning; he had come in late and left early.

"Yes, ma'am, he was here at the break of day," Ned said poetically. "It certainly is good of you to spare him."

"I would have been happy to spare other members of my staff," said Emerson snappishly. "Is that fellow Smith painting? Can't imagine why Davis uses him when David and Carter are available."

He went on grumbling while Cyrus, at Ned's invitation, descended the steps and peered into the entrance corridor. When he came back his face was alight. Cyrus was a true enthusiast, and very well informed for an amateur. It did seem a pity he had never found anything worthwhile.

"When will you open the coffin?" Cyrus asked greedily. "Consarn it, I'd give a thousand dollars to be present!"

Katherine gave me an amused smile. "He would, too," she said. "But Mr. Ayrton is incorruptible, Cyrus, you cannot bribe him."

"Now, Katherine, Mr. Ayrton knows I didn't mean it that way."

"Oh, no, sir," Ned said. "That is—yes, sir, I do know. M. Maspero is arriving tomorrow; I'm sure he would give you permission."

Emerson groaned. "Maspero? Well, curse it, that will be the end of the tomb. He'll want to go in, and he will invite everybody he knows to go in, and by the time they finish stumbling about there won't be a scrap left in its original place. How much longer will the photography take?"

Ned shrugged. "I don't know, Professor."

"He doesn't know much, does he?" Emerson said disagreeably— but not until after we were on our way back to our own tomb.

Ramses was quick to defend his friend. "He is not the one who makes those decisions, Father. Once Maspero gets here he will be officially in charge."

"We can ask Sir Edward about the photographs," I suggested. "This evening, perhaps."

"Hmm, yes," Emerson said. "That young man has been conspicuous by his absence of late. I want to have a talk with him."

Since the hour was past midday, Cyrus suggested we go back to the Castle for lunch. This was agreeable to all. The only question was what to do with Horus, whom Nefret had brought with her. He had stayed with us, for a change; usually he went off on his own, hunting . . . something or other . . . and we always had a hard time collecting him when it was time to go home. Now she asked Cyrus if the invitation included the cat.

"Why, sure, bring him along," said Cyrus.

"My dear," Katherine exclaimed. "Have you forgot that Sekhmet is in—er—a delicate condition?"

I knew the cat could not be expecting or Cyrus would have mentioned it, so I concluded that the condition to which Katherine referred was the one that often led to the other.

"We've got her shut up in her room like always," Cyrus said cheerfully.

I had seen Sekhmet's room. It had mesh screens on the windows and was furnished with cat beds, cat toys, and cat dishes. Many human beings do not enjoy quarters as comfortable.

"Don't count on a locked door to keep that feline Casanova out," said Ramses, giving Horus a hateful look.

Horus gave him one back. All Bastet's descendants are unusually intelligent.

Cyrus studied the animal with a new interest. Horus sat at Nefret's feet, his paws together and his head lifted alertly. His resemblance to the felines depicted in the ancient paintings was particularly strong just then; his long ears were pricked, his brindled coat glowed in the sunlight. He might have been the model for the painting of the Cat of Re that illustrated the portion of the papyrus I had recently translated.

Cyrus tugged at his goatee. "Hmmmm," he said thoughtfully.

When the others started back to the Valley after an excellent luncheon, Horus was not with them. Cyrus had assured Nefret he would return the creature next day. I wondered whether Horus would want to be returned, after experiencing all the feline comforts available to him at the Castle, but that was not a subject I particularly wanted to discuss.

I intended to stay and have a comfortable private talk with Katherine. At first Emerson would not hear of it. He finally consented after I agreed to wait there until someone came for me.

"So you are still in danger," Katherine said soberly. "Tell me what has been happening."

Cyrus had gone with the others. We were alone in Katherine's charming parlor, which her doting husband had completely redecorated for her. It combined the finest of Middle Eastern ornaments—rugs, brasswork, carved screens—with the most comfortable of modern furniture. I always felt hospitably welcomed in that room, and I settled down in an overstuffed chair and told her all about it.

Her plump, pretty face lengthened as I spoke. "I wish there were something I could do to help, Amelia. It is a desperate situation and I see no way out of it."

"Something will no doubt occur to me," I assured her. "We have been in situations as desperate, Katherine. I didn't expect you to offer a solution, only the comfort of friendly interest, which you have done. Oh, and Evelyn asked me to pass on her fondest regards and her regrets that they were unable to say good-bye in person."

"We heard they had left," Katherine said. "Was there a reason for their sudden departure, or should I not ask?"

So I told her all about that, too. Her response was limited to a shake of the head and a murmured "What a pity. I am so sorry."

I realized I had hoped she would say more. That surprised me, since I am not in the habit of relying on others for advice.

"It will all work out for the best," I said firmly. " 'Hearts do not break; they sting and ache'—uh—"

" ' . . . for old love's sake, but do not die.' " Katherine dimpled. "*The Mikado*, isn't it?"

"Yes, of course. You know your Gilbert and Sullivan even better than I. Now tell me how your plans for the school are progressing."

She accepted the change of subject and we had a very useful discussion. She could not decide whether it would be more sensible to construct a new building or refurbish an old one, and she was still in doubt as to the best location for the school. Luxor seemed the obvious choice, but she hoped to attract girls from the west bank villages and, as she pointed out, there were already two schools in Luxor.

"The Mission School and what other?" I asked.

"The one Fatima attends. She told you about it."

"Oh, yes. It isn't an actual school, though, is it?"

"Not by our definitions, perhaps, but it has an excellent location, and Sayyida Amin holds several classes each day. She admitted she has not the money to do more."

It was a pleasure to get my mind off matters that were temporarily insoluble and concentrate on a subject that could be solved, with time and money and dedication—all of which Katherine possessed. When the little clock on the mantel chimed I was startled to realize how late it had become.

"I must get back," I declared, rising.

"You mustn't go, Amelia. Emerson told you to wait until someone came for you."

"I refuse to sit waiting like a child whose papa is busy elsewhere. It is broad daylight and I will be well-mounted."

Katherine followed me downstairs, expostulating all the while; but when we reached the courtyard we found Ramses sitting cross-legged on the ground, chatting with the gatekeeper and one of the gardeners. The latter gave Katherine a guilty look and hastened away.

"Why didn't you tell me you were here?" I demanded.

Ramses uncoiled himself and rose in a single motion. "I haven't been here long. Father is still in the Valley, but he said he would leave shortly and that we are to go straight home. Good afternoon, Mrs. Vandergelt."

"Good afternoon," said Katherine, with one of her catlike smiles. "Wouldn't you like a cup of tea?"

"No, thank you, ma'am, Father said we were to go at once."

He insisted on my riding Risha, and mounted my amiable but plodding mare. "What is your father up to?" I inquired.

"He is lying in wait for Mr. Paul and Sir Edward, I believe. With M. Maspero's dahabeeyah arriving tomorrow, he is increasingly concerned about the contents of the burial chamber."

"He would be. I do wish I could persuade him not to interfere. Maspero is already vexed with him."

The horses were picking their way through the rocky defile that led from the Valley when I heard something that made me look round. It took me a moment to locate the source of the agitated bleating, for the goat's dusty coat was almost the same color as the surrounding rock.

Risha stopped at a touch. I dismounted and started toward the animal, which appeared to be caught by the leg.

"Damn it, Mother!" Ramses shouted. "Watch out!"

Since I am not as stupid as my children believe I am, I had immediately realized this might be a ruse, but I was not at all averse to a confrontation. In fact, I had been hoping for some such thing. My hand was in my coat pocket, therefore, when the man appeared from behind a boulder and started toward me. He carried a knife, so I had no compunction about taking out my pistol and firing at him. As I pulled the trigger Ramses flung himself on the fellow and both of them fell to the ground.

"Curse it," I cried, hastening to them. "Ramses, what the devil do you mean by . . . Ramses, are you wounded? Speak to me!"

Ramses rolled over and sat up. His eyes were narrowed to slits and his dark brows had drawn together. I had seldom seen a more impressive scowl, even on the face of his father. He drew a deep breath.

"No, don't speak," I said hastily. "Compose yourself. Heavens, I do believe I have killed the fellow!"

There was certainly a bloody hole in the front of the man's robe. His eyes were wide open, in the unseeing stare of the dead. The rest of his face was hidden by a tightly wound scarf.

Ramses's lips were moving. I wondered whether he was swearing or praying—no, not praying, not Ramses—or perhaps counting to himself, as I had once suggested as a means of controlling one's temper. Whatever he was doing, it achieved the desired result. When he spoke his voice was reasonably calm.

"I doubt it, Mother. This appears to be an exit wound. He was shot in the back, by someone concealed among the rocks. Stay here and stay down."

Before I could stop him he was gone, surefooted as a goat over the tumbled rocks. Within a few seconds I had lost sight of him.

The dead man was not very good company. I crouched beside him, listening anxiously for the sound of another shot. I heard nothing; even the Judas goat, as I believe I may term it, had stopped complaining. I hoped it was not seriously hurt, but I decided I had better not leave the dubious cover of the rocks in order to find out. If Ramses had not acted so precipitately I would have gone with him, or at least insisted that he take my pistol. Young people are so impulsive. There was nothing I could do now but wait.

It seemed a long time before Ramses returned, as silently and suddenly as he had vanished. He was carrying a rifle.

"Ah," I said, as he sat down beside me and placed the rifle on the ground. "The would-be assassin had fled, I take it."

"Yes. He was up there." Ramses folded his arms and rested them on his raised knees. He appeared quite composed and relaxed, except for his hands, which were tightly clasped.

"After shooting this person he dropped his rifle and ran?" I picked up the weapon and examined it. Ramses hastily shifted position.

"Mother, please put that down. There is a bullet in the chamber."

"So I see. That is odd. Why didn't he fire again?"

"He may have counted on one of us shooting the other," said Ramses. Slowly and gently he removed the rifle from my hand and put it behind him. Then he lowered his head onto his arms. His shoulders shook.

It was not like Ramses to yield to weakness, even after the event. I was touched, for I felt sure it had been my danger that had unmanned him. I patted his shoulder. "Now, now," I said. "There, there."

Ramses raised his head. His lashes were wet. Not until then did I identify the peculiar sound he was making.

"Good Gad," I gasped. "Are you laughing?"

Ramses wiped his eyes with the back of his hand. "I beg your pardon."

"Granted," I said, relieved. "Your father does that sometimes."

"I know." He sobered. "Laughter is somewhat inappropriate, however. Look here."

He pulled the scarf from the man's face, disclosing a nasty sight. The jaw was askew and horribly swollen, the mouth distorted.

"I thought his posture and build looked familiar," Ramses said. "This is one of the guards who was at Layla's house."

"No wonder your hand was hurt. You broke his jaw."

"Evidently. He's been going around like this for days, without medical attention. Poor devil." Ramses turned the body over. There was another hole in the man's back, smaller than the one in front. "He was expendable, injured as he was, and he had failed in his job. Like Yussuf. They gave him another chance—a slim chance, as he knew, but you might have been alone and unarmed. And if he failed, this was a more merciful death than the . . . crocodile."

I shivered. "What shall we do with him?"

Ramses bent over the body and began searching it. Aside from the knife and a packet of tobacco there was nothing on the fellow except a cord around his neck, from which hung a silver amulet.

"Didn't do him much good, did it?" remarked my son. "We'll notify the police. Nothing more we can do."

"The goat," I reminded him, after he had helped me to mount.

"Yes, of course."

The goat was not hurt, only pinned by the rock. It went gamboling off as soon as Ramses freed it. I was relieved, because we had enough animals as it was, and this one was of the masculine gender.

Emerson was not pleased when he learned what had occurred. I was prepared to defend Ramses, but I did not have to. Emerson was not angry with Ramses.

"Curse you, Peabody," he cried heatedly. "The old wounded-animal trick, for God's sake! Will you never learn?"

We had retired to our room and I was at that moment held tightly in his arms, so my reply was somewhat muffled.

"It is irresistible, Emerson; it can never fail with any of us. Besides, there is a limited range of possibilities open to even the most inventive adversary."

Emerson was still laughing when he put his hand under my chin and tilted my face up into a more convenient position.

Sometime later I sat on the edge of the bed watching while he performed his ablutions.

"I hope you will excuse me for laughing," he remarked amid his sputtering and splashing. "But really, Peabody, making excuses for the paucity of imagination of an enemy . . ."

"Ramses laughed too," I said.

"Ramses?" Emerson turned and stared at me, water dripping off his chin.

"Yes, I was quite astonished. The alteration of his features was amazing. I had not realized how strongly he resembles you. In fact, he is quite a nice-looking lad."

"He is a handsome devil," Emerson corrected. He added, grinning, "Like his father. I won't ask what you said to provoke Ramses to such an extraordinary reaction, since it wouldn't have struck you as amusing."

"I don't remember. But I believe Ramses's analysis of the event was correct. She is using up her forces rather callously, isn't she? Three so far, if the girl was one of them."

"She must have been, willingly or not," Emerson muttered. "What did she know that made her so dangerous to them?"

"Come and have your tea, my dear. Perhaps inspiration will come to you."

The others were assembled on the verandah when we went out. The only missing member of the party was Sir Edward. His absence was immediately noted by Emerson, but no one could explain it.

"Unless," I suggested, "he has gone to Luxor with Mr. Paul. As you yourself pointed out, Emerson, he is not in your employ."

"He does seem to be losing interest in us," Nefret remarked. "Has he given us up as a bad job, do you suppose?"

She was sitting on the ledge next to Ramses, who had politely drawn his feet up to make room for her.

"One could hardly blame him," said Ramses. "The only thing we have been able to accomplish is running ourselves into one trap after another."

There was, I thought, a decided note of criticism in his voice. "What else can we do?" I demanded. "We are walking about blindfolded, with no notion as to where our opponents are hiding. And there is one positive aspect: she has one less ally now."

"You notified the police?" Emerson asked.

Ramses nodded. "They will collect him eventually, I suppose. If the jackals and the buzzards leave anything."

"Horrible," David murmured.

"Yes, it is, rather," Ramses agreed. "But I doubt they would be able to identify him in any case. He was not a local man, or I would have recognized him on the occasion of our first meeting."

A gloomy silence fell. Then Emerson said in a meditative voice, "I think I may just run over to the Valley for a while."

"Emerson!" I exclaimed. "How can you think of such a thing?"

"Well, curse it, Peabody, there is nothing we can do about the other business, is there? Maspero arrives tomorrow, and the tomb—"

"If you attempt to leave this house I will—I will—"

"What?" Emerson asked interestedly.

Mercifully the sight of an approaching rider provided the necessary distraction. "Here is Sir Edward," I said. "He will tell us what has been happening."

Sir Edward was pleased to do so. At Emerson's insistence he described the day's activities in excruciating detail. "Well," said my husband grudgingly, "it appears we will at least have a complete photographic record. How much longer—"

"For pity's sake, Emerson, leave off interrogating the poor man," I said. "He hasn't had an opportunity to drink his tea."

"Thank you, ma'am." Sir Edward accepted a sandwich from the tray Fatima offered and nodded his thanks. "I don't want to monopolize the conversation. How was your day?"

So the story of our little adventure had to come out. Sir Edward appeared shocked. "I do beg, ma'am," he said, "that you will take more care. The old injured-animal trick—"

"I will lecture my wife if lectures are required," Emerson said, scowling fiercely.

"Will you be here for dinner this evening, Sir Edward?" I inquired.

"Yes, ma'am. I won't be going out this evening. That is . . . You have no other engagements, do you?"

"I had thought," Emerson began.

"You are not going to the Valley, Emerson."

Sir Edward choked on his tea. After wiping his chin with his serviette he exclaimed earnestly, "Please, sir, I beg you won't think of it. It will be dark soon, and the danger—"

"He is right, Emerson," I said, with a nod of appreciation at Sir Edward. His concern was so sincere I regretted having been suspicious of him. "We will spend a quiet domestic evening here. You have not kept up your excavation diary as you usually do, and I have a number of notes to be set in order."

"And I," said Sir Edward, "will give David a hand with his photographing of the papyrus. If he will allow me, that is."

David started. He had been in a brown study, and I knew what the subject of it must be. He replied with his usual gentle courtesy that he would be very glad of assistance, and that he had rather fallen behind.

"If you have time, I would like to ask you about some of the objects in the burial chamber, Professor," Sir Edward added. "I was struck by the fact that the inscriptions on the coffin appear to have been altered. Can you tell me . . ."

That sufficed to get Emerson's attention, and that of Ramses as well. Led by Sir Edward's intelligent questions, the two of them talked nothing but tomb throughout dinner. I put in a word or two, and Nefret added her opinions when she could make herself heard. It was a most fascinating discussion, but I will spare the general Reader the details, which are related elsewhere.*

The only one who did not participate was David. He spoke very little as a rule, because he was too polite to interrupt, and that is sometimes the only way to join in our conversations; but formerly his smiling attention had betokened his interest. Now he sat like the skeleton at the feast, picking at his food. I confess I was relieved when Sir Edward and Nefret took him off to the photographic studio.

The rest of us settled down to work; and very pleasant it was to be occupied with familiar tasks. Emerson muttered and mumbled over his excavation diary, interrupting himself now and then to ask me or Ramses to verify some detail. Ramses, whose hand was almost back to normal, scribbled away at his notes; and I turned again to the Book of the Dead, as it is (erroneously but conveniently) named.

Any scholar would admit the religious texts are difficult. They contain a number of words that are not in the standard vocabulary.

---

*The general Reader may not regret the absence of these details, but the Editor does not doubt they would be of considerable interest to Egyptologists, coming as they did from individuals who had seen the enigmatic burial chamber in its original state, and who had the training to interpret what they saw. Unfortunately, if the record to which Mrs. Emerson refers was made, it has not come to light.

Certainly they were not in mine! I had kept a list of unknown words, meaning to ask Walter about them. It now covered several sheets of paper. I was frowning over one of them when Ramses rose, stretched, and came to lean over my chair.

"The Weighing of the Heart still?" he said. "You were working on that yesterday. Are you having any difficulty with it?"

"Not at all," I said, turning my paper over. I had every intention of consulting Walter about my difficulties, at an appropriate moment, but I could not quite bring myself to ask Ramses for assistance. It was a weakness of character, and I admit as much, but no one is perfect.

"This particular scene fascinates me," I went on. "The concept itself is quite remarkable for a pagan culture that had never known the teaching of the true faith."

Ramses turned a chair round and sat down, resting his arms on the back. "I presume you are referring to Christianity."

Curse it, I thought. Of all things I did not want to get into a theological discussion with Ramses. He could argue like a Jesuit and his opinions, derived from his father, were distressingly unorthodox.

He took my reply for granted and went on, "The idea that an individual will be judged by God, or a god, to determine his fitness for eternal life is not unique to Christianity. In some ways I prefer the Egyptian version. One was not dependent on the arbitrary decision of a single entity—"

"Who knows all and sees all," I interrupted.

"Granted," said Ramses, lips tightening in his version of a smile. "But the Egyptians allowed the dead man or woman the formality of a court hearing, with a divine jury and a court reporter and another judge who watched over the balance. And the result of an unfavorable decision was more merciful than the Christian version. Burning in hell for all eternity is worse than quick annihilation in the jaws of . . ."

He broke off, staring at the photograph.

"Amnet, the Eater of the Dead," I said helpfully.

"Yes," Ramses said.

"Well, my dear, you have made several interesting points, which I will be glad to debate with you—at another time. It is getting late. Why don't you run along and tell the others to stop? Nefret should go to bed."

"Yes," Ramses repeated. "Good night, Mother. Good night, Father."

Emerson grunted.

After Ramses had gone I looked through the messages that had been delivered that day. I had to agree with Emerson; Luxor was becoming too popular. One could, if one were so inclined, spend every day from morning till night in idle social encounters. There were notes from various acquaintances inviting us to lunch, tea and dinner, and several letters of introduction written by people I had met once or twice on behalf of people I had not met at all and did not wish to meet. The only item of interest was a note from Katherine, saying she planned to visit the school of Sayyida Amin next day, and asking if I would like to accompany her.

I mentioned this to Emerson, whose head was bent over the notes he had spread on the table. "I really ought to go, Emerson. Katherine's scheme of starting a school deserves encouragement, and I have been remiss in helping her."

"You may go if you take Ramses and David with you." After a moment Emerson added, "And Nefret."

My poor dear Emerson is so transparent. "Leaving you alone?" I inquired.

"Alone? With twenty of our men, several hundred cursed tourists, and Davis's entire entourage?"

"There are remote corners of the Valley where tourists never go, Emerson. There are empty tombs and hazardous chasms."

Emerson tossed his pen down onto the table and leaned back in his chair. Fingering the cleft in his chin, he fixed amused blue eyes on me. "Come now, Peabody, you don't suppose I would do anything so foolish as to wander off inviting someone to ambush me?"

"You have done it before."

"I am older and wiser now," Emerson declared. "No. There are more sensible ways of proceeding. I'll tell you what, Peabody; put Katherine off for another day or two, and we will go after the bastards who killed that girl."

They had also kidnapped his son and David and attacked Nefret, but it was the horrible death of the young woman that had driven Emerson into action. He tries to hide his softer side, but like all true Britons he will go to any length to defend or avenge the helpless.

"What do you have in mind?" I inquired.

"We are still in the dark as to the motive behind this business. The papyrus is the only solid clue we possess. We never did pursue that lead. If we can find out where it came from we may be able to deduce the identity of the individual who was last in possession of it."

"Bertha," I said.

"Curse it, Peabody, we don't know that that is so. We've put together a pretty plot, but there is no proof that she is the guilty party. Sethos, on the other hand—"

"You always suspect him. There is no proof of his guilt either."

"And you always defend the bastard! I intend to get that proof. I made a few inquiries earlier, but only about Yussuf. I did not mention the papyrus. It came originally from Thebes, so it must have passed through the hands of one of the Luxor dealers. Mohammed Mohassib is a likely possibility. He has been in the business for thirty years, and he has handled some of the finest antiquities that ever came out of the Theban tombs. You heard what Carter said about him the other evening. Can it be a coincidence that he asked to see me?"

"Not you, Emerson. Me."

"Same thing. I will show him the papyrus and promise him immunity and undying friendship if he can give us useful information. We'll leave the Valley early and go over to Luxor."

I slept peacefully and soundly for most of the night. It was near dawn when I was aroused by a piercing scream.

There was no question where it had originated or who had voiced it. It shot even Emerson out of bed. Of course he immediately fell over his boots, which he had carelessly left on the floor, so I was the second person on the scene.

The first was Ramses. The room was extremely dark, but I recognized his outline. He stood by Nefret's bed, looking down at her.

"What is it?" I cried. "Why are you just standing there? What is wrong?"

Ramses turned. I heard the scrape of a match. The flame sprang up and strengthened as he held it to the candlewick.

By that time the others had hastened to the scene. Never had I been so glad I had insisted on proper sleeping attire. They were all more or less clad, even Emerson, though a good deal of bare skin showed. Sir Edward had not waited to put on a dressing gown, but he was wearing a pair of tasteful blue silk pajamas.

Nefret sat up. "I am very sorry," she began; but her voice broke. Helpless with laughter, she bent her head over the enormous bulk clasped in her arms.

"Good Gad," I exclaimed. "How did he get here?"

Ramses set the candle down on a table. "Someday I am going to murder that animal," he said in a conversational voice.

"Now, you know you would never do such a thing," I said.

"I might, though," said Emerson, behind me. "Damnation! My heart is going at twice the normal rate."

"It was my fault," Nefret insisted. "I was sound asleep, and when he jumped onto my stomach he knocked the breath out of me and I thought . . ." She hugged Horus closer. "He didn't mean it, did him?"

I managed to get Ramses out of the room before he said very many bad words. Next morning we found one of Cyrus's servants squatting patiently on the verandah, waiting for us to come out. Lifting the hem of his robe to his knees, he demanded some of the stinging water. He meant iodine, and the condition of his shins justified a copious quantity of that medication, which I duly applied. Katherine had a perfectly adequate medicine chest (one of my wedding presents to the pair) but I suppose the fellow preferred my magical powers. He also wanted to air his grievances, which he did at length. I am sure I need not mention that he was the servant assigned to look after Sekhmet.

BOOK THREE

THE WEIGHING OF
THE HEART

Hear ye the judgement.
His heart has been weighed truly and his soul
has testified for him. His cause is righteousness
in the Great Balance.

14

When we crossed over to Luxor on Monday afternoon I saw the familiar dahabeeyah of the director of the Service des Antiquités tied up at the dock. So the Masperos had arrived! I would have to call on them, of course. I only hoped I could prevent Emerson from doing so, for in his present state of exasperation he was bound to say something rude.

I had sent a messenger to Mohassib earlier to tell him we would come to see him that afternoon. When we reached his house we saw several men sitting on the mastaba bench beside the gate. They stared in undisguised curiosity, and one of them said with a sly smile, "Have you come to buy antiquities, Father of Curses? Mohassib charges too much; I will give you a better price."

Emerson acknowledged this feeble witticism with a grimace. It was well known that he never bought antiquities from dealers. After greeting each of the men by name, he drew me aside. "I believe I will take advantage of the opportunity to fahddle with these fellows, Peabody, and see what gossip I can pick up. You and Nefret go ahead. Mohassib will be more at ease with you, and I feel sure, my dear, that you can persuade him into indiscretions my presence might inhibit."

Like Emerson, I knew most of the "fellows"; several were dealers in fakes and antiquities, and one was a member of the notorious Abd er Rassul family, the most skilled tomb robbers in Thebes.

"Very well," I said. "Sir Edward, will you be good enough to take the—to take that parcel? Ramses, you and David stay with your father."

Emerson rolled his eyes in evident exasperation, but did not protest. Taking out his pipe, he joined the men on the mastaba.

We were greeted by Mohassib himself. He led us into a nicely furnished room where tea was set out on a low table. Not until we had taken the seats he offered did I realize David had followed us into the house.

"I told you to stay with the Professor," I said in a low voice.

"He ordered me to come with you," David replied. "Ramses is watching him. We thought—"

"All right, never mind," I said quickly. Mohassib was watching us, and it would have been rude to continue a whispered conversation.

The usual compliments and courtesies and pouring of tea took a long time. Mohassib did not glance at my parcel, which I had placed carefully on the floor beside my chair. He left it to me to introduce the reason for our visit, which I did in the conventional oblique fashion.

"We were honored to learn you wished to see us," I began. "My husband had other business; he sends his—"

"Curses, no doubt," said Mohassib, stroking his beard. "I know the mind of Emerson Effendi. No, Sitt Hakim, do not apologize for him. He is a man of honor, whom I esteem. I would be of service to him."

"In what way?" I asked.

The question was too blunt. I ought to have replied with a compliment and a corresponding offer of friendship. Mohassib courteously overlooked my blunder, but it took him forever to get to the point.

"You were asking, a few days ago, about a certain man from Cairo."

"Did you know him?" I asked eagerly.

"I knew who he was." Mohassib's lip curled. "I do not have dealings with such people. But I heard—it was after Emerson was here—I heard he was the one found in the Nile."

"The man killed by a crocodile," I said.

"We know, you and I, that no crocodile killed him—or the girl.

Hear my words, Sitt. Do not waste your time looking for these people among the dealers in antiquities. They have nothing to do with us. They are killers. We do not kill."

I believed him. In acknowledgment and reciprocation—and because I had meant to do it anyhow—I unwrapped my parcel and asked David to lift the lid of the box.

Mohassib's breath came out in a whistling gasp. "So. It was said you had an antiquity of value, and that was why Yussuf Mahmud went to your house. But who would have thought it would be this?"

"You have seen it before, then?"

"It never passed through my hands. But I have heard of it. It was one of the first objects Mohammed Abd er Rassul took from the cache at Deir el Bahri."

"Ah," I breathed. "What happened to it after that?"

The old man shifted position and looked uneasy. "I will tell you what I know of the papyrus, Sitt Hakim. It is common knowledge. Everyone knew of it, and of certain other things Mohammed hid in his house."

Everyone except the officials of the Service des Antiquités, I thought to myself. Well, it was not surprising that the men of Luxor and Gurneh should join ranks against the foreign interlopers who tried to interfere with their ancient trade. The tombs and their contents had belonged to their ancestors, and hence belonged to them; most of them were desperately poor, and treasure was of no use to the dead. It made perfectly good sense from their point of view.

"The stolen objects lay in hiding for many years," Mohassib went on. "Once the tomb was known to Brugsch and Maspero, no dealer would dare handle them. But later—a decade later, perhaps—there came a man who did dare. It was said he took the papyri and the royal ushebtis with him to Cairo, where he had established his headquarters, and what he did with them after that no one knows, but one can guess. You can guess, Sitt, and I think you can guess who this man was."

"Yes," I said. "I think I can."

Mohassib had said all he meant to say. He indicated, by thanking me repeatedly for visiting a sick, tired old man, that the interview was at an end. He had suffered a stroke the previous year and did look ill, but when I took his hand in farewell I could not resist asking a final question.

He shook his head. "No, I do not know who they are. I do not wish to know. If you can put a stop to them, good, they dishonor my country and my profession, but I do not want to end up in the jaws of the 'crocodile.' "

From Manuscript H

As soon as the women had gone into the house, Emerson turned to his son. "Go with your mother and Nefret."

Ramses began, "Mother told us—"

"I know what your mother told you. I am telling you to accompany her."

Ramses took David by the arm and led him through the open gate. "You had better do as he said."

"We ought not leave him alone, Ramses. What if—"

"I'll keep my eye on him. Hurry."

Shaking his head, David entered the house. One of Mohassib's servants came into the courtyard carrying a chicken by its feet. The chicken was squawking and flapping; it might not know precisely what was in store for it, but it took a dim view of the proceedings. Ramses beckoned urgently. A quick, silent commercial transaction ensued. Grinning, the servant went off sans galabeeyah and turban, and richer by enough money to buy several of each. He was also sans chicken. Instead of heading for the wide open spaces, the feeble-witted bird began pecking at the hardened dirt. Ramses knew he had won it only a temporary reprieve. An unaccompanied food source wouldn't remain free long in Luxor.

His father was not a patient man. Ramses had barely finished winding his turban when Emerson rose and took leave of his companions. Tucking the end of the strip of cloth into place, Ramses went in pursuit of the chicken. He had to push the stupid bird before it would move. As he had anticipated, his father looked suspiciously into the courtyard. Seeing only the backside of an inept servant, Emerson proceeded on his way.

After addressing a final critical suggestion to the chicken, and rubbing a handful of dirt over his face, Ramses followed his father. It wasn't much of a disguise, but at least he wouldn't stand out in a crowd as he would have done in European clothes.

He thought he knew where his father was going, and he cursed himself for telling Emerson about the small silver disk. He had found it lying near the abandoned rifle. There was no doubt in his mind it had been deliberately placed there. The idea of a woman, jingling with silver and clad in long robes, scampering around the cliffs of the Valley and accidentally losing one of her ornaments, was absurd.

The silver disk was meant to lead them back to the House of the Doves. For obvious reasons, he had been careful to conceal it from his mother. Ordinarily Nefret and David would have been his confidantes, but poor David was half out of his mind with romantic frustration and Nefret couldn't be trusted to act sensibly when her feelings were so deeply involved. Someone had to be told, though, because, unlike his mother, he wasn't fool enough to go back there alone. That left his father. Emerson had nodded and mumbled and said he'd think about what they should do. And now he was doing it—alone, as he believed, and without taking sensible precautions. It would have been hard to say which of them was more difficult, his mother or his father.

The only question was, had Emerson made an appointment beforehand, or did he plan to drop in without notice? If the latter was the case, he probably wouldn't run into anything he couldn't handle, but if he had been stupid enough to warn them. . . . No, Ramses admitted, Father isn't stupid. It's that bloody awful self-confidence of his that gets him into . . .

Speaking of self-confidence, he thought, as a pair of large hands closed round his windpipe and he was slammed up against a wall.

"Damnation!" said Emerson, peering into his face. "It's you!"

"Yes, sir." Ramses rubbed his throat. "What did I do wrong?"

"You were a bit too close on my heels. Thinking of something else, were you?" Emerson pondered the situation. "I suppose you may as well come along. Follow me at a discreet distance and don't come in the house."

"People are staring at us, Father."

"Hmmm, yes." His father cuffed him across the face. "How dare you try to rob the Father of Curses!" he shouted in Arabic. "Thank Allah that I do not beat you to a jelly!"

He strode off. Ramses skulked along after him "at a discreet distance." The carefully calculated blow had looked more painful than it felt, but his cheek stung.

He had not been mistaken about his father's destination. At this time of day there weren't many customers, but a couple of men stood by the door fahddling and smoking. As Emerson strode briskly toward the entrance, one dropped his cigarette and both stared, first at Emerson, then at one another. As one man they turned and trotted away.

The curtains flapped wildly as Emerson pushed through them. Ramses stepped back in time to avoid the rush of another man, who bolted out of the house and ran off. Ramses smiled behind his sleeve. "When the Father of Curses appears, trouble follows." Daoud had a long collection of such sayings, which were now current in Luxor and surroundings.

He picked up the cigarette end the other fellow had dropped, but he didn't put it in his mouth. Verisimilitude had its limits, and he was already unhappily aware of the fleas inhabiting his borrowed garments. Scratching absently, he drew nearer to the door and listened. He could hear only a low murmur of voices. One was his father's. The other was that of a woman.

As the minutes dragged by Ramses became increasingly uneasy. Polite conversation with the ladies was all very well, but it could be a delaying tactic, and there was only one reason he could think of for someone wanting to delay the Father of Curses—the need to collect enough men to overpower him. The hell with orders, Ramses thought. His mother would kill him if his father came to harm through his negligence—if he didn't kill himself first.

Stripping off the galabeeyah and turban, he ran his fingers through his disheveled hair and pushed through the curtain. The room was empty except for the proprietress and his father. The latter swung round.

"Curse it, I told you not to come in," he snarled.

Since the comment was now irrelevant, Ramses ignored it. "What's going on?"

"I have been requesting permission to search the place. Thus far the lady has been reluctant to give it."

Ramses stared at his father in mingled consternation and amusement. It was like him to politely request permission of the old harridan, and just as like him to contemplate searching a rabbit's warren like this without someone to watch his back. Even if they hadn't expected him, they had had ample time to gather their forces.

The old woman's kohl-smeared eyes darted from his father to him and back again. Gold tinkled as she lifted her shoulders and arms in a shrug.

"Go, then," she whined. "Do as you will. A poor weak woman cannot stop you."

Emerson thanked her in impeccable Arabic.

"For God's sake, Father," Ramses exclaimed. "If you are determined on this, let's do it."

"Certainly, certainly, my boy. This is the way, I believe."

The horrible little cubicles behind the main room, each barely large enough to contain a thin mattress and a few utensils, were unoccupied. Emerson indicated the narrow stairs at the end of the passage.

"The more pretentious apartments are up above, I expect," he said dryly.

"Be careful, Father. Wait at the top for me. Don't go—"

"Certainly, my boy, certainly."

He took the stairs two at a time. Ramses followed, looking over his shoulder. The hair on the back of his neck was practically standing straight up. To his surprise, his father did wait for him. There was more light here, from window apertures at either end of a short corridor, and only four curtained doorways. The place was utterly silent except for the inevitable chorus of flies. The air was still and hot. Dust motes swam in the sunlight.

"Hmph," said Emerson, not bothering to lower his voice. "This is beginning to look like a waste of time. We may as well finish, though. I will take this side of the hall, you take the other."

"Excuse me, sir, but that is not necessarily the wisest procedure." Ramses's skin prickled. It was too quiet. The house couldn't be completely deserted.

"Perhaps not," his father conceded graciously. "Follow me, then."

He started for the nearest door, his boots thumping on the bare floor. Walking boldly through a curtained doorway wasn't what Ramses would have done, but obviously it was his father's intention. Ramses caught hold of his sleeve and managed to get in front of him. "At least let me go first."

His father gave him a hard shove. It struck him as an excessively violent reaction until he heard the first shot. The second followed before his body hit the floor. Then his father landed heavily on him. The last of his breath went out in a cry of alarm.

"God! Father—"

"Don't get up," said Emerson calmly.

"I—I can't. You're lying on top of me. Damn it, are you—"

"Dead? Obviously not." He rolled off Ramses and raised himself cautiously to his hands and knees. A third shot rang out.

"Get down," Ramses gasped. "*Please* get down, sir!"

"Hmm," said Emerson. "Something odd about that, you know. No bullet."

"What?"

"That's where the first two hit." Emerson gestured at the splintered holes in the plastered wall. "Where did the last go?"

"Through the curtain opposite?"

"It isn't opposite," Emerson pointed out. "Her aim doesn't appear to be that bad. We'll just wait a bit, I think."

They waited, Ramses still prone, his father leaning negligently against the wall. When Emerson suddenly straightened and whipped through the doorway, he caught Ramses completely by surprise. He had forgot how quickly his father could move, like a cat or a panther, as his mother said. Scrambling to his feet he followed, thinking unfilial thoughts.

But no shot, no outcry, no sound of any kind followed his father's abrupt entrance into the "more pretentious apartment." It was a little larger than the rooms downstairs, and it contained an actual bed instead of a hard pallet, a table, and two chairs. Emerson stood by the bed looking down at something that lay on it. The window over the bed was open and uncurtained. There were flies. Hundreds of flies. The whining buzz rasped like a file. As he went slowly to join his father, Ramses saw the tall green bottle on the table, and the empty glass next to it.

The gun lay by her lax hand. She was dressed in a dark blue garment like the riding habits ladies wore, and she looked neat as a pin, from the velvet facings of the bodice to the elegant buttoned boots. The only mess was on the pillow. She had shot herself through the head.

"**S**top fussing, Peabody, the bullet only grazed me."

It had cut a long furrow across Emerson's back and upper arm. I added a final strip of sticking plaster and sat down beside him. He gave me a somewhat self-conscious smile. "Another shirt ruined, eh?"

"It might have been mine if he hadn't knocked me down," Ramses said. "How did you know she was about to fire, Father?"

We were sitting on the verandah, with Fatima hovering and clucking and trying to get us to eat. It was the first moment we had been calm enough to conduct a sensible conversation.

When we came out of Mohassib's house and found Emerson gone, I was extremely put out. The amiable villains sitting on the mastaba indicated the direction in which he had gone, which was not of much help. Ramses had not been with him. As one explained, they believed he had accompanied us into the house, and he certainly had not come out of it.

I knew Ramses had not been with us, so I felt fairly sure that he had followed his father in some guise or other—which was somewhat reassuring. We had no choice but to wait where we were. The villains kindly made room for us on the mastaba and entertained us with speculations as to Emerson's whereabouts. Since these ranged from suggestions that he had gone to raid the antiquities shop of Ali Murad to sly hints that his destination might have been someplace less respectable, they did not entertain me very much. Sir Edward, cradling the papyrus box as if it were a baby, and watching me with evident concern, finally offered to go and look for him.

"Where would you look?" I demanded somewhat peevishly.

He had no answer to that, of course.

It was David who first saw the returning wanderers, and his low cry of relief turned all our heads in the direction in which he was looking. From dusty boots to uncovered black heads they appeared no more unkempt than was usual for them, but I observed that Ramses was trying not to limp.

By the time we got back to the house our most immediate questions had been asked and answered, and I had seen the rent in Emerson's coat, which, like his shirt, was beyond repair. He removed the coat at my request, remarking that it was too cursed hot anyhow, but insisted he was not in need of medical attention. I was therefore forced to conduct these operations on the verandah while Emerson sought refreshment in a whiskey and soda.

"You first, Peabody," he said. "Did you learn anything from Mohassib?"

"Are you deliberately trying to provoke me, Emerson?" I demanded passionately. "You sent me to Mohassib in order to get me out of the way while you kept another appointment. You did not expect I would learn anything. In fact, he did tell me something of considerable importance, but it pales into insignificance compared with your experience. How did you know she was there? And why the devil didn't you tell me?"

"Now, Peabody—"

"Why did you go there alone? She might have killed you!"

"I wasn't alone," Emerson said meekly. "Ramses—"

"As for you, Ramses," I began.

Emerson cut me off. "Ramses, while you are there at the table, will you get your mother a—"

Ramses had already done so. He handed me the glass.

"Thank you," I said. "Very well, Emerson, I will listen to your explanation. In detail, if you please."

"Promise you won't interrupt?"

"No."

Emerson grinned. "Keep your mother's glass filled, Ramses, my boy."

The clue of the silver ornament had only confirmed Emerson's suspicion that the House of the Doves was the place to look for Bertha. Where could she find more willing allies than among the unfortunates who had good reason to despise men and to yearn for greater independence? The consistent failure of her attacks on us, he reasoned, must be rendering her increasingly angry and frustrated. Giving away her whereabouts was a bold step, a calculated risk, but it was the sort of risk a bold, reckless woman might take in order to dispose of one of us.

"I didn't realize she was that desperate, though," Emerson admitted. "It may well be that she had used up her resources of money and manpower. The revenge of the crocodile . . . A good phrase that, eh, Peabody? Almost as literary as one of yours. The revenge of the crocodile was designed to inspire terror in her subordinates, but it may have backfired. People are inclined to resign from positions that repay failure by torture and death."

"It makes a certain amount of sense now," I admitted. "But you couldn't have known that when you went there."

"No; but I did not suppose there would be any difficulty," said Emerson. "I—what did you say, Ramses?"

"Nothing, sir," said my son. "That is—you didn't answer my question."

"Excuse me," said Sir Edward. "But I have forgot the question."

He looked quite bewildered. That is often the case with individuals who are unable to follow the quickness of our mental processes.

"I asked how Father was able to anticipate the precise moment of her attack," said Ramses. "The fact that the house appeared to be deserted and unusually quiet had aroused my own suspicions, but to judge by Father's behavior—"

"That was designed to mislead our adversaries," said Emerson complacently. "It was obvious that we were expected. I say we, since she could not have anticipated how many of us would turn up. No doubt our approach was observed; she had time to bundle the girls out of the place, if she had not already done so. Finding no one below, we ascended the stairs, and I announced in a loud voice that I had come to the conclusion no one was there. I did that to put her off guard, you see, so that she would expect me to blunder into a trap."

"It was very convincing," said Ramses.

Emerson looked pleased. I had the distinct impression, however, that the statement had not been meant as a compliment. "Expecting difficulty, I heard the faint click of the gun being cocked. So I pushed Ramses out of the way and got myself out of the line of fire as well. We waited a bit. She had fired three shots, and I thought perhaps she would go on until she had emptied the gun, but after a time I— uh—"

"Lost patience and went in anyhow," I said. "Confound it, Emerson!"

"That was not the way of it, Peabody. As I told Ramses at the time, the third shot came nowhere near us. I assumed it was intended to delay us long enough for Bertha to make her escape via a window. It was something of a shock to see her lying there. There was nothing we could do for her, so we stopped by the police station and reported the incident before returning to Mohassib's house."

"Then her body is now in the morgue?"

"I presume so. Please don't tell me you want to have a look at it. I assure you, you would not want to."

"I will spare myself that job, I think. I will always be curious, though, as to what role she had been playing. A tourist, I suppose. I wonder . . ."

"Do not wonder," Emerson said firmly. "Now, then, Peabody, it is your turn. What was this piece of vital information Mohassib gave you?"

"The papyrus came from the Deir el Bahri cache."

"Ah," said Emerson. He started to reach for his pipe, but failed to find it since he was wearing neither coat nor shirt. "Ramses, would you look in my coat pocket for . . . Thank you. Well, Peabody, we surmised that, didn't we?"

"It was only one of several possibilities, none of which was susceptible to proof. Mohassib was certain. According to him, the Abd er Rassuls kept it hidden for years, until it was taken away by . . ." I paused for effect.

"Sethos, I suppose," said Emerson calmly. "Well, that ties up the last loose end, I think. Nefret's theory was right after all. Bertha and Sethos were in league. She took the papyrus when she left him."

A thoughtful silence followed. The sun had set, and the rosy flush of the afterglow lit the eastern hills. From the villages scattered across the plain rose the blended musical voices of the muezzins. The evening breeze stirred Nefret's hair.

"Then it is over," she said. "I can't seem to take it in. We've been on the defensive so long. To have it end so suddenly and so finally . . ."

"High bloody time," Emerson declared. "Now I can get back to work. We must go to the Valley early. Maspero will want to invade the tomb tomorrow, and I have a few things to say to him."

I allowed the ensuing discussion to proceed without me, for I was deep in thought. Everyone seemed to believe Bertha's death had ended our troubles. Even Emerson, who was usually the first to suspect the Master Criminal of every crime in the calendar, had dismissed him from consideration. I was not so certain. Bertha had robbed Sethos of at least one valuable antiquity. She might have taken others as well, and I did not think he was the man to accept this complacently.

Perhaps we had not been the only ones on Bertha's trail. Had it been fear, not of us, but of her former master that had prompted her to end her life? Had *she* ended it? Sethos had once boasted to me that he had never harmed a woman, but there is always a first time. His anger against those who had betrayed him could be a terrible thing.

Fatima came to announce that dinner was served. I observed that Ramses was slow to arise and waited for him.

"Did your father break any bones—your bones, that is—when he fell on you?" I inquired.

"No, Mother. I assure you, I am not in need of your medical attentions."

"I am relieved to hear it. Ramses . . ."

"Yes, Mother?"

I tried to think how best to express it. "Your father is—er—not always the most perceptive of observers when he is in a state of emotional excitability, as I am sure he was at the sight of that unfortunate woman's body. Did you see anything that might suggest she had not taken her own life?"

Ramses's eyebrows rose. I had the feeling that he was not so much surprised by the question as by the fact that I had asked it, and the promptness of his reply was another indication that he had already given the matter some thought. "The revolver was under her hand. There was no sign of a struggle. Her garments were neatly arranged and her limbs straight, except for the arm that had held the weapon. There were powder marks on the glove on her right hand."

"And the blood was . . ."

"Wet," said Ramses, without emphasis.

"It seems to be a clear-cut case, then."

"Sethos claimed, I believe, that he had never harmed a woman."

"I cannot imagine why you should suppose I was thinking of Sethos. He is not in Luxor."

"Unless he is—"

"Sir Edward? Nonsense."

"The possibility had occurred to you, though."

"I knew it had occurred to *you*," I corrected. "Do you suppose I could be deceived? I knew Sethos in London, disguised though he was. I would know him in Cairo—in Luxor—wherever he happened to be. Sir Edward is not the Master Criminal!"

The next morning brought a sight one seldom sees in Luxor—lowering gray skies and wind squalls that blew the branches wildly about. We had risen before sunrise, and Emerson is not at his best in the early morning, so it was not until we gathered for breakfast that he took note of the weather. He started up from his chair.

"Rain!" he cried. "The tomb will be flooded."

I knew it was not our poor little tomb number Five that had roused such alarm, and exasperation for what had become Emerson's idée fixe made my voice sharper than usual. "Sit down and finish your breakfast, Emerson. It is not raining, only dark and windy."

After poking his head and shoulders out the window to check on the accuracy of my report, Emerson returned to the table. "It looks like rain."

"The tomb to which I presume you refer is not your responsibility, my dear. I am sure Ned and Mr. Weigall have taken all necessary precautions."

Emerson's expression showed what he thought of that optimistic assessment. "They ought to have had a door in place days ago. Sir Edward, is the photographer . . . Where the devil is he?"

He was referring to Sir Edward, not the photographer. Emerson glared wildly round the room, as if expecting to see the young man lurking in the shadows.

"He has probably slept late," I replied. "As he is entitled to do, especially on such a day as this. The inclement weather will keep most people away from the Valley today, I expect."

"Hmmm." Emerson fingered the cleft in his chin and looked thoughtful. "Including Maspero and Davis. Hothouse plants, both of them."

"That is neither fair nor accurate, my dear."

"Who gives a curse?" Emerson demanded. "Ramses, haven't you finished?"

"Yes, sir." Ramses rose obediently, stuffing the last of his toast into his mouth.

"I have not finished," I declared, reaching for the marmalade.

"Hurry up, then, if you are coming." Emerson eyed me speculatively. "Er—Peabody, why don't you stay at home today? The weather is unpleasant, and I don't need you. Nefret, you stay with her and make certain she is—er—kept busy."

Gray skies over Luxor are so unusual as to amount to a portent. Perhaps it was the weather that affected my nerves. It could not have been Emerson's crude attempt to distract me, for he does that sort of thing all the time. I flung the marmalade spoon down on the table, spattering the cloth with sticky bits.

"If you think I am going to allow you to go to the Valley and meddle with Mr. Davis's tomb—"

"Meddle?" Emerson's voice rose to a shout. "Peabody, I never—"

"Yes, you do! Aren't you in enough trouble with—"

"I consider it my professional duty—"

"Your profession! It is the only thing that matters, isn't it?"

As soon as the words left my mouth I regretted them. The handsome flush of anger faded from Emerson's face; the lips that had been parted in anticipation of rebuttal closed into a tight line. The children sat like graven images, not daring to speak.

"I am sorry, Emerson," I said, bowing my head to avoid his reproachful look. "I don't know what is wrong with me this morning."

"Delayed reaction," said Ramses.

I turned on him. "You have been reading my psychology books again!"

Unlike his father, he was more amused than hurt at my reproof. I deduced this from the slight narrowing of his eyes, since no other feature altered. "We all feel it, I suppose," he said. "As Nefret remarked, the change in our fortunes happened so suddenly and unexpectedly, it was difficult to take it in. A reaction was inevitable."

Emerson reached for my hand. "Amelia, if you doubt that I would see every damned tomb in Thebes flooded before—"

"I don't doubt it, my dear." I pressed his hand. "I said I was sorry. Run along and—and try not to do anything of which M. Maspero would disapprove."

"Try," Emerson repeated. "Yes, I can do that. No, but seriously,

Peabody, I haven't forgot about that unpleasant business yesterday. There are still a few loose ends to be tied up, and I have every intention of following through on them. I'm not quite sure how to go about it, though. There is even a question of jurisdiction. She was part Egyptian and part European, and how the devil are the authorities to make a positive identification?" He caught my eye, and his old smile curved his well-shaped lips. "No, Peabody, I did not know her that well."

I felt I had apologized quite enough, so I said only, "Very well, my dear. Since I know I can trust your word, I will stay home today. There are a number of little chores to do and little notes to write. I must invite the Masperos to dinner one evening. Have you any preference?"

"I would prefer that they declined," said Emerson, rising.

I rather hoped they would too, for Emerson was sure to get into another argument with the Director. The invitation had to be proffered, however.

Nefret obviously yearned to take part in whatever underhanded scheme Emerson was considering, so I persuaded Emerson to let her go with him. I had to give him my solemn word that I would not "go haring off to the morgue to inspect that grisly set of remains," as he put it.

It was pleasant being by myself for a change. I busied myself with neglected tasks, and wrote a long letter to Evelyn informing her of the happy ending (for everyone except Bertha) to our little difficulty. If I put it in the post this afternoon it would be at Chalfont almost as soon as they were. The postal service had improved greatly under British administration, which was not surprising.

I had meant to say something about the delicate family situation, but for some reason I could not find appropriate words.

The morning brought the usual messages, most of them hand-delivered. There was nothing from Mme. Maspero. Well, but they had only arrived the previous day, and according to the rules of proper etiquette it was up to me to make the first call. I penned a brief, friendly message, asking them to dine on the Friday.

One message was of interest, however, and I was perusing it when Fatima came to bring me another pot of coffee and a plate of biscuits.

"You are determined to make me fatter, Fatima," I said with a smile.

"Yes, Sitt Hakim," Fatima said seriously. "Sitt—is it true your enemy is dead?"

I wasn't surprised that she should know of it. The verbal grapevine operates efficiently in small towns. "Yes, it is true. The danger is over. But where is Sir Edward? I haven't set eyes on him this morning."

"He is in his room, Sitt. Do you want I tell him to come?"

"Tell him he is welcome to join me if he likes," I corrected gently.

She went off, repeating the words under her breath. Such dedication to learning! I really felt quite ashamed that I had not paid more attention to her studies.

Sir Edward promptly appeared, but he refused refreshment. "I am about to cross over to Luxor," he explained. "Unless you or the Professor need me for something."

"The Professor has already gone to the Valley. I decided to have a lazy day here at home."

"You are certainly entitled to one. Well, then, I will see you this evening, if that is convenient."

He appeared to be in rather a hurry. No, I thought; it is not Mr. Paul who inspires such devotion.

The family returned earlier than I had expected, bringing Abdullah and Selim with them.

"Well, did you accomplish what you hoped?" I asked.

"Yes." Emerson was looking very shifty. "Most of it. Why are you wearing that frock, Peabody? I dare not suppose you put on your best for me."

"I am going out to tea," I replied, nodding at Fatima, who had hurried in with her usual food offerings. "I received an invitation this morning from Fatima's teacher."

"In this weather?" Emerson took a biscuit.

"It is not raining."

"It will rain," Abdullah declared. "But not until tonight."

"There, you see? I have been meaning to meet the lady for some time, and have always been prevented. She has asked Miss Buchanan and Miss Whiteside as well, so it should be an interesting meeting."

"Hmph," said Emerson, fingering the cleft in his chin. "Very well, Peabody. Ramses and I ought to make a formal statement to the police. May as well get it over."

We all went, including Abdullah and Selim. Fortunately we are all good sailors; the water was quite choppy and the boat bounced a good deal. I had to tie my hat down with a long scarf. At first Nefret could not decide whether to accompany me or go with the others. Detective fever won the day. I let her go without lecturing her, since I knew she hadn't a chance of convincing Emerson, not to mention Ramses and David, that she should be allowed to examine the body.

Because of the blustery weather and the size of my hat, I decided to take a carriage from the quay. Emerson gallantly handed me in, and then got in with me.

"Now what is this?" I demanded. "Have you kept something from me, Emerson?"

"I have kept nothing from you, my dear," said Emerson, waving the driver to proceed. "Have you kept anything from me?"

"Oh, for pity's sake, Emerson, is it Sethos again? You cannot suppose I am in secret communication with him."

"I wouldn't put it past you." Seeing my expression, he caught my hand and squeezed it. "That was just one of my little jokes, sweetheart. I would never doubt your affection, but I do doubt your good sense. You have such damnable self-confidence! If Sethos summoned you to a rendezvous, curiosity and trust in that man's so-called honor would move you to respond. Admit it."

"Never again," I said earnestly. "My reticence has caused us trouble enough. Henceforth, my dearest, I will tell you everything. And the children too."

Emerson raised my hand to his lips. "I don't know that I would go as far as that," he said, his eyes twinkling.

The school appeared to be closed for the day, but lighted windows shone warmly through the gloomy afternoon air. The streets were virtually deserted; the long skirts of the few pedestrians, male and female, blew out like sails. One guest at least had arrived before me; a closed carriage stood before the door. I wished ours had been of that sort, instead of an open barouche, for the air was foggy with windblown sand.

Our driver drew up behind the other carriage. Emerson helped me out and escorted me to the door. "I will come back for you in an hour."

He was being absurdly overly cautious, but how could I deny him after those loving words? "An hour and a half would be better. À bientôt, my dear Emerson."

A neatly garbed male servant opened the door, and just in time too, for my hat was about to leave my head. He waited until I had untied the scarf and straightened my skirts. Then he opened a door, bowed me in, and closed it after me.

The room was not a sitting room. It was small and scantily furnished and windowless. The only light came from a lamp on a low table. It was sufficient to let me make out the form of a woman who advanced to meet me. I could not see her face clearly, but I recognized her bonnet. I have a very keen eye for fashion.

"Good afternoon, Mrs. Emerson. So good of you to come."

"Mrs. Ferncliffe?" I exclaimed.

With a sudden leap she seized me in a grip as strong as that of a man. I knew her then; I had felt that grip before. It was no wonder I had not recognized Mrs. Ferncliffe, a lady of fashion if not of breeding, as Bertha's formidable lieutenant. Matilda had always worn the severe costume of a hospital nurse and her hard face had been bare of cosmetics. It was my last coherent thought. Her hand clamped over the lower portion of my face and her steely arm defeated my struggles until I had breathed in the stifling fumes permeating the cloth she held.

When I came to my senses my head ached a bit, but the immediate effects of the chloroform had passed. The room in which I found myself was not the one in which I had been captured. It was larger and appeared to be furnished more comfortably, though I could not see much because only a single lamp relieved the gloom. There was a bed, at least; I lay upon it. Ropes bound my ankles and my hands were pinioned in front of me by something stronger than rope. When I tried to move them, a metallic jangle accompanied the gesture.

"Thank heaven!" a familiar voice exclaimed. "You have been

unconscious since they brought you here some hours ago. How do you feel?"

I turned onto my side. There was enough slack in my bonds to permit that much movement, though little more.

My companion was in worse condition. Ropes bound him to the chair in which he sat. His hands were behind him, and I doubted he could move so much as a fingertip. His fair hair was disarranged and his coat was torn, and bruises marked his face. Except when he had been working in the heat of the Tetisheri tomb I had never seen Sir Edward Washington so untidy.

"How did you get here?" I croaked.

"Never mind that now. There is a cup of some sort of liquid on the table beside you. Can you reach it?"

I inspected the bonds on my wrists. They were handcuffs, connected by a rigid bar. A chain ran over the bar and up toward the head of the bed, where it was fastened with a padlock. The chain was not long enough to enable me to touch my bound feet, but I could just barely reach the cup.

He saw me hesitate, and said reassuringly, "The fellow who trussed you up so effectively took a swig or two before he left, so I doubt the stuff is drugged. Unsanitary, no doubt, but safe."

The liquid was beer, thin and sour and warm and not entirely free of flies, but a lady cannot afford to be fastidious when her throat is as dry as a desert. I managed to pick some of the flies out before I drank.

"Amazing consideration," I remarked, feeling considerably better. (The alcoholic content of the beverage may have had something to do with that.) "She hasn't been so tender of you. Did you have a change of heart? If so, it was not very sensible to let Matilda know of it."

"Why, Mrs. Emerson, what do you mean? The fact that you do find me in this position—and a confounded uncomfortable one it is, too—ought to be sufficient evidence that I am not on good terms with that formidable female, or her mistress."

"Not at present," I conceded. "Or so it would appear. However, as soon as I realized Bertha was our adversary, my suspicions of you revived. It is too much of a coincidence that you should appear on the scene only when she appears, and worm your way into our confidence."

I had begun inspecting my bonds. Removing one of my hairpins, I stretched out and began probing at the padlock. Sir Edward watched with interest and, I thought, a trifle of amusement.

"That is clever of you, Mrs. Emerson. However, you are still mistaken. The game is up, it appears, so I may as well admit the truth. I would not like you to believe that I am an ally of Madame Bertha, as we call her."

My fingers lost their grip on the hairpin. I raised myself on one elbow and stared at him. "Don't try to tell me you are Sethos. I would know him anywhere, in any disguise!"

"Are you certain?" He laughed. "No, I am not Sethos. But I am closely connected with him, and Mme. Bertha was too, until she incurred his fury by arranging that clumsy attack on you. It was careless of him to let her get away, but he is a bit of a romantic where women are concerned—as you ought to know."

"Hmph," I said, groping for the hairpin. "I suppose I ought to have suspected that Sethos was your master. Did he send you here?"

A gust of wind rattled the shutters. Sir Edward glanced at the window.

"Since we have nothing better to do at the moment, I may as well answer your questions. Yes, he sent me. But do let us say 'chief,' shall we? 'Master' is really a bit much. After Mme. Bertha got away, with quite a lot of cash and several of his most valuable antiquities, he thought it possible she would go after you. He was rather busy disposing of Mr. Romer's collection, but please believe, my dear Mrs. Emerson, if he had been certain you were in imminent danger he would not have left you to a subordinate, even one as talented as I."

"Curse him," I muttered. The hairpin had slipped down out of reach. I extracted another from my hair.

"At first I believed affectionate concern had misled him," Sir Edward resumed. "For I failed to find any trace of the lady in our old haunts in Cairo. What I did not know was that she had secretly made arrangements of her own. The people she recruited this time were the dregs of the Cairo underworld. They knew of her connection with Sethos and she swore them to secrecy with threats of his vengeance. They were clumsy fools, however. If our people had laid that ambush in Cairo, your son and his friends would not have got away."

"I am not so sure of that," I said.

"Well, perhaps you are right. Ramses is developing into quite an interesting individual, and Miss Nefret . . . My chief is not easily surprised, but he was struck momentarily speechless when I told him of her part in that affair."

"You told him? When was that?"

Sir Edward smiled. "You won't catch me out that way, Mrs. Emerson. However, as you are aware, I did not know of that business until you informed me of it, and it was not until after I had reached Luxor that I realized Madame was here and up to her old tricks.

"What I failed to realize—as did you—was that her crude attacks were feints, designed to focus your attention on criminals and cults, stolen antiquities and—er—fallen women. All the while she sat in her harmless-appearing web, waiting for you to come to *her*. Fatima was the innocent dupe who she hoped would lead you into her hands. One of her tricks almost succeeded. Miss Nefret would never have returned from her visit to the kindly Mme. Hashim if the boys had not called for her. None of them recognized her, naturally. They had never seen her before, and at that time you had no reason to suspect Madame Hashim."

"No," I said. "Why should I have done? There are many women like that, unrecognized and unrewarded, laboring earnestly to light the lamps of learning—"

"Quite," said Sir Edward. "I hope it will console you to learn, Mrs. Emerson, that my chief and I were also ignorant of Madame Bertha's extracurricular activities. He trusted her, you see. She did not trust him. Oh, she loved him, in that tigerish fashion of hers— that is why she hated you, because she suspected he would never care for her as he does for you—but past experiences, I do not doubt, had convinced her no man was completely trustworthy. Several years ago, without his knowledge or mine, she began forming a criminal organization of her own. She found allies, witting or unwitting, in the growing movements for women's rights in England and in Egypt. The school here in Luxor was one of the activities she began at that time."

"I ought to have known," I said angrily. "She used the suffragist movement in England in the same way, cynically and for her own purpose."

"You don't understand her, Mrs. Emerson. In her own twisted

fashion she is genuinely dedicated to the cause of women's rights. She hates men, and believes she is helping women to fight back against male oppression. My master, as you are pleased to call him, was the sole exception; but now she considers he has betrayed her, like all the others."

The hairpins kept bending. I had used four now, with no perceptible result. My interest in his narrative distracted me, perhaps.

"Then the girl who was murdered was one of her students?"

"I believe that is the case. I don't know whether it was Miss Nefret's charm or your son's offer of a reward that won her over, but she was prepared to betray her mistress. It may have been one of the other girls who betrayed *her*." Sir Edward shifted position slightly, trying, as I supposed, to ease the strain on his aching shoulders. "How are you getting on?" he asked politely.

I tossed another bent hairpin away and flexed my cramped fingers. "I have plenty of hairpins."

Sir Edward threw his head back, laughing heartily. It was a strange sound in that dismal room. "Mrs. Emerson, you are a woman in a million. You are wasting your time, though, and putting an unnecessary strain on your wrists. I feel certain Madame is still in Luxor. If she wants to maintain the useful persona of a teacher, she'll have to convince your loving family that you left the school of your own free will and—if I know the Professor—let them search the place from cellars to roof. It began raining a while ago and she doesn't like to get her dainty feet wet. I doubt she'll turn up until—"

"What!" I cried. "What did you say? Still in Luxor? Teacher? Dainty feet? It is Bertha of whom you are speaking, not Matilda. But Bertha is dead. She . . . Oh, good heavens!"

"Forgive me for not being more explicit," Sir Edward said with great politeness. "I thought you understood. But, there, Mrs. Emerson, your normally quick wits are under something of a strain at present. No, Madame is not dead; she is alive and well and impatient to see you. Not only have I spoken with her quite recently, but it was I who examined the body and realized it could not be hers."

"How did you do that? Or should I ask?"

"I am surprised at you, Mrs. Emerson! You may remember that Bertha has very fair skin. Every square inch of the body was covered, except for the face, and there wasn't much left of that, but if your husband had thought to remove one of her gloves . . ."

"Good Gad," I exclaimed. "She deliberately murdered one of those poor women in order to mislead us. Of all the cold-blooded, vicious—"

"An accurate assessment, I fear. I never believed she had killed herself. If she had been cornered, she would have fought to the end, with teeth and nails if she had no other weapon. So we went round to the morgue and had a look at the body. My friendly conversations with Fatima had aroused my suspicions of her teacher, so, like the fool I am, I trotted round to the school and got myself neatly caught."

I too had been suspicious of the circumstances surrounding Bertha's presumed demise, but this particular possibility had never occurred to me. How could I have been so dense? I ought to have known, as had Sir Edward, that a woman of her temperament would not surrender to fate so meekly. A little shiver ran through me as I remembered what she had said about "ingenious" methods of killing me. An even stronger shiver rippled along my limbs when I thought of Emerson. He would be easy prey for her now, his guard down, his suspicions directed elsewhere.

"What are we going to do?" I demanded.

Sir Edward tried to shrug. It is not an easy thing to do when hands and arms are tightly bound. "Wait. I doubt she'll come before morning. Anyhow, she won't harm you until she's tried to collect the other members of the family. As you so intelligently surmised, mental torture is her present aim. She undoubtedly has other plans for me. She didn't have time to finish questioning me earlier, so I expect she'll want to have another go at it. We can only pray he reaches us first."

"Ah," I said. "So Sethos is here, in Luxor."

"That was what Madame wanted to know." Sir Edward's voice was noticeably weaker. He had put on a credible show of nonchalance, but I knew he must be in considerable discomfort.

"Does he know where to look?"

"I certainly hope so," said Sir Edward with genuine feeling.

Sir Edward said no more. Gradually his head drooped and his shoulders slumped. The shutters creaked and shook. Rainwater had seeped through them to darken the floor under the window. I continued to probe at the recalcitrant lock with fingers that had grown stiff and aching. It might be—it almost certainly was—a futile exercise, but it is not in my nature to wait passively for rescue, even if I had been certain rescue would arrive in time. Emerson would be looking for me too. Where was he now? If he did not know Bertha yet lived, he was in deadly danger.

I had used up most of my hairpins when the shutters creaked—not with the sounds they had made under the intermittent battering of the wind, but with a steady straining groan.

Sir Edward's bowed head lifted. The shutters opened, admitting a burst of wind-driven rain, and a man who climbed over the sill and closed the shutters before turning to face us.

He was as drenched as if he had just emerged from the river. His flannel shirt and trousers clung to his body and arms. Slowly and carefully he pushed the dripping hair out of his face, and a puddle began to form around his booted feet as he looked quizzically from me to Sir Edward.

"Well, Edward. This is not one of your finer moments."

15

The voice was Sir Edward's. The admirable frame, defined by the clinging garments, resembled his; the wig was an excellent copy of his fair hair. The only feature that differentiated the two, at least to a casual observer, was the long bushy mustache that concealed the newcomer's upper lip and altered the conformation of his face.

"No, sir," Sir Edward mumbled. "It is good to see you."

"I'll wager it is." Taking a penknife from his trouser pocket, Sethos cut the ropes that bound the other man to the chair and steadied him as he slumped forward. "Where is she?"

Sir Edward shook his head. His insouciance had been a gallant attempt to reassure me—and perhaps himself! Now that rescue had arrived, hope renewed weakened his voice and his body. "In Luxor, I suppose. Sir—I am sorry—"

"All right. Hang on a minute." He crossed to the bed and stood, hands on hips, looking down at me. "Good evening, Mrs. Emerson. May I be so bold . . ."

I stiffened as his hands went to my waist. With a mocking smile he straightened, and let his arms fall to his sides. "Forgive me. I failed to observe you were not wearing your usual arsenal. What fond memories I have of that belt of tools!"

He was taunting me. Sethos did not fail to observe very much. He picked up the cup of beer, sniffed it, and wrinkled his nose fastidiously. "Not as pleasing to the palate as your brandy, Mrs. Emerson, or as effective, but it will have to serve. I trust you will overlook my lack of manners if I suggest Edward is more in need of it than you."

It might have been the loathsome liquid, or the relief of rescue, or even the charismatic presence of his chief. After Sir Edward had finished the stuff, Sethos nodded with satisfaction.

"You'll do. Go out the same way I came in. Thanks to the rain, there's no one about. You know where to meet me."

"Yes, sir. But don't you want me to—"

"I will attend to Mrs. Emerson. Off with you now."

Sir Edward rose stiffly to his feet and went to the window. Pausing only long enough to bow gracefully to me, he unfastened the shutters and climbed out into the lashing rain. I had the feeling that if Sethos had ordered him to climb into a volcano he would have obeyed as readily.

Sethos used the penknife to cut the ropes around my ankles. Then he sat coolly down on the bed next to me and examined the chain and the padlock. "Hairpins, Amelia? You will be the death of me yet. Come to think of it, you almost were. Hmmm. What have we here? A primitive lock, but impervious, I think, to hairpins. Never mind the padlock, I will just remove the handcuffs."

I watched with considerable interest as he unscrewed the heel of his boot and examined the contents of the hollow interior.

"Ramses has developed something of the sort," I remarked, as his deft fingers removed a narrow steel strip less than four inches long.

"Thanks to me," Sethos muttered. He inserted the end of the steel strip into the lock of one of the handcuffs. It sprang open. "Had I but known how that young man would turn out, I would have gone to considerable lengths to prevent him from making use of my equipment. He has become . . . Ah."

The other cuff opened. Sethos's face darkened when he saw the marks on my wrists, but he said only, "A stage magician's trick, my dear. If young Ramses has not turned to that source for inspiration, I recommend it to him. Now let's be going."

I started to ask where, but came to the conclusion that almost any alternative would be preferable to my present whereabouts. Disdaining the hand he offered, I swung my feet onto the floor and stood up. The fine effect of this gesture was spoiled by the fact that my numbed limbs would not support me. I would have fallen had he not caught me in his arms.

He was still extremely wet. The moisture in the fabric of his shirt soaked into my thin frock. For a moment he pressed me close, and I felt his chest rise in a long pent breath. My hands rested on his shoulders, but they were too weak to exert sufficient pressure against the tensed muscles of his arms and breast. I would be helpless to resist if he chose to take advantage.

He let his breath out and turned his head, pressing his lips to my bruised wrist. "You will forgive the liberty, I trust, and remember that it is the only one I have ventured to take. This way."

With the support of his arm I made my way to the window. "I will go first," he said, opening the shutters. "You will have to lower yourself and drop, I fear; there are footholds, but they are difficult to find in the dark. I will try to break your fall."

Without further ado he swung himself out and disappeared into the darkness. Leaning out, I waited for his low-voiced call before I followed. His arms were waiting to catch me, but either he had underestimated my weight or his foot slipped, for we tumbled to the ground together.

Sethos scrambled to his feet and pulled me upright. I had the impression that he was laughing. The rain had slackened, but the wind still howled and it was so dark I could barely make out his outline. Like me, he was covered with a coating of slimy mud. A stream of water ran over my feet. I had no idea where I was. The darkness was almost palpable, for heavy clouds hid moon and stars. The only solid objects in the universe were the wall of the house behind me and the hard wet hand that clasped mine and led me forward.

The wind was from the north, strong enough to make one stagger, cold enough to chill one's bones. Even the level ground was slippery with mud, and very little of the ground was level. We splashed through a dozen small streams, fought our way up slopes that ran with water, fell and rose and fell again. However, I did not regret leaving the dry, sheltered room I had been in.

By the time we reached our destination I had identified my surroundings. We had passed scattered houses and seen lighted windows; the very contours of the landscape had begun to be familiar. I marveled at the woman's audacity. She had taken me back to Gurneh, to the very house that had been her original headquarters in the village. Not so audacious, perhaps; it had been thoroughly searched before, and was now believed to be abandoned. If I had been able to locate myself earlier, I would have broken away from my companion and headed for Selim's house, which was near the other. Where was he taking me? We had been walking—crawling and scrambling, rather—for what seemed an eternity.

Sethos slithered to a stop and took me by the shoulders. His face was so close to mine I was able to make out the words he uttered, though he had to shout. "You are as slippery as a fish, my dear, and as cold as a block of ice, so I won't linger over my farewells. There is the door—do you see it? Don't try to follow after me. Good night."

Following was beyond even my powers. My teeth were chattering violently and my wet garments felt like a skin of ice. I wanted to be warm and dry and clean, to see light and friendly faces. All that and more awaited me within. The house was that of Abdullah. I squelched and staggered to the door and pressed the latch.

The light, from a pair of smoking oil lamps, was so bright after the utter darkness without that I had to shade my eyes. My sudden appearance—and such an appearance!—shocked them into temporary immobility. They were both there—Daoud and Abdullah—sitting on the divan drinking coffee and smoking. The stem of the waterpipe fell from Abdullah's hand. As for Daoud, he must have taken me for a night demon, for he shrank back with a cry.

"I must apologize for my appearance," I said.

I had begun to feel a trifle light-headed or I would not have made such an absurd remark. Abdullah cried out, and Daoud jumped up and ran toward me. I put up my hand to keep him away. "Don't touch me, Daoud, I am covered with mud."

Unheeding, he snatched me up and pressed me to his breast. "Oh, Sitt, it is you! God be thanked, God be thanked!"

Abdullah came slowly toward us. His face was impassive, but the hand he put on my shoulder trembled a little. "So, you are here. It is good. I was not afraid for you. But I am—I am glad you are here."

They handed me over to Kadija, who fell on me with the loving ferocity of a lioness who has recovered a missing cub. She stripped off my filthy soaked garments and bathed me and wrapped me in blankets and put me to bed and fed me hot broth. At my request she admitted Abdullah after I was properly covered, and between spoonfuls of broth I told him what I felt he should know.

"So it was she," Abdullah said, tugging at his beard. "She told us you had gone from the school, she did not know where. We had no reason then to doubt her. We have been searching for you ever since, Sitt. Emerson thought it was Sir Edward who had taken you."

"Emerson must be warned," I said urgently. "At once. He doesn't know that female fiend is still alive. Abdullah, she murdered that woman in cold blood—drugged her, dressed her in her own clothing, and waited until Emerson was actually outside the door before she ... I must get back to the house at once. Perhaps Kadija will be good enough to lend me something to wear."

Abdullah's lips had tightened. Now they relaxed and he shook his head. "Kadija's robe would wrap twice around you, Sitt Hakim. Daoud has gone to find Emerson. I do not know where he is. He made us go home when the darkness fell and the rain came."

"Oh dear," I murmured. "Poor Daoud, out in this weather ... You shouldn't have sent him, Abdullah."

"I did not send him. It was his choice. Sleep now. You are safe and I will keep you safe until Emerson comes."

I looked from his resolute, bearded face to the strong brown fingers of Kadija, holding the bowl and the spoon. Yes. I was safe with them, safe, and suddenly as limp and sleepy as a swaddled baby. My heavy lids fell. I felt Kadija's hands straighten the blanket and another hand, gentle as a woman's, stroking my hair, before sleep overcame me.

Day had come before I woke, to see Kadija beside me. She rose at once and helped me to sit up.

"Were you there all night?" I asked. "Kadija, you should not have—"

"Where else should I be? It rains hard, Sitt Hakim; stay there and I will bring food. And," she added, her face breaking into a smile, "something you will like even better."

But he had been listening for the sound of voices and came before she could bring him, pushing through the curtain at the doorway and dropping to one knee beside the bed. The joy of that meeting was so intense it was some time before I could speak. In fact, it was Emerson who spoke first.

"Just as well I came without the children," he said, wrapping me again in the blanket. "You are in a scandalous and delightful state of undress, Peabody. What happened to your clothes?"

"You know perfectly well that it was Kadija who removed them, Emerson. How long have you been here? What has Abdullah told you? What—"

Emerson stopped my mouth with his. After a brief interval he sat back on his heels and remarked, "When you badger me with questions I know you are yourself again. I believe Kadija is hovering tactfully outside the door; would you like coffee before you continue the interrogation?"

The room was warm and rather dark, since the shutters had been closed against the rain and there was only one lamp. It felt quite cozy as we sipped our coffee together and answered one another's questions. Emerson's tale was the shortest. He had no reason to suspect Sayyida Amin's veracity when she insisted I had never entered the house; the other ladies, Miss Buchanan and her teacher, and the false Mrs. Ferncliffe, had verified the statement and expressed alarm which, in the former case, was entirely genuine. He concluded that I had been seized by someone waiting in the closed carriage, for it was not there when he returned.

In fact, it must have been in that vehicle that I was removed, disguised as a roll of rugs. After a period of agitated inquiry, Emerson had found a witness who had seen such a carriage at the quay. He had hastened back to the school to collect Ramses and David, who were conducting a search of the place. Sayyida Amin had not only agreed to a search, she had insisted upon it.

"I was a damned fool not to recognize her," Emerson declared. "She was veiled, of course, and she had darkened her face and hands, and—"

"And you believed she was dead. Small blame to you, Emerson. Your persistence prevented her from following me across the river."

"We barely made it ourselves. The wind was blowing a gale and it had begun to rain heavily. We came back to the house and tended to the horses—poor creatures, they had been waiting in the open for hours—and changed clothing and tried to think what to do next.

Since I believed it was Sethos who had abducted you, I had no idea where to begin looking. But I would have found you, my darling, if it meant demolishing every house on the West Bank."

I expressed my appreciation. "But surely," I inquired, "you were not under the misapprehension that Sir Edward was Sethos?"

"I wouldn't put anything past that bastard," Emerson said darkly. "And I never entirely trusted Sir Edward. He was too damned noble to be true. Wasn't it you who said everyone has an ulterior motive?"

"I thought his ulterior motive was Nefret," I admitted. "It appears I was mistaken. I—I have been mistaken about quite a number of things these past weeks, Emerson."

"Good Gad!" Emerson put one big brown hand on my brow. "Are you feverish, Peabody?"

"Another of your little jokes, I presume. Time is passing, Emerson, and we must be up and doing. Do you want to hear about Sethos?"

"No. I suppose you had better tell me, though."

The narrative took longer than it ought to have done because Emerson kept interrupting with muttered expletives and expressions of annoyance. When I finished he permitted himself a final vehement "Curse the swine!" before making a sensible remark.

"Who do you suppose he is—was—has been masquerading as?"

"A tourist, I expect. There are hundreds of them in Luxor. His disguise last night was one of his little jokes, I think. He was the image of Sir Edward, except for the mustache."

Emerson went to the window and threw open the shutters. "The rain has stopped. I came last night, as soon as Daoud told me you were here, but the others ought to be along soon. We are rather in need of a council of war."

"It is foolish for them to come here. Why don't we go back to the house?"

"I doubt the children will wait much longer. They were very anxious about you, my dear. I admit it is difficult to tell with Ramses, but he blinked quite a lot. Nefret was beside herself; she kept saying she had been unkind and unfair to you and that she ought to have gone with you to the school."

"Nonsense," I said—but I confess I was touched and pleased.

"Anyhow," Emerson said, returning to my side, "Kadija informed me that frivolous frock you wore yesterday is beyond repair. You can't ride wrapped in a blanket. I could carry you across my saddle, I suppose, like a sheikh fetching home a new acquisition for his harem, but you wouldn't find it comfortable."

He stood smiling down at me. His blue eyes shone with sapphirine intensity, his black hair waved over his brow. "I do love you so much, Emerson," I said.

"Hmmm," said Emerson. "They won't be here for a while yet, I think . . ."

They came only too soon for me. There was barely time for Emerson to rearrange the blanket before Nefret burst into the room and flung herself at me. Ramses and David stood in the doorway. David's face broke into a smile, and Ramses blinked twice before Emerson pushed them out and pulled the curtain.

Nefret had brought clean clothing for me. Only another woman would have thought of that! She had even brought my belt of tools, and as I buckled it round my waist I swore I would never go out again without it. Then my story had to be retold. Some of it was new to Abdullah and Daoud as well, and so it was long in the telling. Before I finished the sun broke through the clouds, casting a watery light into the room.

"That man again!" Abdullah burst out. "Will we never be rid of him?"

"It is just as well we weren't rid of him," Ramses said. "Forget about Sethos, at least for now. Bertha is the real danger."

"That may no longer be the case," I said soberly. "Sethos knows her present identity, and so does Sir Edward. I cannot believe they have failed to take steps to apprehend her."

"We had better make certain," Ramses said.

"Yes, quite," Emerson agreed. "She has eluded Sethos, and us, too often. This time . . ."

His teeth snapped together. There was no need for him to say more. One should temper justice with mercy, but in this case I could find no pity in my heart for Bertha. She would kill as ruthlessly and remorselessly as a hunter dispatching a harmless deer.

It was decided that we should cross at once to Luxor. Daoud and Abdullah were determined to accompany us, and when we emerged from the house we saw a half dozen of our other men waiting, obviously with the same intention. Selim was there; he hailed us with a shout and a smile and fell in step with David as we started down the path.

I was distressed to see what devastation the storm had left in its wake. The ground was drying rapidly but the rain had dug deep trenches into the hillside, and several of the poorer houses, built of reeds and sun-dried brick, had subsided into heaps of mud. The residents of Gurneh were out in full force, surveying the damage and discussing it, and even, in some cases, starting to remove the debris.

"I hope no one was injured," I said to Abdullah, who was walking beside me.

"There was time for them to get out and other places where they could go," Abdullah said indifferently.

"Yes, but . . ." I stopped. Next to one pile of shapeless earth a woman crouched, rocking back and forth and keening in a high-pitched wail. "Good heavens, Abdullah, there must be someone buried under there."

Abdullah's wordless shout made the others spin round, but it was too late; they were only a few feet away, but they could not have reached her in time to stop her. Her finger was on the trigger as she straightened, and she did not even wait to hurl a final curse at me, she fired three times before she was crushed under the weight of several men.

I heard the sound of the bullets strike—but I did not feel them, for it was not my body they struck. One step was all there was time for, and there was only one man who could have taken it. He fell back against me and I threw both arms round him as we sank to the ground together. I was aware of raised voices and running forms, but only as a remote irrelevance; my eyes and my whole mind were fixed on the body of the man whose head I cradled in my arms. The white robe was crimson from breast to waist and the stain spread out with hideous quickness. Nefret knelt beside us, her hands pressing hard on the spurting wounds. I did not need to see her ashen face to know there was no hope.

Abdullah's eyes opened. "So, Sitt," he gasped. "Am I dying?"

I held him closer. "Yes," I said.

"It is . . . good." His eyes were dimming but they wandered slowly over the faces that bent over him, and it seemed to please him to see them there. His gaze returned to me. His lips moved, and

I bent my head to hear the whispered words. I thought he was gone, then, but he had one more thing to say.

"Emerson. Watch over her. She is not . . ."

"I will." Emerson took his hand. "I will, old friend. Go in peace."

It was he who closed Abdullah's staring eyes and folded his hands on his breast. I gave him over to Daoud and Selim and David; it was their right to care for him now. They were all crying. Nefret wept against Ramses's shoulder, and Emerson turned away and raised his hand to his face. Ramses's grave dark eyes met mine over Nefret's bowed head. He had not shed a tear—nor had I.

Bertha was dead of multiple injuries, including several stab wounds. It would have been difficult to ascertain whose hand had struck the mortal blow.

I have no very clear memory of what happened immediately afterwards. We went back to our house to prepare for the funeral, which would take place that evening. My garments were sticky with blood, but I refused Nefret's offer of assistance. After I had bathed and changed I went to my room. The others were in the parlor. There is often comfort in companionship in cases of bereavement, but I did not want anyone's company then, not even that of Emerson.

My eyes were still dry. I wanted to cry; my throat was so tight I could hardly swallow, as if the tears were dammed by an unyielding barrier. I sat on the edge of the bed, with my hands folded in my lap, and looked at the bloodstained garments spread across a chair.

He had not thought much of me, or of any woman, when we first met. The change had come so slowly it was hard to remember a precise moment when suspicion had turned to affection and contempt to friendship, and then to something more. I remembered the day he had led me to the dreadful den where Emerson was held prisoner. When I broke down, he had called me "daughter" and stroked my hair; and then he had gone back to gather his men and join them in fighting to free the man he loved like a brother. It was not the only time he had risked his life for one or both of us.

I remembered my remote, indifferent father. I remembered my

brothers, who had ignored and insulted me until I came into Papa's money—the only thing he had ever given me. I thought of Daoud's warm embrace and Kadija's loving care and Abdullah's dying words, and I knew that they were my true family, not the uncaring strangers who shared my name and blood. And still the tears would not come.

He had so enjoyed conspiring with me against Emerson—and with Emerson against me. I remembered the smug smile on his face when he said, "You all came to me. You all said, 'Do not tell the others' "; his theatrical grumble, "Another dead body. Every year, another dead body!" The way he had tried to wink at me . . .

It is the small things, not the great ones, that hurt most. The dam burst and I flung myself face-down on the bed in a flood of tears. I did not hear the door open. I was unaware of another presence until a hand came to rest on my shoulder. It was not Emerson. It was Nefret, her face wet and her lips trembling. We wept together then, our arms round one another. Emerson's arms had comforted me on many occasions, but this was what I needed now—another woman to grieve as I was grieving, unashamed of tears.

She held me until my sobs had died to snuffles, and I had soaked my handkerchief and hers. I wiped the remaining tears away with my fingers.

"I am glad it was you," I said. "Emerson never has a handkerchief."

"Are you glad, though?" She knew my little joke was my way of regaining my composure, but her eyes were anxious. "I didn't know whether I should come in. I waited outside the door for a long time. I didn't know whether you would want me."

"You are my dearest daughter, and I wanted you."

That made her cry again, so I cried a little too, and then I had to rummage through my drawers for another handkerchief. I bathed my red eyes and smoothed my hair and we went together to the sitting room. Ramses and Emerson were there, and David, who put food on a plate and brought it to me. We talked of inconsequential things, since the important things were still too painful.

"It is a pity about the school," Nefret said. "I suppose it will be closed now."

"Mrs. Vandergelt might take it over," Ramses suggested.

"An excellent idea," I said. "Do they know ... Have Cyrus and Katherine been informed of what has occurred?"

It was David who replied. His eyes were red-rimmed, but he was quite composed; and I thought he had gained a new maturity and self-confidence. "I wrote to tell them. They sent a message back—they want to be there this evening."

"Good." I put the untouched food aside and rose. "David, will you come with me? There is something I want to say to you."

From Letter Collection B

... so you see, Lia darling, it is going to be all right! Aunt Amelia is writing to your parents, and I don't doubt for a moment that they will do *exactly* as she tells them.

Don't grieve for Abdullah. If he could have chosen the manner of his death, this is what he would have wanted. Be thankful that you knew him, if only for a short time, and rejoice as we do that he was spared illness and a long slow dying.

You would have found the funeral moving, I think, despite its strangeness. The cortege was led by six poor men, many of them blind (only too easy to find, unhappily, in this country where opthalmia is so common) chanting the credo: "There is no God but God, and Mohammed is his Prophet; God bless and save him!" Abdullah's sons and nephews and grandsons followed, and after them came three young boys carrying a copy of the Koran and chanting in sweet high voices a prayer or poem about the Judgment. The words are very beautiful. I remember only a few verses: "I extol the perfection of Him who created all that has form. How bountiful is He! How merciful is He! How great is He! Though a servant rebels against Him, he protects."

The Professor and Ramses were among those honored by being permitted to carry the bier, on which the body lay, uncoffined, and wrapped in fine cloths. Fatima and Kadija and the other women of the family were next. The rest of us followed them. The Vandergelts were there, of course, and Mr. Carter and Mr. Ayrton and even M. Maspero! I thought it was rather sweet of Maspero. Fortunately the Professor was too busy trying to keep a stiff upper lip to start an argument with him. How Abdullah would have laughed!

After a prayer service at the mosque we went on to the cemetery and saw him laid to rest in his tomb. I will take you there when you come back to Egypt. It is a handsome tomb, befitting his high status; the vaulted chamber of plastered mudbrick is underground, and above it is a small monument called a shahid. I took Aunt Amelia away before they replaced the roofing stones and filled in the opening.

I don't think she realized how much she cared for him, or he for her, until the end. Hasn't someone said a woman may be known by the men who love her enough to die for her? (If they haven't, I claim the credit myself.) What on earth, then, are we to make of Aunt Amelia?! The Professor (of course), a Master Criminal, and a noble Egyptian gentleman—for that is what he was, by nature if not by birth.

And what of the Master Criminal? you will ask. Well, darling, we haven't found a trace of him. And believe me, the Professor looked *everywhere*! You ought to have seen his face when Aunt Amelia repeated some of the things Sethos said to her. This time she held nothing back, and a good thing, too; I doubt we've seen the last of Sethos. Frankly, my dear, I would *love* to meet the man! He behaved like a perfect gentleman. That's what really maddens the Professor, I think. He would much prefer to have Sethos act like a cad so he can despise him.

Sir Edward has gone too. He never returned to the house, but he wrote to the Professor. It was a very polite and extremely entertaining letter. At least I found it entertaining. The Professor didn't.

My dear Professor and Mrs. Emerson,

I do hope you will forgive my rudeness in leaving you so abruptly and without the formality of farewells; but I feel certain you understand my reasons for doing so. I beg you will think it over before you decide to lay a formal complaint against me. You would find it difficult to prove I had committed a crime, but the proceedings would be unpleasant and needlessly time-consuming for all of us.

Please accept my condolences on the death of Abdullah. I had learned to admire him a great deal, though I fear he did not reciprocate. A certain gentleman of whom you know has asked me to express his regrets as well. He blames himself (you know the delicacy of his conscience) for failing to apprehend the lady in time. The weather being inclement, as you no doubt recall, we were unable to reach Luxor until after she had been warned of your escape and mine. She must have realized the game was up and that our friend was close on her trail—and, I assure you, he was. We reached Gurneh less than an hour after the unhappy event. My friend has also asked me to tell you that a man can ask no greater happiness than to die for the woman he loves—and that he is in a position to know. I cannot say I share that sentiment, but I find it admirable.

Give my regards (I dare offer nothing more) to Miss Forth, and to your son and his friend. I look forward with great anticipation to the possibility that we may meet again one day.

> *Believe me, with sincere regards,*
> *I am (I really am)*
> *Edward Washington*

We were soon back at work, for there is no better way of overcoming grief than to be busy. I sensed a diminution of Emerson's cheerfully profane ebullience. He missed Abdullah, as did we all; it was hard to imagine going on without him. However, Selim was shaping up well. He had the same air of authority his father had possessed in such large measure, and the men accepted him without argument. They teased him a little, though, and he announced to me quite seriously that he intended to let his beard grow.

Life must go on, as I told Emerson. (I will not record his reply.) It was not one single thing that dimmed his enjoyment of the work, it was an accumulation of them: the laborious effort of clearing tomb number Five; the increase in social activities resulting from the arrival of M. Maspero and a number of other scholars, wanting to see Mr. Davis's discovery; and above all, the frustration of watching Mr. Davis wreck one of the most important discoveries ever made in the Valley of the Kings.

"Wreck" was Emerson's word, and so was "important." He does tend to exaggerate when he is in a temper. How important the discovery might be was questionable as yet, but it certainly had its points of interest, and I had to agree that the clearance of the tomb might have been handled better.

When we returned to the Valley on the Thursday, we found Ned Ayrton removing the fill from the entrance corridor. The black scowl on Emerson's face as he stood, hands on hips, surveying the activity, would have thrown anyone into a panic. Ned began to stutter.

"Sir—Mrs. Emerson—good morning, everyone, I am pleased to see you. We could use Abdullah now, couldn't we? But the panels will be all right, you'll see; I am inserting props as I remove the rubble from under them, and I am being very careful, and I—uh—"

"Quite," said Emerson, in a voice like the rumble of thunder. He looked down at the streaked dust on the stairs. "Water. It rained yesterday. Quite hard."

"No damage done," Ned said. His voice cracked, but he squared his shoulders and spoke up bravely. "Really. M. Maspero was here yesterday, and he—"

"Was he?" Emerson said.

Ramses took pity on his unhappy young friend. "Father, the men will have arrived by now; don't you want to make certain the ceiling in the far corner is properly braced before they begin? Selim hasn't Abdullah's experience."

Duty, and concern for the safety of his men, always took precedence with Emerson. He allowed himself to be pulled away by David and Nefret.

With his father's permission Ramses spent most of that day and the next with Ned, though I cannot imagine he was able to do much to assist. His reports were not encouraging. I would not have encouraged him to prevaricate, of course, but I did wish he could equivocate just a little.

"There was some water in the tomb, even before the recent storm," he said. "Condensation or rain, through that long crack in the ceiling. Nothing has been done to stabilize the gold foil on the panels. To be fair, one would not know what to use. It is so fragile, and most of it is already loose, just lying on the surface; even a breath disturbs it."

Emerson put his head in his hands.

"Paraffin wax," I suggested. "I have often used it successfully."

"Ned thought of it, naturally. But it would have to be applied with great care, almost drop by drop, and that would take a long time."

I looked anxiously at Emerson, whose face was hidden, but from whom issued strange groaning noises. "Well, never mind," I said heartily. "It is time we got cleaned up. Katherine and Cyrus are coming for dinner."

I had invited the Masperos, but Madame had pleaded a previous engagement. It was just as well, considering Emerson's state of mind, and the fact that we had a number of loose ends to tie up—matters we could only discuss with our oldest friends.

The school was Katherine's main interest, and for a while she would talk of nothing else. The owner of the building turned out to be our old friend Mohassib, who had been more than happy to hand over the lease to Katherine.

Cyrus was not so happy about having her acquire it. "Why don't we just build a new house? That one's got some pretty nasty memories connected with it."

"Pure superstition, my dear," Katherine said comfortably. "That woman is dead and her assistant has disappeared. She won't dare show her face in Luxor again. The students can't be left high and dry. None of them knew anything."

"Except for some of the women from the House of—from that house," I said. "The authorities have assured me it will be closed."

"For a time, perhaps," my tactless son said cynically. "Places like that have a way of surviving, in one form or another."

"Not if I can help it," Nefret said fiercely. "Mrs. Vandergelt and I are going to find decent positions for those girls, as housemaids and servants, until they can be trained for better things."

Cyrus's jaw dropped. "Housemaids? Where? Katherine, did you—"

"Now, Cyrus, don't fuss. The household staff is my responsibility, you know."

I beckoned to Fatima, who hastened to fill Cyrus's wineglass. "Fatima will be one of your students, Katherine," I said, attempting to change the subject. "It is strange, is it not, that good can come from such great evil? Though it was certainly not her primary aim, Bertha did strike a blow for oppressed womanhood in starting that school and even in arousing aspirations in the most oppressed of our sex."

Emerson said, "Hmph!" and Ramses added, "And murdered them ruthlessly and horribly when it suited her purpose. Even that was a demonstration of her perverse interpretation of justice. Those who had failed her judgment met the fate shown in the Book of the Dead. The monster Amnet had the head of a crocodile."

"Good Gad, what a fanciful idea," I exclaimed. "And yet . . ."

My hand went to the amulet hanging round my neck. Ramses nodded. "Yes. The ape who guards the balance, the symbol she chose for her organization. Justice, which has been achieved. As you say, Mother, it is strange how things work out."

The most astonishing news, which I had heard that evening from Fatima, was that Layla had returned to her house in Gurneh.

"Amazing effrontery," Cyrus ejaculated.

"Not really," I replied, for I had had time to consider the matter. "As soon as she heard of Bertha's death—and such news travels quickly—she knew it was safe to return. We would not take action against her, for we owe her a considerable debt. Perhaps I ought to call on her and—"

A profane remark from Emerson indicated his disapproval of this idea.

"That would not be advisable, Mother." Ramses was quick to add his opinion.

"Then—yes, I think you and David ought to go—for a brief visit, I mean. Gratitude is more important than propriety, and you owe her your lives. You might take her a nice present."

"I have every expectation of doing that, Mother," said my son. And indeed, when I raised the point several days later, he assured me that he had.*

Over the next few days Cyrus rather neglected his own excavations, with which, as he was frank to admit, he had become very bored. He was not the only archaeologically inclined individual who yearned for a view of the burial chamber of Mr. Davis's tomb. Our old friend the Reverend Mr. Sayce arrived in Luxor, Mr. Currelly, M. Lacau—the stream of visitors was endless, and it was augmented

---

*There is no reference to this visit in Manuscript H. The Editor spent many hours searching for it in vain.

by (to quote Emerson) "every empty-minded society person who wants in." Cyrus was one of them—the former category, not the latter—to his great delight. Katherine amiably declined the treat, despite her husband's enthusiastic descriptions of the golden crown ("Pectoral," Ramses interrupted) and gold-covered panels ("What's left of them," muttered Emerson).

The entrance corridor had been cleared by then; the poor panel rested on a framework of wood, and one had only to duck one's head and walk under. When I paid my own visit to the burial chamber—for I saw no reason to decline when every "empty-minded" visitor to Luxor had already been there—I was shocked to see how conditions had deteriorated since my first visit. The floor looked as if it were carpeted with flakes of gold, which had fallen from the panels of the shrine. The photographer had placed his tripod up against the mummy case in order to get a close view of the four canopic jars, which were still in the niche. I fear I forgot myself. Turning to Ned, who had accompanied me, I cried, "The panels! Why didn't you lower the one that is leaning against the wall?"

A few more flakes of gold drifted gently down to the floor, and from under the black hood of the camera came a wordless grumble of protest.

"Yes, sir, at once." Ned tugged at my sleeve. "We had better get out of his way, Mrs. Emerson, he is very touchy about having people in here when he's about to shoot. You can come back tomorrow, when he's finished."

So distraught was I by what I had seen that the meaning of his last sentence did not penetrate my mind until after we had emerged from the tomb. "Did you say he will finish today?" I inquired. "But surely he will come back to photograph the mummy itself when you lift the lid of the coffin. When will that be?"

"I'm not sure. It is up to Mr. Davis."

"And M. Maspero."

"Of course." Ned added quickly, "My friend Harold Jones will be here in a few days, to make sketches and paintings."

"I thought Mr. Davis's friend, Mr. Smith, was doing that."

"He was. Um . . . it's not very pleasant down there, in the heat and dust."

"No. It isn't."

Further inquiry produced the information I had hoped not to hear. Mr. Davis had indeed dismissed the photographer, who was returning to Cairo as soon as he finished developing the last of his plates. As all my Readers are surely aware (if they are not, they have failed to pay attention to my remarks about excavation techniques) this meant there would be no photographic record of the clearance of the burial chamber, or the mummy itself. Mr. Davis, I was informed, had no intention of hiring another photographer.

The individual who informed me of this was Mr. Weigall. I intercepted him that afternoon as he was leaving the Valley, and since I had him backed up against the cliff face he could not get away from me without knocking me down. I pointed out, in my most tactful manner, that as the representative of the Antiquities Department he could insist on this basic requirement. He obviously had no intention of doing so, or of invoking the authority of M. Maspero. When I offered the services of David and Nefret, Weigall bit his lip and looked shifty and said he would tell Mr. Davis of my generous offer.

The last resort was to plead with Maspero himself. Though I had no great hopes of succeeding, I decided I must try. After we had returned to the house I was about to dispatch a note inviting myself to tea with him and Madame—for the situation was desperate enough, I believed, to justify this bit of bad manners—when Fatima handed me a message that changed my intentions. It had arrived that afternoon, and it came from a suprising source—Mr. Paul, the photographer.

The message was even more surprising. Mr. Paul regretted not having had the opportunity to be introduced to me, for of course he knew me by reputation. He had news of vital importance that could be told only to me. He was leaving on the evening train to Cairo; would I meet him at the station, for a brief conversation that would, he felt certain, prove of considerable interest to me?

I am sure I need not repeat the thoughts that passed through my mind. The astute Reader will anticipate them. My decision should be equally easy to anticipate. How could I not go? There was no danger, for the platform would be crowded with tourists and locals waiting for the train. My original notion, of calling on M. Maspero, would serve as an excuse for my absence.

I did take the precaution of assuming my working costume, complete with my belt of tools and my stoutest parasol, instead of the nice frock I had planned to wear. Emerson, the only person I informed of my presumed intention, made no objection; the only condition he exacted was that I allow one of our men to accompany me.

With Hassan trailing me at a respectful distance, I reached the railroad station approximately fifteen minutes before the train was due to leave. The platform was a melee of bodies, loud voices, pushing and shoving. I took up a position near one of the walls of the station, parasol firmly clasped, eyes moving alertly over the crowd.

I had never seen Mr. Paul face-to-face, but when he emerged into sight I knew him instantly. He was wearing gold-rimmed spectacles and a rather vulgar striped flannel suit. Strands of gray hair had been stuck to his balding head. His shoulders were bowed, his walk slow and stiff, like that of a man suffering from rheumatics.

As he came toward me his stride lengthened, his bent form straightened, his head lifted. It was like the transformations in the fairy tales, when the wand of a magician turns a bent old man into a prince. I sucked in my breath.

"Don't cry out, I beg," said Sethos. "For if you attempted to do so I would be forced to silence you in a manner that would please me a great deal but to which you would feel obliged to object. And think of the damage to your reputation. Embracing a stranger on the train platform in full view of fifty people!"

A wall at one's back prevents antagonistic individuals from creeping up on one, but it also prevents one from eluding such individuals when they are standing directly in front of one. Sethos's arms were slightly curved and his flexed hands rested lightly against the wall. I knew what would happen if I tried to raise my parasol or slip aside.

"You couldn't go on kissing me for very long," I said doubtfully.

Sethos threw his head back and let out a muffled whoop of laughter. "You think not? My darling Amelia, I love the way you go straight to the point. Most women would squawk or faint. I could certainly go on kissing you long enough for my fingers to find a certain nerve that would render you instantly and painlessly unconscious. Don't tempt me. I suggested this rendezvous because I wanted to bid you farewell under circumstances more romantic than those that prevailed at our last meeting, and because I thought you might have a few questions."

"And because you wanted to show off," I said disdainfully. "It is an excellent disguise, but I would have known you if I had ever got a good look at you."

"Possibly. I took the precaution of spending most of my time in the depths of that tomb." He smiled mockingly. "I have learned a great deal about photography these past days."

"Confound it! The night Sir Edward had dinner with you—"

"He gave me a quick coaching on a subject of which I was totally ignorant," Sethos agreed amiably. "I am a man of many talents, but photography is not one of them. The plates I took that first day were absolute disasters. They were so bad, in fact, that we decided Edward had better come and 'assist' me. He did the real work after that. But I fear Mr. Davis is going to be rather disappointed by some of the photographs."

A hideous foreboding came over me. "Oh, good Gad! Do you mean there is no photographic record after all?"

"You really do care about your bloody—excuse me—about your tombs, don't you?" His smile no longer mocked me; it was fond and kind. I looked away.

The conductor's whistle sounded. Sethos glanced over his shoulder. "That is what I wanted you to know, Amelia. I can't give Mr. Davis all the photographs Edward took; even a dismal incompetent like him might notice that some of the objects shown in the photographs are no longer in the tomb—or the coffin."

"What! How? When?"

"The night before M. Maspero arrived in Luxor." The strange eyes behind the gold-rimmed spectacles shone. "It isn't difficult to bribe those poor devils of guards, but your husband may consider himself lucky that Edward was able to persuade him not to go to the Valley that night. Now, dear Amelia, don't look so indignant. Robbing tombs is my profession, you know."

"What did you take? How did you—"

"I fear there is not time to answer all your questions. Rest assured I did as little damage as possible—less, I believe, than that heavy-handed pack of so-called professional scholars. I have some of the world's most expert restorers—or forgers, if you prefer that term—in my employ, and the artifacts I removed will be well taken care of. The photographic record is complete. One day, after I am past caring about criminal prosecution, it will be made available to the world—and to you. I did it for you, you know. How true it is that the influence of a noble woman can reform an evil man! Goodbye, darling Amelia. For now."

The train had begun to move. He bent his head, and I thought for a moment he would . . . There was nothing I could have done about it. Instead his lips brushed my forehead, and then he turned and ran. Swinging himself onto the steps of the last car, he blew me a kiss of farewell.

I think the thing I found most flattering was that he had taken it for granted I would not bother telegraphing the authorities in Cairo. By the time the train reached that city, Mr. Paul would no longer be on board.

Did I hasten home and tell Emerson all about it? No. I would tell him, and the others, in due course; I had resolved to keep nothing from them. But the time had not come.

16

The final catastrophe, as I must call it, took place on the following Friday. Nefret was the only one of us who was allowed to be present when the mummy was finally exposed. How she managed it I do not know, and I prefer not to inquire. Her qualifications were as good or better than those of many of the persons who were there, but I suspect it was not her professional expertise that won her permission from Mr. Davis and M. Maspero. We watched them pass: Maspero and Weigall; Ned and Mr. Davis, in his absurd gaiters and broad-brimmed hat; the ubiquitous Mr. Smith.

It was late afternoon before she returned. We were waiting for her—like a flock of vultures, as Ramses remarked—outside our own tomb, for our mounting curiosity had made work difficult, and we had finally dismissed the men and found places in the shade. Emerson was smoking furiously and I was attempting to distract myself by making additions to my diary. Ramses was scribbling in his notebook, apparently impervious to curiosity; but he was the first on his feet when Nefret came unsteadily up the path. He went to meet her and found her a handy rock, while I uncorked my water bottle.

Emerson removed his pipe from his mouth. "Is there anything left of the coffin or the mummy?" he inquired.

The quiet purring voice warned her, but she was too upset to care. She wiped her mouth on her sleeve and gave me the bottle.

"The coffin lid is in three pieces. They've got it on padded trays. The mummy . . ."

The head and neck of the mummy had already been exposed. When Maspero and the others raised the lid of the coffin they found that the body was entirely covered with sheets of thick gold. They removed these, and then they lifted the body.

Emerson let out a cry like that of a wounded animal.

"It gets worse," Nefret said. She was talking very quickly, as if she wanted to get it over with. "There was water under the mummy. And more gold. One of the sheets was inscribed. M. Maspero said it had one of the epithets of Akhenaton. The body itself was wrapped in linen, very fine, but dark. Mr. Davis took hold of the linen and tried to pull it back, and the skin came off with it, exposing the ribs. There was a necklace—a collar, rather. Mr. Davis took it off, and poked around looking for loose beads, and then the rest of the mummy just—just disintegrated into dust. There's nothing left but bones."

"What about the head?" Ramses asked. He sounded quite calm, but he took a tin of cigarettes from his pocket and lit one. I did not comment.

"Mr. Davis removed the pectoral—he still thinks it's a crown. The face was damaged, but there was some skin remaining. At first. One of the teeth fell out when he . . . Well, to make a long story short, they all pranced around and congratulated one another, and Mr. Davis kept shouting, 'It's Queen Tiyi! We've found her.' Only they haven't, you know."

"What do you mean?" I asked. Emerson raised his bowed head.

"They wanted to send for a doctor to look at the bones," Nefret explained. "To see if they could determine the sex. There wasn't . . ." She glanced at me. "At least I didn't see . . . But I might not have."

"No," I said. "Not if the body fell apart so completely and so rapidly. But you were there; why did they want to send for another qualified medical person?"

"Don't be absurd, Aunt Amelia. Do you suppose any of them would consider *me* qualified? A *woman*? Ned did speak up for me, and Mr. Davis consented to allow me to have a look—chuckling merrily at the very idea. I told him it wasn't a female skeleton, but he just went on chuckling."

"Are you sure of the sex?" Ramses asked.

"As sure as I can be after such a brief examination. I didn't dare touch anything. The skull was damaged, but the undamaged portions were typically masculine—the supraorbital ridges, the overall muscular markings, the shape of the jaw. They wouldn't let me measure anything, but the angle of the pubic arch looked—"

"The skeleton was intact, then," I said.

"Except for the head. It was in bad shape," Nefret admitted.

"Then it is Akhenaton," Emerson exclaimed. "The remains of the most enigmatic of all Egyptian pharaohs, pawed over by a pack of vultures looking for gold!"

"Mr. Davis still thinks it's the Queen," Nefret said. "He went out looking for a physician—a real physician." Her sense of humor overcame her professional chagrin; she began to laugh. "Can't you picture him dashing through the hordes of tourists yelling, 'Is there a doctor in the house?' He came back dragging an unhappy American gynecologist, and stood over the poor man exclaiming, 'We've found Queen Tiyi! It's a female skeleton. Unquestionably female, isn't that right, Doctor?' Well, what could the man say? He agreed, and made his escape. And so did I. I couldn't stand it any longer."

Ramses shifted position slightly. "Father, did you get a good look at the hieroglyphic inscription on the coffin?"

"Not good enough," Emerson said sourly. "The cartouches had been cut out, but the epithets were those of Akhenaton. 'Living in truth, beautiful child of the Aton,' and so on."

"Correct," said Ramses, looking as enigmatic as Akhenaton.

Emerson shot his son a suspicious look. "What are you saying?"

"Don't say it," I exclaimed. "They are coming. I think I hear Mr. Davis's voice. Get hold of your father, Ramses."

I blame the entire thing on Mr. Davis. If he had passed on by with the others, I might have been able to keep Emerson quiet. But of course he had to stop and gloat.

"I hope you appreciate your good fortune, my dear," he said, patting Nefret on her head. "To be present on such an occasion!"

"It was good of you to let me be there, sir," Nefret murmured.

"Yes, congratulations," I said, tugging at Emerson, who stood like a rock, and looked like one, too, for all the animation on his face. "We must go. We are very late. Good afternoon, M. Maspero, Mr. Weigall, Mr.—"

"Charming girl," Davis remarked, beaming at me. "Charming! You shouldn't let her mess around with mummies, you know. Bless the ladies, they don't have the brains for such things. Can you imagine, she told me it wasn't the Queen!"

M. Maspero cleared his throat. "Mais, mon ami—"

"And don't you try to tell me any different, Maspero. I know what I found. By Jove, what a triumph!" And then he administered the coup de grâce. "You can all pop down tomorrow if you like and have a look. Just don't disturb anything."

That was when the catastrophe occurred. I will not—I cannot in decency—reproduce Emerson's remarks. Some of them, in his execrable French, were addressed to M. Maspero, but the majority of them fell on the indignant head of Mr. Davis, who, to be fair, had not the least idea why Emerson was being so rude. And after his gracious invitation, too!

It ended with Davis demanding that Emerson be expelled from the Valley altogether. Only his kindly forbearance had allowed us to work there, since he held the firman. He had tried to be accommodating; he had made greater concessions than could have been expected of him. But, by Jove, there was no reason why he should have to put up with this sort of—er—grmph—thing!

Between him and Emerson there was a great deal of shouting. A crowd of curious onlookers gathered. Maspero didn't try to get a word in. He stood stroking his beard and looking from one speaker to the other. Obviously he was too craven to take the necessary steps, and was expecting me to take them. I am accustomed to men doing that. Emerson would never have laid a hand on such a feeble old person as Mr. Davis, but the latter appeared to be on the verge of a stroke or heart attack, and I did not want Emerson to have that on his conscience. So I raised my voice to the pitch few can ignore, and told him and Emerson to be quiet, and Davis's friends converged on him, and we converged on Emerson.

I managed to get my husband's attention by standing on tiptoe and pulling his head down and whispering directly into his ear. "I have something to tell you, Emerson. Something important. Come away, where Mr. Davis can't overhear."

Emerson shook his head irritably, but by that time Davis's party had got away from him and he had calmed down a bit. We were able to remove him to our rest tomb and persuade him to take some refreshment.

He broke out again just as violently when I told him of my meeting with Sethos, and for a time his profane ejaculations prevented a reasoned discussion. Ramses (who did not have his father's prejudices against the Master Criminal) was the first to realize the import of that meeting.

"Do you mean there is a complete photographic record after all?" he demanded. "Surely not of the mummy, though. How would he manage that?"

"I am sure I do not know," I replied. "But he told me that he—or rather, he and Sir Edward—had managed it. It is some small consolation, is it not, to know that the record exists? And David's copy of the shrine panel and door in the corridor may be the only record of those objects."

Emerson shot me a guilty look. "Now, Peabody, I don't know where you got the idea—"

"It was on your desk, Emerson," I replied firmly if not altogether truthfully. "Anyhow, I knew you were up to something that morning you went early to the Valley with the children. You know you will never be able to make it public, don't you? You had no business doing such a thing."

Emerson said, "Hmph."

"A good many of our activities in that tomb can't be made public," Ramses remarked. "Not if we ever want to work in Egypt again."

Emerson deemed it advisable to change the subject. "Curse it, Amelia, why didn't you tell me this earlier? We might have caught the bas—the villain!"

"I doubt that," said Nefret. Laughter brightened her eyes and her voice. "Anyhow, Professor, would you really have handed him over to the authorities after he saved Aunt Amelia?"

Emerson considered the question. "I would much rather have had the satisfaction of beating the rascal to a pulp—and forcing him to return the objects he stole from the tomb. Did he tell you what they were, Peabody?"

I shook my head, and Ramses said thoughtfully, "We may be able to hazard a reasonable guess by comparing what is now in the burial chamber with the list I made after my first visit."

"Ned will be able to do the same, won't he?" I asked.

"Possibly," said Ramses. "But I daresay his memory is not quite as accurate as mine."

False modesty is not a quality from which Ramses suffers. Since the statement was undoubtedly true, no one contradicted him.

"No suspicion will attach to the photographer," Ramses went on. "There have been literally dozens of people in and out of that tomb over the past few days, including Mr. Davis's workers. We may owe Sethos a debt of gratitude after all, for preserving objects that would have been damaged or stolen by less skillful thieves. I wouldn't be surprised if certain objects turn up in the antiquities market."

This indeed proved to be the case. It was Howard Carter who was shown the bits of gold and fragments of jewelry by a man of Luxor. The fellow offered them to Mr. Davis for four hundred pounds and a promise of immunity. Mr. Davis, I was told, was deeply wounded by the disloyalty of his workmen.

From Manuscript H

"What do you suppose the Professor will do now?" David asked.

It was the first time they had had a chance for a private conference since the debacle over Davis's tomb. For reasons known only to her, Nefret had decided to make it something of a celebration. She had given up pretending she liked whiskey, but there was a bottle of wine and some of Fatima's sugar cakes. They met in Ramses's room, since Horus had taken possession of Nefret's bed and refused to let either of the men into the room.

Stretched out in his favorite chair, his feet on a low chest, Ramses shrugged. "He won't tell us until he's damned good and ready. But I can hazard a guess, I think. He'll let us finish our copying at the Seti temple while he and Mother and Nefret go off selecting another site for next year."

"Why me?" Nefret demanded. She was sitting cross-legged on the bed, with the silk skirts of her blue robe spread around her, like a water nymph in a pool. "They would be much happier by themselves, and I could help you here."

"You know better than that," Ramses said sharply. "People would talk."

"You needn't sound so cross. I know they would and I don't care if they do. Goodness, what nuisances 'people' are."

"True," Ramses conceded. "I expect we'll leave for home earlier than usual. That will make one person happy, at any rate."

David hadn't even been listening. Eyes half closed, lips curved, he was in a happy trance of his own.

"Wake up," Ramses said affectionately. He stretched out a booted foot and nudged David's shoulder.

"I heard. Do you think we will? Really?"

Nefret laughed. "Leave it to me, David. How many times have you written her since she left?"

"Every day. But letters aren't very—" He broke off, staring. "Where did you get that?"

Nefret struck a match and held it to the end of the long thin cigar she held between her teeth. Her cheeks went in and out like a bellows as she puffed.

"Mr. Vandergelt?" Ramses suggested, taking firm hold of the arms of the chair and trying to control his voice.

"I wanted to try it," Nefret explained, after four matches and a fit of coughing. "I don't see what's so funny. Mr. Vandergelt laughed too, but he swore he wouldn't tell Aunt Amelia. I don't know, though. Why do they smell so much nicer than they taste? "

"You aren't supposed to inhale," Ramses said.

"Oh, really? Hmm." She blew out a cloud of smoke. "I think I've got the hang of it. May I have a glass of wine, please?"

"So you can be thoroughly depraved?" Ramses said. He let David hand her the wine, though. He was afraid to get any closer.

"This isn't depraved, it's nice." Nefret leaned back against the head of the bed and beamed at them. "It's glorious. I don't want anything to change. I want it to be like this forever."

"What, drinking wine and smoking cigars? You'll get painfully drunk if nothing worse," Ramses said.

"I've never been drunk. I'd like to try it sometime."

"No, you wouldn't." A picture formed in his mind, of Nefret laughing and a bit unsteady on her feet, her hair coming down and her lips parted . . . He gave himself a hard mental kick.

"You know what I mean," Nefret said. "I like us the way we

are, all of us. I could almost be angry with you, David, for changing things, but I'm not really, because Lia is a darling and she won't take you away from us. It's different for men. They bring their wives home, just as they've always done. Women have to give up everything when they marry—their homes, their freedom, even their names. So I'm not going to."

Ramses was speechless. It was David who replied, after a nervous look at his friend. "Not marry? Isn't that a bit—er—dogmatic? What if you fall in love with someone?"

Nefret waved her cigar. "Then he'll have to take *my* name and do what *I* want to do, and come and live with you and Aunt Amelia and the Professor."

"I'm not at all sure Mother would agree to that arrangement," Ramses said. "She probably looks forward to the day when she can be rid of the lot of us."

"You'll bring your bride home, won't you?"

"No," Ramses said. "Not home to Mother. Not . . . Can we please talk about something else?"

David gave him a quick glance and asked Nefret where she thought they ought to work next season. The cigar was a help too; she was a little green in the face by the time she had finished it, and declared she was ready for bed. David went with her to the door and closed it carefully after her.

Ramses was sitting upright, with his head in his hands. David jogged his elbow. "Have another glass of wine."

"No. That just makes it worse." He went to the washbasin and splashed water on his face, then stood dripping over the basin with his hands braced on the table.

"She didn't mean it," David said.

"She bloody well did." Ramses swiped at his face with the towel, dropped it onto the floor and went back to his chair. "She's such a child," he said helplessly. "What happened to her, during those years, to make her so—so unaware? She's never talked about it. Do you suppose someone . . ."

"Is that what's been tormenting you? No, Ramses. I don't believe she's been hurt, she's too loving and open and happy. She'll come round." David hesitated and then said tentatively, "Perhaps you could—"

"No!" Forcing a smile, Ramses added, "Oh, yes, I could. God

knows I'd like to. But it would be taking a chance. I might end up losing what I already have, and it's too precious to risk—her trust, her companionship. You and she are my best friends, David. I want her love in addition to that, not instead of it."

David nodded wisely. "You're right, there's no way of forcing it or even predicting it. It can come on like an avalanche. That day in the garden when Lia . . . But I told you about that, didn't I?"

"Once or twice." Ramses's smile faded. Abruptly he said, "I'm going away."

"What?"

"Not this instant or forever. But I have to be away from her for a while, David. It's got out of control, and I can't—I can't deal with it."

David's dark eyes were warm with sympathy. "Where will you go?"

"I don't know. Berlin, Chicago, the Sudan—some oasis in the middle of the Sahara where I can study asceticism and scratch fleas and learn to control my feelings."

David sat down on the chest. "Sometimes I think you control them too well."

"Outwardly, perhaps. It's what goes on inside that frightens me."

"I understand."

No, Ramses thought, you don't. Not all of it. And I hope to God you never do.

I was not keen on the idea of leaving the boys alone in Luxor, and even less willing to leave Nefret. Her argument—that they wouldn't be so likely to get in trouble if she was there watching over them—did not at all convince me. She made quite a fuss, though, and when Katherine heard of it she proposed a solution that would solve at least one of the difficulties. Gossiping tongues would be restrained if Nefret stayed with her and Cyrus at the Castle.

"Are you prepared for what that entails, Mrs. Vandergelt?" Ramses inquired. "You will have to take Horus too. Nefret wouldn't leave him with us even if we would have him."

Katherine assured him she and Cyrus—and presumably Sekhmet—would be delighted to have Horus. Ramses shook his head.

So I agreed. The fact that Emerson and I would be alone in our ramblings did not affect my decision in the least. It was just as he said: we would have to trust the children sometime, why not now?

There was plenty of room for two on our dear dahabeeyah, even though Emerson soon filled the saloon with his notebooks and the bits and pieces he collected from various sites. Naturally he went about this in the most meticulous fashion, keeping detailed notes of their provenance. Perhaps the best part of the trip was the week we spent at Amarna. We tramped the plain from end to end and side to side, visiting all the nobles' tombs and venturing one day into the remote wadi where the king's deserted tomb was located. What fond memories that arduous but exhilarating stroll awakened! Amarna had been the scene of some of our most thrilling adventures. In the Royal Tomb Emerson's arms had enclosed me for the first time. They enclosed me again as we stood that day in the shadowy entrance; his embrace was as strong and ardent as it had ever been, and when we began the return journey, the three-mile walk seemed long only because it delayed the expression of the emotions aroused in us both. We did not engage in the customary professional discussion that night.

However, at breakfast the following morning, Emerson shook his head regretfully when I suggested we return to Amarna the following season. "There is certainly a great deal to be done here, but the same is true of every other site in Egypt. I am thinking seriously of removing to the Cairo area. The ancient cemeteries stretch for miles, and most have been only cursorily excavated. Even at Giza and Sakkara there are large stretches unexplored and unassigned. We'll have to give the matter more thought." He filled his pipe and leaned back. "We might stop at Abydos on our way back to Thebes. Are you up to another week of strenuous exercise, Peabody?"

"I believe I have demonstrated my fitness, Emerson."

"You certainly have, my dear. I cannot recall ever seeing you in finer condition."

The tone of his voice and the sparkle in his handsome blue eyes gave the words a meaning that made me blush like a schoolgirl. "Now, Emerson," I began—and then I remembered. The dear children were hundreds of miles away. Discretion was not necessary.

I will not record my reply, but it made Emerson laugh a good deal. He lifted me from my chair onto his knee, and out of the corner of my eye I saw a flutter of skirts as Mahmud beat a tactful retreat with the fresh coffee he had intended to deliver. At that moment I realized fully how necessary it is for a fond mother to accept the departure of her children from the nest. It would be a blow, but I thought I could bear up under it.

I was glad to see them, though, when we returned to Luxor several weeks later. They all commented on how fit and rested we looked. I returned the compliment, though privately I was not pleased with Ramses's appearance. Physically he was much the same; it was a certain look in his eyes. I said nothing at the time, but the day before we were to leave Luxor, I took him aside.

"I have a final visit to make, Ramses. Will you come with me? Just you, I don't want the others."

He accompanied me, of course. I think he suspected where I meant to go.

The cemetery was deserted. It was a desolate place, with the wind blowing fine sand across the bare ground, and not a flower to be seen. I had not brought flowers. I had brought a small trowel.

I laid them one by one in the hole I dug—the little figures of Isis with the child Horus, and Anubis, who leads the dead to the Judgment, and Hathor and Ptah and the others. Last of all I unfastened the chain from round my neck and detached the figure of the baboon, the ape who watches over the scales of the Judgment. After I had placed it with the others I gave Ramses the trowel. He filled in the little hole and smoothed the sand over it. Neither of us had spoken. We did not speak now. In silence he helped me to my feet, and held my hand a little longer than was necessary before we turned away. I hoped this would help him. I had known he would understand.

There is no harm in protecting oneself from that which is not true; and who can say what eternal truths are preserved in the mysteries of the ancient faith?

"I am yesterday, today and tomorrow, for I am born again and again. I am he who comes forth as one who breaks through the door; and everlasting is the daylight which His will has created."